A Special Message from The Author

Hello, lovely playmates!

The original *Goldilocks and the Three Bears* fairy tale is a cute story we all heard as children. It's about a girl who stumbles upon the home of a family of bears. She sneaks in and tests out the belongings of each bear to figure out which she most prefers.

Keeping this in mind, I rewrote the tale with a wickedly sexy twist. This romantic and erotic version has her wanting to be bad for just one day by purposely running into three musclebound brothers in the forest, and trying them on for size.

She's known these delicious men since they were children, but they were a forbidden fruit.

These men offer her more than just porridge and a place to rest her head. Not only do they offer her the best sex of her life, but she's soon welcomed into their loving family bond.

The reason I chose this particular fairy tale is a simple one: what erotic romance writer wouldn't want to start with the premise of a beautiful woman and three hot woodsmen? As soon as Goldilocks popped into my head, I knew it had to be mine. I immediately put everything else aside and ran with it.

Hopefully you'll fall in love with each character as much as I did, and enjoy my version of *Goldilocks and the Three Bears*.

Much love,
Pebbles Lacasse

Copyright
The Naughty Goldie Series
© 2023 Pebbles Lacasse

Paperback ISBN 978-1-989979-42-6

Cover design © 2023 cover artist Pebbles Lacasse
Photographs by Pebbles Lacasse
Cover model J. M.
Published by Pebbles Lacasse
www.pebbleslacasse.com
Edited by: Off the Shelf Editing
https://www.offtheshelfediting.com

Pebbles Lacasse

Who better to sin with than three bad boys who share everything

Goldilocks
and the Three
Bear Brothers
book one

Goldilocks & The Three Bear Brothers

Book 1

The *Naughty Goldie* Series

by Pebbles Lacasse

**Originally featured as Book 2 in
LaSasha Flame's
*Torrid Tales: Fairy Tales Retold Collection***

Chapter 1

The summer has been long, or at least it seems so. I've been living with my parents for the past three months and I can't wait to head back to the dorms in the big city. I'll be leaving home for the final time in three days. After this semester, I'll have extra credits toward my degree and will begin my life as an independent adult. I won't lie, it scares me a bit.

My parents are truly wonderful, but overbearing. I'm twenty-three and they still want to know where I'm going, what I'll be doing, and who I'm going to be doing it with. When it comes to dating, the guy has to be parent approved. I couldn't count how many times I've heard the fifteen-minute lecture on how bad boys never change and they'll give good girls terrible reputations. I think they're just worried about how their friends will judge them on their parenting if I date an unsuitable.

I recently ended it with a guy I'd dated for just over a year. His name was Jeff and he was parent approved. He's studying to become a mortgage lawyer and he bored the hell out of me! The guy never wanted to go anywhere that didn't involve his parents tagging along, and he only ever took me to places that were so snooze-inducing I could barely keep my eyes open. The man even made me yawn in bed. I don't think I ever had an orgasm that I didn't give myself.

Before Jeff there was Sebastian, also parent approved. He too bored me. He could make me cum, but he enjoyed missionary position and never veered from it, and always had a lame excuse as to why he didn't want to try a different position. We dated for about six months, but I ended it when I moved away to university. I told him a long-distance relationship would simply be too difficult. He cried. I was relieved to be rid of him but pretended I wasn't so I wouldn't hurt him even more.

Before him was Cody, a good boy from our town. He was also stamped for parental approval. We dated for two years and ended the summer before I became a high school senior. We had sex a few times and it was good but short. He didn't enjoy going down on me and that was frustrating. He loved getting blowjobs though. It didn't take long for me to insist it be tit-for-tat. If he didn't eat my pussy, I wouldn't suck his prick. He fucked hard with his big cock, but he couldn't last more than two minutes at best.

All I've ever wanted is to find a decent guy who knows how to have excellent sex that benefits me as well as him. I don't think it's too much to ask. I want someone who loves to make me cum with their mouth, fucks like the devil himself, and has an endless desire to pleasure me with new and exciting sexual adventures. Maybe I can find a bad boy that knows how to thrill me if I stop dating the good boys.

My room looks exactly the same as it did before I moved away for school. The pictures of my childhood friends still frame the old mirror I spent hours upon hours staring into, trying to make myself look different from who I am. High school and those awful teenage mood-swings were unbearable, but overall the experience was enjoyable.

I choose my senior high school yearbook from the long rows of books on my wall-to-wall shelf. I want to reminisce about the good days when life was easier, but at the time, I thought it was so hard. If I only knew back then how tough it could get, I'd have made it a point to enjoy my teens more.

When I toss it on the bed, the book falls open to the page I've masturbated to many times. Staring back at me is an all too familiar half-page photo of the hottest boy in high school. His wavy chestnut hair and piercing blue eyes make my heart skip a beat. My eyes trace the strong jaw framing the plump, inviting lips, wishing I could taste them. Bash Bear. Yes, it's a funny name for such a ruggedly handsome man. I would never have dated him—he wasn't parent approved. In fact, my parents forbid me to spend time with any of the Bear brothers.

All three still reside in the cottage that sits directly between the house I grew up in, where my parents still reside, and the closest town. I could best describe the area as a thick forest with many back trails we use for dirt bikes, ATVs, snowmobiles, and hiking. There's only one road leading in to town and it's a single lane dirt road that winds around the Bear property.

While driving by, I'd always look through the trees hoping to see one of those hunky guys but rarely did. The only brother I'd see regularly was Bash, the youngest of the three. He took the same school bus as me. They all have wide shoulders, stand quite tall, and are as strong as bulls.

If I missed the bus, I'd walk the trail that leads through the corner of the Bear brothers' fifteen-hundred-acre private property. It's the fastest way to get to town, even though it zigzags the whole way. Sometimes I would see one of them cutting down a tree or hunting with a bow and arrow, but they would only watch me. Never did they try to strike up a conversation. Even if they had, I was too shy to talk to them. I would have likely just kept walking.

Bash would talk to me once in a while in the morning on the bus. He and I were the only two students to board for the next eight minutes when we'd arrived at Stacey's pick-up spot. She always talked to Bash. She was desperately in love with him. He didn't show her much interest other than friendship. That didn't stop her from making a fool of herself by so obviously swooning over him.

I slam my yearbook shut and slip it back in its spot on the shelf. I'm not a silly high school girl with a crush anymore. I'm an adult woman and I can do whatever I'd like. My body is mine to do with as I please, and it's not up for debate with my parents anymore.

My heart pounds as I strip off my clothes and step into the shower. I'm going to go walking in the woods after I'm clean and smell better. Maybe I'll find one of the Bear brothers, the hunky bad boys my parents forbid me to talk to. If I fuck one of them, who will know? Nobody. It'll be our secret, as if it never happened.

They aren't known for boasting about their sexual conquests; in fact, they've denied being with some women who have told tales of incredible sexual romps that only happen in dirty magazines or pornos. Sex that good isn't real life.

I slip on a white summer dress, omitting the panties. I forgo a bra since my round breasts are perky and firm. Besides, the light material allows for my nipples to form stiff peaks that will draw any hot-blooded man's attention. I glide my hands down my small waist, resting them on my full hips. Yes, I look good in this. I usually wear heels with this dress even though I'm plenty tall enough without them. Today, I'll wear the proper foot attire since I'll be hiking.

After quickly drying my long blonde hair, I pull it up into a high ponytail. Makeup isn't something I'm all that skilled at applying. Whenever I try to outline my sky-blue eyes with a pencil, I end up looking like I have two black eyes, so I'll skip it, as usual. A spritz of perfume and I'm ready for an afternoon of forbidden lust, if I'm lucky enough to run into a Bear.

After another quick check from head to toe in the mirror, I go to the bathroom to pee and wash my hands. While the warm water runs over my fingers, I stare at myself in the mirror. "You've always been a good girl. Today, you're a dirty little whore. You are a strong, independent woman who needs a bad boy to fuck her into a coma." I take a deep breath and dry my hands before heading to the kitchen.

"Mom, I'm heading out for a walk."

"Wait, where are you going?" she asks as I quickly walk past her.

"Just for a walk. I want to soak up as much of this nature as I can before heading back to school."

The city is so hustle and bustle. She knows I enjoy the solitude of the vast forest. I'm going to miss the smell of the moss and the dark quietness from the thick canopy of trees.

She smiles. "I wish you didn't have to return to school but it's what's best for you."

Dad walks into the kitchen from outside, carrying an empty mug. He drinks his first coffee on the porch while reading the newspaper. Morning is his quiet time, as he calls it. He's wearing a scowl likely brought on by the political section. "Don't be walking on the Bear property. Those boys can't be trusted. You know all about their bad reputation."

"Dad, I'm sure they won't care if I walk the paths that lead through their property. They're not as bad as you think they are."

"Yes, they are! The middle boy—" Dad starts.

"Mack."

"I don't care what his name is. He's been arrested for despicable offences that we won't talk about."

"You mean drunk and nude in public, right?" My giggling has him pursing his lips.

"Just stay away from those boys, Goldilocks," Mom says, hoping my father will leave it at that.

"Mom, Dad, I don't plan on being home until late. I have my whistle in case I see a real bear that might actually harm me."

I quickly slip on my hiking boots and rush out the door. I can hear them talking to each other, but I pay no attention and head across the yard toward the path that will lead me to a possible Bear sighting. My heart thumps rapidly in my chest as I near the barely-readable wooden sign posted on the tree stating the property is private, no trespassing. It's there only for the purpose of non-locals who think its okay to hunt wherever they want without the owner's permission.

My heart sinks after about twenty minutes of walking and seeing not a single soul. I'm not a slut, but today, I want to be treated like one. I've allotted myself this one day to be bad, and dammit, if I have to go knocking on their door to ask for a cup of sugar, that's exactly what I'll do. Will I have the courage to ask for sex? I doubt it.

I hear a chainsaw rev up not too far from me, halting me mid-step. A warm shiver runs down my spine that I welcome. This is scary, thrilling, and dangerous. Well, maybe not so dangerous.

I step off the path and head toward the sound. There he is, Patch. He's wearing a long-sleeved black and white button-up plaid shirt, but the buttons aren't fastened, allowing it to flow as he moves, showing off his tanned chest. His heavy gloves grip the thunderous tool as it easily slices through the log like a hot knife through cold butter. His muscles glisten with sweat.

The chainsaw idles as he kicks the freshly cut log out of his way using the sole of his heavy black boot. The saw revs up again as his strong thighs flex to steady his body, allowing him to lift the heavy, vibrating machine. He lowers it onto the tree's stump, cutting off another chunk of firewood. It idles once again after that piece falls.

He suddenly turns, locking his brown eyes on me. My fear has me frozen in place. Patch is the oldest of the brothers and the one who is known to have a mean streak. He's never hit a woman, but he sure can clean the floor with a husky man when the need arises.

Patch turns his body to face me, setting the saw on the thick, moss-covered ground. With his eyes assessing me, he slowly removes his gloves, dropping them beside the quiet saw. The breeze feels hotter than it had only a few seconds ago. Maybe it's just me, but the temperature seems to have risen ten degrees.

"Hello, Goldilocks. What brings you out this way? You lost?" His voice is so deep that it stirs the carnal desire I've had locked away inside me for far too long.

I clear my throat, realizing how suddenly dry it is. "No, I'm not lost."

"I thought you were away at school," he says as he opens his jug, taking a long swig of what I assume to be water.

"I've been home for the summer, but I'll be heading back soon."

"Thirsty?" he asks, waving the jug in my direction.

I nod and start walking toward him. It's not a lie, I'm absolutely parched and regretting not taking a bottle of water with me. It's a long walk. What was I thinking? He hands me the jug. I've never stood this close to Patch before and it's been years since I've even set eyes on him. He's more handsome than I remember him to be.

I take a large mouthful and swallow, suddenly realizing it isn't water. Whatever it is, it burns my throat. I grimace and cough, feeling like an idiot.

Patch snickers, taking the jug back when I hold it out to him. "Moonshine. I make it myself. Do you like it?"

I cough again. "It … burns."

He laughs and takes a long swig before putting the cap back on and sitting it on the ground next to his gloves.

"What brings you out this way?"

I suddenly wish I had taken a larger gulp of the poison in his bottle. "Um, I don't know. I suppose I'm just out for a walk in the forest."

"Is that so? You're definitely not a little girl who missed her school bus and needs to cut through my property." His eyes scan my body in an obvious manner. "So, what other reason could you have for trespassing?"

He steps closer to me, his eyes glaring down into mine. I'm shivering despite the heat. I take a deep breath and let it out slowly, hoping to regain some composure.

"No, I'm not a little girl anymore."

His eyes slowly look down to my breasts and back up. "You grew into yourself nicely. So tell me, why are you here, sexy woman?"

I simply shrug and look down, unable to find the words to explain. My heart thumps so loudly in my ears. All I can hear are the leaves rustling in the trees, yet everything he says sounds crystal clear. My eyes land on his strong abs. No matter how hard I try to look away, I can't seem to make it happen.

"You're a good girl, Goldilocks. I'm definitely not good. What the hell do you want with me?"

As if overcome by the spirit of a slut, I reply with, "I am not as innocent as everyone thinks. Maybe I want to be bad for once in my life. I've always done the right thing, said the right thing, and been the best I can be. I don't want to be that perfect little girl today."

Patch takes two quick steps toward me, grasping the back of my neck with one hand, wrapping the other around my back, pulling me against him until my breasts press firmly to his wide chest. I can smell the salt on his sweaty skin and feel his raging body heat.

"Are you a virgin?" he whispers.

I shake my head. "I'm not a virgin, but my experience is limited."

"What does that mean? Has your pussy ever been fucked hard?" His thin lips are so close that the vibration from his voice can be felt on my lips.

"I've been fucked hard, just not good."

"I can fuck you really good."

His mouth presses to mine, spreading my lips with his. He explores my entire mouth with his moonshine flavored tongue. It tastes better this way. His flesh burns through the thin fabric of my dress. He grabs my ass, pinching a whole cheek firmly in his grip. The bulge in his tight, torn jeans digs into my belly and grows larger by the second. In a flash he spins me, grabbing my throat and right breast to hold me against him while his lips rest just behind my left ear.

I whimper when his deep voice rattles me. "Tell me you want me to fuck you hard and fast, Goldilocks."

"I … I want you to fuck me hard and fast," I manage to mutter with an obvious stutter. I'm terrified and thrilled at the same time, much like sitting on a rollercoaster and expecting one hell of a ride.

Patch releases my breast but continues his grip on my throat. He steps back, yanking my dress up to expose my ass.

"Surprise, surprise! No panties. Perhaps you're not as innocent as everyone thinks."

He slides his hand around to the back of my neck, using that advantage to bend me forward. He's holding my hip with the other hand so I can't move away from him. Once my ass is exposed and vulnerable, he releases my neck, dragging his fingertips along my spine, continuing down the crease between my ass cheeks until he reaches my slippery pussy. He smears my arousal up and down the folds of my pussy, purposely avoiding my twitching clitoris.

Holy fuck! This is definitely starting to be a tale I could send to one of those magazines.

I hear his zipper pull down. The thought of him standing behind me with his hard-on in his hand excites me even more. Here we are, surrounded by the forest, nearly nude and about to fuck beneath the silent canopy of tall trees. I've never even had sex outside of a bedroom, let alone outdoors.

His legs part and his boots rest on either side of mine. The tip of his prick lines up to the opening of my eager pussy. My heart is pounding furiously behind my ribs. He rubs the thick head up and down my slick lips. With one long, slow push forward, he buries himself deep into me. I cry out but love the stretch. His prick is a nice size; not too big and definitely not small.

"You fit nice, little girl," he grumbles. "Are you ready?"

"Will you fuck me hard?"

"I sure as fuck will."

"Then yes, I'm ready."

His huge hands grab my waist, nearly surrounding it. He jerks me back while slamming his hips forward. I nearly lose my footing. He snickers but immediately does it again. This time, I'm prepared for it.

Oh yes, this is going to be amazing! He rams me again but doesn't pause this time. His cock fills me, relentlessly pounding into me. I've never been fucked this viciously, nor this fast. My head is spinning.

My moans and the sound of our bodies slapping together ricochet from tree to tree. It takes all the strength I have to keep my legs from collapsing. I'm coming already! He's only pounded into me a dozen times and I'm already crying out. My body freezes in a state of awe, reveling in the glory of my first orgasm from being fucked incredibly hard and fast by a Bear.

"Yes!" In my experience, it'll be over soon. "Please don't stop! Fuck me! Fuck…"

My words stick in my throat when I'm overwhelmed by another body tightening climax. My knees buckle but I don't fall. Patch is hanging onto my waist so tightly that I seem to be dangling off his cock. I am a vessel for him to fuck, a piece of ass willingly given to him to use as he will.

"You're a fucking slut, aren't you? You're not a good little girl. You're a dirty little whore," he growls.

"Yes … I'm a … fucking … whore!" Another raging orgasm tears through me even more violently than the first two. My legs have turned into cooked spaghetti noodles. It's useless to try to stand; I know they can't sustain my weight.

Patch's solid cock slips from my body. He spins me to face him. He grabs my ass in one hand and the back of my head in the other. His lips press to mine while he walks me backward toward a tree.

He pulls my dress up and over my head and tosses it over a branch. Instinct is to cover my nakedness, but I clutch my hands into fists to fight that urge. His menacing eyes ogle my bare breasts and naked mound.

"I've often wondered what you look like under your clothes, after you were grown, of course. You're just as fucking hot as I'd imagined, probably more so. Goldilocks, turn around and bend over that tree trunk. You'd better hang on because I'm going to fuck the hell out of your cunt."

I smile while biting my bottom lip. If it's anything like how he's been fucking me, I want more of it, lots more. Not to seem too eager, I think I'll take my time getting into position. I let my eyes sink down to his chest and further, past his ripped abs. His hand is gripping his stiff prick. I want it back inside of me. I turn, placing my hands on the bark of the tree, and bending slightly while turning my face to look at his. I see him lick his bottom lip as his eyes lock on my behind.

"I would love to fuck that sweet ass of yours," he comments.

I quickly straighten up and spin around. My mood instantly shifts from whore-mode to terrified virgin. "I've never … I mean … you're not going to…"

He snickers. "I'm not going to shove my cock in your ass, if that's what you're asking. I don't do anything without permission. Judging by the look on your face, I'm assuming I don't have your permission."

"No, I've never actually done that."

"Mack would be the best one of us three to de-virgin your asshole. If you'd be interested in trying that, I'm sure he'd oblige you. His cock is thinner than mine. He's gentle despite his rough appearance. He loves to eat pussy but ass is his favorite hole to fuck."

"I'd be interested in trying. I've heard my girlfriends talk about anal but my boyfriends would never try it. They said it was dirty and gross." I can't help but roll my eyes and giggle nervously.

"Okay, let's find him, shall we?"

He pulls his cell phone from his back pocket and taps it. He holds it screen up, touching the speaker icon. I hear it ring.

Chapter 2

A man speaks with a voice similar to Patch's. "What the fuck do you want?"

"Hey, what are you up to?" Patch asks.

"Why? Do you miss me?"

"I don't miss your ugly fucking mug. I'm standing before a gorgeous and naked Goldilocks."

"Like fuck you are! No way is that fine piece of ass coming anywhere near the likes of you. She'd come for my fat tongue long before your limp cock." I hear the phone click. "Fucker hung up!"

Patch presses some numbers before holding the phone flat again.

"What the fuck, man?" Mack yells after answering the call.

Patch tells me, "Say hello, Goldilocks."

"Hello Mack," I say toward the phone. My hand instinctively covers my mouth, hoping I won't burst out laughing.

"Are you fucking with me? Is that really Goldilocks?"

"Yeah, in the flesh and nothing else. She just rode my pole."

"Fuck off! No way! Who is that?"

"Goldilocks! I'm not fucking lying to you. She has a proposition for you."

"I won't believe you until you take a picture of her and send it to me."

I shake my head when Patch holds up his phone. He tells me, "Cover your face if you prefer."

With my hand over my eyes, he snaps a shot. A few seconds later I hear the sound of the photo being sent. I'm suddenly very self-conscious.

"Holy fuck! You weren't bullshitting me! That's really her!"

"Yeah, fucker, that's what I've been trying to tell you."

"Goddamn, she's fucking hot! Okay, so what's this proposition you were talking about?"

"I don't think you really want to know. Maybe I'll just keep her to myself."

"Patch, don't tease me like this, man!"

"Well, the lovely Goldilocks has never had the pleasure of having a cock in her ass, and she'd like to experience it. I told her you were the best."

"Well, I am the best," he boasts. I hear Mack clear his throat. "Are you fucking with me?"

"No, I'm not. So, what do you say? Would you kindly fuck this gorgeous woman's virgin ass before she heads back to school in a few days?"

"It'd be my pleasure! Well, hers too, of course. Where are you?"

"We're about a hundred feet north of where Bash wiped out on the dirt bike and busted his arm."

"Which arm?"

They're both chuckling as if it's hilarious that he's broken more than just one of his limbs. I vaguely recall him starting his junior year of high school with a cast on his left arm.

"His ulna, not his humerus. He broke that at Dog's Creek."

"Oh yeah! That was a hell of a wipe out!" Mack laughs. "I can be there in about ten minutes unless you'd rather meet at the house."

"I'll bring her home with me," Patch replies while handing my dress to me. His eyes study my curves before it slips over my head. He stuffs his hard prick back into his jeans.

"Aren't you going to finish?"

"Not right now," he replies.

"I'm nervous." I don't know why I just confessed that to him.

"Goldilocks, there's nothing to fear. Mack will be very gentle. I'll be there to make sure of it."

"You're going to be there … like, watching us?"

"Were you thinking you and I were done? Woman, I haven't fucked you hard enough yet and definitely not long enough. After he's done with you, you're going to finish me off."

I shake my head. "I don't know about that. I'll probably be exhausted by then."

He says, "I doubt it. You'll want more. Whores always want more." My pussy clenches.

We start walking back to the house after he collects his chainsaw and half-empty jug of moonshine. I lead the way. I'm sure he's watching my ass move beneath my dress. To make things more fun, I pinch the back hem of my dress and lift it, exposing my ass.

"You're a fucking tease, aren't you? I should drop this shit and finish us both off."

"So, why don't you?" I taunt him with a sweet innocence that doesn't suit the situation.

He laughs. "Because, little slut, I'm going to make you wait."

"I thought I was a whore. First I'm a slut, then I'm a whore. I wish you'd make up your mind." I tease partly to make conversation so my anxiety doesn't overwhelm me, thus beckoning me to change my mind.

"Do you have a preference?"

I laugh. "No, I'm just making fun of your unoriginal choices of degrading titles."

"I was only asking out of kindness. I'll call you whatever I damn well please. You said you wanted to be bad today, so be bad, really fucking bad. Be a whore, a slut who needs cocks, lots of cocks. Beg to be filled in every hole like a dirty slut who can't get enough."

I turn and look him in the eye. "Please tell me you don't think I'm actually slutty, aside from today, of course."

He stops walking so he won't slam into me. "I know you're a good girl, but even good girls have needs that should be fulfilled. I don't think anybody has given you the attention you deserve. Today, you can be as bad as you want. Nobody is judging you. You can act like a total cum-guzzling whore if you want to. It wouldn't be the first time a good girl begged us to let her be bad. You just happen to be the good girl us brothers have dreamed of getting our hands on but never thought it possible."

"You all have? Even Bash?" I bite my lip nervously, hoping he'll tell me that Bash has spoken favorably of me.

"Goldilocks, Bash has mentioned you on many occasions. I think he'd prefer a relationship with you, but he would settle for a romp." He tilts his head. "You like Bash, don't you?"

"I've always had a crush on Bash. All three of you are gorgeous, each in your own way. Bash … he's … different. Yes, I really like Bash."

Before he can say anything else, I turn to continue making my way through the forest with Patch in tow and my dress hiked above my waist, Bash in my thoughts. Just before we come to the clearing where the cottage sits, I drop my dress despite Patch's disapproving groan.

My pace must have slowed because he zips past me. I quickly catch up. We round the house to find Mack sitting on the long porch on a heavy, wooden chair with a beer in his hand, bare feet propped on a wooden stump. He seems darker and more mysterious from being shadowed by the overhanging roof. He's bare-chested and his faded, low-rise jeans have tears in both knees.

"Do you want a beer?" he asks while wearing that same sexy crooked smile that used to make the girls fall at his feet.

"I'd love one," I reply.

"Get me one too," Patch adds before Mack slips into the house.

"What's the matter, your moonshine burning a hole in your gut?"

"Keep mouthing off, slut, and I'll put something in that yap to shut you up," Patch says as he winks. He points to a chair across from the one Mack was sitting in.

I sit and lean back, closing my eyes for a moment to fully appreciate the warmth of the sun on my face. Beneath the canopy of trees is much cooler than here in the clearing. When I open them, Mack is standing in front of me handing me a beer. I take it and smile, noticing that his hair is wet from a recent shower. He smells nice too.

"Thank you." The beer is cold and satisfying as it flows down my throat.

Mack sits back in his chair while Patch walks into the house, the screen door slamming closed behind him. He looks at the peaks my nipples have formed in my dress and licks his lips slowly. His eyes lift to mine as he takes a long swig of his beer. I haven't looked away from him yet.

"So, you want to experience a cock in your ass. Is that right?" He's very blunt.

I fight my habit of playing shy. "I've never tried it, but it comes highly recommended by some of my friends. No one has ever wanted to do that with me."

He grunts, his eyebrows furrowing into a scowl. "You're not the type of girl to have random sex with two men in one day. What's gotten into you, other than my brother's dick I'm assuming?"

I shrug and clear my throat to eradicate the puff of cotton that seems to be looming. "I feel as though I've missed out on so much of what life has to offer. People are always telling me about their wild sexual experiences in college, but I don't have anything to boast about. The men I've been with have been rather boring."

"So, you came to visit my brother?"

"Not specifically." I take a long drink of beer, nearly finishing it. I elaborate when he doesn't say anything. "You boys have always been off limits to me. For years, my parents have been warning me to stay away from all three of you. I've heard some stories through the rumor mill about you guys being hot lays. So, I thought I'd start walking this way and see if I'd run into one of you."

As Patch opens the screen door, he says, "She wants to be very, very bad for only one day. Today. I promised her we would let her be as bad as she wants to be. But this little woman has it in for our baby brother."

"Well, they are closest in age," Mack adds.

I whisper, "Yeah, but he'll never want me after I've had his brothers inside me."

"Is that a joke?" Mack snickers.

"No guy wants a girl who slutted herself out to his brothers. Life doesn't work that way." I set my empty beer bottle down on the chunk of tree they use as a table. "So, are we doing this? If I sit here any longer, I'll either get too drunk to give my consent or lose my nerve and run away, regretting that decision for the rest of my life."

I don't wait for his response. I stand and walk past Patch, then pull the screen door open and walk into their house before either of them even gets to their feet. It's cleaner than I had expected, considering three men live here.

The cabin is made from long logs which give it a rustic appearance, but the furniture is what draws my attention. Everything is made from trees that were plucked from the surrounding acreage and built by hand. Even the bed frame I can see through the open door of one of the bedrooms is made from immature tree trunks. I love this house!

I'm startled when a thick hand slides into mine. Mack is looking back at me with eyes more tender than I have ever known them to be while leading me toward a bedroom. He guides me into a large bedroom.

Mack lifts my chin and smiles at me. He brushes a stray lock of hair from my cheek, tucking it gently behind my ear. My knees are shaking and I'm taking deep breaths to help me remain calm.

"I'll be gentle with you, especially since this is your first time. I don't want to hurt you. You'll need to tell me if you're in pain or if you want me to stop for any reason. At first, it'll feel uncomfortable. Stay calm and relaxed, I'll move slowly. As your ass stretches, you'll start to enjoy it more and more."

"Trust me, if I don't like it, I'll definitely speak up," I assure him.

His lips press to mine just once. "Take off your dress."

I wish I had drunk another beer. I came here to get fucked in the ass and that's what I'm going to do. Off goes my dress. I stand before him completely nude while he casually undresses, not giving my body so much as a glance. Mack pulls open a dresser drawer and takes a small bottle out before pushing it closed. He ushers me to the bed and asks me to lie on my back. I do as he asks.

"Do you enjoy receiving oral sex?" he whispers seductively.

"Of course. It feels good, after all."

"Did my brother cum inside you?"

"No, he didn't finish."

He touches both of my knees gently while looking at my eyes. The heat from his hands radiates across my skin, warming my entire body. He lowers his face to my mound and begins lapping at my clitoris. It isn't long before I'm moaning and humping up to meet each stroke of his tongue. Mack teases my ass with a fingertip, and I clench instinctually.

"You have to relax," he instructs as his finger continues to taunt my asshole.

To distract me, he sucks my clitoris painfully hard and I scream. My hands grab wads of his long, wet hair, ready to yank him off me if he does it again. I'm startled to realize that his finger is in my ass, wiggling and cautiously pulling at it. Stranger yet, my clit is twitching wildly because of it.

I concentrate on relaxing while enjoying his lips and tongue. He isn't working my clit enough to bring me to orgasm, but I don't think that's his intention at this point in time. Soon, he has two digits inside my tight hole, both pulling to stretch it wide enough to compensate his cock's girth.

I took a quick gander at his prick while he was getting undressed. Patch didn't lie when he said Mack's cock is smaller than his. It's longer, but thinner. He isn't any larger than what's evacuated my body, therefore I'm not as afraid to have him inside my ass as I would be if he were larger.

He sucks my swelling clit until it's thick and hard, ready to erupt my body into a vicious orgasm. Much to my dismay, he stops and flips me onto my belly, lifting my ass up by my hips until I'm on my knees and shoving a pillow beneath me.

He slides up behind me, kneeling behind me. He presses the head of his slippery cock against my well lubricated asshole. More cold liquid drips onto my flesh as he slowly begins to fill me, stopping each time I tense and patiently waiting for me to relax before continuing.

It isn't long before he's completely buried deep inside my asshole with his pelvis pressing against my ass cheeks. I feel so full, so dirty, so slutty! This is taboo; very raunchy and nasty. I love the mental aspect of it as much as the sensation of being full.

Each time he pulls back, I feel relief. When he pushes back in, that changes the sensation to one that's foreign to me, but I like it very much. My thoughts keep drifting away from reality. My focus is on the pleasure I feel each time his prick glides along my inner walls. It's as if he rubs nerves I didn't know existed, each one shooting tiny tickles directly into in my clit. What a thrill this is!

Mack asks me to lie face down with a pillow under my hips, my legs slightly spread. His thighs are straddling my butt cheeks with his feet draped over the back of my knees, pinning them down. His ass lifts and lowers, drilling into me with an easy rhythmic motion that has me moaning with each deep penetration.

He pulls the elastic band from my ponytail, setting my hair free. His fingers weave into it, grasping it firmly. The heat of his breath on my cheek and the weight of his chest on my back create a scenario of being under his control. I like it. I like feeling as if he can do whatever he wants to me and I am defenseless to do anything about it. I like it because I know I can yell for him to get off of me and he will. I feel safe in my vulnerability, even though I don't know Mack all that well.

His reputation around town isn't a good one. He's been described as a scruffy, feisty guy with strange perversions and a bad attitude. None of which describes the man making love to my ass. Mack is freshly showered, drizzled with a sweet, manly cologne and he's more tender than any lover has ever been with me. His touch is strong but velvety; loving, I'd be willing to say.

Mack's hand slips beneath my tummy and down toward my clit. The instant his fingertips glide over my button, I whimper and grind my hips down onto them. His fingers swirl and stroke my swollen nub, urging me closer and closer to the edge. I don't want to cum. If I do, this will end, and I dread that. I've only ever been able to cum once during play because my clit becomes too painfully sensitive to touch.

My hips lift, desperate to evade his fingers but my efforts are forted. His prick fucks faster, really working my asshole and forcing my pussy down onto his fingers. I can't hold my climax back any longer.

Every muscle starting at my belly button exploding outward begins to tighten until I am rigid and unmoving. My lungs fill and hold. It feels like a balloon is filling with heat inside of me, bloating my entire vagina from within my depths. It's going to burst! I've never had this sensation hold for so long. Orgasms are usually so quick to end, but not this time.

I'm panting short breaths, each one laced with increasingly loud moans until a powerful scream blasts from my core. I'm coming harder and more gloriously than I ever have in my entire life! I seem to be stuck at the height of climax for a long time. Suddenly, something enters my sloppy wet pussy and begins waving. Fingers … they must be Patch's fingers. I don't care who's they are! Just don't stop! Don't ever stop!

With a violent shutter, my orgasm peaks. Only my body exists, nothing else, no one else. Each part of my pussy is twitching, pushing, and gripping with spasms.

Hot! Hot and wet! So wet! Sloshing wet! I am writhing beneath this strong man whose weight is pinning me to the bed. I couldn't get him off me if I tried, not that I want that to happen. I feel light now, as if I'm floating up to the heavens and taking him with me.

His fingers are still twiddling my aching clit, but it doesn't at all hurt. I want him to make me cum again, just like the last time. I need it! I need him to keep going! The fingers are still filling me, stretching my tight pussy and I love the ache they bring.

"Oh, yes! Fuck my ass! Oh, please, make me cum again. Please!" I'm pleading like a desperate whore.

I've never felt anything as completely overwhelming as this. I need to cum again to prove to my mind that it was indeed real and magnificent. The whole experience feels like a glorious dream, a dream that continues to this very moment.

I'm going to cum again! Never has my clit cum again so soon post-orgasm. The fingers fuck me slowly while Mack drills his prick into my ass with a quick, steady pace. Something cold is pressed against my clit. It's vibrating! I don't own a vibrator and have never experienced one. Holy shit!

I'm immediately jerking, thrusting my hips, and wail, sounding like a wild animal in the throes of a mighty battle. I jerk before coming to a statue-like stillness. I'm thrown into a whole-body engulfing, mind-dazing euphoria. I don't know what happens during the next few seconds. My muscles jerk, pulling me back from the distant existence I've drifted off to. I'm exhausted. Every inch of my skin is tingling.

Mack pulls out of my ass as the fingers leave my pussy. He rolls off me, kisses my cheek gently, and gets off the bed. I hear his bare feet slap the floor as he leaves me to the quietness of my mind. All I can hear are my satisfactory whimpers and the pounding of my overworked heart.

Chapter 3

I hear a scuffling of shoes on the floor and it startles me. I thought I was alone. Mack left the room so who is here with me? It must be Patch getting ready to finish fucking me like he said he would do after Mack had his way with me.

"Patch, have you been here the whole time?" I ask with a fatigued voice.

"No and I hope you're not disappointed, but I'm not Patch."

I quickly flip over and sit up, pulling the sheet with me to cover myself. Bash is leaning against the doorframe with his hands in his pants pockets and a quirky grin on his face.

"How long have you been standing there? Were those your fingers in me?"

He nods. "Yes, those were mine. I came home and Patch told me you were in here with Mack trying anal for the first time. I had to come see if he was bullshitting me. When I saw that it was you, I wanted you to have the best first anal sex experience possible. So, I helped out. I hope you don't mind."

"Um, no, I suppose I don't. I'm sorry you had to see me like that." I pause, shaking my head rapidly. He looks at me strangely. "I'm sorry, I don't know what I'm supposed to say right now."

"Goldie, I like you. I've always liked you."

He walks over and sits beside me on the bed. I'm extremely uncomfortable because I'm nude beneath this sheet and suddenly emotionally vulnerable, regretting my decision to fuck his brothers. Does he think I'm a whore now and wants nothing to do with me? I pull the sheet tighter over my chest, dreading that thought. If he were disgusted with me, he wouldn't be sitting on the bed with me after having fingered me into one of the best climaxes of my life. It makes no sense, him saying he likes me after having just watched me get my ass pounded by Mack.

He takes my hand in his. "I respect you, always have. You're a nice girl with a solid head on your shoulders. You know what you want in life and you aren't afraid to go after it, no matter what anyone tells you. To be completely honest, you intimidate the hell out of me."

"I am? You really think I ... do I?"

He snickers. "Yes, you do. You've always been better than me and I like that. To see you here enjoying yourself like this is wonderful. Patch said you had your heart set on experiencing what it's like to be a bad girl by doing some taboo things. I think that's great. Everyone should let their hair down now and then to break up the monotony. Life can be boring, but it doesn't have to be."

"Maybe you did like me in high school, but after what just happened, you aren't going to see me in the same light."

"No, I won't. I'll see you in a better light. It makes me want to know you more."

"Oh, I see. You only want to fuck me now."

"Yes, I do, but there's more to it. I'd like to take you out to dinner, get to know you better."

I smile and ask, "Where did Mack go? He just left without a word."

"He's probably in the shower."

"I'd like to ask him if he came in my ass or not."

"No, he didn't finish," Bash states matter-of-fact.

"What is it with you Bear brothers? Do any of you like to cum or do you all prefer to avoid it?"

"We like coming just fine, thank you. We prefer to make sure the woman is completely satisfied before we take our pleasure."

"So, they're going to come back in here and do me again?"

"Is that such a bad thing?" he asks with a salacious smirk.

"No, but with you here, it feels wrong for some reason. I mean, if you want to explore a relationship with me, I shouldn't be having sex with your brothers."

"It's okay, we like to share each other's toys." His teasing snicker has me laughing but doubting his statement.

I look at him and ask, "Do you want to have sex with me today? I mean, if I'm being bad and experiencing new things, you're new."

He leans his face very close to me, his lips nearly touching mine. "Would you like to be with me?"

I can feel my body quivering. I whisper with a shaky voice, "I've always wanted to be with you."

A shock of wonderment rips across his expression a second before his warm, puffy lips press to mine. I've hoped for this since I was a little girl and the teacher introduced him as a new student to my class. I was only eight years old, but I had the biggest crush on him. Now, in this moment, I am his to do with as he pleases.

The heat from his palm on my cheek seems to radiate down to my breasts and further. My thighs instinctually squeeze together when my pussy twitches, alerting me that she wants him.

Our lips part, enabling him to pull off his shirt. As it falls to the floor, I'm shocked to see the large tattoo he has. It engulfs his left pectoral muscle up to his collar, over his shoulder and down his arm ending near his wrist. The detail is incredible, telling a story that I hope to learn in the future.

Fuck! He is thin but his chest is strong, abs are washboard ready and his arms bulge with muscles. It's obvious that he grew up slinging lumber in the woods with Patch and helping Mack build custom log homes.

"Wait, I want you in my mouth. I've dreamed of this moment for a long time, and I want to pleasure you first."

His face perks up in a sexy grin before he rises to his feet. With his eyes focused on mine, his jeans drop to his ankles followed by his underwear. A very large, stiff cock springs forth, ready for me to suck. He snickers when I gasp, shocked at its size.

"I get that reaction a lot."

I pry my eyes from his enormous prick long enough to glance up at his face. Since I was old enough to know what oral sex was, I've dreamed of what Bash would look like from this angle. The view is so much more thrilling than I had imagined it to be. He's even more desirable than I had thought possible.

"I heard the stories, but I didn't believe them. I mean, people sling a lot of shit when they've had a few drinks, most of which isn't to be taken at face value. I don't know if I can get much of it in my mouth."

"Changing your mind?"

I shake my head while studying his thick cock with my eyes, daring to clutch his prick in the tender grip of my palm. My hand looks small in comparison.

"You are so fucking beautiful. Do you have any idea of how many times I've jerked off at the thought of this exact situation? I don't think I can count that high."

"Really?" I ask, more shocked from the confession of his jerking off than the amount of times he claims he had.

"You really have no idea, do you?" Bash whispers with a crack in his voice.

His strong hand gently caresses my cheek while I look up at him. His expression has softened, erasing the roughness of his exterior to expose the emotion within him. He never struck me as a soft-hearted man, but I've only seen what he's allowed people to see. Right now, alone together, he's letting me see a side of him that not many likely do.

"Tell me," I whisper.

"You are the woman every man in this town has dreamed of making love to. When you walk into a crowded room, people take notice. Women are jealous of you and men dream of having you look at them the way you are looking at me right now. How am I so lucky to be here with you?"

My face slowly drops as I shake my head. "I'm not me today, not really. Casual sex is not something I've ever done, and yet I was with both of your brothers. That makes me no better than a common slut, taking what I want and not caring who hurts from my actions. Doesn't it bother you that I was with them?"

"No, it doesn't. I share everything with my brothers and vice versa. We're close, very close. Since our parents died, it's only been the three of us. We rely on one another for everything in life. Patch's first girlfriend was the one who taught Mack and me how to please a woman. I'm grateful to her for those lessons. It's not uncommon for us to share women. Maybe one day that'll come to an end, but I hope not. I think it keeps us close."

For a moment, I imagine myself living here, dating Bash, and having sex with his two brothers any time the mood hits. My pussy twinges at the thought. It's the variety that has my womanhood damp. Each brother's cock is a different size, as are their bodies; each magnificent, strong and drool-worthy in its own way.

"Do you want me?" I ask with my eyes fixed on his.

We stare into one another's eyes for what seems like an eternity. He slowly leans down, lifting my chin with his finger. Ever so tenderly, his warm lips touch mine. My body instantly reacts. My nipples stiffen, and my thighs press tightly together. I want him, all of him, including his heart.

"Let me taste you," I whisper.

Bash stands tall, offering his thick prick for my pleasure. My hand is small against the thickness of his shaft. I kiss the tip, tasting a drop of his sticky arousal and I lick my lips before wrapping them around the head, teasing his pee-hole with my tongue and tasting his sex. A soft moan escapes him as I lean forward, taking as much of him as my stretched lips will allow. Fuck, his cock is huge!

I grip the base of his thick shaft firmly and suckle on as much of his length as I can manage to fit in my mouth. The spongy head of his shaft presses against the back of my throat and I want more, but my gaping mouth will only compensate so much.

I moan with delight when his heavy hand caresses my head. His thick fingers comb through my hair, pulling it off my face into a loose ponytail which he holds in his grasp. I'm grateful because now I can lick and suck him without my hair wrapping around his cock, thus making me gag. It's hard enough taking his size, I don't need any further intrusion making this more of a challenge.

Bash moans loudly and then pulls my mouth away from his engorged prick. He leans down, wrapping his strong arm around my back. He lifts me, pulling me with him as he crawls onto the bed above me. His mouth hovers over mine but he doesn't kiss me. Instead, his eyes meet mine.

"Goldie, I'm going to make love to you. I want your heart to belong to me. Your body is yours to share as you will, but never your heart, that's mine. Promise me."

A sensational warmth washes over me, leaving me feeling safer and more protected than I have ever felt. His eyes are kind, alluring and familiar in a way that doesn't seem possible. It's as if we've already shared a life together. Perhaps his yearbook photo is why but I feel like I've known him as my other half for years upon years. Is it possible to feel this close to someone I've seldom spoken with before today?

Our lips entwine as he lowers himself between my legs. His erection presses against my inner thigh. I've wanted him inside of me for so damn long. I shift my hips, but he moves with me, not yet allowing himself the pleasure of entering me just yet. His forearms rest above my shoulders, his fingers weaved into my hair. I could kiss this man all day, for the rest of my life and be very grateful to do so.

He lifts his face and his hips. The tip presses against the slick opening of my sex. I tilt my hips just enough to push the tip between my labia. Our lips part, readying for the moan soon to escape us both. He doesn't push in right away, he savors the moment while his eyes peer deeply into my soul.

Slowly, so slowly, he lowers his hips, burying himself completely. My eyes flutter, unable to remain linked to his. A long moan seeps from my core. At this very second, both my heart and body are being taken by this man.

"I'm yours," I whisper. "Please, don't hurt my heart."

"I've been waiting for you for so many years. I love you, always have. Hurting you … I never could."

His hips wave against me, pressing him so deeply into me that I think he may get stuck inside forever. I hope he does. I don't ever want him to slip out.

The room around us fades away as the friction between us seems to be building a fire deep inside of my belly. My hips leap up to meet his downward thrusts. With my legs wrapped around his thighs, I hang on, not letting him get too far away from me.

We are spinning out of control and my heart has given itself to him for safe keeping. Perhaps it was his all along and that's why I've never fallen in love. The lights have faded from my vision, only his face seems illuminated. My walls tighten around his thrusting shaft, begging him to never stop.

My fingernails dig into his back, begging him to take me! Take all of me! I'm fallen away now, lost in the vastness of my climax. My lids squeeze shut but my mouth gapes, willing to take in air if only my lungs should ever resume function. I'm frozen in time, stuck at the peak of my orgasm as his prick swells inside of me, stretching my already full vagina.

With a hard jerk, Bash spills his hot seed deep inside me. I cry out as I'm drawn back from my euphoria. My entire body shutters beneath him as the walls of my pussy twitch around his throbbing cock.

His eyes remain closed as the pained expression of orgasm eases from his face, replaced by a level of calmness I understand so well. Slowly, his eyes open to discover that I've been watching him.

We remain joined together as his sweet kisses ease away the tensions of my life. I could do this always, with him. With great regret, he rolls off me and onto his back, pulling me against him.

Chapter 4

I rest my head on Bash's tattooed shoulder. My finger traces the outline of the wolf's head that stares out from the left side of his chest, its teeth sharp as if protecting what hides beneath.

"Is the wolf here to protect your heart from women who want to break it?"

"It's there because it's already broken and vulnerable, so it needs to be protected."

I look up at his face, but he doesn't look at me. I ask, "Why is your heart broken?"

"When my parents died, it nearly destroyed me. It took a long time before I could even talk about them without a burning pain in my chest. The wolf is there to remind me that Patch will always protect me. The wolf on the back represents Mack, because he always has my back. If it weren't for Patch willing to watch over me, I would have ended up in foster care. He was only eighteen when they died."

"You were twelve. I remember the principle and guidance counselor coming into the classroom to get you. Nobody knew what was happening. When she whispered in Mr. Heavest's ear, his face fell sullen and his eyes darted straight at you. He wore an expression of pity. I just knew something bad had happened and it involved you. I wanted to go with you right then but was afraid to anger my parents. The teacher told us what happened after he was sure you were out of earshot. I cried all afternoon." The memory causes a lump in my throat and bringing tears to my eyes.

"Why did you cry? You didn't know my parents very well."

"I cried because I could imagine how much pain you were in. My parents were called to come pick me up and bring me home. I didn't know why it hurt me so much."

He places a kiss on the top of my head. I felt his pain that day, and still. I'll never forget it, as I'm sure that day will forever haunt him.

"I know they died in a car accident two weeks before the end of the school year, but what actually happened? You don't have to tell me if it's too painful. I've heard so many farfetched stories."

"Farfetched? Like what?"

"Well, one person said a Bigfoot ran out of the bush and they swerved to avoid it. Another said the truck driver, or the driver of the other car, was drunk. Then some said your father was a mean son of a bitch and did a murder/suicide. I didn't believe any of them."

"Wow! A Bigfoot, huh? That's one I hadn't heard," he laughs.

"My parents wouldn't even talk about the accident. They said it would bring bad luck to speak of the dead. That made no sense to me. They simply told me to stay away from you boys because you were wild to begin with, and without parental guidance, the three of you were going to end up in prison or dead."

"Sounds like your parents never liked my family even when my folks were alive."

"Well, you didn't go to church three days a week and you boys hated wearing proper clothing like shirts and shoes." I roll my eyes and shake my head while my fingertips trace the valleys between his washboard abs. "So, what really happened?"

"They were on their way to get groceries when someone appeared to be trying to pass them on the highway. A witness said that woman was swerving all over the road just before she ran into the back of their car, sending them head-on into the grill of a semi coming in the opposite direction. They all died instantly. It was determined the woman who caused the accident was having a seizure and that's why she was driving so erratically. I take comfort knowing it was sudden death and they didn't suffer. The caskets were closed, so I didn't get to say goodbye. It's like I haven't had closure yet. Anyway, wolf tattoos are my brothers and they protect me."

"I'm sorry about your parents. That must have been very hard for you."

"It was harder on Patch than either Mack or me. Patch took on all the responsibility of raising us. Mack was sixteen, so he pretty much took care of himself, but I needed parenting. I regret giving Patch such a hard time. Maybe that's why we still argue a lot. If you keep touching me like that, I'm going to take you, hard this time."

"Is that so?" I ask, teasingly scratching my nails along the sensitive skin below his belly button.

"Do you think you can handle another fucking or is your pussy sore now?"

"I've had three men inside of me today, so yes, I'm a bit sore. It's wonderful but taxing. I should be getting home."

"I can walk you," he says as he sits up.

"No, you can't. If my parents see me with you … well, it won't be a good thing."

"True. Your dad might shoot me," he says with a jest.

Little does he realize my father just might. I'm his little girl and Bash is a Bear brother, a dangerous Satan worshipper who has soiled my good reputation. Well, they're probably right about that last part.

I slip my dress over my head and straighten it by gliding my hands down along my hips. Bash has his jeans on in no time. He arranges my boots so I can slip into them easily. I follow him through the living room. The unmistakably delicious scent of someone working hard in the kitchen fills my nostrils, making my mouth fill with saliva.

"Hey, what's for supper?" Bash asks Mack, who is standing over a pot holding a heavy ladle.

"Rabbit stew. Can you set the table? Goldilocks, you're staying for dinner," he insists without giving me the courtesy of posting it as a question.

"No, I can't. I wish I could, but I must get back. Thank you for the invitation. It smells great."

"Are you sure? You can call home to let your parents know you're here," he says as he offers up his phone.

I pull mine from the pocket of my dress, showing it to him. "I'm set, thank you. But no."

"She can't stay. Her parents would freak out if they knew she was here. They don't care for us all that much. We're wild boys, don't you know?"

"Wild boys?" Mack repeats as he drops the ladle in the pot and grabs Bash around his waist, pinning him against the wall as if wrestling in a professional cage match. "We are a bit wild."

Mack fakes a few punches to Bash's kidneys while they laugh.

"It's true, they think we're Satan worshippers because we don't go to church."

Mack releases him, tussling his hair in the process. "Well, we are doing our best to get their daughter into some trouble."

"Yeah, we're corrupting her with our bad-boy, seductive ways," Bash teases me with a wave of his eyebrows. I smile agreeing with him.

Patch walks up behind me, slapping me on the ass as he passes by. "You're both wrong. This hot, young thing is corrupting us."

Mack walks up to me and says, "Hell yeah she is! And, I for one, like it a lot." He kisses me gently on my lips and then looks me up and down. "I hope we get to play again soon."

My eyes shoot to see Bash's reaction but he's sampling the stew and adding salt while Mack is distracted. Patch grabs the spoon from Bash and pushes him out of the way so he can scoop up a taste for himself.

"I ... I don't know. Bash asked me to date him ... so, I'm not sure it's appropriate," I reply shyly.

Mack looks at Patch and then they both look at Bash. Mack asks, "Did you pee on her to mark her as your own?"

"I think he came on her, not peed on her, dumbass," Patch corrects him with his deep voice that vibrates my chest.

"He didn't do either," I reply. "He came inside me, not on me, and there was certainly no urine involved."

"It's not unheard of," Bash tells me with a look of expectation.

"What?" The look of shock on my face has all three of them laughing. "Oh, fuck off, all of you! Nobody does that!" I reply with a flushed face, embarrassed about my gullibility.

Patch kisses my forehead before whispering in my ear. "Some people are into golden showers, but you can relax, we aren't. I would really like to fuck you again before you leave for school. Come by any time."

My breath catches and I find myself biting my bottom lip. My face is flushing again, and my pussy is instantly hot and wet. He's a fun, hard fuck, and I want him again too.

"I'd like that, but it's up to Bash whether he wishes to share me or not," I whisper, but Bash and Mack both hear.

Bash takes my hand. "Goldie, you can fuck whoever you want. I told you that. I want your heart. The rest of you is yours to do with as you choose. If you want to fuck Patch and Mack right now, right here, it's your prerogative. I won't be upset. In fact, I might help out again."

All three of the smoking hot brothers are looking at me with their chests bare and bulges in their jeans. My mind is whirling with thoughts of having all of my three holes filled at the same time. I swallow hard. My face is still flushed but its cause isn't so much embarrassment as it is arousal. My pussy is dripping wet. I can feel my walls clench and it wakes me from my fantasy.

"I, um…" I clear my throat. "I have to go."

Bash reaches out for my hand and I join it. "I'll make sure she gets home safely. Keep supper hot for me."

"Take too long and we'll eat your share," Mack teases with a wink. "See you soon, Goldilocks."

"Bash can give you our phone numbers so you can call us any time the urge hits you." Patch's grin is wide and friendly, which seems unsuitable for his perpetually dangerous scowl.

"Thank you for … you know," I say, and then wave nervously as I slip through the doorway behind Bash.

As we walk, Bash says, "My brothers really like you."

"I like them too," I say with a crack in my voice.

"What are you doing tomorrow?" he asks as he takes a few wide strides and then starts walking backwards in front of me.

"Careful, you'll trip," I warn him.

"As long as you fall on top of me, I won't mind."

I smile and flutter my lashes in a nervous gesture. "I don't know what I'm doing tomorrow. Nothing is set in stone. My mother mentioned shopping for school supplies but I have everything I need, so I might just pass on that."

"You shouldn't," he says.

"Shouldn't what? Pass?"

"Yeah. She loves you and just wants to spend time with you before you move back to school."

"You're probably right. I'll go if she asks. I can say that I need a new laundry hamper or something."

He smiles and turns, slowing his pace until I am at his side. We walk hand in hand, in silence and lost in our own thoughts. I'm thinking about how hard and ruthlessly Patch fucked my pussy. And how Mack pleasured my clit with his mouth and then carefully slid his cock into my ass for my first time ever. But my thoughts are focused around Bash and the tenderness he showed me while our bodies and hearts became one. Even if our momentary love affair fades too quickly after I leave him, it will forever be instilled in my heart, totally and completely having taken me.

"Goldie, promise me that you'll come see me before you go back to school," he begs with sadness behind his words. His eyes look straight ahead as if looking at me will utterly destroy him if I should deny him his request.

"I promise to see you again before I leave. Maybe I'll visit your brothers again too, if you're sure that would be acceptable."

"Yes, Goldie, I'd like that too."

"Can I ask you why you call me Goldie and not Goldilocks?"

"Because nobody else does," he replies with a silly smile. "It'll be my pet name for you. Goldie. It has a nice ring to it. Don't you think?"

"Sure, why not? Normally I'd hate it but as long as you're the only Bear brother to call me Goldie, I'm okay with it."

"Do you not like the nickname?"

"I do as long as it's you're the one saying it," I reply after taking his outstretched hand so he can help me over a tree trunk that fell during the last storm.

"It's mine and only mine."

"When do you return to university?" I ask him.

"I only have one more course I'd like to take before I agree to graduate. I don't have to take it but I think it'll benefit me. It doesn't start for a few more weeks. How many credits do you need?"

"None, actually. I was wanting to go back to get a few extra credits. I'm worried I may not live up to the expectations of life. But now I'm rethinking that idea. I'd like to stay here with you. I won't because that would be ridiculous! I've worked my whole life for my education." I look at him and look away, wondering if I should confess something. "I didn't tell my parents this, and I hope it stays between us, but I already wrote the final exam to get my degree."

He looks at me with surprise. "You did? How did you do? And, the better question would be, why are you going back?"

"I wasn't ready to start my life, I suppose. I really like knowing that I can if I want to. Maybe I'm afraid to fail at real life. You probably think I'm an idiot."

"Of course not! You're a very intelligent woman, definitely not idiot material. So, if you're not taking classes, why return?"

"I'm signed up for additional classes to bump my qualifications."

"Do you not think you'll be a good nurse?"

"Of course, I do. I was working at the nursing home two blocks from my school and they've asked me to come on full time, but I don't know where I want to be. I have to decide whether to take that job offer, which is a good one, or look for something closer to my parents. I don't want to live with them forever and I fear that's what they'll expect if I decide to move back this way."

"Move in with us! There, issue solved!" Bash isn't laughing.

"Is that a joke?" I ask. "I think my parents would disown me or, at the very least call me a heathen."

"So?"

"I love my parents, but I don't think they'd accept that decision. Besides, before today, you hadn't said more than a dozen sentences to me, and all of a sudden you want me to move in? I don't think so."

"Well, the offer stands. Mack can design a log cabin for you on our property and you can live there rent free as long as you want. I can live in the big house with my brothers. No pressure!"

"That's very kind. Excessive, but kind. Why don't we take it a little slower than that, shall we?" I stop walking and turn to look at him.

"Slower? It took us fifteen years to get here. How much slower can we go?"

"Well, this is where I leave you."

"I know," he says, looking very disappointed that we've arrived near to my parent's home. "Give me your phone."

I hand it to him and watch as he puts all of their phone numbers in it. He hands it back to me with a silly grin.

"I named us Fucker, Eater, and Lover. That way, if your parents happen to look through your phone, they won't know it's us."

I roll my eyes and scan for their names. He really did use those titles. "Right, because Fucker, Eater, and Lover won't give cause for concern."

He laughs, kissing me once before turning me toward my parent's house and cracking my ass with his palm. I gasp, having not been expecting it. I rub it as I make my way across the yard. I'm sure he's laughing as he watches me try to soothe my butt.

"What's the matter with your bum?" my mother asks.

I jolt, not realizing she was standing behind the sheet hanging from the clothesline and swaying in the breeze.

"I fell and landed on my... do you need help?" I ask, hoping to change the subject before she can see through my lie.

"Sure!"

As we hang the remaining sheets, I catch her glancing at me more often than one should.

"What is it?"

"Hmm?" she asks, trying to seem innocently oblivious that she was staring.

"You're staring at me."

"Oh, it's nothing."

"Spill it, Mom!"

She turns to look toward the house as if making sure nobody is within earshot. "I know where you were and I'm all right with it, but don't tell your father."

"What?" I ask nervously. My body quivers with a strange childhood fear of getting caught. She can't possibly know where I was.

"You were with Bash Bear."

"H-how do you ... what makes you think I was..." I look toward the trail that I just came from to see if he followed me into the clearing.

"I saw you with him. The trees aren't as thick and bushy as you might have thought. Besides, I heard him laughing as you came into the clearing. Don't worry; like I said, I'm not upset. You're an adult and can do as you please. Your father would disagree, however, so let's keep this between us."

"Um, okay. I'm … ah," I'm stumbling to find the right thing to say.

I had no idea my mother was so liberated in her new way of thinking. She's always hissed the Bear name when she spoke of them. Perhaps it's my father who doesn't like them and not my mother at all. I must be looking at her with a confused expression because she smiles.

"I had a flat tire up the road about three years ago. The rain was pouring in sheets and it was hard to see ten feet in front of me. I pulled over and got out of the car. I had the car up on the jack, but the wind was blowing and I was afraid the jack wouldn't hold. Just as I was about to take the spare from the trunk, Patch came walking up. I hadn't noticed that he'd pulled up and stopped behind my car. Like I said, it was raining heavily. He lowered the jack and tossed it back into the trunk of my car. He walked me to his car and opened the door. I climbed in and sat. Water was dripping from my hair and I was shivering. He started to drive me home but the big oak tree that used to be at the bend had fallen and blocked the road, so he took me to his house. I wasn't afraid of him like I thought I should be. He gave me some dry clothes and offered me a hot shower, but I only took the clothes. He made us some tea and we sat at his kitchen table and talked while the storm passed. He earned my respect that day. Since then, we've chatted in passing."

"Did you tell Daddy?"

Her eyes widen. "Oh no! You can't tell him either!"

"I won't, I promise."

"So, you see, it's all right by me if you want to spend time at their place. I don't know the other boys but if Patch raised them, I'm sure they're respectful men. Are they?"

"Yes, they are. I got to know each one of them today," I'm not lying, "and they all were very good to me." Again, I'm telling the truth.

"You like Bash, then?"

I can feel my face flushing. "Yes, I've always liked Bash."
"I know. Mom's always know.".

FFBI

Chapter 5

After dinner, I help tidy up and then soak my sore pussy and ass in the clawfoot bathtub filled to the rim with hot water, Epsom salts, and lavender oil. I breathe in the calming scent, but I'm too wound up for it to take effect. Picturing all three of them naked might have something to do with its failure.

Afterward, I slip on a nightie and flop on my twin sized bed, checking my phone to see if one of them has called but then remember that they don't have my number so it would be a small miracle if they had. I close my eyes for a moment and picture Bash Bear waiting at the end of his long driveway where the school bus would stop to collect him. My heart always beat a little faster when we rounded that corner and I'd see him hop off the huge tree stump wearing rip-knee jeans and a simple t-shirt with his backpack slung over one shoulder. He used to wear Mack's hand-me-downs until he grew taller than him.

I open my eyes and search my list of contacts for "Lover" and press the green dial icon. It rings only once before he answers.

"Hello, sexy woman. It took you awhile to miss me. I was wondering if you were ever going to call."

"It's only been two hours!"

"Yes, but I missed you. Mack said he wanted to put you up on the table and eat your pussy and ass for dessert but you left too soon. He said his tongue is lonely now. Come back! I'll meet you in the woods and bring you to our house for the night. I'll make sure you get back before sunrise. You might be exhausted by then, but I'll carry you home if I have to."

"That's an intriguing thought, but I'm going to have to pass."

He pulls the phone away from his mouth. "Hey Mack, she said she doesn't want your worthless, dried-up, abrasive tongue." He laughs.

"Hey! His tongue is marvelous," I whisper, hoping my parents don't hear me.

"Should I tell Patch you don't want his lame cock inside of you?"

"Um, no!"

"So, you do want his cock?"

"I ... wait, you're putting words in my mouth!"

"Words, cocks ... you choose," he jokes.

"What?"

"You said I was putting words in your mouth so you can either have words or cocks in your mouth. You choose."

"Smartass! I can't win with you, can I?"

"Sure you can! You can win over and over again but you have to be here for us to make that happen."

"That's not going to be possible tonight." I hear his exasperated exhale. "Did you know that Patch helped my mom with a flat tire and they had a lengthy conversation? I wonder if it went any further than that."

"He can be very seductive and irresistible, so I've heard." He pulls the phone away from his mouth again. "Hey, Patch! So you banged Goldie's mom?"

I hear mumbling in the background and then Bash start laughing.

"What did he say?"

"He's just teasing. Nothing happened between your mom and Patch. Can you picture it though? Your mom sprawled on the kitchen table while Patch nails her? Shit, I think I just grossed myself out."

"Eww!" I shake my head to remove the thought from my mind. "Keep talking like that and I'll never be in the mood for sex again!"

"Oh shit! We don't want that. I'll shut up. So, how did you find this out?"

"She told me after she said she saw me with you in the woods." Silence follows. "It's okay, she's not upset. That's when she told me about her chance meeting with Patch."

"What did your father say about us?"

"He doesn't know about Patch and my mom, or you and me. He wouldn't even try to understand."

"Okay, enough about your parents, my cock has gone soft. I much prefer to have it stiff with you being the cause. Tell me how many times you orgasmed today."

"Why, so you can jack off to my voice?"

"Yes, exactly," he replies with a chuckle.

"No phone sex. I think I've had enough new experiences for one day, thank you. However, I was considering coming to visit you tomorrow around noon. Mom wants to go shopping but said it's okay if I'd rather be with you. My father will be at work all day so she won't have to make up a cover story to tell him. If I simply walk away from the house, she won't know for sure where I'm going if he should care to ask her where I've been all day. Mom doesn't like to lie to my dad."

"We'd love to have you."

"*We,* or *you?*"

He chuckles. "You know I want you always. The guys would love to borrow you, if playing with them is something you'd like to do again."

"This sharing me idea will take some time to get used to," I confess.

"The option is there but not expected, and nobody would throw a temper tantrum if you don't want to play with them. Well, that's not completely true. Mack will whine like a toddler, but give him some cookies and he'll get over it soon enough."

"If the mood hits..." I don't finish my words because my pussy tightens at the thought of having all three of them naked and available at the same time. But then I wonder if I could even handle three men simultaneously invading my body.

"What's on your mind? You fell quiet all of a sudden."

"Um, nothing. I was just thinking." Again I pause too long.

"Thinking what?"

"Never mind, I don't think I could handle it anyway. Okay, so I'll stop in tomorrow. I'm not sure when exactly."

"Text me when you're getting ready to leave and I'll meet you halfway."

"You don't have to do that. I know my way around the forest."

"I know you do, but I'm a gentleman."

"Good night, Bash. Tell the boys I said to sleep tight."

"Goldie says to sleep tight." He pauses then laughs.

"What did they say?"

"Mack is in his room with the door shut now, but Patch said he'll sleep nice and relaxed tonight after giving you a good fucking."

"I doubt Patch will be relaxed since he didn't get to ejaculate." I'm glad he's not here to see me blushing.

He tells him what I said and then relays his reply. "Patch said he jerked off when he watched Mack fuck that sweet ass of yours, and that he'll be dreaming about the many ways he'd like to use your body."

"He did? I didn't know that," I reply, taking a few seconds to imagine him fucking his fist. "So, were you watching Patch jerk off?"

"Um, no! I don't prefer to watch my brother jerk off. He was standing behind me while I put my fingers in your pussy."

"You don't think it's weird to have your hand that close to your brother's cock?"

"I promise I didn't touch him. We're close but not that close. We drew that line in the sand a long time ago."

"I never understood that reference, 'drawing a line in the sand,' because sand is always shifting."

"Okay then, we drew that line in cement."

"I'll see you tomorrow. Good night Bash."

"Good night, lovely Goldie."

I hang up and then go downstairs to sit with my parents in the living room and join them in the silence as we each read for a while. After an hour and I've read the same page three times, I decide to go to bed. I'll need my sleep because I might require a lot of energy for tomorrow.

Chapter 6

The sun is beaming too brightly for my tired eyes so early in the morning. The weatherman is calling for a severe storm in the early afternoon. I've been lying awake in bed for about an hour but I keep closing my eyes so I can better imagine the Bear brother's sexy eyes. If I look too eager to start my day by primping myself now, Dad will question my enthusiasm. Besides, it's too early to head over to the Bear house. I don't want to come across as being overzealous.

The seductive scent of coffee drifts into my nostrils, revving up my brain and urging me out of bed. I flip onto my back and recall the dream I had last night where I was looking into Bash's eyes while he was inside my pussy. One of the brothers was fucking my ass at the same time, but I'm not sure which one. I didn't want to tear my eyes away from Bash's loving gaze long enough to find out.

I sit up, stretch and yawn. As I walk to the door and pull it open, my nightie unravels. This is when I take notice of how dripping wet my pussy is. I quickly make my way to the bathroom to pee and clean myself up before heading to the kitchen to suck back half a pot of coffee.

The instant after Dad's car disappears down the driveway, my mom asks, "So what time are you heading over to the Bear house?"

"Are you sure you don't want me to come with you today? We could make it a girl's day."

"No, love. I want you to go have fun with your new teddy bear."

"Ha ha! I like the play on words, Mom. But are you sure?"

"Of course I'm sure. I want you to have fun with Bash. Let your hair down for once, Goldilocks. You're always so held together. Don't think I didn't notice how lazy and relaxed you seemed when you came home after being with that young man. I don't want to know what he did that led you there, I just want to see you happy. You were happy yesterday with him. You were never like that with anyone you've dated. It looks good on you." She brushes a lock of hair off my shoulder and then smiles while her eyes admire my face. "Yes, definitely more beautiful now."

"Thank you. I take after you."

"Hmm, maybe, but I can't take all the credit. When can you be ready?"

"I'll need a shower before I go."

"If you can be ready in fifteen minutes, I'll drive you. Otherwise you'll have to walk."

"I won't be ready by then. You go ahead. I enjoy the hike anyway."

"All right, bring the whistle with you."

"It's extremely rare to run into an actual bear but I'll bring the whistle anyway."

Mom jokes, "The Bear brothers look scarier than any bear I've ever seen."

"Well, Patch looks scary. Mack and Bash look dangerous but in a seductive way."

"Is there something you aren't telling me?"

"What?" Does she somehow know that I've had all three of them inside my body? No, there's no way she could know that.

"Have a great day. I'll see you for dinner?" She poses that statement more like a question, but I know better than to be late.

"I'll be here, or I'll call in advance."

"If you don't, your father will question your whereabouts."

"I know. I'll keep tabs on the time."

After my shower, I skip the bra and panties, choosing to slip on a halter top and a free-flowing short skirt. As soon as my hair is pulled into a high ponytail, I give my reflection a once over in the mirror and head off to the Bear residence.

I didn't text Bash to let him know I was on my way because I know how to get there and decide to surprise him instead. He needs to realize I'm a strong woman who doesn't need a male escort. This forest is where I grew up. I know it well and enjoy the solitude its foliage provides.

I'm lost in thought about the possible coming events when the sound of a cracking branch nearby startles me back to reality. My feet halt in place. All I can hear is the thunderous pounding of my heart. I scan left and right, trying to hear every sound that isn't typical of the lonely forest.

I hear it again and spin around to look behind me. My eyes are wide as they peer into the dark shadows cast by the roots of the fallen trees, each one taking on the shape of a rather large bear. I suddenly regret not bringing the whistle. I can picture my mother yelling at me while I lie dead in a casket. My fucking heart is so goddamn loud!

The noise has stopped. I should continue the trek to the Bear house making double time, keeping my senses more aware of my surroundings. I take a deep breath while scanning the area one more time. Nothing is moving that shouldn't be but my knees are shaking.

I spin and slam face first into something hard. A scream lodges in my throat but the hard landing on my backside jerks it loose. I hear running behind me but my legs are like cooked pasta noodles with no strength to lift my body. I can't run away from whatever is after me.

A large human hand grabs my forearm, yanking me to my feet. My mouth is suddenly covered by another hand, muffling my screams. I open my eyes to see Patch, blurry and standing in front of me with a wickedly sexy sneer.

"Do you want to play rough, Goldilocks?"

My heart is on fire from trying to break itself free from my chest. My glare should alert him that I'm not impressed with them having hunted me, but he doesn't seem to care in the least. I'm furious that he gave me such a start and I want him to know it. I can't turn to see who's holding me hostage because I'm not able to spin my head. It is held back against a strong chest by a hand over my mouth. My right arm has been pulled behind me and is being restrained unnecessarily high. When I groan in protest, it's lowered but not released.

"I asked you a question, Goldilocks, and I expect an answer," Patch says with a deep and seductive voice.

My anger is subsiding and I can think clearer now that my adrenaline isn't flooding my brain. I nod my head slowly. My curiosity about what they have planned for me has my pussy tightening. I'm desperate to know who's behind me, but sort of hoping the answer isn't revealed until after I'm fucked by the stranger. The uncertainty has my nipples pressing hard against my soft cotton halter top.

"He's going to release your mouth and you're not going to scream. Are you? It doesn't matter if you do, nobody will hear you this far into the woods." I try to say that I won't, but my voice halts behind the hand. "Have you ever had a rape fantasy?"

I shrug my shoulders. I have but saying it out loud seems wrong. Too many women and men are raped, so a fantasy of it happening to me shouldn't be arousing even if it's only a game. I don't want anyone to have sex with me without my consent, but the idea of someone I'm willing to play with taking me while I play the helpless victim sounds rather thrilling.

"We don't often call it rape because rape refers to non-consensual sex and we'd gladly destroy someone for doing that. Nobody would ever find their body. But, back to what I was saying. We call it consensual non-consent. That means that we pretend it's against your will, but you have a safeword in case it gets too hairy for you. Are you willing to play along?"

I nod my head.

"Red will be the word that makes everything stop immediately. If you say it, we will let you go, and no one will

touch you in a sexual manner after that. Do you understand?"
I nod. "Let's get started, shall we?"

***

My arms are pulled around in front of me by the man at
my back. They're held together while Patch begins skillfully
wrapping a thick rope around them in a rather appealing
design. He ties it off. The hands release my arms, giving me
the opportunity to turn but Patch tugs the rope, redirecting my
attention. I step forward with a nervous giggle. I've never been
bound before. It's scary and that makes it seem so taboo. I
seem to like taboo lately.

The rope is looped around an overhanging tree branch and
pulled taught. My body is stretched tall. My boots rest
comfortably on the mossy foliage, but my arms are raised high
over my head. I can't go anywhere. Again, nervous laughter.

Patch smirks and then grasps my top, pulling it up to
expose my breasts. He lifts it until it covers my eyes. I can't
see but the rope keeps me from losing my balance and toppling
over. My skirt is yanked down, and each boot is lifted until the
material and boots are freed from my body. My bare feet rest
on the cushioned layer of soft moss. I remain nude, blind, and
vulnerable for all to see.

My heart is throbbing and I can just barely see the moving
human shapes through the tight fabric weave. A figure I
recognize to be Bash is a few feet away from me and taking
off his pants. I turn my body so I can get an idea of who's
around me and that's when I see two more figures. One is
Mack and the other Patch. Mack is sitting on a rock or stump
behind me, but not undressing. Patch stands behind me,
folding my skirt.

"I'm going to be rough with you." Patch's deep voice
vibrates my chest like the roar of a powerful motor.

"Rough? Like how?" I ask, suddenly rethinking this
bondage/consensual non-consensual game I've agreed to play.

Patch's unmistakable voice comes from directly behind my head. "Spanking, pinching, swatting."

"Swatting?" I ask in barely a whisper.

"With a switch taken from a tree. It stings and will likely leave red welts on your body, but they'll go away."

"I don't think I'll enjoy the switch." My heart is pounding furiously again.

"I'll let you know when it's coming and you can decide if you don't want to try it, or be a brave little girl and give it a try. If you don't care for it, you can say orange and I won't use it again."

He presses his hot chest against my back and glides his fingers down my tummy, sending shivers that stiffen my nipples. They slowly ease their way down between the slippery folds of my pussy, and begin gently stroking my clitoris.

"I'll reward you well if you take the punishments."

"What if I scream?"

"Your screams are my reward. No one will hear your desperate pleas, so scream until your mouth runs dry. Just remember your safewords. What are they?"

"Orange and red," I tell him with a mouth that suddenly feels very dry.

"Saying yellow means you've reach your intensity level. Do you understand?"

"Yes, I do."

"I'll start with a spanking using my hands. I'm going to swat you twelve times. Eight of those will be on your ass."

"And the other four?"

"You'll see," he replies in his typical stern and assertive manner.

I feel safe with these men, even though one of them is about to physically hurt me, something I never thought I'd permit a man to do. His fingers leave my pussy, disappointing me.

"Open your mouth and taste your excitement."

I do as instructed, opening wide. His fingers slip into my mouth and I close my lips around them, sucking my flavor from each digit. He pushes them deeper into my mouth, so far I fear I may gag. Ever so slowly he retracts out.

"I want you to count the spanks. All of them. If you miss one, I'll add two to the count."

His hand cracks down on my right ass cheek and I yelp. My heart is pounding so hard in my chest that it might break free!

"You aren't counting. This is your one warning."

The figure I'm fairly sure to be Bash stands a few feet in front of me and I believe he's stroking his cock. He's watching Patch punish me and it's arousing him.

"One," I retort. Another crack on the same cheek. I immediately yell, fearing he'll add another. "Two!"

The anticipation of the third has me quivering. He pauses, remaining still and silent. I jolt when his fingertips brush across the burning handprints on my ass. I wait for another touch, not knowing if he'll spank me or touch me tenderly. The anticipation of it builds butterflies in my tummy.

Crack! Yelp! "Three!" Another immediately follows. "Four." The final two alternate ass cheeks. "Five, six!"

I'm gasping, tears welling up behind the makeshift blindfold.

"Your ass is turning a lovely shade of pink and I can see my giant handprints on your shapely ass. It's making my dick hard." He pushes his bare, rock-hard cock between my tightly squeezed legs. I tilt my hips toward him. I want him inside of me.

"Eager little bitch, aren't you? You're so fucking wet!" he purrs behind my left ear.

He reaches around me, cupping both of my breasts in his slap-happy palms. His hot fingers pinch my nipples, gradually increasing the intensity of the pressure, making me cry out. I'm wiggling to get away but it's useless. He has them held firmly. The more I squirm, the harder he pinches and tighter he holds me against his chest.

I whimper, hoping he'll take pity on me. He doesn't. Instead, while he squeezes my nipples, he pulls them as if he's trying to rip them from my breasts. I scream when the pain is too great. He releases them and then tenderly rolls them between those same punishing fingers. This feels really good, surprisingly hypersensitive to his touch immediately after the inflicted pain.

Bash walks toward me and the silhouette of his thick, erect prick swings with each step. He has a great cock. Having him inside of me makes me feel full, but it's more than just a physical fullness. It's a total mind-altering feeling that I can't explain. All I know is I want more of that, more of him.

He slides the halter top higher up on my arms to expose my mouth, leaving my eyes shielded, and then presses his to mine. He has the softest lips of all the brothers and his kisses are more tender despite his efforts to seem aggressive. Even in the height of his passion, when most men's kisses are more eager, his puffy lips are like pillowed bumpers, protecting me from the harshness of the assault.

Bash slips his fingers between my sex, quickly finding my clitoris. His easy circles rim the hood in a tantalizing tease. I moan softly into his mouth.

Whack! Whack! I scream. The sharp burning of my ass cheeks combined with the arousal of my clitoris is thrilling!

"Count," Bash whispers.

It takes me a moment to remember what number I'm at. "Ah ... seven, eight," I manage.

My hips tilt toward Bash's hand, pleading with him not to stop. His fingers slip further back and into my pussy. With the palm of his hand pressing against my clit, I'm coming closer and closer to orgasm. I hump against it, taking his fingers into me while simultaneously arousing my clit. I'm so fucking close!

He pulls his hand away just before my climax erupts. I beg and plead but he only steps away from me. Patch takes Bash's place in front of me. He's just as tall as Bash but so much larger and therefore more intimidating. I like the fear his size awards me, especially when I can't get away. I know I'm safe, so the fear is more of a thrill than anything.

"Spread your legs wide," he tells me, while caressing my silky breasts with his gruff hands.

I do as he's instructed but only able to spread my legs about shoulder width, otherwise I'll be on my tiptoes. I'm sure to step cautiously on the soft moss. Getting a stick poked in the bottom of my foot would be a mood wrecker for sure. I stand with my legs apart. The cool air caresses my hot, swollen clit.

"I'm going to spank your pussy."

"No!" I shout. Before I can close my legs in protest, his thick hand swats my pussy lips, stinging my clit like a bolt of electricity zapped me.

I shriek from the shock of the sting and don't want another, not yet anyway. My legs are shaking so hard I can't lift them to pull them closed. Instead, my knees buckle inward, shifting my weight and putting more strain on my wrists.

"Open your legs or I'll add another. Don't forget to count." His words ring loudly in the quiet forest, even though they were spoken in his normal tone.

"Nine," I whisper. Realizing it wasn't as painful as my mind had lead me to believe, I do as he orders, spreading my legs as wide as before.

"Ready?" I bite my bottom lip, as if that will make what's to come less shocking.

Slap! My pussy stings and burns. He doesn't remove his hand after that slap, which seems to make the pain dissipate quickly because of his hand's heat. Two of his fingers easily slide into my drenched hole, burrowing so deeply into me that I can feel his knuckles pressing against my opening. I'm not surprised by how soaking wet I am.

He waves inside of me, wickedly assaulting my g-spot. The speed of his movements have me coming in a matter of seconds. I wail through a powerful orgasm that begins deep inside my body and finishes with a blast of my hot cum coating his hand. It continues to spirit, splashing against my thighs, tickling my flesh as it trickles downward. His fingers withdraw, leaving me panting and shaking.

He slaps my right tit, likely thinking I won't enjoy it, but I do. *Swat!* "Ten!" I scream with a taunting laugh quickly following. I push my chest toward him, inviting another. I'm so fucking turned on that he could slap me anywhere and I'll likely invite him to do it again.

Another slap, this one to my left tit. *Slap!* "Eleven!" I growl in a very uncivilized way. I've always thought of myself as a lady with very feminine tendencies but right now, I'm a horny bitch with a need for satisfaction.

Swat! I lurch toward him and scream, "Twelve! Fuck me!"

Bash rushes behind me, grasping my hips in his tough hands and lifting them until I'm balancing myself on my tip-toes. He lines up his cock and rams its full length into me, forcing the breath from my lungs with a loud, appreciative moan.

He pounds himself into me with a fierceness that I'd been hoping for. My head is spinning, the darkness is pulling me further from reality as orgasms ripple through me, one after another. I have no concept of how long he fucks me, but it seems like forever yet not long enough. He slides his gorgeous prick from my twitching cunt and I whine like a child who dropped their sucker in the dirt. "More!"

My hands are untied and set free. They feel heavy and tingle as my blood rushes through them. The shirt covering my eyes is yanked off, but I can't seem to open my lids. The brightness of the sun has me squinting as my lashes shield my protesting eyes.

My hair is grabbed and I'm forced onto my knees. After my head is yanked back, a cock is shoved between my parted lips. Whomever it is is fucking my mouth quickly but not deeply. I wrap my lips around it and suck as it pulls and pushes. The sound of someone to my right unzipping his pants seems very loud.

The hand releases my hair, but another quickly takes its place. I can tell it's someone else because of the easiness of this guy's hair-pulling. This man isn't as brutish in his guidance. His cock pushes into my mouth and I can tell it belongs to Mack. Its smaller size gives him away. It's long but thinner than his brothers' pricks. He glides in and out of my mouth as my lips encircle him.

My hair falls free, but I continue to ravish Mack's hard cock. My forehead bounces against his strong belly as I take him deep into my throat, amazing myself with my ability to control my gag reflex. His moan is lengthy and appreciative of my talent.

Two hands grasp me under my arm and I'm suddenly being lifted to my feet. This is disappointing; I wanted to make Mack cum down my throat. Mack lines up my boots for me to step into, wiping the dirt and moss from my soles before guiding them in.

Bash takes my hand and walks me over to where Patch is standing, fiddling with a rope. I can finally see clearly without the sun burning my eyes. Seeing three extremely handsome, well-built men walking naked through the forest with their stiff cocks wagging free in the breeze has my pussy twitching. I want them, all of them.

Chapter 7

Patch waves me toward him. He stands on the opposite side of a downed tree. The trunk is thick and level at my hips. I stand with my hands resting on its bark, admiring its texture.

"Give me your hands," he instructs.

Without hesitation, I lift them and put them together just as they were before. He binds them with a slight difference from the last time. He slowly pulls the rope, forcing me to step forward until I'm leaning over the trunk. My tummy rests on the scratchy bark. It's not very comfortable, that's for sure.

He squats down, tossing the rope ends through a gap under the trunk. I feel it hit my boots. My calves are wrapped separately using each end of the rope. I can move my feet wider apart but can't step back without my hands being pulled further beneath the trunk. I'm bound around this tree, vulnerable and unable to fight back—not that I'd want to.

Large hands separate my ass cheeks and then a thick cock is pushed between my slick pussy lips until its forced deep inside me. Bash pounds into me and all I can do is lie here and take it. The warm bark digs into my soft skin, scratching its top layer. It hurts but it's adding to the whole experience. Oh fuck! This is so incredible!

Just before I cum, he pulls out of me, leaving me panting and grunting in protest. Another cock is buried into me and this time I know its Mack's. He slides easily in me. His cock being slimmer allows for me to focus on its firm tip poking at my cervix with each thrust. I like it, a lot. He also isn't kind enough to let me cum.

He pulls out and is quickly replaced by Patch. His thrusts are relentless and much more powerful than those of his brothers. The thunderous pounding of his thick thighs is painful, but I want more. The bark feels like it's cutting into my skin, but I don't care. At this point, I'd let a wild horse fuck me. Without giving him any warning, I start coming—hard.

He yanks his cock out of me and cracks my ass with a widespread hand, reigniting my burning ass cheek. The sting is incredible, more electric than before. It adds another level of intensity to my already, all-consuming orgasm, ending it with my shrieking wail that echoes back at me from the deepest pockets of the surrounding forest.

As I gasp to catch my breath, something long and thin trails down my spine. My head jerks up, turning as if I'll be able to catch a glimpse of what it is.

"It's a switch," Patch informs me.

"Are you going to hit me with that?" I pant.

"Yes, I'm going to swat you five times. If you accept all of the swats without telling me to stop, we will all fuck you until you can't discern one cock from the other. Are you ready?" Patch explains.

"This is going to hurt a lot, isn't it?" I ask, not really needing him to confirm what I already know.

"Yes, but you might like it," Bash suggests. He's standing several feet behind me.

Patch swats me with the switch and it fucking hurts. The sharp sting overwhelms me. I can't scream. I was expecting the pain but when it tears through my body the way it does, my mind snaps back to reality. I'm no longer lost in the delirium of an orgasmic fog.

"Breathe, Goldilocks," Patch instructs. He places a warm hand on the small of my back and it helps to ground my mind. I inhale slowly, letting it out in silence. He rubs my lower back. "Prepare for another, a little harder."

Twack! Aargh! My head is spinning. I've never felt anything so abrupt in my entire life.

"Take in the pain. Absorb it. Don't let it overwhelm you." Patch is leaning over me, whispering in my ear. "You are stronger than your pain."

I breathe slowly, my eyes blinking away the eruption of tears that are starting to blur my vision. To stop them from building, I close my lids. I nod slowly, letting him know I'm ready for more. Two down, three to go.

The third swat hurts like hell but I don't cry out. I'm trying to take his advice, to absorb the pain and not allow it to overwhelm me. I'm shaking, thankful the ropes are holding me in place, otherwise I'd be on my ass.

Another *whack!* I wasn't ready for this one. I scream, letting the pain escape me through my voice. The sound of my scream drifting into the thickness of the forest draws my mind away with it.

Another crack, this time harder than all the others. My wail is that of a woman lost in her pain. The sound seems to come from someone else, not me, definitely not me. This woman's voice sounds different; deeper and more animalistic.

My ass is caressed, each welted scar from the switch traced with the feathery touch of a tongue. Fuck! It hurts but my pussy is tightening, begging to be touched, licked or fucked. I can't focus my thoughts on any one particular thing. It's as if I've left myself; my inhibitions, fears and insecurities and escaped to a freer state of existence.

Suddenly, my pussy is plundered with a very hard cock. Mack stabs at my cervix, thumping against it in a sensational way that forces me quickly into orgasm. Oh yes! I want more!

His hips bounce off my sore ass cheeks, but I don't care how much they hurt or how the bark scraping the flesh on my body irritates. I want to be filled, to feel the closeness of a warm body. I want Bash!

Mack humps erratically, groaning and panting like a man taking his pleasure. His prick pulls from me, but I hear the whimpering sounds men tend to make when they orgasm, and it pleases me to know that my body was a vessel he used to give himself that much pleasure.

Patch slams his thick dick into me and immediately begins humping into me like a wild animal taking what's his. My pussy spasms around his cock within seconds. I'm overwhelmed, lost in another orgasm, and then another and yet another. I hear him cry out just before his thickening prick yanks from my depths.

At some point, and I don't know when, my ankles and wrists were untied. I could have moved at my own will, had I chosen to. If I had, I'd have been a fool to deny myself this pleasure.

I'm lifted off the fallen tree and carried in a pair of strong arms. My body is laid down on the mossy patch beneath the tree branch I was hanging from originally. It seems like it began so long ago.

Bash's lips press to mine, and the world seems to disappear around us. My arms wrap around his neck, holding his face to mine so my lips can easily reach his. The softness of his hot skin feels like cotton compared to the roughness of the warm tree bark.

He slips his huge cock into me and rests his hips between mine. Instead of fucking me, he holds himself inside me while he lovingly kisses me. His breath fills my lungs and mine his. He is mine, the one I truly wanted. The others don't matter, they're only bodies there for the purpose of my entertainment.

My legs fall open listlessly. His hips gently roll between my thighs, burrowing his hot thickness deep into my soul. My fingers weave into his thick, dark hair. We are panting together, loving the way our bodies move perfectly to complement each other's motion.

My thoughts are fading into darkness as I allow myself to drift away with him. It is only us that exist. We are here together as one. Nothing matters—life and death are irrelevant. I only want to feel the way his heart is thumping harshly in his chest in perfect sync with mine.

"Goldie," Bash whispers under his breath.

My tired legs wrap around his back, ankles linking together to pull him in deeper. Our bodies mold into one. I don't know where I begin and he ends. There is no him and I, it is only us—one being—one heartbeat—one mind.

"I have always loved you," he whispers.

I'm spinning, barely able to keep myself from being thrown off the earth. Our bodies are welded together as if we fear being torn apart by some strange, unforeseen force. His hands clutch either side of my face. His lips continue to touch mine, but not in a traditional kiss. Our breath is one. If he pulls away, neither of us will be able to breathe and we will die. He needs me. I need him.

I've become very small and insignificant beneath him. I just know I am forever lost to this man. A warmth rushes over me, followed by the most amazing orgasm I have ever had the good fortune to experience. His pleasure is also mine. His seed spills into me as wave after wave of the most incredible emotional and physical euphoria overcomes us both.

We lay here, locked together on the mossy floor until his withered manhood slips from my depths, disconnecting our souls. We both sigh heavily as if the separation is excruciating.

His head lifts enough so he can look into my eyes. "I meant what I said, Goldie. I love you, always have. From the first time I saw you, I knew you'd be mine one day."

"I was always drawn to you, too. I just thought it was a childhood crush. It's so much more, isn't it?"

"Yes, for me anyway." His eyes search my face for any doubt that our feelings are mutual.

When a smile creeps up on my face, his expression softens. My hands slowly glide down his sides. He twitches as if ticklish. I giggle and purposefully tickle him.

"That's enough of that!" he says, lifting his tired body off me. I suddenly feel very cold and alone.

Bash helps me sit up and that's when I realize just how weary and well-used my body feels. I look around expecting to see Patch and Mack watching us, but they are nowhere to be found. I'm relieved that our bonded lovemaking wasn't witness by anyone, shared for future ridicule should one of them choose to poke fun at the most favored moment of my life thus far.

I stand on wobbly legs and giggle at how depleted I am of energy. As soon as my hands touch my ass, I'm reminded of the punishment I was given.

"Does it hurt a lot?"

"No, it's not so bad that it'll annoy me. Each time I sit down tonight I'll be thinking about it, and maybe tomorrow too. Does it look bad?"

He ganders at my ass but doesn't say anything, he just continues to stare.

"Well?" I ask impatiently.

"You might not think it looks okay but to me, it's sexy as hell."

"Do you like seeing red lines on my skin? Does it turn you on?"

"I like it because it reminds me how your face looked after each swat. You were so strong, and you overcame. Disciplining you isn't my thing, but Patch really gets off on it. Mack enjoys how aroused some women get from it and I've learned to appreciate it."

"Appreciate it?"

He shrugs, "Yeah. I've been told that the pain and arousal that comes from it can take a person deep into themselves, leaving them feeling emotionally, physically and mentally fulfilled."

"Have you ever been whipped?"

"Patch took a switch to me the day I took his truck out for a joyride and dumped it in the creek." He scratches his head and smiles as if recalling the memory of that day brings him joy. "I didn't enjoy it though. He really let me have it. I remember how those purple lines on my ass burned for days. I tried to make him feel guilty for it but he only smiled at me. He told me he'd gladly whoop me again if I ever needed a refresher."

"He must've been overwhelmed suddenly being the guardian of his two younger brothers. You guys weren't exactly well-behaved boys."

"Yeah, trouble always found us. One day when Patch got angry and stormed off into the woods, I followed him. When I caught up to him, I saw him crying like a desperate man needing help. He was begging for someone to help him, but nobody was around to hear him other than me. I just remember how he looked so small despite his massive size. That's when I realized how hard we were on Patch. That moment changed me."

"Did you ever tell him you were there?"

He shakes his head as he pulls up his jeans. "Hell no. That was a private, desperate time in his life. We all have at least one. I didn't tell Mack either. If I'd have brought it up to Patch, he would've stopped his façade of being the strong parental figure we needed him to be. He didn't have to know I saw his vulnerability. Why am I'm telling you all of this?"

"What about Mack? What was he like growing up?"

"How did he seem to you?"

I think back, trying to remember what my perception of Mack was, but I didn't really know him very well. Since he was a few years older than me, I didn't share classes with him either. I only saw him getting off the school bus and lighting a cigarette before walking up the driveway. I can't smell smoke on him now so I'm sure he quit.

"He always seemed to be sad. He didn't talk much but the girls were always hot for him. Then again, they were for you too, and Patch."

He snickers, sarcastically saying, "Fuck yeah! They all wanted a piece of the hot Bear brothers." I shake my head and roll my eyes at his feigned attempt at egotism. "Mack was a depressed teenager. I think he got into trouble just so someone would give him attention, even if it was the wrong type of attention. Patch took pity on Mack because he was Mom's favorite. She took him everywhere and he loved it. Dad usually had Patch by his side and I always tagged along with them. Mack had the hardest time adjusting after they died."

"And what about you?"

"What about me?"

"What are your future plans?"

"Well, I have to finish one course at school and then I suppose I'll write a book, maybe about our adventures. I'll never leave this forest though. This is my home and I'll live and die here."

Bash walks me most of the way home and then kisses me before sending me on my way. The rain is just starting to fall, creating the sound I refer to as the forest's orchestra. I love this sound but the darkness that comes with it is quite eerie.

$\mathcal{GTB}$

Chapter 8

My father is already home from work by the time I walk in the door. Unfortunately, my mother isn't. As far as he knew, I was supposed to be with her today.

"Where's your mother?"

"Um, I'm not sure. I walked home."

"From the city?"

"No, I was just walking." Why am I lying to my father? I'm a grown woman.

"To where?" His expression has changed from curiosity to irritation.

"I was at the Bear residence." There it is! I stand before him, waiting for his wrath.

After he clears his throat, I watch his Adam's apple bob when he swallows down his anger. "Well, you're a grown woman who can make her own decisions. I thought you were intelligent enough not to lower yourself to be with a Bear boy. They're so beneath you, Goldilocks. They'll only tarnish your good name and reputation."

"Don't you mean *your* good name and reputation? I'm no better than them. Had you two died in a car crash, I wouldn't be nearly as strong or self-sufficient as they are."

"Do not compare yourself to them. They have a long list of criminal behavior that will follow them their entire lives. You will stay away from them if you know what's good for you!"

"Is that a threat?"

"Take it as you will. Whichever scumbag you're about to give yourself to will only use your body and throw you away.

Each one of them is a filthy, vulgar boy in a man's body. You will stay away!"

"I favor Bash, the youngest one. He's a wonderful man with a great future in front of him. He's about to graduate university, in case you didn't know. He has a strong future and he's good to me. Maybe he has a criminal record. I don't know, and I don't care. I feel safe with him, safer than I ever did with the other guys I've dated. Bash actually wants to make me happy. Nobody else ever cared or respected me enough to ask what I wanted. I'm not going to stop seeing him, Daddy."

"If you don't stop seeing him, I won't support you any longer. You'll have to finish school on your own and you won't be welcome in my home. He's bad for you, Goldilocks. I love you and only want what's best for you, and that boy is not it."

"You're kicking me out?" I'm shocked that he would cast his only child aside so easily.

"No, I'm asking you to choose between a promising future and a future loaded with disappointment."

Dad stands up, taking a deep breath and letting it out slowly. I can see the distress in his eyes and it's breaking my heart. Why doesn't he trust my opinion of Bash? I've heard most of the rumors involving the Bear brothers and some I believe to be true, but most are embellished tales to intrigue the gossiping townsfolk. But they would never hurt me. They would defend me if I needed them to. I'm sure of it.

"I feel sorry for you, Daddy. I'm sorry you don't trust me enough to make the choices that are best for me. If I'm to fall, let me fall. You raised me to be strong and independent. Now that I am, you don't like it. I love you but if you won't even try to see things from my perspective, I don't know what else there is to say."

I walk to my room and quickly pack what I'll need into a backpack while choking back tears. The only sounds I hear coming from the other side of my bedroom door is the kettle's obnoxious whistle.

My father is standing at the counter with his back to me when I enter the kitchen, hoping he'll tell me that he was wrong and will try to get to know Bash. But, he doesn't. He doesn't even turn around.

With a soft voice, I say, "I wonder what Mom is going to say about this. They're good, hardworking men, Dad. You should reconsider your intolerance. I'm sure you'd like them if you were to have a conversation with them."

I stand in the silence waiting for something, anything. He sighs heavily but keeps his back to me.

"Daddy, I'm twenty-three years old. Mom was twenty-one when you two married. She was twenty-two when I was born. Are you saying she wasn't wise enough to know you were a good man? Grandpa didn't like you much back then. Mom told me that he begged her not to marry you, but she knew differently. She knew you were good for her. Okay, I'm leaving now. Do you have anything to say?"

Silence.

"I love you, Daddy."

I push open the screen door and walk out, letting it slam behind me. I half expect him to chase after me, his one and only child, but he doesn't.

Evening is setting in and getting darker as I enter the forest. The shadows all look like creatures that are ready to eat my flesh whether I'm dead or not. It's eerily quiet except for the scuffling of my boots on the path. I feel safe here but when I look into the thicket of the trees, knowing I have to walk that way leaves me a bit uneasy.

I dig through my pockets and then the backpack for my phone. It's nowhere. Dammit! I left it on the dining room table along with my keys. Looks like I'll be going it alone.

The thought of an animal chasing me down and eating me has my knees shaking. As proven earlier, I'll likely be too afraid to attempt to outrun a hungry animal. Mom will believe I'm at Bash's. Bash will think I'm home, ignoring him for whatever reason. Maybe he'll find my remains. Hopefully the scene is not too gory.

I listen with a sharp ear while searching the shadows of the forest for anything large and carnivorous. My tiny flashlight just isn't strong enough to cast sufficient light to reflect the eyes of a hungry beast. During the fifteen-minute walk, I trip twice, cursing my clumsiness each time. When I come to the open path, I start to walk quicker, less fearful of uneven ground.

Their house is quiet with only the sound of a television breaking through the silence of the night. I shouldn't be here. What if Bash wants me to stay but his brothers don't? Worse yet, what if my father is right?

My knuckles tap lightly on the heavy wooden door as my broken heart races. The television quiets so I rap again, louder this time. I clear my throat when Mack opens the door.

"Did you come back for more?" he teases, ending with a quirky grin.

"No, my father kicked me out."

His smile sags. "Well, come on in then." He stands aside, allowing me to walk through. "Here, let me take that." I hand him my backpack and he set it on the table.

Patch strolls out of his room, which is right off the kitchen. "What's going on?" He looks concerned.

"Her father kicked her out." Mack shrugs.

"You didn't tell him what we did to you this afternoon, did you?" Patch grins.

"Hell no! If I had, he'd be here with his gun cocked and ready to take you all to your graves."

"I hope your pussy isn't too sore from earlier," Patch says with a crooked grin.

I smile shyly. "No, it's fine."

"So, what happened with your father?" Patch asks while pulling out a kitchen chair and offering it to me. He picks up my backpack and puts it in his room while Mack grabs a few beers from the fridge, handing one to each of us. I look around but don't see Bash, but the bathroom door is closed.

"He asked where I had been all day so I told him I was with Bash. He said that I shouldn't be seen with you hoodlums because you're a bad influence and you'll ruin my innocence."

Patch is quick to remind me that's not so. "As I recall, you came here begging me to take your innocence."

"Yes, I remember. He knows I'm not innocent, but he doesn't like the reputation associated with the name Bear. Now that I'm an adult, I don't think he should tell me who I can't spend my time with."

Patch takes a long slug from his bottle. "And what did you mother say about it?"

"She wasn't home. She'll be so angry with him when she finds out. Of course, I doubt she'll tell him about you rescuing her on the side of the road that rainy day."

"You know about that?"

"I do. She told me," I reply.

This is obviously news to Mack. "What? You rescued her mom? When was this and how did I not hear about it?"

"It was nothing. Her car broke down during a bad storm so I brought her here. I later fixed her car and cut the downed tree blocking the road so she could get home. It wasn't a big deal, still isn't." Patch isn't the type of guy to boast. Mack leaves it at that.

"I'm sure she'll help him come to realize how wrong he is without revealing her pleasant afternoon with you. You two didn't…"

He hisses, "No, absolutely not! She's a married woman and I'll never get with another man's wife behind his back. I have absolute respect for the vows they swore to."

"I'm happy to hear that you didn't fuck my mother." I take a long swig of beer before setting the bottle on the table. "Where's Bash?"

"He's in the shower," Mack replies.

"I probably shouldn't have come here. Just say the word and I'll leave. You guys don't need to take on my bullshit."

Patch frowns. "Where else would you go? No, you'll stay here where we know you'll be safe."

"I could stay at the Presley residence. Kim is back at school so her room is available. They love me."

Mack asks, "Wasn't she your best friend in high school?" I nod. He snickers. "I nailed her on prom night."

"You didn't go to your prom," Patch says.

Startled, I ask, "You what?"

"Not my prom, hers," he corrects him. "I was getting off my shift at the mill when I saw her walking on the side of the road at night in a very fancy dress. I wasn't about to leave her alone on a highway. She said that she always thought I was sexy and didn't want to waste the opportunity. I thought maybe she was drunk, but she swore she hadn't drank anything and I couldn't smell booze on her breath. So, I pulled off the road and we spent a very memorable few hours steaming up the windows. I think about it often."

"She didn't tell me about that!" I'm shocked by her secrecy. "How did she ever keep that from me?"

"Well, maybe she thought you'd judge her harshly, like your father did to you tonight."

"I'd never judge her. I would've drilled her for details though," I say with a guilty grin and lifted brows. "I'm going to be asking her about this the next time I talk to her."

"Are you going to tell her about the past two days?" Patch asks.

"Hell no!" I gulp my beer, finishing the bottle. "Hmm, I guess I can't be upset with her for not telling me about you if I have no plans to tell her about my adventures with all of you. Maybe I'll let the past stay in the past. Perhaps one day when we're old and grey, I'll bring it up."

The bathroom door swings open followed by a cloud of steam. His eyes dart to me and immediately fill with concern. "What are you doing here?"

"I told my father that I was seeing you. He sort of kicked me out." My words are spoken with an overzealous shrug.

Mack hands me another beer and one to Bash, who is standing beside me in just a damp towel. The bulge from his unaroused cock is quite impressive. My mouth waters. I want to suck him until he's rock hard. My pussy is sore from the fucking the three of them gave me this afternoon, but I want him to tenderly make love to me again.

"Well, you'll have to sleep in my room with me, Goldie. I hope that's all right. These hounds won't keep their paws to themselves if I don't protect you." His joking words and evil glare have everyone laughing.

"Bash, I will be honored to share your bed tonight."

Patch states, "If he doesn't keep you warm enough, you can slide in with me."

Mack quickly pipes up. "Lady, my bed is available too. I have a great tongue, as you know."

"I'm sure Bash will keep me very warm and satisfied. But thank you for your offers. I know where to find you should either need arise." Yes, I am flattered by all the attention.

We chat about our high school days and the trouble that seemed to always find them. Patch talks about a few of the sexual adventures he's had with some of the town's women but refuses to stake any names to his claims.

"I know you guys have shared women. Tell me about that," I ask. All three of them shake their heads.

Bash says, "No, those times are just for us and the ladies involved, of course. Our filthy, dirty sexual ménages will remain between us."

"But why?"

"Would you want us to tell others about our trysts with you? They might put two and two together and figure out who you are," Patch says with a raised brow.

"Never mind then. I'm no longer curious," I respond, gulping down the last few drops of my beer. "If it's okay with you guys, I'd like to take a shower. I still have all your scents on me."

"Here, I'll get you a towel," Bash says as he scurries toward the bathroom. I follow him after collecting my backpack.

I forgot to pack a nightie so Bash loans me one of his t-shirts. It just barely covers my ass but I'm grateful nonetheless. I half expect my mom to call the strangely named phone numbers listed in my contacts but she doesn't.

The night is dark and silent other than the soft snores from the beautiful man sleeping beside me. For so many years, I dreamed of being exactly where I am. I wonder if I'm going to wake up somewhere else and realize the past two days were nothing other than something incredible my lonely subconscious imagined.

I admire his lashes that seem to dance along his lids. The slope of his nose is almost perfectly straight which is odd. I remember when he broke it in grade ten. His lips are slightly parted and relaxed, allowing the deep breaths to slip freely in a soothing, rhythmic song.

His eyes pop open and look directly at me without first searching the room. It makes me uneasy. How did he know I was watching him?

"Are you okay? What's wrong?"

I smile and shake my head. "I'm fine. I couldn't sleep so I was watching you, hoping to give my brain incentive to shut down."

"Wasn't working?"

"No," I pout.

"What can I do to help you sleep?" he asks innocently enough. "Do you want something to eat?"

"No, I just want to look at you."

Bash brushes his fingers along my cheek to capture a stray tress of hair and ever so lovingly tuck it behind my ear. The gentleness in his eyes is something I'm sure few have ever seen. How lucky am I?

"You are so beautiful. What are you doing with me?" he asks.

"I was wondering the same of you."

He looks confused. "Goldie, you are the perfect woman, someone I thought should never given me a moment of her time. You're beautiful, smart, driven, strong and sexier than anyone I've ever met. Why are you here … with me? What did I ever do right to deserve this moment with you?"

"I think we're both lucky and deserving of each other."

"If this is a dream, I don't ever want to wake from it."

I lean toward him and quietly press my lips to his. My hands cradle his cheeks as I gracefully straddle him. His cock is already thick and hard when I sit on him. I feel his hand reach beneath me, so I rise up. He aims his shaft between my folds and I slowly lower myself, enveloping his full length with merely a shudder.

Bash's hands glide along my thighs, coming to rest on my hips. I nearly melt when I lift and lower for the first time and feel his fingertips dig into me as a moan escapes his depth. My pelvis rocks on him as he lifts and lowers his hips. It isn't more than a minute before I'm on the verge of losing myself to him once again. I sit straight up so I can rock much quicker and bury him deeper inside me.

With the moonlight casting its shadows upon his face, he looks more innocent than he does in full light. Most people look more dangerous in the darkness, but not Bash. I see him for who he is. I know how fragile his heart is. If I'm not careful, I will break this man's spirit. What a tragedy that would be.

His blue eyes appear darker than the bright blue the daylight proves them to be. This man is mine for as long as I allow him to be. I own him as much as he owns me. We are one, bound by this beautiful night which only the sweetest dream could have created.

He sits up, pressing his mouth to my right nipple and sucking it between his lips. As he rolls it with his tongue, the sensation shoots from my breast straight to my clitoris. I drop my weight onto him, forcing as much of his cock inside of me as possible, and grind my pussy against his strong stomach.

Both of us are breathing heavily. We're lost in each other. His body feels hard and yet so soft. He's abrasive but smooth. Strong bodied, but he is so very fragile. I look down into his eyes only to see them watching my mouth.

"I want you," I whisper. "I want all of you."

I can't hold back any longer. My body rocks wildly as if with a mind of its own. His arms wrap around me, trying to gain some level of control but I'm uncontrollable. I hold his head against my chest, hugging him to me as my hips buck feverishly. The room spins around us as my body tenses and my orgasm shreds me.

I can't tell if his cock is twitching and swelling inside of me or if it's my pussy torturing him with a multitude of wicked spasms that have me clawing my nails into his scalp. His muffled growl proves beyond a doubt that he couldn't prevent the eruption of his pleasure. When my pussy started milking his cock, it was simply too much.

He sits beneath me, his muscles clenching and his breath repeatedly catching in his throat. His cock twitches inside of me, expelling every drop of his seed in my depths. One final heavy exhale ends his climax.

I roll off him and curl up under his arm, my face resting on his chest. We lie here quietly as we slow our breathing. With a kiss to the top of my head, I am left feeling loved.

Chapter 9

A sudden brightness jolts me from my thoughts. Is it morning already? I wasn't even sleeping, or was I? I don't remember falling asleep.

I roll over, pushing my face into the pillow. His scent fills my nostrils and a smile creeps across my face. I'm in Bash Bear's bed. We made love last night. I was his and he was mine. My hand glides along the sheet in search of him but he isn't here. I want him. Starting the day in the same loving way we finished last night would be wonderful.

My thoughts veer toward my father's stubbornness and my mood begins to sour. I flop onto my back and try to remember exactly how it felt to have Bash so deep inside of me. Yes, this eases my worries. Where the hell is he anyway?

I open my eyes, frustrated that he left me without so much as a good morning kiss. My senses liven up when I smell food and hear the hushed chatter of male voices from behind the closed door. With my breath held, I try to hear what they're saying.

"I'm telling you, she's mine. That girl is mine."

"No way, brother! That girl is going places. You're meant to be here, not in a big city, and you know it."

"He's not lying. Enjoy her while you can but you know she won't stay. She's meant for bigger and better than this lazy fucking town. Let her be who she's meant to be. If you hold her back, she'll only resent you later."

"I know, but I fucking love that woman!"

"You've always loved her, even when she didn't know you existed."

"She said she's always wanted me but thought I didn't want her."

"She's just saying that so you won't feel stupid for drooling so much over her tight little ass."

I quietly open the door and lean against the frame with my arms folded over one another. "I really did like him but he seemed unapproachable, as did you all. Is that a collective attribute, or did the three of you just decide one day to start acting standoffish for the sole purpose of keeping people at a distance?"

The three of them stop dead in their tracks and look at me. It's obvious they weren't expecting me to be awake and listening in on their conversation. They seem suddenly shy, none of them choosing to respond. I snicker as I make my way toward the coffee maker. Mack holds up an empty mug which I gladly reach for. He kisses my forehead before letting me take it from him.

He whispers, "Sorry if you heard something you probably shouldn't have. It's just brother-talk."

I pour myself a mug full of the aromatic bean juice. I'm hoping this will jumpstart my weary mind and body.

Patch asks Bash, "Can you hand me that plate?"

After handing it to him, Bash walks over to me and kisses my lips with the same tenderness I felt last night. Nothing in his eyes has changed. He adores me.

Do I love him or is this simply a burst of endorphins from a new and exciting experience that fascinates me, as new relationships do? Am I simply in love with the dangerous excitement these three men incite? If it were only he and I, would the fascination still exist? I want to believe it would, but how can I be sure? Time will tell.

"You should have woken me," I whisper.

"But you were sleeping so soundly."

"You still should have woken me," I say as I attempt to walk past Patch. He wraps his huge hand around my forearm, pulling me closer to him.

With his face inches from mine, Patch's dangerous brown eyes burn hot. He hisses in a chest quivering tone, "Sit down, young one. You're our guest and will sit that pretty little ass of yours at the table while we feed you."

My pussy twitches when the grip of his hot hand eases and trails down my bare arm. I nearly melt from the tender caress. He's a brutish man that stirs my animalistic urges like no other man ever has. Bash doesn't scare me while thrilling me as much as this man-beast seems to do so easily, but it's purely a physical reaction as my heart belongs elsewhere.

I shiver when my hot ass touches the cold wooden chair. I can feel the dampness building between the folds of my pussy. As tired as I am, my body still craves Patch's ability to fuck me with a fierceness that turns me inside out.

The best distraction from my desirous thoughts is the liquid gold in the cup I'm clutching so lovingly in my hands. I cannot wait to get this fuel into my body. Morning coffee is a habit I got into when I moved into the dorm. The late nights and early mornings beckoned for caffeine. One day I'll break the habit, but today is not that day.

Mack and Bash have begun eating before Patch even sits down. He finishes cooking the last pancake and flops it on his plate before setting the pan back on the stove. I quietly eat while watching the three of them interact as if I'm not in the room. The love between these brothers is so deep that it has me wondering what it would be like to have a sibling. When my parents have passed on, who will be my family if I'm not yet married with children of my own? They're lucky to have one another.

"What are you thinking?" Mack asks while tapping my arm.

I'm suddenly aware that all three of them are staring at me. "What?"

"You seem lost in thought. I was wondering what you're thinking?" he repeats.

"Oh, um … I was just observing how you three interact. It's foreign to me … having siblings, I mean. So, what are all of your plans for the day?"

Mack replies, "Patch has to go to work and I have to work on the plans for the new cabin I've been hired to build for a couple who currently reside in China."

"China? Why'd they buy property here of all places?"

He shrugs. "They claim it's quieter here and that's what they want."

"It seems like a long way to travel for vacation."

"They plan to retire here in about five years. In my experience, no matter the great intentions, they never stay. I build it, they come a few times and then sell after they realize their family will never take the time out of their daily lives to travel this far for a week-long visit. It's a pity really. They spend so much time and money to make the home to their exact specifications, but don't get to enjoy it as they'd hoped to."

"That is sad," I whisper while seeing the similarities of that scenario to my father's recent behavior.

"What about you, Bash? What are your plans?"

"I have a bit of work to do on the computer and then I have to go to town, but otherwise I'm all yours. What would you like to do today?"

I reply sarcastically, "I'd like for my father to come to his senses but that's not likely to happen, so I suppose my day is wide open."

"Will you come to town with me?"

"You want to be seen with me?"

He bows his head slightly and places his hand over his heart. "I would be honored to have you next to me for the whole world to see."

Mack and Patch start making cooing and kissy noises to tease him for his tender-heartedness. I laugh at their silliness. I can picture them as young boys doing exactly the same thing if one had mentioned a cute girl in his class he had a crush on. I can almost see their mother telling them, "Stop that!"

I wish I knew them better when their parents were still alive. These boys must have driven them crazy at times. I can't imagine raising three boys, each one different from the other but just as wildly spirited. What a challenge that would be.

"My father won't like it when he hears about it from nosy onlookers who don't know how to mind their own damn business."

While wearing a confused expression, he asks, "He knows you're with me, right?"

"Yes, but he won't like that I'm letting everyone in town know. He'll think I'm doing it purposely to rub it in his face. It'll make him angrier. I'm sure of it."

"You don't have to come with. If you're not ready, I understand," Bash sympathizes.

"I'll think about it, okay?" Bash nods while forcing a smile. I don't want him to think I'm ashamed to be with him because I'm not willing to shout it to the whole town. I should've said I would go and proudly wear him on my arm. But I fear my father will permanently shun me if I don't give him time to accept my decision to be with Bash before announcing it to everyone.

I quickly say, "I want to come with you."

"Are you sure? You don't have to."

"Yes, I'm sure. I want everyone to know I'm with you and that I'm not ashamed to be with you. That didn't sound right, did it? I just … I want people to know that I trust you and that you guys are good men. People love to spread gossip, so, like the song says, let's give them something to talk about."

"Okay," he replies with a solid nod. "Should we make out in the center aisle at Baneck's Drug Mart? Better yet, we could fuck in the car in the hardware store parking lot."

"Um, no! I don't mean a nasty rumor." I shake my head and roll my eyes. "You're hopeless!"

Bash leans toward me and says, "But you want me."

I swallow and clear my throat. "I do."

With a tender kiss to my forehead, he says, "Then it's settled, you'll come to town with me."

It's quiet for a moment while everyone shoves pancakes and strawberries in their mouths. They are not delicate eaters. They can shove half of a pancake in their mouths and still close their lips to chew, but their cheeks are puffed out like chipmunks collecting nuts. I take smaller bites and try not to burst out in laughter. Had their mother been around, she would've broken them of their bad habits.

Patch says, "I think you should go home and try to talk to your parents at some point today."

The three of us stop chewing and look at him. He's right; I should, but I really don't want to. My eyes meet his expression of conviction. He wants me to settle this issue with my parents.

"It's not that I don't want you here. You're welcome to move in if you'd like. But I think you need to make peace with your family. After that, come back here and spend the night with me." His expression shows purely wicked intentions.

"Uh, she'll be staying in my room, but nice try!" Bash announces.

"As interesting as that sounds, I'll be spending my sleepover nights with Bash." My bottom lip finds its way between my teeth suggestively.

His words are spoken slowly and seductively. "You can always visit me in my bed, you know, to test its firmness. Is it too hard? No, it's just right."

My lips curl up at the edge while my eyes fixate on his. He growls, literally! He has me instantly breathing heavily, my pussy tightening and my nipples desperately trying to poke holes in my borrowed t-shirt.

"Do you want me to fuck you right now?"

I shake my head. Shit! I haven't even finished a cup of coffee yet. My body is defying me. It wants him, desperately.

"You want me, admit it," he hisses.

"If I said yes, how would you go about it?" I'm a woman playing with fire.

He sets his fork down slowly with his still eyes locked on mine. I sip my coffee delicately, hoping to bluff my way through this nerve-wracking conversation without choking on my coffee. He needs to know I can handle myself and resist him, even when my body begs otherwise.

Patch replies, "Little girl, I'd walk over to you, grab you by the arm and stand you up. I'd bend down and toss you over my shoulder and then carry you to my bed while spanking your bare ass." I swallow hard but try to appear calm. "Keep talking to me with that sassy attitude and you'll learn firsthand not to test me."

"Do you not like a woman to challenge you? Did your cock get hard when you told me what you'd like to do to me?"

"Keep it up, woman!" he threatens with eyes so dangerous, like a dog about to attack.

Mack and Bash sit back in their chairs looking from Patch to me and back, as if they're watching the most dangerous tennis match being played with a grenade. Perhaps they've never witnessed a woman taunt Patch in a battle of wills.

"I don't want to play right now," I say with conviction. "If or when I do, I'll let you know. But I'll talk to you with whatever attitude tickles my fancy and you can do nothing about it. You will not touch me against my will, I know that for a fact. So, maybe you've met your match. Back down, you won't win with me." I have no idea where this strong-willed, tough-ass woman came from, but I love her!

He leans back in his chair and takes a deep breath, letting it out very slowly. What's he thinking? I can almost see the raging inferno in his eyes. The seething dominant within him must be twitching with a need to punish me for my, what did he call it? Sassy backtalk? He's rubbing his palms together, no doubt his way of easing the need to crack my ass a dozen times while I count each one.

"I'll let you win this battle, Goldilocks, but I will have you over my knee one day soon, and you'll be begging me to spank you before I fuck you hard."

"If I ever do, you'll thank me for giving myself to you, won't you?" Who is this woman speaking out of my mouth?

His eyes twitch but as he grips the edge of the table, he calmly replies, "I'll be honored for the privilege of being allowed to touch you."

I smile proudly as if I've just won a glorious battle. I suppose I did, in a sense. Bash and Mack are still looking at him and then me, both wearing shocked expressions.

Mack says, "Hey Patch, it looks like you've met your match."

Patch glares at him but looks down at his plate, forking half of a pancake and ramming it in his mouth. Bash sits quietly chuckling to himself.

Chapter 10

"Are you sure you don't want to go see your parents?" Bash asks as he turns into the parking lot of the grocery store. He pulls into a spot and shuts off the truck. "Maybe Patch is right, you should try to settle this."

"I haven't decided."

He takes my hand and lifts it to his mouth, kissing the back of it. I smile and open my door. He hops out and runs around the truck, holding the door as I step out. He puts his hand up to help me, but I opt for the assist handle instead. He shuts the door and then puts his hand out for me to take. When I only look at it, undecided whether I want to hold hands or not, he lets it drop to his side.

"It's okay if you're not ready for that yet," he says with an understanding smile.

We walk side by side through the automatic doors. They still open with the same irritating swooshing sound that hurts my ears. Bash walks over to the carts and separates one from the others. He spins it around and then quickly catches up to me. I look to him to lead the way and then follow as he makes his way toward the fresh vegetables section.

Bash doesn't seem to care at all that the middle-aged woman holding two cucumbers has her attention on us, not the vegetables. She's rudely staring with her mouth gaping.

"Goldie, how much do you want to bet she's going to take one of those cucumbers home to fuck herself? Hang on, I'll be right back."

Bash walks over to the woman. He says something to her and then proceeds to choose a cucumber from the display and examines it. He says something else to her and I watch her expression change from curiosity to shock. As he's walking back to me, he grins and waves his eyebrows.

"What did you say to her?"

"I said I was picking you a cucumber for later. And then, I said that you like the fat ones as opposed to the long, thin ones, and how you like them juicy and hard. Before I walked away, I told her I prefer to have mine thinly sliced with salt and a little cayenne, but women tend to like them for other reasons. Then, I looked at her cucumbers and told her to have a pleasant night."

"No, you didn't! Tell me you didn't!"

He's laughing.

"I did! Look, people stare at me all the time in this town. I'm sure most of them think I'm a badass who might steal their wallet if they don't watch me closely. Others, especially women, see me as a bad boy they secretly want sneaking into their bedroom to have sex with them."

"You can't possibly know what people are thinking."

"True, I'm not a psychic, but I've seen the way some women look at me and when they think I can't hear them, they say nasty shit to their friend who is also looking at me with that same expression." He tosses a bundle of apples into the cart before leaning on the handle. "Look, for some reason, people either hate us Bears or they want to have sex with us. Everyone has their perceptions, but nobody takes the time to get to know us. We may have been wild when we were young, but we've matured. So, when we get the opportunity to fuck with those who stare at us, we do. You should stop worrying about what people think of you. Odds are they're talking about you behind your back anyway. Why not give them something to talk about?"

"I can't just pretend nothing bothers me. Maybe you don't care what people think, but I do."

"Well, I think your reputation is tarnished now that you've been seen with a Bear. You might as well fall to your knees and beg their forgiveness."

"Don't be ridiculous," I hiss.

Bash shrugs and then continues pushing the cart toward the oranges. We're being watched by a teenage stock-boy, the middle-aged cashier, an older man with a cane, and Mr. Abler, the store's owner. It's creeping me out. The cucumber woman couldn't wait to get far away from us.

I hate being the reason for gossip. He's right, I shouldn't worry about what people think of me. My parents drilled it into me that I have to be pretty and well-behaved, intelligent as well as ladylike. If I didn't act accordingly, I was given a very long talking to that bored me to tears. To avoid it, I learned how to behave *properly* in public.

We finish food shopping and drive down the street to the drug store. Again, he attempts to assist me as I'm getting out of the truck.

"Look, you don't have to run around the truck to open the door for me or take my hand to ensure I don't fall. I'm quite capable of doing these things for myself. I appreciate that you're a gentleman, but it really isn't necessary."

Too matter-of-factly for me to argue with him, he states, "I was raised to be a gentleman and I'm not about to change now. You'll just have to get used to it."

He opens the heavy glass door and waves his hand for me to take the lead. I enter the family owned drug store, the only one in town. Bash follows me in and walks down the first aisle in search of something without a care in the world. I'm busy looking around to see if anyone is watching.

The owner, Mr. Baneck, is a pharmacist and his wife does everything else, including passing along gossip regardless of the content of which may be false rumor. She has a talent for embellishing stories until they resemble only a shadow of the truth.

They have twin daughters which are about the same age as Patch. It's rumored that one of them partied with Patch one night and ended up in his bed, but it's never been confirmed nor denied by either person. The townsfolk like to believe the girls are innocent and polished young ladies who would never have given away their virginity before marriage, especially to a vulgar, no-good, piece of shit like Patch. They were actually quite slutty but pulled the wool over everyone's eyes. I hate how most people in small towns are so incredibly naïve and judgmental.

I notice Mrs. Baneck at the counter writing something in a book. She glances up casually but quickly takes a sharp notice of Bash. Her eyes follow him as he walks down the aisle. The look on her face is one of disgust. I can't believe it. Maybe I am naïve. Did I really not notice how people look at Bash? If they only took the time to have a real conversation with him, they'd know he is an intelligent, well-spoken man who has had more education than most of them. People are assholes!

I walk up to her with a smile that could light up a room. "Hello, Mrs. Baneck. How are you this morning?"

"Oh, hello dear. I'm just fine. When do you leave to go back to school?"

"Soon. A few days," I say before looking toward Bash.

"You'd be wise to keep your distance from that boy. He's trouble," she warns.

I'm so disappointed in her. I smile again and ask, "Mrs. Baneck, do you think I'm a smart woman?"

"Yes, of course you are."

"So, you think I'm wise enough to make smart choices for myself and not be easily swindled by a snake."

"Yes, dear. What is this about?"

"If I said it looked like rain will be rolling in soon, would you go to the window to take a look for yourself or would you trust my assessment?"

She sighs heavily. "I would trust your assessment."

"Hmm," I nod thoughtfully.

Without another word, I walk right up to Bash and throw my arms over his shoulders, planting my lips on his for a very lengthy, romantic kiss. The woman gasps so loudly I fear she might be having a stroke.

He wraps his arms around my waist, holding me against him. He didn't even hesitate to kiss me back. How shallow am I to have been so concerned that people would judge me for being with him. He's more honest and worthy of my affection than anyone in this damn town, or the ten towns surrounding it. Damn her for judging him!

"Oh my god!"

Bash pulls his lips from mine and we both turn to see who said that. Mindy, the oldest of the twins, is staring at us with a shocked expression.

I've had enough of being nice. "Really Mindy? Have you forgotten who you gave your virginity to?"

"Pfft!" she scoffs, glancing nervously at her mother. "My husband on our honeymoon."

Bash corrects her. "Wrong! You might have everyone else fooled, but I know you begged my brother Patch to make you a woman when you two were in your senior year of high school. If I'm not mistaken, it happened after Vinny Lexor's beach party."

Her eyes open wide, confirming his statement without saying a word. She looks again at her mother, whose mouth is gaping. Mindy's skinny finger points at Bash as if she's going to shoot electricity from it if she can only purse her lips hard enough.

Bash takes my hand and walks up to Mrs. Baneck, dropping a box of condoms on the counter in front of her. For a split second, I'm horrified. I had no idea what he came into the store for. Now she's going to know we're having a sexual relationship. I have no doubt that she's going to call my father the instant we leave the store. Without hesitation, the rest of the town gossipers will get their ears full as well. I'm quiet on the drive out of town. Bash is kind enough not to disrupt my thoughts. I appreciate his patience.

"Can I ask what that was all about?"

I shrug. "I had enough. She was nice to me but so rude when it came to you. I didn't want her to think it was okay to talk about you like that when she so obviously doesn't know you."

He sighs. "I'm used to it. You don't have to defend me. They mean nothing to me. Therefore, their opinions and judgments are irrelevant. But I appreciate your concerns for my honor."

"Will you take me to see my parents?"

He looks over at me as if to ask if I'm sure. I nod and he smiles nervously. The remainder of the drive is spent in silence, lost in our own thoughts. No doubt he's wondering whether my father is going to chase him away with a shotgun. I keep running conversations over in my head, trying to decide how I should start the dialogue once we get there. If I tell him to have a conversation with Bash before passing judgment, maybe that'll be best. Perhaps I should tell him he's being a fool just like the ignorant people in town. Maybe not.

When we pull up and get out of the truck, I'm still not sure of what I'm going to say. Bash follows closely behind me as I make my way up the porch and up to the screen door. Before we reach it, my father slowly pushes it open and makes his way through it. I can't read what he's thinking but he isn't happy, that I'm sure of. He looks tired, as if he's aged overnight.

"Dad…" I can't find the right words, any words!

"Goldilocks, sit down," he calmly says. He looks at Bash and asks, "And you are?"

"Hello, sir. My name is Bash Bear. It's nice to finally officially meet you." Bash stands before my father with his hand extended.

My dad looks him head to toe and then reaches for his hand to briefly shake it before offering him a seat as well. They sit opposite one another. My mom leans out the door to see who is here. Her face lights up with a smile but she quickly pinches her lips together before waving at me to go in the house with her.

"I'm going to go say hi to Mom," I say softly before standing quickly and scurrying inside before either Bash or my father have a chance to protest.

Mom whispers, "Let the men talk. There's a lot they need to work through."

"Why does Dad hate him so much?"

Mom takes the jug of cold lemonade from the fridge while I line up four glasses on the counter. She begins to pour.

"Well, he doesn't hate Bash, he doesn't know Bash. You can't hate someone you don't personally know, at least, that's what your father has always said. You know, he's always saying that you might hate the actions but not necessarily the person."

"Then why did he kick me out of the house when I told him I was spending time with Bash?"

"He was upset, that's all. Your father doesn't want you to be with someone who is known to have a bad reputation. He only knows what he's heard. And that's why I asked you to come in the house. Let them have some time to talk to one another."

"Dad doesn't have his gun with him, does he?"

She jokes, "No, I hid it yesterday."

We sit at the kitchen table looking at one another. "I really like him."

"I can tell just by looking at you. Last night when your father wouldn't stop yammering on about how awful the Bear brothers are, I told him about Patch helping me during that storm."

"I'm sure that didn't go over very well."

Her eyes widen. "No, not at first. He was angry I'd kept it from him for so long. But after he calmed down, he wanted to know what Patch was really like. So, I told him that he was a perfect gentleman, very cordial. I also told him about the intelligent conversation we had while we waited for the storm to pass. I know he didn't go to college because he had to be home to raise his brothers, which is honorable. I told him that Patch said he's read at least one book a week since he was twelve years old. He loves to read because learning helps to keep his mind sharp."

She stands and takes a prepared tray of cheese and crackers from the crisper in the refrigerator. I'm not surprised. She must have cut up the cheese and laid out the crackers when my father was otherwise occupied. She knew I'd be coming home today and bringing Bash with me.

"Oh these?" she points at the tray. "I knew you'd show up at some point today. I raised you to know better than to let things stew for too long."

I look toward the door while chewing the hard skin beside my fingernail. What are they talking about? I don't hear any yelling. In fact, I don't hear anything.

Mom calmly takes my hand away from my mouth. "Don't worry, Goldilocks. They're getting along wonderfully."

"You can't possibly know that."

"If they weren't, your father would have been rushing through that door in search of his gun. Trust me, it's going to be okay. Now, grab those glasses and follow me."

I take three of them and follow Mom outside. After handing one to my Dad and one to Bash, I sit beside him while my mother sits in the lone chair closer to my father.

Dad seems calmer and Bash doesn't look as nervous as he did when we first got out of the truck. They aren't talking though and that concerns me.

"So did you two work out your issues?" Mom blurts out, cutting through the silence.

My father sighs heavily before taking a sip of his lemonade. "Well, Goldilocks, do you plan on continuing to see this man?"

"I do, yes," I reply, not liking the direction this seems to be heading in.

"And what about school?"

I clear my throat after taking a gulp from my glass. "I'm still going back in a few days. My plans for school haven't changed. I'll get my degree before I make any life-altering decisions pertaining to my future. But, as for dating Bash, I hope to continue seeing him."

"Hmm," he grumbles. After setting down his glass, he sighs again. "Bash, you seem like a decent enough young man, but I suppose time will tell that to be true or not. Your past reputation isn't a good one, but you already know that. You seem to have your head squarely on your shoulders now and you aren't afraid to work hard for what you want. In my book, that shows character. As long as Goldilocks finishes her education, I won't interfere with your relationship. If you hurt my little girl, I will not hesitate to riddle your backside with buckshot."

"I'd have it no other way," Bash replies with a smile. "Goldie is a very smart, independent, and stubborn woman. I know nothing will stop her from achieving what she sets out to do and I would never stand in her way of reaching her goals. That, sir, would be a pity."

"Bash, tell me about your brothers," Mom asks. She always knows when it's time to change the subject. She's a wise woman. I aspire to be just like her.

We sit on their porch until late in the afternoon discussing everything from childhood memories to future plans. Dad laughed hard a few times when Bash told stories about dumb things he and his brothers did as children. Some of the stories he tells us are the much more innocent versions of the terrible falsehoods the gossiping townsfolk had spun to further ruin their reputations. Bash isn't surprised to hear the false stories told about them.

Chapter 11

Back at the Bear residence, Mack and Patch are sitting on the sofa watching a car restoration program on television. Bash tells them how it went with my parents while I take a quick shower and slip into the same t-shirt I wore this morning at breakfast.

Bash takes a shower and meets me in his bedroom. He takes the hairdryer from me and finishes drying my hair while running his fingers through it to keep it from getting too tangled. Our eyes meet now and then in the mirror.

When his towel falls off, I reach for his lazy cock and palm it. He threatens to shut off the dryer, but I insist he finish, otherwise I'll stop touching him. The second it's dry, he shuts it off, setting it on the dresser.

In a flash, he's picked me up and tossed me onto the bed. I shriek and laugh like a high school girl on a carnival ride. We make love, our bodies moving in unison. How are we so perfectly matched, knowing how the other is going to move and moving accordingly? Maybe we were meant to be together all along.

The house is quiet and our breathing has calmed. We're lying in the darkness, entwined. His bedroom looks different as the moon casts dancing shadows from swaying trees. I feel at peace, like I belong here, like I've *always* belonged here.

Bash kisses my head then whispers, "Are you tired or do you want to have some fun?"

"We just had some fun. Didn't we?"

"Uh huh! We certainly did but I'm thinking of a different kind of fun. How would you like to slip into Patch's bed?"

"You want me to make love to your brother?"

"Not make love, no. But I want you to do what you want to do. Could you use a good hard fucking?"

"And you didn't just give me a good fucking?" I continue to tease him.

"No, Goldie. We made love, we didn't fuck. Patch fucks hard, emotionless and rather barbaric. As I recall, you really enjoyed how he fucked you over the log. If you want to sneak into his bed, I'm okay with that. Besides, it'll be a great way for you to gain some control over him."

"How do you figure?"

He snickers. "This morning he threatened that he was going to pick you up and take you to his bed. If you just go on your own and hop on him, he can't say that he took you kicking and screaming."

"He wouldn't take me if I were kicking and screaming. That would be against my will."

"Yes, but anything goes until you use your safe words."

"Uh huh, I see. You wouldn't be upset at all if I go to his bed? Like, not even the tiniest little bit?"

He looks at my face and brushes his thumb along my cheek while he cradles my face. "Goldie, I've loved you from the moment you first set your beautiful eyes on me and then smiled, making my knees weak. I'm pretty sure you love me, too. I know you're coming back to me. He won't have you forever. He and I are in no competition over your affections."

"I have a question."

"Ask me anything."

"If Patch or Mack get a girlfriend and you and I are a couple, will you go to bed with her?"

"Would that bother you?"

"If I like the woman, I don't think so. You obviously adore me." I grin conceitedly. "If I couldn't stand her, I'd have an issue. Otherwise, do as you will to her. Just remember to come home to me, okay?"

"Always! My heart will belong to you forever whether you choose to be with me or not. I've loved you from the moment

I first saw you and nothing will change that." He grins. "Would you ever be with a woman?"

"I don't know. I've thought about what that would be like. How about I get used to sleeping with three men before introducing yet another new adventure?"

"There are so many adventures to be had," he says with a loving kiss on my lips. In a whisper he suggests, "Now go ride my brother."

*** Continue Goldie's Story in Book 2 ***

If you enjoyed book one in the Naughty Goldie series, please leave a review on your favourite book purchasing site. Feel free to boast the book online and tag Pebbles Lacasse.

Goldilocks
and the Three
Bear Brothers
Book 2

Trifecta

Pebbles Lacasse

Goldilocks & The Three Bear Brothers: Trifecta

Book 2

The *Naughty Goldie* Series

by Pebbles Lacasse

Chapter 1

Since Bash thought it would be best for us to follow through on our educational plans before settling down together, it's been tough. Not so much my courses; it's being away from him that has me feeling lonely. Even though we talk most nights, I feel his absence when I lie in bed and don't have his hot body to snuggle up to. Neither phone nor video calls compare.

Tomorrow, I'll leave this campus for the last time. The one thing I won't miss is my lousy roommate. She is awful! Not only does she keep weird hours, but she spends most of her life on her computer and rarely showers. At first, I thought she was depressed, but she's just a weird girl.

Patch will pick me up from the airport when I touch down. No matter how much my father insisted he would be the one driving the two hours to collect me, his one and only daughter, Patch would not budge. His argument was that he sets his own working hours so it would be wiser if he made the trip rather than my father taking a day off work. I never thought I'd see my father agree with Patch Bear about anything pertaining to the bad boy spending two hours alone with me in a truck.

My clock reads 12:38 AM, two hours since I put in my earplugs and slipped an eye-mask on, hoping to block out the light flickering from my roomie's endless stream of YouTube videos. My jaw aches from clenching. I do that when I'm tense. My stomach is growling up a storm too. The apprehension about boarding a plane in the morning has me all tied up in knots. I dread flying.

Most of my belongings fit in my suitcase, which I'll be taking with me on the plane. I shipped everything else home via UPS. It's scheduled to arrive in a few days.

It's not the move back to my hometown that has me so concerned. It's telling my parents that I won't be living with them. They will not like my decision to move directly into the Bear residence where I'll be alone with Patch and Mack until Bash returns in three weeks.

Everyone in town sees the Bear brothers as being bad boys with wicked intentions. Sure, there is some truth to the rumors spread about them, but it would be wise not to listen to every nasty thing said.

My stomach tightens, and bile rises to my throat. In an instant, I'm sitting up, clutching at my chest. I rip the mask off my head and pluck the earplugs from my ear canals. Taking slow deep breaths helps.

"You okay?" Lenora looks up from behind her laptop while the bright images reflect off the lenses on her wide-framed glasses.

"Yeah, just anxiety."

"About the move?"

Yeah, idiot, about the fucking move!

"Likely." A gulp of water from the glass on my nightstand seems to push the bile back into my stomach. "I'm not moving home and haven't told my parents yet."

Intrigued at the possibility of new material for her creative writing course, she closes her computer and sets it down on the bed beside her.

"So, where will you be living?"

"My boyfriend and his two brothers live together but, as you know, Bash is away at university for a few more weeks. I'm moving into his room. I haven't told my folks yet. I don't know how they'll take that news."

She nibbles the end of her pen in a way that would likely arouse any man with a raging sexual appetite. I think I still have a ginger ale in the fridge, but the package of saltines I had for dinner is buried deep in my suitcase. Feeling the bile rising again, I dig to find them.

"Few men would ask their little brother's hot girlfriend to move in with them unless they have ulterior motives."

If she only knew! Not to let on that both of them will fuck me in every way possible many times before Bash returns home, I scoff and roll my eyes. My cheeks heat from the insinuation of her questioning leer. The discovery of the saltines calls for a quick laugh in celebration.

"Do you have a picture of them? You never showed me what they look like. I mean, your boyfriend is hot as fuck, judging by his picture on your desk, so they must be hot too, right?"

"Um…" My shoulders lift, and for a second, I wonder if showing her their picture will only urge her to question me more about my *innocent* relationship with them and if I'll be able to hide my raging sexual thoughts. "Yeah, it's the last one taken before I left to come here."

Several quick gulps of cold ginger ale urge an angry burp that I stifle. My stomach feels better in an instant. After shoving a cracker in my mouth and beginning to chew, I sit on my bed cross-legged and scroll through the vast collection of photos in search of the one I've stared at many times since we took it.

There it is: Patch, Bash, and Mack standing in a line. I'm horizontal across the screen with my mouth wide open, laughing like a fool with my blonde hair hanging in my face.

The tallest, Bash, is in the center, smiling wide while supporting my hips. The gorgeous, blue-eyed Mack hugs my calves. The only person not sporting a happy expression is Patch, who rarely smiles anyway. That's okay, it suits his persona as a mysterious, dangerous man with a lot of pent up sexual frustration. Even still, he looks unusually distant, and his normally dangerous dark-brown eyes seem softer somehow. Patch's strong arms support my shoulder and chest.

I cross the room and hand her my phone as I sit at the edge of her bed with one leg tucked beneath me.

She whistles. "Damn, girl! They are all fucking hot! How are you going to live in a house with these men and not want to fuck all of them? I wouldn't even bother wearing clothes if I were you." With her fingers on the screen, she zooms in to get a better look at them. "Shit! Can I move in too?"

Fuck no! I've had enough of her. I smile and shrug while shaking my head. She hands me my phone.

"I'd love to crash with the angry motherfucker on the end. He looks like he'd be the wildest one. I can never find a guy who's as crazy as me without him turning out to be a psychotic asshole."

Laughter escapes me, not at her comment but at a guy being crazier than her. Is it even possible?

"Patch." My fingers stretch the screen so I can see his face better. "His name is Patch. He's not crazy, just has a lot on his plate. When their parents died, he took it on himself to raise his little brothers. He was still a teenager at the time, barely eighteen. Somewhere along the line, I think he forgot how to have his own life."

"Sounds rough," she says as she picks her computer up, setting it on her lap and flipping it open. That's the cue that she's done talking, but so am I. This is the longest meaningful conversation we've had in three months.

I stand and slip on my housecoat, putting my phone in the pocket, and then slide my feet into my slippers. "I'm going to go for a walk. Don't wait up!"

The door shuts behind me, and I snicker. She'll still be up when I come back. The woman almost never sleeps. It's fucking annoying!

Chapter 2

Having the talk with my parents weighs heavily on my mind as I stroll along the corridor coming to the general lounge area on the main floor. Three people look up as I enter the room. Their stares are vacant, zombie-like. The pale faces, exaggerated by the heavy eyelids and dark purple circles hanging below their sunken eyes are a dead giveaway that they've been hitting the books hard. The look is familiar to me as I've seen it staring back at me from the mirror more often than I care to admit.

I snuggle up on the worn-in sofa perched in front of the imitation log gas-run fireplace. It's not a real fire, but the audio sounds emitting from it create the illusion of sap heating and crackling as it escapes the embers via tiny eruptions. With my legs tucked beneath me and my plush housecoat warming my body, I open the photo which is still zoomed in on Patch's face.

The night Bash sent me to Patch's bed didn't play out how I thought it would. Every time Patch had sex with me before that night, he was rough. His sexual perversions teeter on the verge of being sadistic. He loved hearing me scream in pain as he whipped me with a switch taken from a tree or when he spanked me with his lumberjack-sized hands. He fucks hard, impossibly hard. I'm not complaining! I love it!

But that night, alone in the dark with him, was not at all what I had expected. I stare at the fire and let my mind drift off to that night.

After Bash sent me off to be with Patch, I took a quick shower and then tiptoed through the house and into Patch's room.

He was snoring softly as I made my way toward his bed. Fuck! He looked so damn huge beneath the thin sheet. One arm was under his head while the other hand rested over his crotch as if protecting it from danger as he slept.

It was dark, aside from the moon's rays. I slid in, right up against his super-heated body. Without waking, he wrapped his arm around me and held me in a loving hug. I wasn't there to cuddle—I wanted his cock.

My hand slid down along his washboard abs in search of his manhood. My fingertips grazed the tender flesh and stroked along its length. At first, he didn't even stir. I slid down his body and engulfed his limp member in my mouth. Within seconds, his cock was fat and erect, filling my mouth and throat.

Patch jolted awake and hissed, "What the fuck?" The sheet flew off my head, revealing my identity to the panting man.

"What brings you to my bed at this hour?" His fingers tenderly stroked my hair as my head bobbed over his cock. Only a moan escaped me. He whispered, "Come up here."

I knew better than to deny his wishes. A harsh spanking wasn't what I sought that night. My knees rested over either side of his pelvis, my hands on his thick chest as I leaned forward to kiss him. He grabbed the back of my head and pulled me in, kissing me with romantic affection. I lowered myself on his cock, burying his full length in one thrust. Its girth filled me, stretching my walls. We both moaned in each other's mouths.

I don't know how long I rode him before he rolled us over and began fucking me in a slow, gentle rhythm. He touched me with a tenderness that night which seemed suitable at the time but left me feeling guilty in the morning, after having woken nestled in his strong arms.

When my weight shifted in the bed, he woke. He was quick to sit up. I shook Bash's t-shirt and slipped it over my head, having not yet met eyes with Patch. He cleared his throat before saying that he shouldn't have made love to me.

I turned the door handle but didn't open it right away. The sound of dishes tapping against the table had frozen me in place. I wasn't supposed to spend the night with Patch. I should have returned to Bash's bed.

"Last night was exactly what I needed. It's been three years since my last relationship. I..." Patch paused and cleared his throat. "It won't happen again."

"That's too bad. It was nice."

Both Bash and Mack were standing in the kitchen, looking at me when I did my walk of shame.

Bash followed me into his room. "Goldilocks. Good morning. Perhaps you'd like to shower before breakfast."

Bash always calls me Goldie, never Goldilocks. It's his pet name for me. When he said my full name, a shiver went up my spine.

I remember crying and shaking as the water rinsed Patch's scent from my flesh and hair. I feared Bash would end our relationship. My guilt about making love with Patch overshadowed my sleeping offense, but Bash didn't know about that part, yet. It was wrong, no matter how I tried to spin it, but it felt right last night.

Patch and Bash were having a hushed conversation in the kitchen that immediately stopped when I came out of the bathroom. Bash looked upset while Patch stood wearing a stoic expression. He's forever impossible to read. Mack flipped pancakes on the griddle, keeping himself out of the conversation completely.

In Bash's bedroom, I quickly dressed. As my dress slipped over my head, Bash opened the door and stepped inside. His eyes looked everywhere but at mine.

"You're breaking up with me, aren't you?"

"What? No!" His panic was obvious. He quickly pulled me into a tight embrace. "God, no! I love you! I waited a long time for you and I'm not about to let you go."

My hands clutched at his back. "I thought you were dumping me. I'm sorry about spending the night with Patch. We fell asleep so quickly and before I knew it, morning had arrived. It won't happen again."

"Good." His lips pressed to my forehead. "If I'm home, I want to reach for you in the night to feel your soft skin. I want to wake with you beside me, even if I fall asleep in your absence. When I opened my eyes and you weren't there, my heart sank. I thought you'd left me. Please, always come back to me."

"I am yours and you are mine."

"Patch told me that he made love to you last night. It's okay to go through the actions. I just need to know that you belong to me—that our hearts are bound."

"My heart is yours. I'm sorry."

"Look at me with those beautiful blue eyes." I look into his blue eyes that seem to always be happy. "Don't be sorry about love. You shared a moment with my brother, a loving moment, and I'm okay with that. He loves you. We all do. I can't blame him for wanting to drown in your affection now and then. When Patch told me, I'll be honest... At first, I wasn't sure if you would choose him over me, but Patch assured me that wasn't the case. I promise that I'm all right with you being romantic with my brothers, as long as I know your heart truly belongs to me."

"I will always be your girl."

A loud sneeze startles me awake and back to the here and now. I'm still in the dormitory and not being adored by Bash's loving gaze. A heavy sigh takes the vivid sharpness of the memory from the forefront of my mind. A yawn has me aware of how late it is. The clock over the mantle claims it to be 4:32 AM. I unlock my phone to confirm the time and immediately see the magnified image of Patch staring back at me. I really miss them.

The corridor is deathly still as the students rest in slumber behind closed doors as opposed to the mixed variety of music, constant talking, and loud bursts of laughter that will surely grace these walls during daylight hours.

My bed feels softer than it did earlier, probably because I'm absolutely exhausted now. I surpass the earplugs and mask since Lenora is fast asleep. I'm quick to drift into a dreamless sleep.

Chapter 3

The screeching of my alarm yanks me from sleep, infuriating me. With a slap to the screen and a low groan, I lift my head to see Lenora curled into the fetal position and mumbling as she often does when she sleeps.

Forcing my tired body to roll onto my back is like dragging a wet carpet on grass. I have to get up. The airport shuttle will be here to pick me up in forty-five minutes and they won't wait for me.

As I sit up, I pull off my bedding and stuff the bundle into my suitcase. I strip off my nightgown and toss it in as well. A quick shower helps to wake me, but I have to hurry. I only have fifteen minutes to get the main building next door.

"Hey." Lenora's voice jolts me from the silence. "Have a good flight. Thanks for not being a bitch to me. I know I have issues and that makes me a shitty roommate, but I appreciate you not making my life more miserable than it already is."

"Yeah, no problem. You're not as bad as you think you are. If you weren't so negative all the time, I'd bet your outlook on life would improve. You're a nice woman when you want to be. Don't cut yourself down so much."

"Wait." She climbs out of bed and digs through the pile of unfolded clothing in her armoire, pulling out the light blue dress she wore when she went on a date that ended with him dropping her off and quickly driving away. She climbed further into her shell after that. I loved the dress and told her as much at the time. She buried it and I never saw it again. "Here, take it. It'll look better on you."

"Are you sure?"

"Yeah, I'll never wear it."

"Thank you." I smile and lay it atop the pile of clothing in my suitcase.

She slips her hand into mine, which I wasn't expecting. We've never purposely touched. "You deserve to have a good life. You are the person I wish I was." Her smile seems forced. Her demeanor suddenly shifts. "Enjoy those boys of yours! If I were you, I'd savor the weeks alone with them before your boyfriend comes home and ruins it."

"Um… yeah, that's not how it is." The lie sticks in my throat.

With my suitcases in hand and my backpack slung over my shoulder, I quickly scan the room to see if I've left anything behind. Seems not.

"Well, this is goodbye then."

She waves. "Yeah, see ya!"

"Good luck to you too!"

The elevator doors finally slide open with a low ding. I head to the building next door, which means trudging through the snow-covered sidewalk and bearing the blowing cold air. Without a coat, I'd surely freeze before I get there. Just as I open the door to the main building's lobby, the shuttle drives up.

Chapter 4

My flight wasn't on time because of back-ups from a heavy snowfall that made the departing runways require clearance. When the plane finally made it to our destination, we were almost two hours late. Before I even departed the plane, I fired off a quick text to Patch, but he isn't replying.

What will I do if he isn't here?

A cluster of over two-hundred people is waiting for their luggage to make its way slowly around the carousel. Just as I reach out to grab mine, a huge hand beats me to it. That hand is Patch's. I'd know it anywhere just by the size of it. My arms fling around his neck as he lifts the heavy case with ease, setting it on the floor beside him.

"Hi, little girl. How was the flight?" His voice is deep and gruff, but his words flow smoothly as if practiced a hundred times. His thick arms wrap around my waist and lift me off my feet. His roaring growl has people looking at us. He grabs my ass while I remain suspended and unable to push away.

I squeal, embarrassed that he did that in front of a huge crowd of onlookers.

"Put me down!" I insist. Once on my feet, I step back and scan the crowd to see if anyone is wearing a disgusted expression, but nobody seems to care. They're too exhausted from the two-hour delay and three-hour flight. "We were delayed because of the snowstorm, but otherwise it was uneventful. I slept most of the way."

"So, what you're saying is you're rested up for us horny fuckers?"

I tilt my head down from embarrassment, but he carries no concern over the scoffs from the people within earshot. He smiles while biting his lower lip. It's obvious what's on his mind. My pussy clenches, letting me know that it's been too long since I've orgasmed.

He takes my suitcases and my backpack, refusing to let me carry anything. I follow his lead out to the truck. He opens my door and makes sure I'm in before putting my baggage in the backseat.

***

As soon as we get in the truck, I shoot off a text to Bash to let him know that I've safely arrived in the protective arms of his brother. He'll be relieved when he reads it after his class has finished. Being the respectful man he is, he doesn't answer his phone during class.

We ramble on about what's happening back home, how my classes were and how I must have drawn the short stick when picking out roommates. Time flies by; more than an hour has passed. I love his truck because his windows are tinted very dark, making it seem like its own private room. It also blocks out the sun that's not only shining from above but the reflection of the pools of water that have built up from the overnight rainstorm they received. Without the tint, the outside world would seem blindingly bright.

Patch is still as sexy as ever. It's only been three-months but somehow, I thought he would look different. The night we spent together weighs heavily in my thoughts and I'm craving his touch; the soft touches I know he is capable of. Him fucking me hard and spanking my ass pink will come soon enough, I'm sure, but it's not what I want, not yet. His tenderness will do perfectly right about now.

He pulls the truck into a spot at the far end of the line of cars and hops out, rushing around the truck to open my door and help me exit. I'm grateful because the running boards are wet, nearly spilling me on my ass had he not been there to grab my arm.

"Quit messing around, woman. I have to pee." If someone didn't know Patch, they wouldn't think he's joking around. He refuses to release my arm until we are indoors, safe from impending wipeouts.

By the time I emerge from the bathroom, he's been through the coffee shop line-up and gotten two coffees and some sandwiches. He grips my arm to escort me safely back to the truck. Does he think I'm clumsy?

He lets the truck run while we eat and watch people trying to avoid the puddles. Two children trip and fall in the same puddle and start crying, but their father stands them up and urges them to keep moving. We burst out laughing, of course. Watching people wipe-out is great entertainment.

After we're finished eating, he looks over at me. "Are you ready?"

The way he's looking at me sideways with his dark brown eyes, my body flushes hot. I can't hold myself back. Quicker than he can react, my mouth is on his, kissing him and tasting his sweetened coffee on his tongue. One of his hands grips my head and holds my face to his. The seat quickly slides back, giving extra room for me to straddle his lap. My skirt is long and flowing, easy to lift out of the way.

As he fights to undo his jeans, my hands cradle either side of his strong jaw. He releases my head, rushing to his button to aid his other hand in freeing his cock from its prison. He lines it up against my dripping pussy and grabs my ass, forcing me down on him. My body swallows him completely, and I gasp.

We're both moaning in each other's mouths as I lift and lower at his beckoning. His massive hands guide my ass, setting the pace. His hips lift off the seat hoping to plunge deeper into me. He's getting close to coming. So am I.

"Cum, Goldilocks. Cum on my cock." His hearty whisper is like fire igniting a fuse, shooting me into orbit.

The truck fades away, out of my line of sight. All I see is his ruggedly handsome face. All I hear is our heavy breathing. His eyelids weigh heavily, lips slightly parted, nostrils flared. Despite the chill in the air, his cheeks are flushed.

"Oh, God! Yes… please…" My words drop off as a much-needed climax overwhelms my mind and body. He holds me down on him and fills me with his jizz. His cock swells thicker and harder, nearly stretching me beyond my capabilities, and holy fucking hell, I love it!

A loud grunting moan vibrates the truck as his last wad spits into me. Having no strength left in my body, I flop forward, resting my head on his strong shoulder. His arms surround me, making me feel safe and loved. We rest until his withering penis slips from my saturated pussy, causing us both to shiver.

My phone chimes and I'm sure it's Bash returning my text.

After handing me a wad of tissues, we clean away the evidence and gather ourselves before continuing on with the journey. I reply to Bash, saying that I love him, miss him, and I'll call him later. He is on his way to another class and doesn't have time to text anyway.

Patch interrupts my thoughts. "I've been waiting for that since you left to head to school. I'm glad you initiated because it was becoming damn near impossible for me to drive. My cock has been rock hard all day. It was aching for you."

"We could have waited until we got to your place."

He speeds up as we enter the on-ramp back to the highway. Once settled into the middle lane, he responds, "Yes, but then I would have had to share you with Mack."

The smile on my face screams my twisted thoughts. "And would that be so terrible? I mean, it's kind of awesome for me."

He glances at me just as I look away. "I wanted to have you to myself first. That night… in my bed… it was, ah…" His words fall away. I see his lips move but silently. He quickly presses them together as if searching for the right thing to say and then deciding to say nothing.

To make it easier on him, I whisper, "It was a lovely night."

My excellent peripheral vision sees him turn his head several times, quick to look back at the lane he's driving in. If I look at him, I might as well say that I love him. That night was so beautiful—our bodies molded into one, moving in perfect sync, touching just right, breathing as one and losing ourselves together. It was nothing like it should have been. And not how my boyfriend expected it to be when he sent me to be with his brother. I expect Patch to fuck me hard, cold and emotionless, as is his way. That night was different and neither of us could stop it, nor did we want to.

He clears his throat. "That night was, um... But it shouldn't have been that way. And, ah... just now, that shouldn't have been so gentle either."

"I know," are the only words I can muster.

The rest of the drive is spent in silence. For nearly an hour, only the sound of the wheels on the concrete and the creeks and clunks from his old pickup truck entertained us. It was awkward, and I hated it but didn't know what else to say.

Chapter 5

Patch parks next to the house and sprints around the front to open my door which is a trait all the brothers gained. Not needing to, I take his hand and hop out. Our eyes meet but he quickly looks away. As he takes my bags from the back of the truck, I can't help but inhale the calming familiar scent of the forest's many musky, pollinated aromas. I've missed this place! It's cool here but no snow, thankfully.

The door swings open, smacking against the wood siding. Mack rushes through, skipping down the stairs Fred Astaire style, and then wraps his arms around me. He plants a giant kiss on my lips. When he pulls back from me, he looks me up and down while I taste the sweetness from his mouth, trying to guess what he last ate or drank.

His whistle is loud but makes me feel sexy. "Damn, woman! You look hotter than before you left. How is that even possible? Have you been working out?"

The pink in my cheeks is darkening. "A little, yes. I did a lot of walking. It helped to relieve my stress."

His hands perch on his hips. "Sexual tension, no doubt."

"Hey, asshole!" Patch hands Mack the big, heavy suitcase.

"You think that's an insult? I'll have you know that I love assholes. Isn't that right, Goldilocks?" His exaggerated wink seems silly. I have not forgotten that he took my anal cherry.

Mack's tongue flips wildly between his spread lips, making my clit twitch. The perverted gesture aimed in my direction ignites my desire and I want to drop my panties right here and now, but I won't. I have more class than that. Besides,

I'd rather wash his brother's cum off my pussy before he puts his mouth anywhere near it.

Patch shoves Mack's shoulder, as brothers often do. "Is that the only way you plan on being useful?"

"Oh, I plan to be extremely useful in the very best ways possible, but first, I'll bring your suitcase in." Mack laughs in his joking way before kissing me like a friend kisses another friend.

His arm pops up, bent at the elbow. With a slight bow, he says, "My lady…"

My arm slips through his. He picks up my suitcase and ushers me, releasing my arm once we're on the porch. He brings my suitcase into the house. Patch stands beside me as I soak in my surroundings.

"You love it here," Patch says.

I smile softly and nod slowly. "I do."

"You should call your folks to let them know you're here, safe and sound. Maybe I'll drop you off later."

"I don't need you to drive me. I can walk. To be honest, I'd love a taste of solitude. You're welcome to come with."

His face grimaces despite his efforts not to. "I don't think they'd be too excited to see me. Come on, let's get you unpacked." He turns and walks into the house with my small suitcase in hand and backpack slung over his shoulder, making it look much smaller than I know it to be.

"Why don't you think they wouldn't want to see you?" I question as I sprint to catch up. He doesn't give me an answer.

Chapter 6

After I've unpacked a few things, I choose a clean towel from the closet and strip off my clothes. A quick shower will wash all the smells of the big city from my hair and skin.

My thoughts drift away for what seemed like hours as the hot water washes my troubles away. Until muscular arms slowly slide around my shoulders. My fingers glide along the thick forearms, enjoying their manly girth. Had he quickly grabbed me, I would have jolted, but he was slow and deliberate.

"Patch," I whisper.

"Not Patch. I hope you aren't disappointed?"

The strong body presses against my back. His skin feels cooler than mine because I've been cooking under the water for however long. He feels like comfort itself, as strange as that might sound. He kisses my neck as he holds me. The water flows between our bodies. He eases his grip, so I turn to face him.

While I admire his chest, abdomen, and penis, he steadily admires my face. When our eyes meet, his smile is faint.

"I have a girlfriend. She'd like to meet you." As he speaks, I can't help but feel a tinge of jealousy. I have no right to this emotion, and it confuses me. "Are you all right?"

I'm suddenly aware I've been staring blankly at his chest.

"What? Oh, yeah, I'd love to meet her." No matter how hard I try to make my smile seem believable and unforced, I don't think I'm all that convincing.

He steps back, concerned. "Are you upset that I have a girlfriend?"

"No! No, not at all." *Liar!* "I wasn't expecting it, that's all. Bash didn't tell me, so I... I didn't know."

He seems relieved. "Oh, okay. So, you're all right." I nod. "I met her shortly after you went back to school. I mean, we'd been talking online before that, but hadn't met. I hope you'll like her."

"I'm sure I will. When will I meet her?"

"She'll be here for dinner tomorrow. Will you be here?"

Is he seeking my approval of her? "Tomorrow? I can't see why not. My interview isn't until Monday, so I'm wide open until then."

He furrows his brow. "Interview? Where at?"

Mack turns the tap so it sprays on the wall, taking away the heat. I pout but he ignores my pleas and picks up the soap, lathering his hands. After placing them on my shoulders, he turns me away from him. I haven't the heart to tell him I've already washed. I collect my wet, blonde hair and move it off my back, laying it down my chest. The ends hang down to my belly button. I really should get it trimmed soon.

With great skill, he tenderly massages the muscles in my back that have had me popping Ibuprofen like candy for over a week now.

Between winces, I reply, "Metropolitan Hospital, Day Surgery."

"Day Surgery," he repeats as his hands wrap around my body and begin massaging my breasts. I lean back against his chest, resting my head against his shoulder.

"I got lucky that they have an opening, otherwise I might have had to move elsewhere. The job calls for part-time hours with opportunity to advance, which isn't easy to get these days."

"That's great! I'm happy you'll be staying here, provided you get the job. They'd be fucking idiots not to hire you."

"Thanks." When his fingers pinch my nipples firmer than he had been, my moan slips free. He kisses my neck, and I nearly melt into him. "What does your girlfriend think about me coming to live here?"

"I can't remember if I told her you'll be living with us or not." His lips continue to peck away at the side of my neck and behind my ear, but I clasp my hands over his, holding them against my breasts. He adds, "Don't worry, she's okay with us brothers sharing everything. She's a smart woman. I'm sure she assumes you'll be living here."

My heart pounds loudly in my ears as my thoughts run wild. "Has Bash met her?"

"Yes, they've met." His kisses continue, uninterrupted. Between kisses, he adds, "He came home for the weekend recently. She was here."

I still haven't released his hands. "Did he like her? I mean, did they…"

My heart is desperate to escape my chest. Sensing my distress, he slowly turns me back around to face him. Concern riddles his handsome face.

He asks, "Would it bother you if they had fucked?" His smile isn't mocking, but I feel like a jealous schoolgirl and I hate myself for it.

"So, they didn't…" I try to read his face, but he's unflinching, giving me no cues. "Why am I jealous?"

Did I just say that out loud?

His expression softens. "You're new to this type of lifestyle. You can't expect yourself to find your groove without hitting a few bumps in the road. You're a good woman, and you love him. If you didn't, you wouldn't care in the least. I know how much you care about him."

I shrug my shoulders at the confusing analogy, then jokingly brush it off as though I don't really care for Bash.

Mack snickers before leaning in to kiss me but hesitates just before our lips touch. He whispers, "Is it okay if I kiss you?"

"She won't be jealous?"

He slowly shakes his head before leaning closer. His lips are soft and warm, tender in their approach. It isn't over thirty-seconds before Mack is on his knees in the shower, licking and sucking my clitoris. It couldn't have been a full minute to pass and I'm gripping his hair in my fists and humping his expert mouth.

"Holy fuck! I'm coming!" I yell. As if my body is experiencing the most pleasure it's ever felt, intense waves erupt from my core tickling me, one after another, rocking my body and soul until my knees are weaker than a newborn giraffe and I'm twitching uncontrollably.

Mack stands and hugs me, slowly turning us until I'm no longer under the water. He releases me, smiling at me with a wave of his eyebrow. He tips his head under the water for only a second. He looks at me again as he blobs shampoo in the palm of his hand and rubs it into his hair. I stand dumbfounded and weak while I watch him clean his body. There's nothing stopping me from exiting the shower, I'm just too wobbly-legged to attempt the feat.

Chapter 7

As I make my way to the bedroom, Patch calls out to me, "Deer steaks, yams, salad, and cornbread for dinner. How do you like your steak?"

"Sounds great! Um, medium."

He gives me a thumbs-up before looking down at the chunk of yam with a huge knife protruding. As I'm just about to close the door to Bash's room where I will lay my head each night, Mack reaches in and takes my arm.

I jolt, not realizing that he'd followed. His body still glistens from the water droplets dripping from his hair. The fluffy forest green towel around his waist does nothing to hide his arousal. His eyes are dreamy and seductive. His face is so handsome that one could almost say he's pretty. Although shorter than Patch and Bash, his body is strong, fit and ripped with muscles, but his face could easily look out from a magazine cover.

"Come with me."

I follow him to his room, not that I have much choice since he's gripping my arm. I could tell him no, but why would I? Going to his room to receive more of what I had in the shower sounds heavenly!

He shuts the door and removes the towel from my head, tossing it to the floor. He then tosses our body towels. His lips meet mine as his fingers glide along my waist and around to my back, where they grip me, pulling me against his body. He walks, forcing me to walk backward. The bed catches my knees and I topple back, but Mack doesn't let me fall. His eyes, filled with desire, lock onto mine. With his arm around my back and the other bracing against the mattress, he lies me back with a strong easiness that would turn on any red-blooded woman.

My legs open but Mack pulls them together before flipping me onto my stomach. His hot mouth pecks down my spine sending shivers radiating outward along my skin from each gesture. His tongue slithers down my tailbone and between my ass cheeks. It's so seductive that my ass instinctively lifts, urging his strong, wet tongue to fidget with my puckered bud. He laps teasingly and I'm immediately taken back to the day all three brothers sampled me, each in their own way. He took my anal cherry that afternoon.

Mack kisses up my spine before flipping me onto my back. The tips of his fingers glide along my calves and grip my ankles. He guides them until my thighs press against my abdomen. He squirts some lubrication onto his right hand and then tosses the bottle aside while coating his solid cock in the clear lotion.

Our lips peck at one another. Between kisses, he whispers. "I want your ass. May I?"

"Yes," I reply.

Having him in my ass again has been the subject of many of my dreams since the first and only time he's done that to me. The instant the tip of his prick slips into my tight hole, I'm reminded of how awkward it initially feels. Perhaps I've tightened up because he remains still.

"Shh, try to relax. Just breathe, beautiful woman." The calming words and kisses to my neck are working. I feel less pain despite more pressure. Before long, his pelvis is resting against me. He's completely buried inside, and it feels so fucking full.

Mack lifts his hips and gingerly lowers several times as I clamp my jaw closed and squeeze his biceps tightly. There's pain, but it's more of an enjoyable ache. Every sexual nerve in my body is at the peak of arousal. My clitoris is twitching and aching for release.

"Mmm, yes!" Pleading moans float through the air, urging him onward.

He lifts himself onto his knees, taking my ankles in his grasp. He is a handsome man, not as imposing as Patch, but definitely prettier, if one can say that about a heterosexual man without it being weird.

Mack's attention is on watching his cock slide in and out of my asshole, giving me ample time to admire the way his muscles ripple and jump with each thrust. I could watch his body move like this all day and not get sick of it. His abs are intoxicating!

"Play with yourself," he whispers.

My hands leave my thighs and travel to my chest, taking both breasts in my hands. He seems torn whether to watch the left breast or the right, shifting between the two.

He doesn't alter his rhythm for a second. "Touch your clit."

My hand slips down between my legs, quickly zeroing in on the tiny button between my labia. I roll tiny circles over its stiffness while tilting my hips, allowing him easier access. He shifts his weight to gain a more comfortable position, still not altering his rhythm. His gentle tempo pulls me deeper and deeper into a transient state.

Mack releases my ankles, and my thighs fall to either side of my chest. He pinches my nipples between his thumbs and forefingers, slowly rolling them.

Oh! Fuck! Yes!

"I'm going to cum. Oh, I'm…" My words fade into the distant voids in my mind.

Every nerve in my body is ablaze. It's a burn so hot that it can't possibly last without killing me. It's fantastic! My muscles gradually ease but my mind takes another minute to return. When my eyelids finally open, Mack is still above me, his lids squeezed shut, and he's wearing a pained expression. His nostrils flare, teeth clamped together, and eyebrows furrowed.

His sudden, exhaustive exhale seems to take with it all of his energy, collapsing the spent man on top of me. Hot rapid breaths caress my sweaty neck. I run my fingers through his damp wavy hair. His tension eases slightly, but his breathing remains labored.

"You didn't answer me when I asked if Bash fucked your girlfriend." Perhaps this wasn't the right time to bring it up. He didn't even have time to enjoy the afterglow.

He snickers. "Nothing like changing the subject, huh?"

"Sorry," I mutter.

He shifts himself up onto one elbow so he can look at my face. "Does it really matter if he has?"

I feel foolish suddenly. "I have no right to be jealous, especially under the circum—"

He cuts in, "No, you really don't."

My throat feels tight, so I clear it. Dammit, don't cry! "This is so new to me. I mean, I knew this would most likely happen, eventually. Bash and I have briefly discussed it. I didn't think I'd have any issue with it. I am having sex with you and Patch. So, please tell me why I feel this way and what I can do to stop it."

His chubby fingers pick strands of my hair off my sweaty neck. "You're entitled to your feelings. Remember that. You should talk to Bash about your insecurities because that's where your concerns and emotions stem from."

"Insecurities? Like what? Like, fearing I'll lose him to her?" This hadn't even crossed my mind. I shake my head. "No, I know he loves me and will not choose her over me."

"He loves you dearly. Try to keep that in mind."

Mack's hand glides up and down my thigh. "Do you think Bash doesn't worry about you falling for either Patch or me?"

"No, why would he? You guys have done this often and with many women." He shrugs.

"Why? Do you think he worries?"

"Of course, he does. He's human, and he loves you. The thought is always there but trust outweighs it. He trusts that if you or Patch or I start to feel more than we should, we'll go to him to get everything out in the open. Most often, those romantic emotions develop during lustful activities and quickly subside outside of the bedroom. It's human nature to feel a bond during heated sexual moments. Sex causes a release of endorphins that create a sense of euphoria, which makes us happy. We assimilate that happiness with feelings of love. Learning to compartmentalize those emotions can be difficult sometimes."

I flop my arms over my head, onto the bed, and sigh. "That makes sense."

With a kiss to my forehead, he climbs off me and sits on the edge of the bed. He leans forward to collect his towel. He wipes my tummy with it. I hadn't realized he'd pulled out of my ass to cum on me and not in me.

"So, tell me about her."

"She's awesome; great personality, outgoing, intelligent and hot as fuck! You'll like her." He offers his hand to help me sit up.

"I'm sure I will." With my towels in hand, I stand and make my way toward the closed door. "Can you at least tell me her name?"

"I sure can… tomorrow, when you meet her."

"Is she hideous or something?"

He laughs. "No."

"Then why all the secrecy?" I glare at him while opening the door.

He shrugs. "Maybe I like watching you squirm."

My finger waves at the bed. "And you're so fucking good at making me squirm."

Chapter 8

After showering for a second time and then tossing on a lightweight, pale green dress, I dial Bash's phone number. It rings twice before he picks it up.

"Hi, Goldie," he blurts.

"Hi, Bash. Are you busy?"

"Well, I'm on my way to the library. How are my brothers treating you?" He snickers. "They missed you."

"So, it would seem. They have both been very good to me."

"I'd bet money that you didn't make it home without Patch putting his mitts all over you. Am I right?"

I shrug, dropping my shoulders quickly because he can't see me. "I initiated."

He laughs loudly but immediately apologizes to someone. "Okay, I'm in the library now, babe. No cellphones allowed. Have fun with my brothers, don't miss me too much, and I'll talk to you soon. I love you."

"I love you too."

The three of us eat the delicious deer steaks Patch cooked for us while I answer all of their many questions. Each time I ask them a question, they either give shallow answers or evade it without giving me a chance to repeat myself. Are they always like this?

Mack will not allow me to help him clear the table or wash the dishes; instead, he insists I go visit my parents. He tells me I can use Bash's truck or his, but I'd rather take the time to enjoy a hike through the forest. With my hiking boots on and phone in hand, I come out of Bash's room and notice Patch sitting on the armrest of the sofa with his hiking boots on.

"Are you coming with?"

"If you'll have me." His voice is so deep it rumbles my chest.

"I thought you said my parents wouldn't want your visit. You never told me why. What is it with you Bear boys today? You're both being so evasive."

Mack snickers as he wraps the remaining deer steak in foil. Patch stands and looks down his nose at me. "We are a secretive bunch." His snicker frustrates me.

Patch leads the way down the path toward my childhood home or their hunting grounds, but I stop when we come to the large boulder perched by the slow-flowing river, right where the path forks. Memories of myself flopped back on its cool hardness while listening to the water rush past floods my thoughts. For a moment, I close my eyes and tip my head back, feeling the heat of the sun's rays through a clearing in the trees. This is my favorite spot in the forest.

"Are you coming?"

The peacefulness disappears in an instant, leaving me feeling sad. I make a mental note to come back here, alone.

Our boots thump on the packed dirt as we walk side by side on the wide section of the path. We've been walking in silence, mostly, other than the odd warning of slippery rocks or low-hanging branches.

He breaks the silence. "You'll spend tonight with me. We'll have another night like we did before you left for college." His voice is deep and steady, but it doesn't hide the question behind his statement.

I toss the dandelion I was slowly pulling the pedals from into the thicket of a fallen tree. "You want another romantic night with me?" He looks at me and furrows his brow, questioningly. "Oh, come on! You were gentle and loving with me, which is the very definition of lovemaking. Isn't it? We probably shouldn't. I mean, I'm in love with Bash, not you."

He scoffs and continues toward the narrowing path. A few moments of silence later, and he finally speaks. "I love you, Goldilocks. You know we brothers all do. I'm not in love with you and can't ever allow myself to go there. You belong to my little brother and I intend to keep it that way."

I lead the way into the dusk of the overhanging trees and prickly bushes that cross our path, tangling around our legs with each step. I turn to glance at him while pushing a chest-high branch away. He's holding something back. I can feel it!

He interrupts my thoughts. "But I would like to imagine... um, to enjoy your body tonight."

I stop and face him with my arms crossed over my chest. I ask, "Imagine what... that we're in love?"

He tries to stare me down, but I don't even blink. He mumbles, "I miss it."

"Miss what?" I drop my arms and my forceful attitude. He scans the forest behind me. "Just tell me."

With my hand in his, he clears his throat before giving in to my urging. "I had a steady girlfriend for a while. This was some time back. I loved her. I still love her." His sights drop to look at our clasped hands. "Her career led her across the country. There's no way I could move, so we broke it off. I really miss having that closeness with someone. You brought back those same feelings that night. I want that, again."

"The picture taken the day I left for school; the one with you three holding me up—you looked distant. Did you have a lot on your mind?"

He glances at my face then back to our hands. "I didn't want you to go. You woke up my heart and I was angry about it, and yet, I wanted to take you back to my bed and do it again."

"Were you falling in love with me?"

"No, I was in love with the idea of you. You don't belong to me. I know this to be true. But that doesn't mean I don't love you." He pauses. "I think I needed time to harden my emotions before I was with you again. Now that I have myself all sorted out, I want to experience that again, even if it's only in that moment. I'll think of her, not you. If that's not okay, I'll be rough with you instead."

I look up to the sky and tip my head side to side, playing up my inner banter. "I enjoy you however I can have you."

He stands tall, tucks his fingertips in the front pocket of his jeans and struts as if he is a sex god. He teases, "Yeah, you do! I'm fucking awesome! I know you want more of this!"

My laughter stops his over-exaggerated peacocking. He shrugs. "What does a man have to do to get a compliment around here?"

I roll my eyes. "So, why didn't you move with her?"

His smile fades and his dark brown eyes reveal the heaviness in his heart. "My brothers. They still needed me. Besides, this is my home. Living in the cement jungle would be a fucking nightmare for me. I had to let her go."

Who knew the tough and ruggedly handsome, slightly sadistic Patch is a secret sentimentalist? I knew there had to be a soft spot in him somewhere because he cared so much for his brothers. Besides, he was loving and tender with me, whether he meant to be or not. Either way, it was very memorable, and I liked it… more than I should have.

His huge hands grasp my shoulders and spin me around. The slap to my ass is his way of urging me to walk.

"Cement jungle?"

He replies, "The city."

My laughter fades into the dark corners of the forest as our boots pound the dirt beneath them.

Chapter 9

As we enter the clearing in front of my parent's home, the brightness of the sun has us both squinting. Through my tears, I can see my mother in her vegetable garden. She must be harvesting dinner ingredients.

"Mom," I yell as I quicken my pace.

She startles and spins around quickly. Her arms lift to the sky in excitement and then drop to brush the dirt from her shins.

"Goldilocks!"

We hug, rocking side to side while Patch slowly approaches. With his hands in his front pockets, he appears smaller than I know him to be. Mom finally releases me and focuses on the standoffish man. She hesitates, then puts her hand up to shake his. He takes her hand while sporting a forced smile. Mom does the same.

What's with these two?

"This seems awkward," I suggest, both are ignoring the comment.

"Come, sit on the porch. I'll get us something to drink." She looks at both of us and asks, "What are you thirsting for?"

I reply first. "A beer would be nice."

Her sights shift to Patch. He nods. "Sounds good to me. Thank you."

Mom scurries into the house, letting the screen door smack shut behind her.

"Okay, what's going on?"

He sits on the wicker chair, shifting the purple, flowered cushion behind his back until it's in a better position. "I don't know what you're talking about."

I drop my ass onto the chair next to him, not taking my eyes off him. "Something's up and I want to know what it is."

"Nothing's wrong. Let it go, Goldie."

Quickly, I correct him. "Goldilocks. Only Bash calls me Goldie." I straighten my skirt and shove my hair onto my back instead of leaving it to hang over my breasts. "You'd better tell me."

"It's nothing important…" His voice becomes deeper and more threatening. "And I'll call you whatever the hell I want; slut, whore, cunt, Goldie. I choose, remember?"

That familiar warmth washes over me, arousing my womanly desires. My pussy dampens at the memory of him viciously fucking me in the forest while calling me a slut. It was sexy, dirty, and oh, so taboo! I loved it! Before I can retort, the door slams behind my Mom, carrying three beers on a tray with crackers and some dip. That woman can easily juggle a ten-course meal without breaking a sweat. I've seen her do it.

She sits in the chair across from us with an exhaustive sigh. As she cracks open her bottle, she asks, "So, when did you get into town?" She takes a small swig before beginning to pick at her label. She has a habit of tearing it off.

I open my bottle and take a swig while Patch follows suit. "A few hours ago. Patch cooked up an early dinner, so we ate before coming here. Otherwise, I would have been here earlier."

Her reply is quick. "Did he?" Her sharp glare at Patch has me even more curious.

"Okay," I say as I slam my beer on the wooden table. "What the hell is going on here? And don't tell me it's nothing." I frown at Patch who raises his hand in a gesture toward my mother. She frowns at the foam volcano erupting from my bottle.

Neither says anything. My constant stare has my mother huffing and crossing her arm over her chest, tucking her hand under her armpit while she remains holding her beer in the other. She looks out toward the forest to evade my leer. After what seems like a full minute passes, with only the robins chirping in the nearby tree to break the deafening silence, she looks at me with her lips pressing tightly together and her eyebrows nearly meeting in the middle.

In my peripheral, I see Patch shake his head when her eyes veer in his direction. When I turn to look at him, he is looking at his beer, avoiding me.

"Your father wanted to pick you up at the airport, but once again, a Bear boy steps in and gets what he wants. Seems like they get to have you anytime they want." She clears her throat and gulps her beer. She looks at Patch, who seems concerned and is shaking his head slowly as if hoping she won't continue. "What I mean is, you're living with them, they get to do wonderful things for you, and they won't let us take part. You're pushing us out of her life, and we don't like it."

Patch sits forward and gently sets his beer on the table beside mine, which has a beer-moat surrounding it. "Causing issues was not our intention. We want to make Goldilocks as happy as possible and sometimes it's not always thought out." He clears his throat, taking the time to choose his words carefully. "If there's anything you two can do, we'll let you know, but everything is under control."

"What's under control?" Both remain silent. "Someone, tell me what's going on." I'm prepared to throw a tantrum. "Is this all because Patch picked me up at the airport and not Dad? This is silly."

Mom is looking at me and I can tell she wants to spill, but she shifts her sights to Patch, who's rubbing his thighs and shaking his head. He leans forward, resting his elbows on his knees. Mom leans back in her chair, looking and picking at her label.

Patch clears his throat. "We have a surprise for you. It should have been finished by the time you came home, but we ran into a snag along the way. It'll take another week, maybe."

"What kind of surprise?" My attitude has shifted 180 degrees.

"It's more of a gift than a surprise. Can you hold off on insisting I tell you what it is? That was likely your next question."

Should I pester him to tell me? No, I'll let it go for now, but my curiosity has piqued.

"If you don't want me to ask, you shouldn't have said you had a gift for me." I bite my bottom lip when he casts a dominant gaze my way. The sun catches one of his dark brown eyes, revealing a lighter shade than I'm used to seeing.

Fuck! He's so ruggedly handsome.

Patch turns his attention to my mother and shakes his head. "We aren't trying to push you out. She's your daughter. We would never intentionally ruin that bond. You're welcome to help…" he pauses, realizing that I'm listening with great curiosity, hoping he'll slip up. "Actually, there is something you can do. I'll call you later when this nosy one isn't near me." He aims his thumb at me.

Two beers each and Patch announces that he has to get going. I've done most of the talking while he sat, quietly listening. He asks if I'm ready to head back, but I want to stay with my mother for a while longer. I'm picking up on his vibes; he wants me to go with him. Mom begs me not to go. He's disappointed when I decide to stay. He says his goodbyes and rushes off into the woods alone.

Chapter 10

She listens while I tell her all about school. She's so proud of me. She married my father young and worked to put him through school. The plan was that she would continue her education after he graduated and got a good job. But then I happened. She stayed home and raised me while my father worked. She's taken odd jobs here and there but never finished her schooling. This is why she glows each time I talk about school.

"There's not much else to tell. Nothing prolific happened while I was there—no wild parties and no crazy stories to reminisce about when I'm older."

Mom drinks the last of her beer and frowns from the disappointment of its demise. "Want another beer?"

"Um, no. If I have another, the walk back to the Bear house will be challenging. Fun, but challenging."

"Tea?" she asks as she stands, taking our empty bottles.

As I rise, I pick up the tray containing the remnants of a few crackers and only two remaining pieces of cheese and follow.

"Sure, but then I have to go. I might bake some cookies for them tonight. It's the least I can do for them since they're letting me stay there." The door slams behind me and I cringe, expecting my father to hiss at me for it, but he isn't home.

"You know, you are welcome to stay here. We'd prefer it, actually." She rinses the brown bottles, leaving them upside down in the drip tray. "People talk, and... they say awful things."

"So, let them talk. I don't care what those judgemental—
It's okay for me but not you—people say."

She shrugs. I shove the rest of the crackers and cheese into
my mouth and chew quickly because I'm annoyed about the
busy-bodies constantly sticking their noses where they don't
belong. As soon as I'm able to speak, my hand covers my
mouth to shield her from seeing the mashed disaster within.

"No, it wouldn't seem right. After college, I always
thought I'd be on my own, even though I'm not actually on
my own." I swallow the mushy wad, taking several attempts
to get the mess down my throat. "Bash will be home soon,
anyway. I want to live with him, so it wouldn't make much
sense to move here and then there in two weeks."

She leans against the slate countertop after plugging in the
kettle. Her hesitation screams volumes.

"It isn't right; you, living with them while Bash is away.
Even when he comes home. You're not married, and you
haven't been dating all that long. What will people think?
They talk, you know. They say things... reputation destroying
things."

I set the mugs onto the slate and cringe at the sound it
makes. Slate countertops generate a grinding sound that
affects me like nails on a chalkboard does to most people. I've
hated it ever since they installed it.

"Let them say what they will. They know me and my
character. If they don't like me because Bash is in my life...
well, fuck them!"

Mom's eyes dart to mine. That's the first time I've cursed
in front of her. I'm half expecting her hand across my cheek.

"Sorry!"

Her disappointed grimace has me wishing she would have
slapped me instead. Mom pours the hot water into the mugs
with a heavy sigh. Her eyes meet mine then slowly drop.

"They talk is all I'm saying."

She takes both mugs and sets them on the table. As we pull
out the wooden chairs, the familiar screech has me cringing
again.

"So, how's Dad?"

Mom shrugs and blinks several times. She does that when she's evading a conversation that makes her uncomfortable.

"He's fine. You know your dad; always busy and will forever have something to complain about."

"Okay, can we talk honestly?" I ask, and she hesitantly nods. "Something seems off. Ever since I got back into town, there's this itch in the back of my mind that I can't quite get at. What's going on?"

"There's been some talk around town." She sips her tea, setting the mug down slowly. Her eyes have yet to meet mine. "You know how people make stuff up to entertain their small minds... well, that's likely all it is."

I slouch back in my chair and smile. "Those people have nothing better to do with their lives. They're a bunch of uneducated, self-absorbed windbags. You can't believe half the shit they claim to be fact."

Mom smiles quickly before sipping her tea again. I sit straighter and furrow my brows.

"Tell me."

"There's a rumor of sex outdoors."

I suddenly feel lightheaded. There were two instances where I had sex outside. The first time, Patch fucked me really hard. The second, all three of them had me, and then Bash made love to me without Patch and Mack present. What did this person see? There had been bondage and spanking involved. Did they see that too? It might be a false rumor started by a jealous ex-lover. No matter, because the truth behind it is hard to hide from my mother's examining stare.

I roll my eyes and snigger. "Who said that?" I try not to over-gesture with my hands, which is something I do when I'm nervous. "You know me; I'm so uptight. Sex outdoors? Nobody who truly knows me will believe that bullshit."

Matter of fact, she states, "It doesn't matter who said it, just that it was said. It only takes one accusation for people to think you're a tramp. It's just talk... right?"

Come on, Goldilocks, make it believable!

"Do you believe the rumor?" I stare at her questioningly.

She studies my unwavering expression. "No, not completely."

"Not completely?" I chuckle.

Mom simply smiles before getting up to fill a pot with water and setting it on the stove. She begins washing beans in the sink.

"You're a grown woman, Goldilocks. If you want to have sex outside the bedroom and with whoever you choose, you're welcome to do so. I love you no matter what. You could have sex with the whole town if you want to. I'll be disappointed, but I will always be your mother." She stops washing the beans to glance at me. "Just be careful. Be sure of what you're doing and with whom and where you're doing it. Someone could be watching."

She turns to set the colander of beans on the drip tray and then checks on something she has cooking in the oven before adjusting the temperature dial.

"I'd ask you to stay for dinner, but you said you already ate. I should warn you that your father heard the rumor and isn't too happy about it. If you're not willing to listen to him go on and on about your reputation, you might not want to stay." She looks up at the clock.

"When is he expected home?" A cold sensation runs through me, awakening the nervous knots in my stomach.

"Five minutes."

I stand and set my mug on the counter beside the sink, cringing again. "I think I'll go. It's been a long day and I'm not sure I'll be able to mind my manners while he gives me the three-hour speech. Maybe I'll leave that for tomorrow after we're all rested. Just let him know I'm back in town."

"I will. Letting it lie for another day won't change anything. But, it's Saturday tomorrow. He won't have to work, so he'll be in a better mood." She groans. "He's been coming home from work grumpy every day this week. He's... distant."

She waves her hands, letting me know that I shouldn't worry about it. She pulls me in and hugs me as moms do; tight but loving.

Despite the squeeze, I say, "I'd better go before he comes home."

"It's getting dark. Should you be walking alone?" She calls out. With a wave of my hand, I start toward the door. She insists, "At least take the whistle and flashlight! I love you!"

"I love you too!"

With whistle and flashlight in hand, I wave and smile before backing through the screen door and flinching at the thud.

The woods are darker than the clearing, making it look very intimidating. Here I am again, walking to the Bear house in the dark, knowing I've disappointed my father with my life decisions. I've let him down, and it's breaking my heart.

With each step, my anger toward the unnamed rumor spreader grows. A bear would likely fear me by the cursing rage I'm spewing to the trees as I stumble down the overgrown path.

Lightning cracks seconds before huge raindrops find their way past the thick canopy of leaves above me. The sound is intense, blocking out my raging curses. I'm cold and drenched within seconds. The only thing comforting is the stench of wet moss I've learned to love over the years. The last thing I need is a tree coming down on my head, so I step it up to a faster pace.

Chapter 11

By the time I reach the Bear house, I'm fully enraged and soaking wet. The wind is whipping so strong the door is challenging to close. My chest heaves from the run. I can't catch my breath. My skin prickles with tiny bumps and my fingertips have shriveled.

Both Patch and Mack's heads spin around to observe the soggy mess before them. I'm dripping, and respectfully, don't step off the welcome mat. They come to their feet while holding back their laughter. I'm not laughing.

Patch speaks first. "You know, if you had called, I would have picked you up."

Mack heads to the bathroom, probably to get a towel for me. I hear his distant laugh.

My jaw quivers, making it hard to form words. "Why the fuck didn't you tell me someone saw us having sex in the woods?"

Patch tips his face toward the floor and scratches his temple while he peeks up at me. He knows I'm about to ream him a new asshole. He doesn't stop his approach, but he slows his pace. Mack unfolds a thick red towel while stifling a laugh. As he walks toward me, he looks at his brother, hoping he'll take the lead on this one. When Patch doesn't, he explains while handing me the towel.

"We were hoping you could have one night of peace before we threw that at you. It's been a long day for you."

"Well, that worked out well, didn't it?" I'm being very sarcastic. Snatching the towel and burying my face in it, I muffle my lengthy groan.

Patch grips the towel and lowers it so he can see my eyes. "This was the main reason I didn't want to go see your parents today. Your father came here one day after hearing the rumor. He went off on us."

My eyes are wide, and now I'm shaking for a different reason—fear. "Wha... What. Did. He. Say?"

Mack leans against the table, crossing his arms and head shaking. "A lot, and nothing good about us Bear brothers."

"Oh. My. God!" I bury my face in the towel and kick off my boots, sending them in different directions. I pace while Patch lines my boots beside the others. Everything must be in perfect order around Patch. I instantly freeze as a thought seems to explode in my head. "Did the big mouth say they saw me with just Patch or all three of you?"

Mack drops his head again and bites his top lip while peeking at me through his long, wavy brown hair. Patch has one hand on his waist, the other scratching the back of his head, also looking up from his brows. His expression foretells what he's about to say. "All of us," he whispers. "Her account is accurate, aside from a few embellishments the rumor-spreaders have thrown in. But, overall, it proves she saw everything."

"She?"

Mack lifts his head. "Ginger." When I look at him questioningly, he adds. "Ginger Linden."

"I don't know who that is."

Mack adds, "She's a middle-aged redhead that works at the bank. She is a long-distance runner and often runs the paths around here. I didn't think anyone came this far onto our property."

"A redhead named Ginger? Her parents didn't like her, did they?" I wrap the towel around my body and hug it close to my chin. "Have either of you talked to her?" Both men shake their heads assertively. "Why not?"

They snicker as if I've missed out on a private joke. Patch replies, "We feel bad for her, in a way. Can you imagine telling one person, which is what we were told she did, and having it spread like a wildfire with your name attached to it? I'm sure she's scared that we'll come knocking since we are the evil Bear brothers. To answer your question, no, we did not confront her and have no plans to do so."

Mack adds, "Besides, if we make a big deal of it, it'll just add kindling to the fire. Just let the embers burn out, Goldilocks. People will soon move on to ruin someone else's life. Best to just let it go."

I glare at him, tilting my head. I'm fucking angry, so angry that I'm filled with hot rage. "I will talk to her then. She will regret ever saying anything. You boys might be afraid of a little redheaded woman, but I certainly am not."

I scurry to the bathroom quickly, turn on the shower and strip off my wet clothes. It doesn't take long before the tiny bumps on my skin have flattened and my seething anger has also simmered. I'm slightly disappointed that neither man joins me to help ease my frustration with their seductive ways. Maybe they're afraid I'll try to rip their throats out or something. I should apologize for flipping out.

After dressing in one of Bash's long t-shirts, I slip on a pair of panties and warm, wool socks, and dry my hair. I walk past the boys, who are sitting in the living room. As I tie my hair into a loose bun, I open and close the kitchen cupboards. Mack stands up from the couch and comes to assist me. He stands in front of me, smiling. He's so fucking handsome, with chiseled features, seductive, sky-blue eyes and dark wavy hair that hangs longer than his shoulders.

"What are you looking for?" His finger brushes a loose tress of hair from my cheek, tucking it behind my ear. "Damn, girl. You smell sweet and fruity." He moves closer and takes a long sniff of my hair.

I pause momentarily and then step back with a smile. My hands block his approach. "Baking supplies? I'll bet you boys wouldn't mind eating some homemade cookies."

Without turning his head away from the book he's reading, Patch yells, "Fuck yeah! Love me some cookies!"

Mack opens a tall cupboard and pulls out a few plastic tubs and some plastic bags, contents unknown.

I yell back. "What is your favorite kind, Patch?"

"Oatmeal raisin but they have to have cinnamon in them or don't bother."

He turns the page and continues reading. How can he read and still follow this conversation?

"What about you, Mack?" I say as I pick up each thing to see what they are. Most of these perishable ingredients look too old to use. Baking must not be a common practice in this house.

"I like chocolate chip, but not just any chocolate chip cookie will do. It has to be crunchy around the outside but soft and gooey in the center. Mm-mmm! I can almost taste them. But I can't find any chocolate chips. Dammit!"

"And you don't have any oatmeal, vanilla, or flour. These are old and should be replaced."

He scans the products on the counter. "Damn! Now I'm craving cookies. It's all your fault, Goldilocks. If the weather clears, we can take a trip into town tomorrow to pick up what you need. If you want anything specific that we don't have here, like lady stuff, make a list."

"Thank you. I'm set for lady stuff, for now. I do have a few things I can add to a list other than baking supplies."

We put most of the old stuff in the trash and settle for popcorn instead. It isn't long before I fall asleep on Mack's shoulder on the couch. I feel him shift and it jolts me awake. They are both looking at me.

Mack whispers, "I was going to carry you to bed."

I yawn and sit up, pulling the blanket with me. With a shy smile, I reply, "I just needed a catnap. I'm awake now."

"You can go to bed if you're tired, nobody will stop you," Patch says with his deep voice.

"What time is it?"

Mack points to the massive clock on the wall above the television. How had I not noticed the oversized, hand-carved wooden clock? It has to be five feet across and still retaining the dark-grey bark from the tree trunk it was sawed from. The hands are long, gold, and very fancy in their design. The hands don't jolt with each movement; they sweep with silent ease.

"I love that clock!" It's only eight-thirty, too early to go to bed.

"Maybe I'll build you one someday," Patch says before flipping another page of his book.

"It's beautiful."

Patch looks at it and says, "It's a great piece of wood. Seemed like a waste to burn it." He's a humble man. He looks at Mack. "Would you mind if I ask for her company tonight?"

He sighs but waves his hand. "Fine."

"Goldie, would you like to…" He starts, but I cut him off.

"Goldilocks, not Goldie. We discussed this already."

As he's closing his book, he shifts in his chair making it easier for him to glare at me. "We did, and what did I tell you?"

"That you get to choose what you'll call me; slut, whore. But I put my foot down at Goldie, or did you forget me telling you that? Only Bash can call me Goldie."

Our locked stares have us in a battle of wills, yet again. He and I seem to find ourselves in this position often. He leans forward, resting his elbows on his knees after setting his book on the table.

"Fine. I will call you something else. Perhaps cunt. Would you prefer that?" He's testing me.

I stand, picking up the bowls as I do. "Sure! Just as long as you don't call me Goldie."

Chapter 12

Patch groans as I turn to walk past Mack and into the kitchen to put the bowls away. For such a big man, Patch moves stealthily. I see him coming in my peripheral and spin, putting my hands up to stop him. I try to back away, but my high-pitched laughter has me moving too slowly. He bends forward and scoops me over his shoulder. He hangs onto the back of my knees while he turns one way, then the other as he dumps the bowl's contents into the trash and sets them in the sink.

I'm laughing harder now. He cracks my ass with his lumberjack-sized hand. Both ass cheeks heat instantly and my pussy twitches. I grab onto the waistband of his denim pants and try to lift my face off his back, but I'm laughing too hard to hold the position for more than a few seconds. He cracks me again. I try to cover my ass with my right hand, but somehow, he grasps my wrist and gives me two more. My ass is on fire!

I fucking love this!

Patch carries me into his bedroom and kicks the door shut with his foot. Before putting me down, he steps out of his slippers, undoes his pants and lets them fall to the floor, kicking them to the side. He tosses me onto my back on the bed. He's on me, between my legs before the second bounce.

His mouth presses to mine with passion behind it. I could disappear into this man if I let myself. It would be as simple as closing my eyes and pretending he's Bash. I miss him so much.

I whisper, "Tonight, you can pretend I am her."

His expression softens. It's as if he's suddenly lost ten years of stress off his face. He nods slowly, brushing his thumb along my lips. The dominant man inside him is shadowed by his kinder side.

His voice flows with a deep whisper. "If we keep our eyes closed, we can pretend. This isn't wrong, is it?"

My fingertips trail down his forehead and cheek. "We'll keep our eyes closed. It won't mean anything between you and me, other than two bodies pleasing each other while holding the image of someone else."

"Agreed. Thank you," he whispers before his lips press tenderly to mine.

He's passionate and romancing *her* with his kisses. The otherwise rough, workingman's hands seem softer than silk as they brush along my skin. He cups my breast, kissing down my neck with slow, deliberate pecks. My fingers weave into his short, dark hair as his lips surround my areola. As his tongue warms and teases my nipple, the full weight of his chest presses onto my pelvis, pinning me to the bed.

He rocks his body. Between the nipple play and the pressure on my clitoris, I'm moaning between deep breaths. His gentle hands wrap around both breasts, pushing them closer together so he can alternate between them quickly, nipping and flicking until my womanhood drips with need.

I'm lost in his tenderness. His sensual movements are as smooth as a ballet dancer. My hands slide along the bed, down beside my butt until our fingers weave together. An easy moan slips from his throat.

His tongue laps at my folds, sucking and flicking at my clitoris until I'm on the edge of letting myself fall into the abyss of glory when he suddenly stops. I groan my disappointment, but his mouth is on mine quickly, suffocating my protest. His left elbow rests beside my head while his right hand caresses my thigh.

With one quick movement, he's deep inside me. Both of us gasp into each other's mouths. His halted breath proves his pleasure. When my hips lift to meet his slow, deliberate thrusts, he pushes against my cervix, causing shock waves to ripple through me. The way our bodies mesh so perfectly, anyone watching would believe us to be deeply in love with each other.

He's building me slowly toward orgasm. Nobody has ever moved this expertly with me, including him. I'm slipping away, becoming light and yet so heavy. I'm warm, cradled, and desired. I know it's not me he's dreaming of, but how lucky I would be if I were. She is a fool to have left a man who loves her this much. I can feel his heart breaking for her. He does not aim his compassion at me. I'll be wise to keep that in mind.

In a flash, he rolls us both, our mouths never separating. I'm above him, straddling his pelvis, his rock-hard cock buried deep into me. His massive hands grip firmly on either side of my waist. I sit up and try to buck but he won't allow me to move. His eyelids are closed, mouth open, chest heaving.

The weather outside pelts against the window creating a song that mirrors the moment between us; deafeningly peaceful, serene but treacherous, absolutely flawless with the possibility of disaster. At any moment, either of us could forget who we're connected to and let our hearts break wide open.

I glance at him but only for a second. I cannot allow myself the pleasure of falling deeper under his spell. He watches me. His teeth are clenched, eyes seem darker, and his face has taken back those years he had lost earlier.

His Adam's Apple bobs. "I'm going to fuck you hard now because I can't do this with you." I nod, knowing how close we came to bonding with more than just our bodies.

"Should I make you work for it?" I reply with a sassy tone.

His nostrils flare. "If you're up for it."

Before he can react, I slap his face and then fling my leg over him, attempting to escape his wrath. He growls like a madman, grasping my ankle just as I'm about to hop off the bed. I topple forward, catching myself before I hit the floor. I pull at the rug and kick, trying to yank my ankle out of his hand, but his mighty grip is inescapable. I kick with my other leg, hitting him in the chest, forcing him to let go. We both laugh; mine brought on with a hint of fear while the battle enthralls him.

I run to the door while he leaps off the bed and strides toward me. Quickly, I whip open the door and run through, slamming it behind me. He thuds against the wood and growls like a wild beast. He gives me time to hide while calling out to me from behind the closed door. "Goldilocks... I'm coming to get you!"

Which way do I go? Shit! Shit! Shit!

I run out the front door, closing it quietly behind me. It's damn cold out here and dark as hell. I can't see my hand in front of my face unless the lightning sparks, momentarily blinding me with the darkened shapes of the surrounding objects. I feel like someone is taking pictures of me and I keep looking at the flash.

I'm careful not to make any noise, but I'm unsuccessful when I bump into the table, knocking an empty beer can onto the wooden porch. I shuffle my feet, waiting for the lightning to light a path to the other side of the porch. It's too dangerous to slip into the thick of the forest. If a tree falls, it could kill me.

I hear a sound behind me and spin to look just as a bolt of lightning lights up the entire porch. Patch is standing a foot away from me. My giddy yet terrified shriek seems to fizzle out between the fat raindrops as if it didn't exist. I spin to run but he has my hair in his fist.

His voice sounds distant, drowned by the sheets of rain. "I found you, bitch! You're in trouble now, whore!" He's naked, his cock harder and thicker than I've ever seen it. His huge hand grabs my throat, pulling me toward his face. "Slap me, will you? You won't do that again."

A tinge of fear trickles into my laughter when his hand tightens. Blood rushes to my face and it's harder to breathe. He glares fiercer with each bolt of lightning. It's terrifying, sexy, and holy fuck, I want him!

His hands release my neck and hair, but he picks me up over his shoulder and carries me into the house. The heavy door slams behind us. His grunts are loud and raging like a barbarian. When he spins, walking here and there, I see Mack sitting on the couch but his attention is no longer on the television. He's snickering, as though we're purposely entertaining him.

"Hi, Mack," I say with a wave and a giggle. "I slapped his face!"

Mack's face drops, and his mouth hangs wide. "Oh shit! You didn't, did you?"

I'm laughing, slapping Patch's firm, naked ass as hard as I can but my energy is depleting quickly. "Yes, and then I kicked him!"

"This will be good!" Mack stands and turns one of the sofa chairs so he can watch the wrath of Patch play out in comfort.

Patch flips me quickly and I scream, thinking he's going to slam me onto the floor, but he stops me just before I hit the wood. My cackling annoys him. I can tell by the flushing of his cheeks and his clenched jaw.

With expertise, he quickly fashions a binding around my wrists and tugs it, forcing me onto my feet. He flips the free end of the rope over one of the thick bulkheads. As he pulls the rope, the stress on my wrists intensifies. He eases it slightly, but I'm still left to stand on my tiptoes. I wobble back and forth, not far, but like I can't find my balance long enough to hold still.

Patch pulls open a drawer in the kitchen and I wonder if he's about to get a knife, but rethink that. He would never really hurt me... would he?

He pulls out a rubber spatula and bends it so it's in line with the handle. As he saunters toward me, his hard cock swings from thigh to thigh. I glance at Mack, who watches with his head tilted and a disturbing grin on his lips.

Patch circles me, pinching my skin in several spots, forcing me to jerk away from him and yelp. I'm still giggling, which is likely frustrating for him. I hear the loud crack before the pain registers. He hit my right ass cheek with the spatula and it stings like it's on fire. My yelp is loud and sharp.

He cracks my left butt cheek just as hard and I jolt, trying to escape another possible slap. *That fucking hurt!* He comes around the front of me, staring deep into the eyes. His eyes are dark and seem uncaring, almost inhumane. I'm no longer laughing.

"I'm sorry. I shouldn't have slapped you..."

"Shut the fuck up, slut!" His thick fingers grip my nipples and pull, forcing me to arch my back until my toes barely touch the floor. He doesn't release them until I squeal. He asks, "What are your safe words?"

"Um, what?"

"Safe words. What are they?" He roughly wipes the hair off my face.

"Red and yellow," I whisper, fearing I may need to use them tonight.

He grips my chin and lifts my face while leaning in until our lips are almost touching. "Let's see just how fucking tough you really are. Shall we?"

"No, it's okay. I'm not that tough. Really! I'm a banana; you touch me and I bruise." I laugh at the analogy. He isn't.

"Then expect to be black and blue tomorrow." That statement has him snickering. He's such a sadist. I can easily say *red*, but I don't want to. Not yet.

Patch steps back and reaches out, touching the tip of the spatula to my nipple. As he lifts his arm, I hollow my chest. He shakes his head, holding the spatula out until I relax and place my nipple at its edge. He lifts and swings downward, thwapping just my nipple. I yelp and twist, hoping to avoid another.

His fingers glide around my waist as he circles me before doing the same to the other nipple. This time, I don't move away. I stand and stare him down, trying not to show any pain or fear. I will beat him at his own game. He snickers and repeats the action three more times to each nipple before slapping the backside against the tender skin on the outside of each breast. It's more of an uncomfortable sting than it is painful.

After tossing the spatula onto the kitchen's island, he stands inches in front of me. His lips peck onto mine with more affection than I'm expecting at this point. He winks and then leans around me, bracing my tummy with his hip. He forcefully slaps my ass at least a dozen times while tears drip down my cheeks. I'm yelping with each hard crack. When he stops, it's not only me who is panting. He's aroused from the act of spanking me.

He stands tall, his quick breaths flowing over my face. His eyes are hooded, his lips glistening. Two of his fingers slip between my labia. His digits are strong as they dip into my wetness. He pulls them back then holds them up between us, separating them slowly so I can see the strings of goo spanning between his digits.

My breath catches when he opens his mouth, pushing his fingers in and closing his lips around them. His eyes slowly droop, savoring the taste like a well-aged whiskey. He quickly bends forward, shoving his arms between my knees and standing quickly, lifting my legs out from under me. My wrists ache, but I grasp the rope above the knot to ease the strain.

In a flash, my thighs are resting on his shoulders and his strong hands brace my hips. My back arches with my head hanging lower than my hips. His mouth presses firmly against my clit. He's slurping, sucking, and flicking at the swollen button and surrounding flesh. When I open my eyes, I see Mack but he's upside down. He reaches into his pants to readjust his bulge and smiles at me. My eyelids close. It feels so good.

Patch lowers my legs. I'm pouting but happy to be right-side-up again. He disappears into his room but only for a few seconds. He reappears behind me holding more rope and something small clutched in his hand. I watch as he quickly wraps the rope around my legs and pelvis until I'm wearing a strange-looking harness. Patch flips the rope over the ceiling log and pulls until my pelvis lifts equally in height to his. He releases the rope connecting my hands to the bulkhead. I fall backward, screaming as I go.

The pelvic rope prevents me from falling to the floor, but I'm upside down again. That was scary as hell! He tugs the wrist rope, letting me know that he had me the whole time and would not have let me hit my head should the harness fail.

He takes my wrist and pulls until I'm sitting up as if resting on a swing. He lifts my arms over my head and behind me, bending them at the elbow until my hands are against the back of my neck. He wraps the rope around my chest, just beneath my breasts. It circles me, enveloping the rope supporting the harness, holding me upright. After tying it off, he steps back to savor his creation. I cannot move anything above my calves. It seems strange to me how the supporting rope running between my breasts excites me.

With Patch standing between my spread thighs, he buries his swollen prick deep into me. Without hesitation, he steps forward as he does, like he's pushing me back on a swing. He thumps his hips against me, using gravity as a way for me to come crashing back against him. The depth of his cock feels like he's deeper than my belly button.

I can't utter a word, but strange *eep* sounds seem to lurch from my throat with each thrust. I'm spinning out of my mind and away from my body. He owns me and I can't fight him off. I don't want to fight him off. If this continued for a full day, that's okay with me.

The room whirls around my head as if the storm has ripped the walls from the house, leaving us amid the tumultuous noise and chaos. My clit is so alive, as if being tickled by the most powerful lightning bolt. Everything is loud and spinning as if I'm swimming in a washing machine. I want to let go; to allow myself to sink to the bottom and give in—to permit death to take me, should she wish to.

I stiffen, straining the ropes as my body is sweetly tortured by the wrath of Patch. My thoughts; nothing—absolute nothingness. I'm free from the anarchy that was drowning me.

It's the sweetest euphoria. True nothingness has enveloped me and I'm floating.

I'm jolted and I gasp, wailing on the exhale as my body continues to be thrashed from Patch's brutal fucking. He grunts like an injured bear before holding motionless, his muscles seeming to vibrate as he clutches my thighs with a constrictive grip. His wail slowly builds inside his body, finally ripping from his depths. The sound intensifies, filling the room in a deafening pitch that vibrates my chest.

Patch's legs wobble, causing me to swing free. He holds my calves to stop my swinging. Both of us are twitching and gasping for breath. He quickly sets my arms free and then my pelvis while Mack holds me from behind, preventing my spent body from slumping to the floor. I can barely focus on Patch while he frees me from the harness. He's standing, but his weakened legs have him struggling to do so.

Mack releases me, leaning me on Patch who hugs me, allowing me to disappear against his muscular body. He walks me to Bash's bedroom and pulls back the sheets. As I lay on the bed, he smooths the comforter over me and kisses my forehead. This is when I notice how wet his thighs are.

"Someone was really working hard," I comment. "You're all sweaty."

He looks at his legs and grins crookedly. "That's from you." My eyes widen with disbelief. "That's your cum. You exploded and nearly strangled my cock. It was fucking sexy as hell. I couldn't hold off after you did that. I can usually contain myself, but not after that."

"Wow!" I'm shocked. Never have I been so excited that I've saturated someone. "Maybe I'll slap you more often." I chuckle, pulling the covers under my chin.

He smirks. "Be careful, little Goldilocks. This big, bad Bear might hurt you if you poke too hard."

I laugh. "As long as you don't huff and puff and blow my house down."

He grimaces. "I think you're mixing up the fairy tales." Before he walks out, he turns and without looking at me says, "Thank you for earlier."

"You're welcome," I whisper. It isn't long before I'm drifting into a deep sleep.

Chapter 13

I wake, still smelling the mossy heaviness brought to life by the rain and humidity. It must have poured all night. The room is dim, proving the clouds have yet to lift. As I roll, sleepiness fades and clarity swoons in. Someone is cooking, and it smells very appetizing. I close my eyes, hoping to hear men chatting. There's only silence, aside from clanking dishes.

As I stand, I search for something to wear. The t-shirt I took off in Patch's room last night is tangled in the comforter which I kicked onto the floor during the night. Patch must have tossed it on the bed after he found it in his room.

Mack is cooking while Patch reads the newspaper at the table with a steaming mug suspended by his two huge fingers wedged in the cup's ear. His eyes follow me as the paper sags to the table. He sips from his mug, expressionless. I head to the bathroom to pee and brush my teeth. When I open the door, Patch watches me again. I wink and then slink over to the cupboard to retrieve a mug.

Mack leans toward me, pursing his lips. I peck my lips on his and we both say good morning. After filling the mug with coffee, I stand beside Patch and sift through his paper. I smile at him and then kiss the top of his head before taking a seat across from him. He grimaces at the disheveled newspaper before him.

I'm going to sift through the want ads to see how much it is to rent an apartment around here. Maybe Mom is right in that I shouldn't be living with three men. I can see how people might judge me, especially after the rumor... the true rumor.

Hopefully, it won't ruin my chances at getting the job at the hospital. Small towns have many secrets that never stay secret.

Before my first sip of coffee, I say, "I hope you guys will let me cook breakfast once in a while." They both snicker. "What's so funny?"

Mack teases, "We will if you wake up at a decent time." I grimace.

Patch says, "A man could starve to death in the morning while waiting for you to drag your lazy ass out of bed."

"Oh, come on! It's not even 7:30 yet."

Mack widens his sky-blue eyes and says, "Exactly! We've been up for an hour already."

Patch asks, "How'd you sleep?"

I slurp my coffee and then shake the paper to get it to fold on the seam. "I wouldn't call it sleep—more like I temporarily died. Seriously... wonderful. How about you?"

He smiles at me but doesn't comment. Mack cuts in. "I heard him snoring from my room, so I'm going to say that he slept very well." Being the jokester that he is, in a higher, more feminine voice, he asks, "How did you sleep, Mack?" Replying to the strange voice but in a deeper, more masculine tone than his own, he says, "I tossed and turned all night. Thank you for asking."

Both Patch and I shake our heads and laugh. I ask, "Why didn't you sleep well, Mack?"

He waves the spatula and then uses it to flip something in the pan. "My cock was so hard it hurt."

Patch drops his paper to the table. "Why didn't you jerk off? It's not like you've never done that before?"

He shrugs. "I should have just done it. Maybe I would have slept better. To be honest, I was too damn tired to put forth the effort."

Chapter 14

Around nine o'clock, Patch takes off in his truck to go to work. Mack asks if I'd be interested in going into town to shop. I'd love to go talk to that bitch at the bank with the big mouth. Logic warns me that I should just avoid her as the guys suggested, but she needs to explain why she would say anything to anyone in the first place.

I need to make the effort to see my father today. It's inevitable that I'll get the morality speech. He'll condemn my actions, treat me like a little girl who is too innocent to understand the ruthless ways of men. It'll be tough, but I will have to keep my lips held tightly together. If I lose my temper and blurt out that I'd like him to let me live my life, it'll turn into a fucking war!

We make a shopping list and then head out. His truck is so new I can still smell the factory scent. He travels often, so he requires a reliable vehicle. Mack designs the plans to build custom log homes for people. He's an architect, a very good one. Patch and his crew help hunt down the logs they'll need to build it, according to Mack's specifications. Patch loves doing the heavy lifting grunt work while Mack handles the office work, which Patch despises. Still, he loves to be out in the forest despite the intensive labor it entails. Give him a chainsaw and he's as happy as he can be.

Bash is away at school taking extra courses toward his degree. He plans to return here to begin his book editing career and possibly write one of his own. There is already a job lined up at the local paper where he will write obituaries. It sounds grim, but he believes everyone deserves an honorable announcement. He also said it's a great way to get his foot in the door at the local paper so he can work his way up the ladder, if he stays in that industry and not follow in his brothers' footsteps and work the family business.

In nine days, he will be home. I miss him so much. It's been three months since I've seen him. Three long months since he's held me in his arms and told me he loves me. His brothers will keep me company until his return, but they don't compare to Bash Bear.

The grocery store is nearly empty, which is just fine with me. We pick up everything on our list and then head to the checkout. The young woman scanning our products is unfamiliar to me. I used to know everyone in this town.

"Can we stop at the bank?"

Mack nods without thinking and then stops bagging the groceries to give me a reprimanding look. "What are you up to, Goldilocks?"

"Who, me?" I feign innocence. "Whatever do you mean?"

He glares at me. "I know damn well what you're up to. So, no, we are not going to the bank."

The cashier stares at me. I look at her. She glances at Mack before shaking her head.

"What?" I ask the heavyset, late-teen girl with blue hair.

She looks at me and questions, "You're Goldilocks?"

"Yes, I am. Why?" I place my hands on my hips, ready to go to war. *I'm not in the mood today, bitch!*

"Nothing." She looks me up and down while scanning the bag of chocolate chips.

"You heard the rumors about me and believe every word, don't you?" She shrugs. "And what if the rumors were true? What if they were *all* true?"

The girl is holding the box of baking soda and staring wide-eyed at me.

"Would it make a difference in your life if I was the town slut? Or would your life go on the same as always?" I pause, but not long enough for her to reply. "I guarantee my sexual behavior has zero effect on your life. Therefore, my suggestion to you is to keep your opinions to yourself. Don't dumb yourself down by believing what the bullshitting, pathetic, uneducated people are spewing about other people. Chances are what they say is a lie or a huge embellishment of the truth. You're young. In time, you'll learn of the small-town mentality."

Mack swipes his debit card and we scoop up the bags without another word, leaving her chewing her fingernail and watching us leave the store with our heads held high.

"You embarrassed her," Mack scolds me.

I drop the bag on the backseat beside the two he carried. "And?"

"She's just a girl."

I roll my eyes when he opens the truck door for me, as all the Bear boys do. "She needs to learn to make her own decisions about people and stop trusting every rumor to be factual."

He rounds the hood and gets in his side of the truck and corrects me. "What is being said is factual."

My arms lift as does my voice. "She doesn't know that." He laughs. "I would like to go to the bank now, please."

"No, I'm not taking you to the bank." His sexy, pretty boy looks along with his crooked smile have my anger easing. "Where else would you like to go today?"

I think for a minute and ask, "Are there any other secrets that I should know?"

He clears his throat and looks into his rear-view mirror but not at me. "Why?"

We drive past the bank and I glare at the front door, wishing he would pull in the parking lot so I can go in and give Ginger a piece of my mind.

"Sweetheart, there's nothing you need to concern yourself with at this very moment, other than the sexy as fuck man sitting next to you."

He turns into Baneck's Drug Mart and parks. As he's opening his door, he asks, "Are you coming in?"

I shake my head as Mack hops out and closes his door. My door suddenly flies open, startling me. I thought he was heading into the store. He puts his hand out to me, inviting me to go with him.

"I'd like you to come with. Leaving a lady waiting in the parking lot is rude. Besides, I don't trust you not to take off running to the bank. I might have to tie your hands to the steering wheel."

With a loud huff, I take his hand and step out, leading the way into the store. Mrs. Baneck will judge me because that's what she does. I hold the heavy door for Mr. Lennysman. To me, he has always seemed old and fragile. Mack takes his arm to assist him down the two cement steps.

"I don't believe the stories people tell about you boys. You're all nice fellas. You've been nothing but kind to me for as far back as I can remember. I might be old, but my memory is still as sharp as a whip. One of you boys stole some of my flowers once. I followed you to the graveyard. They were for your parents. Well, you might not have been good boys, but you do have big hearts."

He takes a small, shuffling step, then stops. "Don't let this town eat you up. You all deserve the very best out of life. Don't have regrets for not doing the things that would have made you happier. You'll be wise to keep that in mind." He shakes his cane at us to stress his point.

He's a cute old man with thick glasses and only a few strands of feathery soft hair that dance in the mild breeze.

"Do you need help getting home?" Mack asks, but the man declines, claiming he's old, not invalid.

Chapter 15

Mack is smiling when he follows me into the store and then passes me to scurry up an aisle. I look to see if Mrs. Baneck is lurking behind the counter, ready to condemn me for hanging around another wicked Bear boy. She isn't. Mr. Baneck sees Mack walking up an aisle. He lifts the counter leaf and sets it down behind him.

"Hello! How are you two today?" We both nod and mirror his wide smile. "Is there anything in particular you're looking for?"

Mack says, "Yes, actually. Ah, we're looking for antacids, the extra strength kind, and lubrication." He knows he's embarrassing me and his smile proves that was his intention. "My guts turn something fierce when Patch cooks deer steaks. I was suffering with acid reflux and heartburn all night. Goldilocks, your stomach must not have been bothering you because you slept well." All I can do is shake my head to beg him to stop while wearing a horrified expression.

He takes my hand and follows Mr. Baneck. The pharmacist, despite knowing who we are and that we should not be holding hands since I'm dating Bash, didn't even bat an eyelash when asked for the sexual aid.

After asking which type he recommends as being the longest lasting and most effective lubricant—further embarrassing me—Mack chooses the bottle in the purple box. The older man walks to the antacids, taking one off the shelf and handing it to Mack with a few instructions on to help ease his symptoms without medication. I didn't know marshmallows ease heartburn when you suck on them. Mack picks up a bag of marshmallows on the way to pay for his items.

"Have a great day. Welcome back to town, Goldilocks. Say hi to your parents for me." Before I'm out of the door, he yells out to me. "Goldilocks! Since you're going back that way, you can save your father a trip into town. Hang on a minute while I get his prescription."

I didn't know my father was taking any medication. He rushes down the aisle, seeming a bit winded when he nears me. "If he has questions, ask him to call me."

"I will. Thank you."

Mack opens my door and closes it once I'm seated. He gets in, laughs, and starts driving without an explanation for his embarrassing behavior. Two blocks down the road, I punch him in the arm. I know I didn't hurt him, but he reacts as if I've slammed him with a sock full of pennies.

"Shit! Woman! Save it for the boxing ring. Geeze!" He looks at me with a smirk and then bursts into hysterical laughter. "What? We needed lube. You didn't find that funny?"

"Hell, no!"

"Bash said you loved it when he did it. A little *deja vu* was just what you needed to take your mind off the redhead." When I don't smile, he adds, "Well, it worked for a few minutes."

"You're an asshole!" I turn my head to hide my growing smile. That was funny and just as humiliating as what Bash did.

This town has changed little over the years. The same pale blue shutters frame the windows of the ice cream parlor. Dying red rose bushes still line the front of Mr. and Mrs. Geller's tiny white house that somehow housed twelve kids. He passed away last year.

The windows on Canter's Flea Market have all been boarded up since it closed in November. It'll open again in April. People still walk down the main street and the elderly who sit on their front porches, hoping someone will spare a moment to chat about the old days. Nothing changes in this town, even as the generations do.

"What has you so far away?"

"Hmm?" I look to him and see his concern.

"You okay? Did I really piss you off back there? If I did, I'm…" He places his hand over his heart.

I shake my head. "Yeah, no, I'm over it but you pissed me off. And yes, it was funny."

I stare at the red streetlight halting us and then look to the left and the right. No cars are coming in either direction. "It never made much sense to put this damn light here."

He snickers. "I remember when they put it up. Everyone ignored it."

"Maybe you should drop me off at my parent's house? I really should go to see my father. It's better to get this over with sooner than later."

He stares at me, even after the light turns green. I shrug and point to the light. He leers in his rear-view mirror after hearing a horn honk behind us.

"Drive!" I say in a slight panic. He slowly drives, likely infuriating the driver behind him.

"You want me to take you? Wouldn't Patch be better to do that? Your mom seems to like him. Your father won't be too pleased to see me if he's heard the rumor." He takes a deep breath and lets it out with a groan. "I'm not good with parental confrontation." He swallows hard.

"What does that mean?"

He seems to sag while shaking his head. "I was seeing this girl in high school…"

I cut in. "Leslie?"

"Yeah, her. She wanted me to meet her parents, so I agreed to go home with her. We were sitting on the couch, making out with my hand in her pants when her mother came home. She blew up, called me all kinds of awful names, threatened to call the cops if I ever came near her again. It was a fucking nightmare. I got the hell out of there and never went back."

"Is that why you two seemed to break up suddenly?"

"Bingo. So, I avoid parents. Then, your Dad freaked out on us…"

I nod sympathetically. "Look, you don't have to stay if you think it'll be too hard for you. There's a ninety percent chance this will be another bad experience for you. Just drop me off."

"I won't do that. It's rude and disrespectful." He runs his fingers through his shaggy hair and groans. "Fine! I'll take you, but you owe me!" His lips press together and his brows furrow as he playfully glares at me longer than he should when operating a motor vehicle.

"Only if you want to," I tease.

"I don't."

Chapter 16

Mack groans after he puts the truck in park and turns the engine off, leaving the keys to swing in the ignition. "Let's go before I change my mind."

"You don't have to go in." I pull Dad's prescription from my purse.

He turns to grimace at me. "Yes, I do. It would be rude not to."

I rap at the screen door and then slowly open it. "Hello. Anybody home?"

Mom calls out from the bedroom. "In here. Get yourself something to drink. I'll be out in a minute. I'm just putting some clothes away. I was…" Her words fade into a low mumble. I hate it when she does that.

I yell back while setting his prescription on the table. "I didn't get that last part. Where's Dad?"

She yells, louder than necessary. "He's outside. Didn't you see him?" She comes out of the bedroom and sets the empty basket on the sofa chair. She turns to peek out the window just as my father opens the screen door. He pauses in the threshold with a bowl of raspberries in hand. He glances at me but locks his sights on Mack with fury in his glare.

"What the hell is *he* doing here?" His monotone speaks volumes. I've only ever seen him this deeply angry a few times.

"Dad," I rush toward him, putting my body between him and Mack. "You can't believe everything you hear in town. You know they make shit up all the time, so don't…"

His hand cracks me across my face, sending a lightning bolt through my eye and pain radiating from my cheekbone outward. I'm shocked.

"Why?" I beg through a broken heart.

He screams, "I don't know who you are anymore. We raised you to be a good woman, not someone who has sex with three men in the forest! Three brothers?" His fist is clenched at his side—the other still clutching the bowl of berries.

Mother shoves herself between me and Dad. Her gentle push urges me to walk away. I turn and see Mack with his jaw clenched, nostrils flared, eyes full of rage, with his fists clenched. He's seething and ready to defend me. I place my hands on his chest to draw his attention. His eyes dart to mine and then my reddening cheek. Mom attempts to calm Dad.

"Don't! He's my father. You will respect him. I'm okay, it's just a bruised cheek." He glares at my father. "Look at me. Dammit, Mack!"

He hisses, "He hit you. Father or not, he had no right to do that."

"He's upset. He'll apologize later. Just let me handle this. Please?"

He folds his arms over his chest before sucking in a deep breath. "Fine, but if he slaps you again..." His eyes narrow.

"He won't. Please, sit. Let me go talk to him. Just stay here, please."

He sits on the sofa's armrest. I turn to see my mother with her arms on her hips talking to my father. She steps aside, arms crossed over her chest. She nods at me and then casts her sights over at Mack.

"Goldilocks, come here," Dad speaks in his disappointed, fatherly tone. He sets the berries on the end-table and clasps his hands in front of him.

I take a deep breath before walking toward him and my mother, who stands close, ready to intervene if he should lose his temper again.

"Dad, I..."

He puts his hand up, and I flinch. My reaction disturbs him. He slowly raises them up in surrender.

"What you did is wrong, Goldilocks. How do you expect people to respect you if you're giving your body away in such a disgusting fashion?" He looks up toward the ceiling as if asking the heavens for help. I remain quiet. He clears his throat. "Did you have sex with all three brothers in the forest? I was told they all had their way with you, one after the other; used like a cheap whore at a frat party."

"Do you really want to hear what I have to say? Dad…"

Shall I lie and save him the heartbreak? I pace back and forth, gesturing with my hands as the words start to flow like verbal diarrhea.

"What I do in my personal life is nobody's business. I'm not saying I did what the rumor claims, but if I *do* want to have sex with *every* unmarried man in this town, it's my business. It's *my* life. You don't like the Bear brothers, that's obvious, but don't hate them because you heard a stupid rumor." I stop and stare at him, my chest heaving, fearing his reply.

He speaks calmly, which scares me more than his yelling. "So, the rumor is true; you had sex with all of them. You would have denied it outright if it weren't. Bash is not a respectable man if he allows this. You need to get your priorities in check, young lady." His eyes meet Mack's. "And you, *piece of shit*, can get the fuck out of my house." I've never heard him swear before.

Dad walks away in a huff. He puts the berries in the sink and begins washing them. Despite his anger, he's very gentle with the fruit. Mack makes his way toward the door but turns, refusing to leave without me. Dad slams his hand on the faucet handle, shutting off the water. He spins to look at me, clamps his wet hands on the backrest of a wooden kitchen chair.

"So, you're not only having sex with Bash, but you're letting Patch and this *son-of-a-bitch* use your body." He points at Mack. "Are you fucking my little girl? Is your brother, Patch? You need to learn to respect the sanctity of the union between a woman and a man. You're a goddamn loser! So are your no-good brothers! Pigs, all of you!" He feigns spitting on him.

Mack becomes stoic. "If you want me to leave, I will, but she comes with me. She's your daughter, and a very intelligent, quick-witted, independent woman. You raised her to have her own mind."

Mom cuts in and speaks softly to my dad. "Apologize now or we could lose her forever."

Mack remaining calm and in control, contends. "We love Goldilocks. If you tell us to never come around, we will respect your opinions and wishes, but I beg of you not to push your daughter away."

Dad turns away and begins washing the berries again. I walk across the living room and look out the bay window to collect my thoughts.

Mom approaches me and quietly says, "No matter what you do in your life, whatever choices you make, I will always love you. I'll do my best to accept the way you choose to live even if I don't understand it. Well, I can understand the desire for the boys; I have seen them." She takes a deep breath and asks, in a lower whisper, "Did you have *fun* with Patch? Never mind, I shouldn't ask that!" She's sporting flushed cheeks.

So, Mom is curious about what Patch is like in bed? It's strange to imagine my mother as a sexual being. She's my Mom, not a woman who has physical needs. It's all too clear that Dad isn't into having adventurous sex. Then again, what do I know? A shiver runs through me from the image in my mind.

"Do you really want to know about my sex life?" I feel ashamed discussing this with her. It's silly, I know. I force myself to look at her.

Mom bites her lip, her eyebrows lifting high on her forehead. "Well, I... I mean... Yes, I'm curious... about them."

Embarrassed, I reply, "I have been *with* him."

"Lovely Goldilocks, you're not a child anymore." She brushes a lock of hair from my forehead and tucks it behind my ear. "Did you have a good time with him?"

My shy snicker grows into a huge smile that shoves my cheeks up to my eyes. The slight swelling on my left cheek is a quick reminder of my father's rage and forces my smile to fade.

"To which time are you referring?"

A groan lodges in her throat. "Really? More than once?" She points over her shoulder toward Mack, who stands outside the screen door. "And that gorgeous hunk of meat?"

"Yes, him too."

She sighs and glances toward Mack, who has his back to us, revealing his denim-covered, hard as a rock ass. "Who's better?"

"Mom!" My face flushes to match the shade of my reddened cheek. She widens her eyes and waves her eyebrows. I snicker. "They're all very good in their own way. Bash is more special to me, so it means more."

"Of course." She pauses while biting her bottom lip. "This will sound bad, but who has the biggest..." She looks down at my vagina "...dinky?"

"Dinky?" I laugh louder than I should, causing both men to turn and look at me. I lean in and whisper, "Bash."

"Really?" She's surprised by my answer. "I would have thought it would be Patch who had the biggest..."

"Dinky?" I tease.

She snickers. "Okay, he should be calmed down now."

Mom pats my back and urges me to talk to him. She makes her way out the door while I approach the stubborn man still washing the berries in the sink.

"Dad, I love you. No matter what I do or where I go, that will never change. You'll always be my father; the first man I ever loved. Please, don't hate me."

He suddenly stops washing the berries when I place my hand on his shoulder. As if struggling to do so, he turns his head to face in my direction but he doesn't meet my eyes, which are tearing up. I feel like a child about to be scolded, and I don't like it.

"Goldilocks, you are my daughter. You'll always be my daughter. But this…" He waves his hand in the air, splashing water on the window. "These dangerous games you're playing? This is going to ruin your life."

I try to speak but he puts his hand up, suggesting I don't.

"You should move home until you and Bash can get your own place. You must deny the rumors outright! It's settled. You'll go pack your things and move home."

Sedately, as if all my energy has drained, I reply. "I'm not moving home. I'm going to stay where I am. Bash will be home soon. Dad, you can accept me as I am, or you can choose to push me out of your life. It's in your hands."

He shuts off the water, dries his hands, and pulls me into one of his loving hugs I remember disappearing into when I was young. He kisses the top of my head and then releases me.

"I'll never accept what you're doing with those assholes. Until you change your ways, I think you should go."

Dad quickly makes his way to his bedroom and closes the door, leaving me stunned. Tears stream down my cheeks. My chest feels like it's exploding. My feet shuffle me toward the door. I've never felt so alone in my life. I want to run and jump in his arms like I used to do when I was a little girl, but that was then, and this is now.

Chapter 17

I swallow down my tears, wiping away the wetness from my face before pushing open the screen door. Mom and Mack are standing on the porch. I blow right past them without saying a word.

"Goldilocks, wait!" Mom yells. "What did he say?"

"He doesn't love me unconditionally." The tears are streaming again but I angrily wipe them away before they fall from my chin. "He told me to leave."

Mom hugs me to console me, as moms do. "You are always welcome here. This is my home too and he will never stop my daughter from visiting me." She steps back and wipes my face with the palms of her hands. "He's a stubborn old fool, but he'll come around. Just give him some time. Now go, enjoy your life!"

My mom hugs Mack longer than she probably should. He looks at me over her shoulder while I pull my lips between my teeth. He sighs defeatedly, understanding that she knows of our dirty little secret.

He clears his throat. "I'm sorry if my actions have hurt you. And for…" He points to the house where my father hides away.

Mom shrugs, scoffs, and passively waves her hand toward the house. "No, it's not your fault he's a buffoon stuck with the 1900s morality. You two should go." She hugs me again before cradling my sore left cheek and sighing. "I'm sorry, Love. He can be an emotional asshole sometimes. Try not to hold it against him."

My head drops back and I look up at the heavens, just as my father did earlier. A groan escapes me. When Mack opens my door for me, I look back at Mom before climbing into the truck. I wish my father could see how good the guys treat me, but I doubt he'll ever take the time to see that.

Mack slides in behind the wheel and fires up the engine. "Are you okay?"

I smile and nod, sniffing my runny nose. "Are you? He didn't mean what he said about you and your brothers. He's just upset."

He takes my hand. "I'm fine. It's not anything I haven't heard before. I just want to know if you're okay."

I grimace and shrug. "No, but I will be." As he drives down the driveway toward the road, I ask. "Do we have any more stops?"

He gazes at me, having only half heard what I said. "Oh, ah, no. We should get back. Our afternoon date is arriving in an hour."

"Date? What? What do you mean by *our date*?" Holy fuck! Does he think I'm going to join him and his girlfriend's sex-capade after having just been ostracized by my father?

He shrugs innocently while my anxiety level is about to erupt. I feel light-headed. I need a quiet place, like a dark closet, so I can hide away for the rest of the day and cry. I press the button to lower the window, close my eyes and aim my face into the cool air.

My father hates me.

Mack shakes my hand, drawing my attention. "It's going to work itself out. You'll see. Give him time. I can cancel tonight."

"No, I want to meet her."

He kisses the back of my hand. "There are no expectations for tonight. We will have a nice dinner and maybe a campfire when it gets dark. If she and I have sex, you're welcome to join in if you want to... or you can watch. That's always entertaining after-dinner excitement. If you're not up for that either, nobody will be insulted."

"We'll see," I say despite my suddenly parched throat.

Chapter 18

I help Mack harvest some beets, beans, carrots, onions, lettuce, peppers, and raspberries from the garden. I clean them while he unthaws the fish they caught last month in the nearby river. As soon as it's in the oven, he takes the knife from me and urges me away from the counter.

"Go take a shower and do whatever it is women do that takes them an hour to get ready. Off you go!"

"But I can help you."

He aims the knife in the bathroom's direction without looking up at me. I turn and head for the bedroom to strip and gather my towels and shower kit.

As I'm walking to the bathroom, he announces, "I cleared off the second shelf in the cabinet for your stuff. It closes so you can put whatever you want in there and nobody will see it."

"Thank you." He waves the knife again, so I continue on my journey to the bathroom, clutching the towel around my body. I note how cold the floor is on my feet and make a mental note to buy slippers the next time I go to town.

After setting some things in the cabinet, I hang my towels and start the water. She isn't expected to arrive for forty-five minutes, so I'm in no rush to get out. After I'm clean and shaved, I stand under the hot water, enjoying how it flows over my face, washing away my woes.

Cool hands brush my arms, startling me. I jolt and screech.

"I'm sorry! I didn't mean to scare you." Mack pulls me against him, wrapping his arms around my shoulders. "You're shaking. You must have been deep in thought… your Dad?"

"No, I wasn't thinking at all."

His eyes stare deeply into mine as he shifts us until he is under the running water. He releases me and begins running his fingers through his dark, wavy hair.

"Oh, so that's all you wanted… to shower."

He looks at me and wipes the water from his face even though it's still dripping down. His smile is sneaky, but his waving eyebrows have me snickering.

"Well, you were in here for a long time and I need to shower before she gets here."

"You mean before the water runs cold."

"That'll likely never happen." He shrugs, glops shampoo on his hand and rubs it in his hair. As the water rinses it, he adds, "Patch installed a system that heats the water as we need it."

"So, you really did just need a shower. Okay. It's all yours." I slide the curtain aside, but he grabs my waist and pulls me back in.

He's hoping to seduce me with his baby-blues. "I was thinking…" He pulls me toward him. "Since we have a bit of time, maybe I should take your mind off everything." He brushes his hand over my breast while his tongue glides along his upper lip.

I whisper, "I have a better idea."

He tilts his head to the side. I know he's hoping to drop to his knees to pleasure me, but I beat him to it. I look up at him. He looks down at me, his chest rising and falling quickly.

"You don't have to." He sucks in a deep breath when I glide his prick deep into my throat. He slams his hand on the shower wall and groans in appreciation. "Oh, Baby!"

Mack's hips tilt forward while his head tips back. I look up as I bob on his cock, admiring the V leading from just above his cock, up and over his pelvic bones. The grooves are deep. His belly button is small amid the well-formed abs that match the intensity of the V. His chest and arms, shoulders and back are equally impressive.

My right hand slides up his thick thigh and grips his ass. With my left hand, I cup his balls and gently squeeze at the base, and just as gently pull down while taking him into my throat. His fingertips press to the back of my head. I stop.

"Put your hands on the back of *your* head and don't touch me. I know what I'm doing." I can give orders to Mack and maybe Bash, not Patch; he's too dominant.

He rethinks whatever he was about to say, instead following my instructions. It isn't more than two minutes before he's moaning, his hips swaying to my rhythm.

"Do you want to fuck? If you do, stop now."

To answer his question, I take him deep into my throat and swallow, which I'm told squeezes the shaft.

"Oh, fuck! Hell, yeah. Oh, that's good." He takes three quick, deep breaths before warning me. "I'm going to cum. Oh… shit!"

I release his testicles. His body jerks, cock lurching as it spills its seed deep into my throat. I fight away my body's urge to wretch out my stomach contents. My eyes fill with tears but I wipe them away before he gathers himself enough where his vision comes back into focus.

He offers me his hand, helping me to my feet. I glide past him and fill my mouth with water and swish, repeating several times before swallowing the last mouthful. His head drops against the nape of my neck while wrapping his arms around my shoulders. He's groaning and still winded.

"Was that good or should you have held my head to guide me?"

Mack laughs exhaustively. "Touché! Your turn."

"No, I'm good."

Before he can argue, I step out of the shower and quickly dry off, leaving the bathroom before he finishes rinsing himself off.

I pull on a light blue dress that flows well when I walk. Before buttoning the bodice, I send a text to Bash.

I saw my dad today. He disowned me after slapping my face. Sad emoji. *Mack was there. I should warn you; Mom knows I've been with each of you.*

I slip on a pair of pink panties and then blow-dry my hair. Deodorant, a spritz of perfume, and a pair of fuzzy socks and I'm ready to meet Mack's girlfriend.

My phone alerts. It's Bash, replying.

I'm so sorry, Goldie. Angry emoji. *I should be there with you.*

You will be, soon. I'll be meeting Mack's girlfriend shortly.

So, your mom knows? Shit!

He's avoiding the subject. I want to ask him about his rendezvous with Mack's girlfriend, but texting isn't the best way to do that.

She was curious who was the better lover and whose cock was bigger.

I hope you said it was me on both accounts.

I send a shrugging woman emoji.

He replies with only a heart, so I send one back.

I'm nervous to meet Mack's girlfriend.

Chapter 19

When I open the door, I see the back of a woman who's being embraced by Mack. Her simmering, jet-black hair hangs long. Her hips are wide, accentuating her small waist. The tight stretch-denim pants she wears do nothing to hide her strong, thick thighs. She's tall, like me, but seems shorter because of Mack's towering height of 6'3".

He whispers something, and she spins. She's a gorgeous, big-breasted black woman with skin the shade of cocoa. I'm captivated by her beauty. Her eyes are lined in coal, lids topped with purple shadow. Her lips are ruby red, plump, and inviting. What best draws my attention is how perfectly sculpted her cheekbones, nose, and chin are, as if her makeup had been professionally applied. Maybe she can teach me that trick. Properly applying makeup has never been something I excelled at.

We both walk toward each other and attempt to shake hands, but it seems awkward. "Fuck it," she says and throws her arms around me. "Mack's told me so much about you that I feel like we're already besties. I'm Shaina."

"Goldilocks. It's nice to meet you. He's told me a lot about you too." I rethink that. "Actually, he didn't. He only said that he has a girlfriend and that you were coming for dinner today. Other than that, he left me hanging."

Mack still leans back against the counter with his hands resting on the edge and one foot crossed over the other. He grins as he watches us. She turns around to look at him but quickly returns to look me up and down.

"Damn, Mack! You didn't tell me she was a goddamn beauty cut right out of a Hollywood movie. But you are pale as fuck, girl. Don't you like the sun? I'm just fucking with you. I like making people uncomfortable."

"I can see you've spent *a lot* of time in the sun." I try to maintain a stoic expression, but can't help cracking a smile when she looks at me with wide eyes. "I'm good with uncomfortable."

She laughs. "What are you drinking tonight?"

Mack snickers. When we both look at him, he holds his hands up in submission before turning to peek at the fish in the oven.

"I'm thinking white wine. Do you want some?"

"I'll get the glasses," she replies, waving her perfectly manicured fingernail my way. I look down at my nails and cringe at how short they are.

"So, are you from around here, Shaina?" I twist the corkscrew into the cork and pull. She sets the glasses down after checking to see if there are any smudges on them.

She sees me watching her and explains. "Habit I picked up at work. I work at a strip bar about an hour's drive from here, which is a five-minute drive from my apartment. I'm paying my way through school and the job pays well. I'm a bartender, not a dancer. I tried dancing, but it's not in me. I mean, I can dance. I just don't like taking my clothes off in front of a bunch of horny, sweaty men."

"Ah, that tells me you've never been naked with three Bear brothers at once."

She bursts into a hard laugh. "I fucking love this girl! She's so funny!" She looks at Mack and lightly slaps his arm. "Why didn't you tell me she was so funny?"

"Get out of the kitchen and let me cook. Go do your female bonding somewhere else," Mack teases while waving his arms.

We head to the living room. I hand her a half-filled glass and then compliment her on the low-cut, snug-fitting red shirt she's wearing. She thanks me as we make our way. Just as we sit, Patch comes stomping into the house and sits on the stool at the door to remove his muddy boots.

"Hi, ladies. You two look lovely tonight." He struts toward us, kissing her before continuing over to kiss me. "How are you two getting along?"

"What are we, children?" she hisses. "Go away. It's not like we'll start throwing punches. We don't need male supervision."

"Not until we've drunk at least two more glasses of wine." I lift my glass while she snickers.

"You two are trouble." He makes his way to the kitchen to pluck a pepper off the table and pop it into his mouth. He asks Mack, "Why did you want those two to meet? They'll be the death of us. You wait and see!"

"We'll be fine." Mack pounds his chest and stands tall. "We're men; strong, virile, powerful men. They are mere women; frail, gentle-spirited, and pretty. I think we can overtake them should we need to."

They both stand with their hands on their hips, chests bloated as if to show off their masculinity. Patch grunts like a wild beast. Mack follows suit. They walk around the kitchen puffed out. I can picture them as children doing the same thing with their father urging them on.

Shaina jests. "You guys don't stand a chance against both of us. One on two... maybe, but not together. We will overrule you every time."

I concur. "We're women—seductive and convincing. You know you don't stand a chance."

They both deflate and grimace. Mack pouts. "They're right."

Patch grunts in agreement and then hurries to the bathroom for a shower before it's time to eat.

Chapter 20

Dinner was delicious and now we're sitting around the blazing fire Patch created. The blankets help to keep the chill out when the fire and drinks don't. Mack and Shaina snuggle in the same blanket. I stare at them while missing Bash. Patch sits in another chair beside me, wearing only his lumber jacket to keep the heat in. He is a walking furnace.

I'm still chilly despite the wool blanket that surrounds me. The night air is nipping at my face each time the breeze picks up. I've had three glasses of wine and I'm feeling a bit tipsy. Patch wanders over to the woodpile and picks up half a dozen pieces and dumps them beside the pit, tossing two thick ones into the fire. He leans back in his Adirondack chair and takes a big swig from his beer bottle.

He's a big man, burly and thick. He's strong as an ox and very intelligent. Whenever he isn't working, cooking, cleaning or all over me, he's reading. There are books in every room of the house. He likes every genre. I've caught him reading a book with a shirtless man on the cover who physically dulls compared to himself. He'll read any book he can get his hands on. Me, I avoid reading unless I absolutely have to.

I stand, hugging my blanket while making sure it isn't dragging on the ground. "I'm going to go for a little walk along the river and then turn in for the night."

Patch stands while the other two groan hoping I'll stay. Patch rounds the firepit and starts walking after me. "I'll come with."

My snicker is enough to have him looking disappointed. "No, I'll be fine on my own. Stay, enjoy the fire." I smile, then set off alone.

The three of them whisper to each other but the sound quickly fades in the distance as I pad toward the path that leads to the rushing stream flowing through their property. Just as I make it to the blueberry bush, I hear feet run up behind me. I shriek while spinning around, tossing the blanket to the ground, prepared for fight and/or flight. Most likely, I'll weaken at the knees and stand here, my feet stuck in the invisible tar that holds us all prisoners in our dreams.

"It's me," Patch shouts. "It's okay. Just me."

My heart pounds and I'm sure the color has left my face. I slap his shoulder and swear. "Fucking asshole, you scared me!"

"Did the slap mean you want me to chase you down like the last time, or not? Asking for clarity." He's waving his hands as if teetering invisible weights.

"No! Fuck! Why do you insist on scaring me?" I scoop up the blanket and shake it. "You know I hate that."

"Sorry. I didn't want you to get lost out here on your own." I look at him and roll my eyes with great sarcasm. It's not likely he can see the action, but he might sense it. "Why don't we head back to the house?"

"You don't have to be here. I just want to listen to the stream at night. It's something I miss doing."

He takes my arm and pulls me against his chest. "I want you." He plants his lips on mine.

"That's lovely, but I want to hear the stream."

He pulls his lips from mine and then flips me over his shoulder. He's quick about it.

I hiss, "Put me down! Goddammit, put me down!"

"No," he insists and then swats my ass twice. "You're mine now."

I go limp because there's no point in fighting him. He's much stronger than me and will win every time. I must outsmart him, somehow.

"If you take me to the stream, I'll suck your cock." Will he turn around?

He stops walking while he mulls it over. "No." He resumes his quick pace.

"You know, I'll just sneak out later, or go tomorrow night. You can't watch me continuously. Would you like me to call you Daddy since you're treating me like a child?"

He halts and drops me onto my feet. The scowl he wears has me questioning what I said that was so awful.

"I am not *Daddy* to anyone I'm fucking. One day, I'm hoping to have a daughter. The last thing I want is some woman ruining the moment my daughter first calls me Daddy by using the term with sexual innuendo." He points his finger in my face. "Don't do it again!"

Knowing I've touched a nerve, I apologize to him and vow to never repeat it. He takes my hand and pulls me behind him. We're walking faster than we should since it's so dark we can't see where our feet are landing.

In seconds, we're back at the firepit. Shaina is straddling Mack, facing him with the blanket wrapped around them both. It's obvious by her movements that she's fucking him.

My face flushes with the embarrassment they should be feeling. Why do I keep staring at them? *Dammit! Look away. Look away.* Shit! I'm still staring.

With a tap on Patch's arm to get his attention, he looks at me instead of them. I whisper, "We should leave them alone."

"Nah! They don't mind if we watch." Patch has me sit on one of the Adirondack chairs before crouching in front of me. "Can I ask something of you? But, you can't ask why I'm asking this of you. I'll need you to trust me and swear you won't break that promise."

I slump back on the chair and look past him to see if his talking interrupted the erotic act playing out before us. Patch's line of sight hasn't wavered from mine despite the distraction of Shaina's increasing moans.

"Okay, I agree, depending on what you want me to do or not do." He tilts his head, raising his eyebrows questioningly. "Fine. I promise."

"Don't walk the river path until I say it's okay to do so."

Is he serious? "Why not?"

He smirks. "I asked you not to ask that." I shrug, and he continues. "Just promise you won't go. It'll be well worth the wait. I swear."

With my attention locked on the breech in trees leading to the forbidden path, I can't help but wonder what's out there that he doesn't want me to see.

He takes my hand and cups it on his cheek. "This isn't a punishment. I'm *asking* you not to go, not *demanding* you don't."

My sigh is heavy, and I nod.

"Thank you." He kisses my palm. He slides into the chair beside me and cracks open a beer he had stashed beside it. Together, we watch the two lovers fuck.

I whisper, "Do you have another one of those?"

"No." He hands me the bottle. I sip it and hand it back.

Shaina's fucking Mack at a good tempo. The blanket has fallen from her shoulders and now hangs about her waist. She's still wearing her sweatshirt. Judging by his erratic breathing, he sounds like he's going to cum soon. She slides off him until she's kneeling on the cold ground. With the blanket pulled up and draped over her shoulders, we watch her head bob above Mack's lap.

Lucky man—two blowjobs by two different women on the same day. Men have killed for less. Patch hands me the beer. I take a long pull before returning it.

I focus on watching Mack's face. He's watching her mouth engulf on his cock, but when he looks up, he catches my eye. With his head leaning against the backrest, he looks down his nose at me. His arms span out over the backrest. He holds my stare. The tip of his tongue caresses his lips. His moans quicken with each exhale. His teeth clench, eyelids hang heavy, but he's still locked in my gaze. I'm breathing heavily from watching him experience so much pleasure from another woman's doing.

An exhaustive moan precedes Mack's twitching as she noisily sucks every drop of semen from his shaft. His attention veers from me when she comes off her knees and sits beside him. He tucks his withering member back into his pants while she slips her legs into hers. She stands, not allowing the blanket to gap nor reveal her nudity beneath. After some fussing with her clothes, she sits, sharing the blanket with Mack as she settles in beside him on the wooden loveseat.

Mack looks utterly spent. Even his grin seems like it's taking him a lot of effort. He glances at me. His voice is even sedate in its tone. "Twice in one day. I'm a lucky man."

Shaina turns to him and asks, "She sucked your cock today?"

His head tips in her direction. "Yup, in the shower just before you came over. Don't be jealous."

"What? Jealous? Not at all." She waves her hand while wearing a toothy grin. "Girl, I know what these boys are like. They love to play and I'm cool with that. I know you belong to Bash and you'd never step on my toes. As long as we know our places, we can do what we want with whoever we want."

"In all fairness, Goldilocks was here first."

She sneers at Mack. "Is this a seniority situation?"

Mack laughs and shakes his head. "I'm just messing with you."

She smiles, but it's obvious she didn't find that to be humorous.

Patch adds, "Maybe one day the two of you will gang up on us boys, or each other."

I quickly state. "It could happen." Everyone looks at me as if I told them I am about to grow a second head. "She's a gorgeous, sexual being. Even I can see that."

She points her long nail at me, then spins her wrist, as if waving me toward her. "You just let me know when you're interested in having some fun. If you don't want to go in that direction, I'm cool with us being friends and sharing boys. I like you. You and I are a lot alike. We could become good friends."

"I'll keep that in mind. It's good to have options. On that note…" I stand, wave at the two lovebirds, and start walking toward the house. "Patch, are you coming or not?"

I hear his feet trampling the lawn as he dashes toward me. "Water down that fire before you turn in."

Mack replies, "This isn't my first time in the bush, big brother."

"Nobody likes a wise-ass, little brother."

He rushes past me and turns to face me with his arms spread out to the side like he's on a cross. His ruggedly handsome face wears a challenging expression making him look like an immature college frat-boy and not the grown man I know him to be. When he crouches, I know what's coming.

"No!" I stop walking and glare at him, but he slowly slinks toward me, holding his arms outstretched while wearing a devious grin. "Don't do it!"

My glare alone should have him halting in his tracks, but he thrives on tempting fate. He scoops me over his shoulder, and I scream in protest. My arms are pinned in the blanket that surrounds me. I feel like a burrito. I enjoy the restraint, not that I want to tell him that. It's more fun fighting him because I know he enjoys it when he wins the power struggle.

Patch carries me into the house, letting the screen door slam behind us. His boots thud on the floor as he kicks them off but uses his feet to straighten them on the mat.

He's carrying me toward his bedroom, but I don't want me sleeping with him to become a habit. Do I want to have sex? Hell yes, I do! I just watched two people get it on. That's a first for me. I'll admit, I enjoyed it. Once the shock of seeing it happening wore off, so did my good-girl politeness. I wasn't shy about watching them after that.

Chapter 21

"Not tonight, Patch."

He stops just in front of his bedroom door. "But you invited me to come with you."

"Yes, but that was to give them some privacy, not to have sex with me."

He questions, "Is there some wiggle room for convincing?"

I shake my head. I don't want our feelings to grow toward something more than they should be. Last night was very intimate, before the rope suspension, of course. He sets me down onto my feet and fixes the blanket so it covers my shoulders. His disappointment is obvious, but I appreciate that he's at least attempting to pretend it isn't.

With a kiss to my forehead, he disappears into his room, closing the door behind him. For a moment, I stand in front of the closed door and silently argue with myself, debating whether one more night with Patch could even alter my feelings for Bash. I know it won't because I love him so much. But would Bash be upset or jealous because I'm spending so much time with his brother?

I dance a jerky frustration jig while debating whether I should just go to bed or open the door and have another hot, dirty sexual experience with Patch. He will distract me from my thoughts about my father. I'm not feeling tired, anyway. One more night won't hurt anything.

***

After Patch fucked me so hard that I feared his bed might break, he quickly fell into a deep sleep. I'm still wide awake despite my exhaustion. My father's words continue to plague me. An hour passes before I hear Shaina's car drive away. It's so quiet in the forest that I can hear the motor slowly disappear down the laneway. A few minutes later, Mack comes in the house and shuts the door, kicks off his boots and uses the bathroom. The running shower has my bladder urgently pleading with me to empty it.

Patch is sound asleep, his eyelashes fluttering as his eyes seek the images flashing through his mind. His gentle snores are low and constant.

In the darkness, I feel around for my clothes that he nearly tore from my body before tossing them in every direction. It doesn't take long before I decide the effort is futile and wrap the smoke-scented blanket around my nude body. I find two socks but only one is mine. Not caring, I put them both on and quietly giggle at how his sock hangs off my toes. Knowing I'll probably wake him by searching for my belongings, I decide to give up the hunt and come back for them tomorrow.

With the lights out, the moon casts its brightness through the window, creating shadows about the bedroom. Everything looks so different at night. It seems more serene but also promising that the new day coming will differ from all the others, perhaps be even better than any before it. Everything changes, and the night brings that on. A heavy sleep, waking to the brightness of a new day, and knowing I can do whatever I want with it gives me hope that all my woes will disappear.

The door creaks as I exit and then latch it closed behind me. The floor is still cool on my feet despite the mismatched socks. The illumination from the moon is barely enough where I can safely maneuver through the house without bumping into anything.

With Mack still in the shower, I make my way to Bash's room—our room—and change into the t-shirt I've seen him wear many times during our stint in high school. Finding it hanging in his closet brought back a lot of memories. Most favorably, I remember he was wearing it when he walked onto the bus and winked at me, sending my whole body into a fit of cold tingles. I had such a crush on him back then… still do!

I know Bash's bed is comfortable, very soft, and inviting, but I'm parched and have to go pee before I settle into it. I hope Mack hurries up and gets out of the bathroom. If things become urgent, I'll have to invade his privacy. I really don't want to pee in front of him. A girl has to draw a line somewhere.

While drinking from the glass of water I just poured, the picture of Bash on the mantle seems to call to me from across the room. I mosey toward it and stare at the handsome face smiling back at me. The man in the photo is a few years younger than the man I know him to be today, but I remember this picture. It's the same one from the yearbook—the one I memorized so well.

Tears fill my eyes and drip down my cheeks when I blink. I quickly wipe them away. I pick up the frame and hold it to my chest as I stare out the window at the stillness lurking within the night's shadows. If he were here with me, I'd be snuggling up beside him, warm, safe, and feeling loved. At this moment, I feel alone. I miss him.

My mind flashes back to the intimate scene at the fire. Shaina is so beautiful and sexy. She's secure within her own self, unlike me. She's the type of woman who can walk into any room and instantly own it. That's not me. I'd rather remain off to the side and let everyone else take the spotlight.

How was she when she and Bash had sex? Was he on top or did she ride him like she so superbly rode Mack? Did they have oral sex or just fuck? Did he take her from behind? Did he make her cum on his cock or his tongue? My mind races, and I can't stop my imagination. Not knowing has my imagination running wild.

Why didn't he tell me about her in one of our lengthy phone conversations? Was he trying to hide it? Did he think I'd never find out?

Chapter 22

"What are you doing awake? I thought you'd be out cold by now."

I startle. "You fucking scared me, again!" Deep cleansing breaths help calm me.

He chuckles. "Sorry. You didn't hear me walking up?" His hand brushes my bare arm, hoping to soothe me. "Why are you still up?" I find myself staring at his Adam's Apple. It bobs when he swallows.

I look down at the photo in my hand and smile faintly. "I had to pee."

"Oh, sorry. I guess I was in there for a while." He walks toward the kitchen, and I follow. "Want a shot of Vodka? It'll help you sleep."

A laugh escapes me, louder than I planned. My hand covers my mouth as I look toward Patch's closed door.

"Don't worry, he's dead when he sleeps. Short of a shotgun blast, nothing wakes him."

"He's likely a miserable bear when he's woken up, so I don't want to be the one interrupting his sleep. I'm sure he'll punish me or something." I laugh and roll my eyes. Mack laughs, but we both know I'm right. It'll be playful punishment, but I'm too tired to play tonight.

"I like your footwear."

I look down and scrunch my face. Tilting my head up, I announce, "There's another pair just like it somewhere in Patch's room."

"One is a bit big for you."

"Nope, one foot is just smaller than the other." I gesture with my finger and thumb as if it's just a tiny bit smaller. He raises his eyebrows and chuckles.

He pours us each a man-sized thumb's length of vodka in a small glass and hands it to me before putting the bottle back in the freezer.

"Cheers," he says, clinking our glasses together.

It's so cold that I can't take the whole shot in my mouth. Besides, this is more like three shots. He downs his and then looks at my glass and grins.

"You're not a fan of Vodka?" he asks.

With my head shaking, I swirl the clear liquid before gulping it down. My face contorts as the icy fluid rushes down my throat, leaving it tingling and hot, yet cold… freezing cold.

"That's our girl!" he praises. After setting the glasses in the sink, he asks, "So, what did you think about what happened at the fire?"

"Oh, um…" My good-girl shyness has suddenly returned. "Yeah, um… good. I enjoyed watching."

"What did you like about it?" His hand slips around my waist, pulling me against him.

"You, watching me…" He looks at me with dreamy eyes. "While she made you cum."

"I was thinking about you sucking my cock in the shower. I wanted you to watch me cum. You didn't look away, which surprised me. Are you not the shy and innocent Goldilocks anymore?"

"I think you guys have fucked the innocent out of me, don't you?" My laugh drowns out in my throat.

"Would you like to spend the night with me? We can just sleep if you don't want to play."

The shadows of the night have his cheekbones seeming more pronounced from the darkness pooling beneath them. The tiny cleft below his plump bottom lip seems cavernous. His seductive blue eyes seem to glow almost neon from the brightness of the moon's rays. There's a softness in his expression that has me wanting to say yes, but I gently release myself from his hold instead.

With a scratch to my temple, I reply, "No, thank you. I think I'll spend tonight alone." I look down at Bash's photo. "I don't think I'll be good company tonight. I miss him."

Mack's fingers brush my cheek with a loving tenderness. I'm sure he misses his brother, too.

"He'll be home soon," he whispers. I nod then make my way toward the bathroom. "Can I ask you something?"

"You just did." When I turn, he sees my smile and shakes his head.

"All right, I'm going to ask you another question." I turn and lean on the bathroom's doorframe. He seems nervous, if I were to judge by his fiddling with his fingernails.

"Go ahead." I take a few steps closer to bridge the gap.

"I've had a crush on you since high school. I know you're younger than me by a few years, but you didn't even notice me."

I take another step toward him. "What? You don't think I noticed you? I was just a silly young girl who had a huge crush on your younger brother. You... Oh, my god! You were this wild, over-the-top, sexy-as-sin, slightly older badass, who barely knew I existed. You paid me no attention either."

"I wasn't that wild." He rolls his eyes and tilts his head. "Scratch that... I was a crazy motherfucker back then. But I liked you. Every time I'd meet your eyes, you'd look away from me." He smiles but it fades quickly. "I thought you hated me, but I liked you and wanted to get to know you better."

"How would that have worked out? I'm sure you would have left me in the dust after realizing I was a very good girl and didn't play sex games. My father never would have allowed me to spend time with you... with any of you Bear boys." I scoff because nothing has changed in that respect.

"I didn't know you liked Bash at the time. I don't think Bash did either, otherwise, he would have asked you out." He shrugs and clears his throat. "I never told him how much I liked you." His hands perch on his hips. "Besides, you were a good girl back then, and I didn't want to ruin that perfect reputation with my wild, bad-boy ways. That might have fucked you up for life."

Our laughter fills the room. "It's funny but you're probably right. My morals would have slipped, and I might have become a slutty little whore after you tired of me. I'd have to if I were craving more and more sexual excitement. It's a slippery slope, you know."

"Well, I hope you'll always be our slutty little whore." With his fingers propped up like a Boy Scout, he adds, "I promise to do my best to keep you entertained even if you ride that slippery slope right into the depths of depravity."

I point at him and say, "That is where I seem to be heading. You've been there. What's it like?"

He chuckles and points back at me. "Haha! You joke, but it's actually quite nice there."

I laugh as I enter the bathroom, closing the door as he turns to head to his bedroom. After peeing and washing my hands and face, I brush my teeth then head back to Bash's—our—bedroom.

Chapter 23

The mattress is pillow-soft, and the sheets are even softer, but it's not comforting me from the stress of my inner monologue. If only I knew for sure what happened between him and Shaina, I know I'd feel better. Why is this bothering me so much? I can't decide if not knowing how he had sex with her is bothering me, or if the fact that he had sex with her in the first place and didn't tell me about it is what is plaguing me.

I pick up my phone. It's 2:30 AM. He'll be asleep. Should I wake him? I turn to look at the photo I now have propped up on the nightstand. *He's so fucking cute!* My fingers tap the screen, and it rings. I tuck the phone between my head and the pillow, pulling the covers over my shoulder. It rings twice.

"Goldie! What's wrong?" an exasperated Bash gushes.

"Nothing's wrong. I just miss you." The panic in his voice has me regretting calling him.

His relieved sigh precedes the lengthy throat clearing. "Sorry, It's dry in the dorms. So, you miss me?"

"Yes, you know I do." My whisper is low, but he hears me.

"Baby, I miss you too. I'll be home soon though." I can hear his covers rustling. He groans, likely from rolling over or getting out of bed. "Just a little more than a week before I get to hold you and never let you go."

"I can't wait."

"Aren't my brothers keeping you company?" A snicker escapes as my face flushes hot. "Judging by the laugh, I'm going to assume they are."

"They are, especially Patch. He's keeping me *very* busy. Mack, too. He invited his girlfriend over tonight. She seems nice. She fucked and blew Mack while we watched. That was a new experience for me… fun, but awkward, at first. I liked it, but…"

"But what?"

I swallow the cotton ball forming in my throat. "Watching her with him had me wondering what the two of you have done. It's been digging at me like a tick."

He's quiet for several seconds before speaking. "Does it bother you that we had sex or that you weren't present at the time?"

It's my turn to pause because now I know they had sex. Until now, I wasn't sure. "I don't know." I clear my throat, suddenly feeling foolish for my idiotic feelings. "The thought of you fucking her and making her cum excites me… honestly, it does. But not knowing how you fucked her keeps my mind racing. And you didn't tell me about her."

He sighs loudly. "Okay, let me just say that I'm glad you're asking me about this and not letting it fester inside you." His covers rustle again. "Do you want to know the details?"

"Yes… yes, I do." I roll onto my back and stare at the dancing shadows on the ceiling.

"Mack had introduced us in passing a few times before anything happened. If she's just a playmate, we share right away, but otherwise, we hold off a bit to let him have bonding time with her." He clears his throat. "She came over, but Mack wasn't home from work yet. I offered her a beer. She said she knew that we share our women. She said she was horny and didn't think she could wait for Mack. I asked her if she could use a hard fuck. When she nodded, I rushed her, grabbed her, and bent her over the table. I yanked her skirt up over her ass and jerked down her panties while I held her hair, pressing her head onto the tabletop." He pauses.

"Keep going," I whisper, my heart leaping in my chest.

"I fucked her... hard. So hard the table slid up against the cabinets." He chuckles.

"That's a heavy table!"

"It is, but as I said, I was fucking her hard."

I swallow then ask, "Did she cum?"

"Did she ever! She gushed all over my pants. I had to change out of them after." He seems entertained by the memory. "She screamed through her first orgasm, but when the second was about to erupt, Mack came in the house. She seemed nervous and tried to get up, but I held her down and kept fucking her. If she'd have told me to stop, I would have. I wasn't raping her."

"What did Mack do?"

"He stood beside the table, scowling, and locked eyes with her while I kept hammering away. She came within seconds, soaking me more. I backed up, pulled up my pants, and walked out the front door with my beer. Then, I swapped my soiled pants for a pair of jeans hanging dry on the clothesline."

Silence. "What? That's it? What happened after that?"

"I chopped some wood. I don't know what they did, but I heard her cum a few more times before they both came outside to drink beer on the porch."

I huff, now sitting up in bed, blankly searching about the room. "Okay... But, what did you do about your hard-on?"

"Nothing. It softened after a few minutes." He sounds so nonchalant about the whole thing, meanwhile, I'm about to lose my mind.

"Are you serious? You didn't jerk off? Holy fuck! You must have been aching to cum. What about blue-balls? Is that a real thing?"

He chuckles. "No, it's not a real thing, at least not in my experience. I didn't cum because she was done with me. I served my purpose, and it was time for me to move aside and let Mack take over."

"Is that why Patch and Mack didn't orgasm the first time I was with them? Were they saving me for you?"

"No, because you and I weren't starting a relationship at that time. If I recall correctly, you were out to get laid." He yawns. "They did know how much I liked you. We all wanted you, but I think they knew you were mine even before you were."

"You're tired. I should let you go back to sleep. I shouldn't have called you. I'm sorry."

"Goldie, never apologize for calling me. I love hearing your voice and don't care what time it is. Besides, I'm glad you called. This way, I can get a few hours of study time in before the exam."

"Oh, shit! You have your exam today, and I woke you. Had I remembered I wouldn't have called."

"It's okay, Goldie. I like that you woke me. Talking about this with you feels good. Keeping the lines of communication open are key to a great relationship. I should keep that in mind."

"Why didn't *you* tell me about her?"

He's quiet. I hear him take a deep breath and release it slowly. "I didn't want to tell you over the phone. I didn't want you to freak out and me not be there to ease any of your concerns." He pauses, taking another breath. "Are you all right with what happened?"

"I sort of have to be, don't I?" I snicker but he doesn't laugh with me. "If I'm having sex with your brothers while you're away, how can I be jealous of you having had sex with one woman? That's not fair."

"Sweetheart, don't deny your feelings. They matter to me. You matter to me. If me having sex with other women bothers you, then I won't do it."

"No, I don't want that. I want you happy. It's just so unusual for me. All of this is so bizarre. I don't come from this world of free love. I was always so limited. Just give me a minute to catch up, that's all I ask. I don't want you to stop yourself if the opportunity strikes. Just... just tell me about it, okay. Hearing it from your brothers really sucks."

Bash groans. "Yeah, I was hoping to tell you before they did. I'll be home soon."

"Not soon enough," I pout.

"Oh, so tell me what happened with your father. That text was vague."

I yawn. "Not tonight. I'm nice and relaxed now and don't want to get upset again."

"All right. Why don't you climb into bed with one of my brothers and let them spoon you? You can pretend it's me behind you. Maybe you'll fall asleep that way."

"That's a great thought, but I think I'll stay in your bed tonight. I'm already warm and cozy right here. Thanks for talking with me. I feel better now." A yawn has my mouth gaping and my eyes watering.

"I'm glad. Good night, Goldie. I love you."

"Good night, Bash. I love you." I press the red circle and hug my phone to my chest.

Not discussing my abolishment from my father's life was me being considerate. The last thing he needs is to have that haunting his thoughts while he's trying to write exams and finish his projects to earn his final grades.

As if weighted, my eyelids float down, awakening the dreams that hide behind them.

Chapter 24

Two more days have passed with no word from my father. The guys have tried to keep me distracted, and my Mom and I have texted a few times, but it's my dad I want to talk to. It would be great if he would apologize, but I'll accept a casual conversation if apologizing is too difficult for him.

"What has you troubled, Goldilocks?" Patch asks after rolling over, flopping his thick arm over my side and pulling me until I'm tucked up against him. "Did you not sleep well again? I tried my best to tire you out last night."

"You did a good job, as always. I was just hoping my father would have come around by now. It looks like that will never happen."

"Never say never! People change. Until he does, just go on with your life." He kisses behind my ear before sliding his hand up and clutching my right breast. His huge hands can either be brutal or have a seductive, delicate touch. This morning, he's delicate. Last night, he was rough.

I push his hand away. "Stop! I have to pee."

"Go, then come right back. I have a raging erection with your name on it."

I laugh. "Yes, I can feel it poking my thigh."

He snickers and then leans back and slaps my ass cheek.

"Ouch! Are you seriously hoping for rough play? It's 6:18 in the morning, for fuck sakes! Have a little consideration for the non-morning zombie who's been tossing and turning all night. Ass!" I'm so cranky this morning.

He rubs his eye before glancing at the clock hanging on his wall. "I slept in. See what you do to me. You're making me lazy."

I smirk. "Looks like you tired yourself out last night."

I slide out of bed, rolling my neck to stretch away the stiffness. A lasting yawn plagues me as I shuffle my feet all the way to the bathroom. After relieving my bladder and brushing my teeth, I shuffle to the coffeemaker and take a mug from the cupboard. Mack takes the mug away from me while handing me a bigger mug already filled with coffee made exactly how I like it. My smile presses to his lips and then to the lip of the mug where it remains until I'm seated at the table. It's going to be a rough day.

"Mmm. You have no idea how much I need this today."

Patch overhears me as he makes his way to the bathroom. "Don't you mean every day? Zombie girl!" He jokes but I hate happy morning people.

Mack says, "Speaking of exhausted people, Shaina might stop in this afternoon before she goes to work. That woman keeps a busy schedule and seems to never sleep."

"She should be just about finished with her semester at school." I form that as more of a question.

"Yup!" Mack flips a pancake onto a plate, then pours more batter in its place before flipping another half-cooked pancake.

"Are you nervous about your job interview today?" he asks.

I sigh, feeling my stomach acid pooling in my throat. "Yes, I'm a little nervous. Thanks for reminding me!"

He laughs. "You'll do great. They'd be foolish not to hire you on the spot."

He sets a plate in front of me containing two eggs over hard, two pancakes, and four slices of bacon along with several banana slices and a few strawberries.

I inhale its aromatic scent and swallow a wad of saliva. The nausea immediately subsides. "Thank you! Everything smells delicious!"

Just as I pick up my fork, he places a bright white rose beside my plate. "Oh, my! That's beautiful. Thank you!"

"It dulls in comparison to your beauty." He flirts, leaning in for a soft, lengthy kiss.

Patch exits the bathroom and heads for the cupboard, taking out the same mug I chose a few minutes earlier.

"Get a room!" he hisses, jokingly.

"If I take her to my room, you'll have to cook your own breakfast," Mack replies. Patch grunts his disapproval.

Mack sets a plate down for him and then one for himself. They both sit at the same time and start shoveling huge forkfuls of food in their mouths. I pick at mine, enjoying each item's flavor. They finish eating long before I do.

I'm in no hurry to get started on my day. My interview at the hospital isn't until this afternoon. Both Patch and Mack have to work today, so I'll have the house to myself for a while before I have to head into town.

Chapter 25

The guys have left for work, so I wash and dry the dishes, do some dusting, and hang a load of laundry out on the line to dry while I start another. After stripping all three beds and applying fresh sheets and pillowcases, I spritz my perfume on their bedding so they'll think of me when they slip into them tonight.

Bash wrote me an email wishing me good luck at my job interview along with a picture of him lying on his bed wearing a dreamy expression. His hand is tucked down the front of his well-worn jeans. He suggested I recall the picture in my mind when I'm feeling nervous at the interview. As if that will calm me down!

My belongings arrive via UPS around nine-thirty. I'm just leaving it packed. Besides, there isn't much room for Bash's things and mine. When he returns from school, he'll bring more stuff with him. I decide to stack the three boxes in the corner of the living room.

I spot a smudge on the window and lift my nightshirt to use as a shammy. As I'm wiping, I see the path leading to wherever it is I promised Patch I wouldn't go. No, I won't break my promise. I'm still wiping even though the smudge is long gone. Should I go and simply not tell him? No, I won't.

I shower at my leisure, dress, wearing the light blue dress my college roommate gave to me, because she said it looked better on me than her. It flows nicely when I walk. I'll top it off with a white sweater. With my hair in a ponytail and only a bit of pressed powder on my shiny t-zone, I'm ready, but ready for what, exactly.

Before I realize it, I'm walking down that forbidden path. At first, I move slowly until I pass my favorite rock, and then I start to speed up. Whatever is waiting down this path, I need to know what it is, now! My feet stomp the dirt as I hold my skirt up to my knees so I won't trip.

I can hear people talking and noises I'm not used to hearing this far back in the forest. There isn't anything here! I burst into a clearing and stop dead in my tracks. My lungs burn as I suck in full breaths, trying to ease my panting.

I see several men and one woman. All are wearing reflective vests, hardhats, and work boots. They pause only slightly to take notice of the woman who suddenly burst from the trees.

A beautiful log cabin rests in the middle of a circular, carved out clearing in the forest. It's a tall house with a wraparound porch lined with a log railing. Huge picture windows will allow for a lot of sunlight, which is something I would look for in a home. It's absolutely beautiful and in a picturesque setting suitable for a postcard. Down the hill and through a thin line of trees, I can clearly see the river.

I search the reflective vests for any familiar faces. I spot Mack through one of the bay windows. I scale the five steps and turn to look around. This place is heavenly.

A hand-carved wooden door is propped open with a basketball-sized rock. My hand brushes along the fine detail on the door until my breath feels like it's been sucked from my lungs.

BASH is inscribed near the top of the door, above a big fish covered in tiny scales. In the center reads the words *BEAR HOUSE*. Beneath that, surrounded by carved roses is my name, *GOLDIE*.

I'm confused, to put it mildly. While I point at it, I look up to see Patch's shocked expression. Mack wears a similar face. I search the door again and back to their faces.

"What... wh... what's this? Why... why is my name on... on the... door?"

Both men seem to deflate as they shuffle toward me. Mack puts his arm around my shoulder and leads me further into the house. His arm waves a wide circle as if revealing the room to me.

"Welcome home, Goldilocks." Mack's words sound like a song, a tune that makes my heart swell. I'm overwhelmed and the tears begin to flow like the river outside.

"No way!" I scream. Mack smiles. Patch, silently standing with his arms crossed over his thick chest, nods. "This is Bash's house? Oh, my god! Does he know?"

Mack corrects me as I sail around the kitchen, touching everything. "No, Goldilocks... the house belongs to Bash *and* you. You can live here together." I pause and squeal.

Patch adds, "Bash chose the location."

"Oh, my god! I love him! I love you all!"

The open concept home has a winding staircase leading to the upper floor, which is open to look down into the living room. I run up the stairs, my breath continuing to catch in my throat, bursting from me with sobbing tears. The upper floor is unfinished but there's plenty of room to build two bedrooms up here, for guests or future children.

I run down the stairs, nearly tripping at the bottom when I skip the last step. My feet can no longer move because I'm shaking so violently. I stand, holding onto the pillar at the base of the stairs, looking all around, at everything my eyes can take in.

"This is my home?" I speak in a whispered tone. Patch nods again. "I can live here with Bash?"

"Goldilocks," Mack says with a gentle softness in his voice. He takes my hand and kisses it. "We built this house for you and Bash to live, have children if you care to—and grow old together."

Patch's deep voice rings through the house. "What do you think? Do you like it?"

I'm surprised he's even questioning that. I run and fling my arms around his neck.

"Woah, woah, easy girl. I'm glad you like it." He plants a long, heavy kiss on my lips.

He lifts me, and I wrap my legs around his waist. At this very moment in time, I don't care who sees. Let the rumors fly! I don't fucking care!

I have a house!

"We can make any changes you'd like. You know, if you need more storage shelves or whatever. Your bedroom is this way." Mack reaches out for my hand, gently pulling me from Patch's arms. "We upset your parents by not bringing them in on this. They caught wind of it after they heard the rumor. It's just one more reason for them to dislike us Bears. We didn't intentionally keep them out of it..." He pauses. "That's not completely true. After your father freaked out on us, we didn't think they would want to work with us."

Patch, who walks behind me, adds, "I arranged for your mother to come yesterday to measure or something, so she can coordinate color, Feng Shui, or whatever the fuck she was mumbling about. I kind of blocked her out after a while. She talks a lot."

"I'm sure that made her happy," I say. He grunts and shrugs.

Mack leads the way down a short hallway with a small laundry room on one side and a pantry on the other. At the end of the hall is a wooden door with carved hearts and ribbons, along with the words, *LOVE LIVES HERE.*

I'm melting!

Chapter 26

Mack pushes the door open to reveal a large room with a huge picture window facing the forest. That will be a beautiful view during winter. Patch follows as Mack leads me through the room and past another door. It's a bathroom containing a shower big enough for two people, a jacuzzi tub for two, a counter with two sinks, and a separate stall with a toilet inside. Off to the side of the bathroom is a huge closet capable of housing my clothes and Bash's, and will also store plenty of other things.

Patch pulls a string, illuminating a dim lightbulb over the door. My lips press onto Mack's, and my tongue immediately searches for his. My fingers weave into his thick, wavy hair, pulling him into me. He returns my affection.

Patch's hand brushes my back and I spin, planting my lips onto his. He kisses me with heated passion, with more of a bestial hunger than his brother. I allow his tongue to dance with mine while one of his fists clutches my hair, pulling me to him.

Mack lifts my skirt. His fingers weave their way into my panties and slip between my heated folds. I moan into Patch's mouth. He responds with a firmer grip in my hair and more urgency in his kiss. Mack's fingers dance on either side of my clit, teasing it to plump fullness.

They spin me around. Patch's thick arm crosses over me just beneath my neck and holds me firmly against his chest. My hands grasp his forearm instinctively as if fearing he'll hurt me. His free hand hastily pulls at the buttons securing the bodice of my dress.

Mack drops to his knees and pulls down my panties. He lifts my right leg and rests my thigh on his shoulder. His mouth sucks at my clit and pussy lips. His tongue flips and spins, teasing my clitoris until tiny tingles tempt me closer and closer to climax.

One yank and my tits pop free from the bottom of my bra. Patch's hand cups my breasts, squeezes each one and then he wraps his forearm beneath them. He pulls me tightly against him while pinching my breasts between his forearms. It doesn't hurt, but the restrictive feeling is intense. It's hard to take in a deep breath, intensifying a sense of helplessness.

Patch kisses my neck, just behind my right ear. With his rustic, deep voice, he whispers, "Cum. Let go and fucking cum. Don't forget… you're our little whore. You're ours to fuck, suck and take as we please. Your body belongs to us. We fucking own you. Cum, Goldilocks. You know you want to. Give Mack your orgasm. Give it to him."

My mind slips away as my body tightens. The closet around us blurs as my mind is about to fade into the darkness of euphoria. Patch covers my mouth and nose, forbidding my lungs from releasing their breath. I struggle but when the orgasm hits me like a tidal wave, breathing no longer seems necessary. My body falls limp in his arms, aside from the spastic twitches radiating from deep within my belly. Mack stands and steps back.

While still pinned to his chest by one of his forearms, Patch spins. My hands flatten against the wall built of cedar planks. He fusses with his pants, but only for a few seconds. In one smooth motion, his thick cock is buried deep within me. He fucks me, hard but not brutally so. It's glorious! His hand covers my mouth, preventing my passionate moans from being heard by the building crew. I cum twice before he pulls out of me and cums in his hand.

Mack turns me to face him. His strong hands cup my ass cheeks and lift me. My legs wrap around his waist. His cock finds its path into me. I press my back against the wall, our lips locked in a passionate kiss, his hips humping against me.

His prick is long, poking my cervix with each thrust. I'd swear he's burying himself into my uterus, and I fucking love it.

Light fills the room, but only for a moment. Mack hammers into me, our whimpers muted by our kiss. With my fingers weaved into his hair, he continues his assault on my cervix. My lips fall away from his when a moan escapes me. His hand presses down on my mouth, stifling my screams as a powerful orgasm sweeps my mind away from reality. His body stiffens, copying mine. His cock swells inside me, forcing me into a body bucking, world spinning orgasm.

We both seem to wither as the pleasure leaves us weakened. His hand slowly falls away, dragging my bottom lip down until it pops free. He gasps, jerks one final time followed by a heavy sigh.

My legs drop and he holds onto my waist to stabilize me, and maybe himself too. I place a lasting kiss on his lips while taking in a deep breath. He pulls back, a soft smirk remains where my lips just were.

"Welcome home, Goldilocks."

Chapter 27

My legs are still weak from my romp, but I'm still floating on cloud nine. Nothing can spoil this mood. I mean nothing!

With my qualifications in hand in case they need to see my certificates and diploma, I close the door and climb behind the wheel of Bash's pickup truck. It's an old truck; a 1965 Ford. It takes a few turns of the key for it to rev to life.

I park in the only parking spots available at the far end of the lot. I don't mind; the walk will help me expel some nervous energy.

A handsome man in a dark blue business suit is standing at the circular desk in the main lobby when I walk up. The dark-haired receptionist he's chatting with notices me before he does.

I smile before interrupting. "Hello, could you point me toward Dr. Janson's office?" She lifts her finger, aiming it at the man.

"Hello," the salt and pepper haired man says while greeting me with an open hand. I shake it. "Come with me, I'll show you where you'll be working."

I follow the pompous man, catching up quickly. He walks fast. "I thought this was an interview."

He stops and looks at me. This is when I see how pale his sky-blue eyes are. Although scarred with the years of a middle-aged man, he's very attractive. His nose and chin are sharp amid prominent cheekbones, hovering above a squared jawline.

"You are mistaken. You already have the job. You're overqualified for the position you applied for, but when a position better suited to your qualifications opens up, you could advance. So, you'll fill this position temporarily. Let me be the first to welcome you aboard." He stands, smiling while holding an iPad at arm's length over his crotch.

"I'm willing to fill any position you need me for." I blush as soon as I realize what I've said. His smile fades, seeming uncomfortable. He turns on his heels and immediately speeds off. It takes some long strides for me to catch up to him. "What is it I'll be doing, exactly?"

"For now, we'll have you in the surgical ward, tending to the patients post-administration." We walk down a long corridor and then take an elevator that requires swipe card access.

Dr. Janson shows me around the hospital, introducing me to Lizzy; a short redheaded woman with a big smile and a happy-go-lucky attitude. She and I will get along wonderfully. Another nurse, Mary, seems like a total bitch. She's not rude to me, exactly, but the way her eyes keep looking me up and down while she scowls is a dead giveaway. Her hesitancy to shake my hand doesn't earn her any friendship points either.

I'm introduced to my boss, the head nurse, Laura. She seems very pleasant and I think we'll get along just fine. She's blunt and to the point as she explains the rules. I follow as she shows me where the break room is, patient waiting rooms number one and two, and explains what tasks I'll be in charge of. After introducing me to several of the nurses I'll be working with, she brings me up to room 315 so I can fill out the proper paperwork. This is where she leaves me.

It takes me a half-hour to fill out the forms, but afterward, my photo is taken and put on my ID card. I'm given an information booklet to look over before I begin my first shift. It's a thick booklet, but I don't mind.

The nurses on this floor didn't hesitate to shake my hand. They were pleasant with me, and that eases my anxiety. Because of the rumor, I was worried that I'd be met with resistance; that they would be rude and give me nothing but attitude, making my daily life at this hospital miserable. It doesn't seem to be that way and I'm relieved.

With my homework in hand, I decide to roam around the hospital to get a better assessment of where everything is. Pushing a patient around while searching for a specific place I was asked to bring them wouldn't go over very well.

Chapter 28

After about an hour, I get back in Bash's truck and fire off texts to Bash, Patch, and Mack.

I got the job! I start next week.

Bash doesn't reply right away, but he's probably writing an exam or studying. Mack writes one word, *Congratulations!* Patch writes. *I knew you'd get the job. Now go pack your belongings and bring them to your new house.*

I'm giddy as I drive. It doesn't take more than a few moments for me to pack my things. I consider packing some of Bash's items but figure there will be time later to do that. For now, I'm too excited to waste another minute!

When I arrive, most of the workers have already gone home. With my suitcase dragging behind me, I scale the steps and look out at the water. I can't shake the smile that splashes across my face.

Inside, Patch is setting a new coffeemaker on the counter. Lots of boxes from new appliances and Amazon are scattered about the living room. Some have been broken down while some hold their structure. He looks up and smiles, spanning his arms as if showcasing the house with the new furniture, appliances, and rugs.

"How the hell did you get all this done so quickly?"

He curls his fingers toward his mouth and blows on them smugly before brushing them on his chest. "We're fucking awesome! That's how." I grimace and he says, "We had a lot of help."

I rush toward him and wrap my arms around his neck. He lifts me, hugging me close.

"Thank you so much. This is incredible!"

He looks over my shoulder at my bags. "I see you brought your belongings."

As he sets me down, I say, "Yes, but I left some in the truck."

He brushes a lock of hair off my cheek before kissing me with a slow tenderness that makes my tummy tingle. "Congratulations on the job. Mack is in the bedroom setting up the bed."

"I have a new bed?" My enthusiasm has me rushing toward the bedroom. "Mack!" I squeal, he jolts from his crouched position and whacks his head on a dresser.

"Fuck!" he hisses while rubbing his new lump.

I cover my mouth as I approach him, but soon snicker at his pain. "The bedroom looks great! I can't believe you guys did all this in only a few hours."

"Not to burst my own bubble, but we are pretty great!" He smiles boastfully but then leans in to give me a kiss and hug.

Instead of letting me go, he holds me tighter and rushes toward the bed, dropping both of us onto it. I laugh like I've lost my mind. He's on top of me, kissing my neck. His hand pulls at my skirt until it's raised enough where he can reach into my panties. I'm not laughing anymore.

"I want you," he whispers.

I reply, "I want to get fucked hard, right now, by you."

He lifts off me and flips me onto my hands and knees. While he's fussing with his jeans, I lift my skirt and drop my panties. In seconds, he's buried into me, fucking me with incredible speed. His strong hands grasp my hips, using them as leverage to fuck me harder. Each slam urges me closer to climax, but I don't quite get there. He erupts before I can, leaving me panting and slightly disappointed.

"I'm sorry. Fuck! I've never… That never happens." His apology is met with heavy breathing. He lifts enough where I can roll onto my back. He adjusts himself beside me on the bed so he can look at me. "Give me a few minutes and I'll get it back up. I'd love to lick your pussy while we wait."

My smile has him ready to slide down my body. "No, that's not necessary. That was fun, and it'll leave me wanting more later."

He squints. "Shaina is coming to the house later... my house... the main house. Damn, I don't know what to call it."

"The main house sounds appropriate. Don't worry about it. I'm good for now." My hand cups his flushed cheek. He leans in and kisses me. I whisper, "I'm moving into my new house."

"I'm almost done here. You can start unpacking if you'd like. We can move the furniture wherever you'd like." He leans up on one elbow and looks toward the big window. "I just thought this view of the lake, when you open your eyes in the morning, will start every day off right."

"It's perfect. I can't thank you guys enough."

"It's our pleasure."

Chapter 29

Over the next two days, Patch hardly leaves my side, unless we're at work. He's been helping me rearrange furniture, set up the washer and dryer, and put up shelves. We even discuss where I'd like the food garden to be. He took me shopping for groceries, kitchen and bathroom supplies, and bedding. Basically, we bought just about everything Bash and I will need from a toaster to a television. He paid for everything himself, saying it comes from the Bear money stockpile saved up over the years. All the guys contribute to a fund and have to agree when the money is to be used for something.

I feel guilty that I couldn't contribute anything. Once the wages from my job come into play, maybe they'll let me chip in.

Patch has fucked me in every room of the house, even carrying me while his cock is inside me, to go from room to room. It's been thrilling, to say the very least. He bound me to the kitchen table and fucked me with a cucumber while he licked and sucked my clit. I nearly lost my mind! I must have orgasmed four times before he untied my legs, hopped onto the table and fucked me until I couldn't cum anymore.

He's cooked every night and held me while I slept. If I didn't know any better, I'd swear he built this house for him and I. Sometimes, when I think about him moving back to his house when Bash comes home, my heart feels like it might explode. I love him. I love all of them, but my love for Patch is much deeper than it should be. Bash will be my husband. He will own my heart. I know this to be true. It's what I want. But... I want Patch too.

My job has been going well, only a few mess-ups along the way, but I haven't killed anyone or caused any harm. That's a good start, I must say. Lizza is becoming an excellent friend of mine. She's so full of energy that she tires me out just by having a ten-minute conversation with her. She's great! Most of the other nurses have been helpful but there are a few who've heard of my bad reputation and refuse to see me as anything but a dirty whore. It hurts, but I try not to let it bother me.

At five-thirty, I arrive home to the smell of something stewing in a slow-cooker. I lift the lid and use the ladle to sample a taste. Deer stew. Yum! Nobody cooks deer better than Patch.

He isn't home, so I take a shower to wash the hospital smell off my skin and slip into a light dress that hangs to mid-calf. I set the table for two and head to the bedroom to collect the dirty clothes from the hamper, so I can start a load of wash.

Patch strides into the bedroom, startling me. He kisses me before stripping off his clothes and handing them to me. He hops in the shower while I put the clothes in the washer, getting them ready to start later when he won't be scalded by the shift in water temperature.

A cloud of steam puffs from the bathroom when he opens the door. As he strides out, naked, rubbing the towel over his short, army-style haircut, he doesn't notice me lying on the bed, also naked. He reaches into his duffle bag, choosing a pair of pants, t-shirt, socks, and underwear. As he's about to toss them on the bed, he sees me, lounging beneath the covers.

"Well, hello there, Goldilocks." He licks his bottom lip. "So, what you're saying is that dinner can wait."

I smile and raise my eyebrows while flipping the sheets back, inviting him in. His cock grows by the second. Slowly, he slips in, pulling the covers back over to cover his body. His lips meet mine with incredible tender lovingness. He's too gentle with me, more than he should be if he isn't after my heart.

He leans up, slipping himself between my legs, and easing his manhood between my slick folds until he's buried completely. His lips have yet to leave mine as our tongues dance together in an explorative tango. Patch rocks on me slowly, in no rush to push me toward climax. His fingers weave into my hair before he kisses down my neck and chest, taking a nipple between his lips and tonguing it perfectly.

A moan slips from deep in my chest, urging him to increase his tempo. His movements flow smoothly as my hips lift and lower in perfect sync with his. I'm so close to orgasm. My arms wrap around his back, clinging to him, hoping to hold his hot body against mine for as long as possible. I don't want this feeling to end; this need, this desire that's building to an unforgettable, monumental moment that is sure to make the world disappear around us.

"I love you," he whispers. "I'm so fucking in love with you!" His lips press to mine before I can say anything in response. This is probably a good thing because I want to tell him how much I love him too.

"What the fuck!"

I shriek just as Patch leaps off the bed, ready to beat the hell out of whoever just broke into the house. He's naked, hard-on still protruding, fists clenched, one knee on the bed, and one foot on the floor. He and I are both panting furiously. I have the blankets yanked up at my neck and I've scurried up the bed to get as far away from the intruder as possible.

As if realization claims us both at the same time, we cry out in excitement. "Bash!"

I shuffle toward him on the bed as Patch reaches for his towel, likely to wrap around his waist. "Brother!" he calls out, enthusiastic to greet him.

Bash rushes across the room and clocks Patch, throwing him off balance. I scream, shocked, not knowing what to do. Bash pushes Patch before punching him again.

Patch puts his hands up in defense. "Brother! What the fuck? Settle down!"

"You're in fucking *love* with her? With my Goldie? You fucking backstabbing motherfucker!" Bash yells before sucker-punching Patch, whose knees buckle, toppling him to the floor. Bash looks at me and I don't recognize this person. He kneels over Patch, hitting him several times in the face. Patch tries to grab Bash's arms but keeps missing as they come down with each blow.

I scream. "Stop! What the fuck? Bash, stop! Please, Bash!"

Patch's fist meets Bash's jaw, jolting him back. Patch is up on his knees, even with his brother, and they begin wrestling.

Patch yells, "Stop, little brother! What's wrong with you? You asked me to stay with her. I was doing what you asked."

"No, motherfucker! You're falling in love with her, trying to take her from me. You're supposed to be my brother!" Another blow to Patch's eye lands.

"I'm sorry," he yelps, stopping Bash's next swing from connecting with his jaw. He lunges forward while swinging but doesn't connect his blow. Bash lands another on Patch's bottom lip, splitting it open. Blood spews down his chin and onto his chest before another blow is blocked. Patch shoves with his weight until Bash is on his back.

Bash rolls until Patch is on the bottom. He pulls his fist back quickly, catching me in the chest with his elbow. As I fall back onto the floor, Patch, having not seen, takes advantage of Bash's distraction, punching him in his stomach.

I lie on the floor trying to get some air into my lungs. Bash screams, "Goldie!"

The next thing I know, both of them are above me, looking down with concern in their eyes.

"I'm okay."

Patch shoves Bash, "What the fuck is wrong with you?"

"Me?" Bash yells back. "I don't like coming home to find my brother making love to my girl, in my bed, while telling her he's in love with her. How the fuck did you think I'd react? You're a fucking piece of shit!"

"It's not like that, brother." Patch runs his hand through his hair and then puts out his hand to help me up. Bash leaps forward, shoving Patch away from me.

"Get the fuck away from her! You're done! Say goodbye because you'll never touch her again."

I stand under my own power, furious that they are fighting over who's allowed to love me. "You two are fighting over me? It's true, you both love me. It's different between us, but it's still love, and how can that be wrong?" They glare at one another, surely not listening to me. "I can't do this!"

They yell at each other while I put my dress, socks, and hiking boots on. After throwing some clothes in a bag, I leave the house unseen. They are too busy yelling at each other to notice me leaving.

Chapter 30

I walk toward the main house to see Mack. Bash will need his truck back. It's his, not mine, so taking it seemed criminal. Mack is home when I arrive, crying having swollen my eyes and lips. He looks up from his desk when I toss my bag onto the floor.

"What the fuck?" He stands slowly but quickly rushes to hold me. "What happened? Are you okay?"

Tears pour as I whine through the incoherent, gasped explanation. How he understands anything I'm saying is incredible. Without a word, he takes my hand and walks me to the washroom where he wets a rag with cool water and carefully dabs my face until I've stopped crying. His calm, yet concerned demeanor eases my worry.

"They will work it out. Don't worry, Goldilocks. They've been at odds before. They're both strong-willed and somewhat stubborn, so it might take them a while. Just hang in there and don't give up on them. I'm sure it'll work itself out one way or another."

I'm exhausted; mentally, physically, and emotionally. Maybe my father was right in thinking that I shouldn't be involved with more than one man. Have I been playing with fire, setting their family ablaze, one heart at a time? What have I done?

"You'll stay here with me until they resolve this issue between them. We can stay at the cabin resort I designed for Wolf Lake. I'm sure they'll allow us to test run one of the finished cabins. Let me make a phone call. You can lay in my bed and rest. I'll come get you when I'm ready to go."

He kisses my hands one at a time and then walks me to his room. After tucking me under the covers, he closes the bedroom door and quickly clears the length of the house until he's outside. I can hear him talking, but I'm too tired to listen in. I drift off quickly.

"Goldilocks. Wake up. We can leave now." Mack is sitting on the edge of the bed, rousing me.

"Okay," I whisper with a hoarse throat. All that crying has it aching.

He helps me up and into my boots before walking me out to his truck. We drive without a word, for about half-hour before cutting off the main road. Five minutes of winding dirt road brings us to the first set of cabins, which look unfinished. He parks in front of the last cabin we come to, situated beside the lake, away from the other buildings.

He wasn't exaggerating when he described the picturesque scenery. The mountain across the lake is crown land, and therefore uninhabited. It's lined with trees that seem to glow orange as the sun sets, casting its glow upon them. The water remains still, seeming like a mirror has laid upon it, reflecting the orangey tones. I would cry at the marvel of its beauty if I weren't completely cried out.

He ushers me inside after carrying in our bags. I'm surprised to see it fully furnished, right down to the cozy-looking bedding.

"You look surprised. It's the model cabin we had prepared for the financer's visit. What do you think?"

"It's more beautiful than I had imagined. The blueprint doesn't do it justice. I'm impressed."

"I brought some food, not much, but it'll get us started. I'll start some coffee brewing. Are you hungry? I can whip up some sandwiches for us in no time at all. Just say yes and you shall receive." He smiles in his comedic way, but I only smile meekly. "Sandwiches it is!"

I watch him tuck his hair behind his ears before washing his hands. He butters the bread while I watch, his eyes darting up to mine from time to time. "It'll be okay, Goldilocks. I promise."

We spend the night together, my butt pushed against his belly, his arm slung over my shoulders. I don't sleep much, and Mack keeps stirring each time I yawn. It takes a full minute for me to slowly ease my way out of his grasp without waking him.

After peeing and washing my face, I head to the kitchen to find something alcoholic to drink. In the freezer is a full bottle of tequila. Score! I reach up to take a glass from the cupboard but wince from the pain of the bruise on my chest. "Ouch, fuck!" I whisper in the darkness, pulling the collar of my nightgown down so I can see the darkened skin. Just as I turn to get a better look with the light from the full moon, Mack is standing right behind me, startling me.

"What is that from?" he inquires.

I'm afraid to tell him. Will he freak out and go after Bash or Patch? "It happened during the fight. I got in the way. It wasn't their fault. It looks worse than it is."

"Let me see it."

"No," I say, pulling away. "Let it go. I'm heading to the porch to watch the lake and drink until I forget what happened today. Care to join me?"

He reaches over me to get a glass for himself. We sit on the porch and drink, talking about everything from when we were children to some of our heartbreaks. I had no idea Mack was such a deep-feeling, loving soul. He's always joking around and seldom shows his tender heart. Tonight, I'm seeing him, for the first time.

"You're a beau—ful man, Mack. Has anyone ev—ver tole you that?" I slur most of that but he understands. He's just as drunk as I am.

He snickers. "Yup! Once'er twice. I'm careful not to give m'heart away too eez-ly. It's bin brok'n a lot. You, Goldi-locks, are a beau-ful woman too. You could eez-ly break my heart."

His phone vibrates. "Answer it," I tell him.

He picks it up. "Hello. No, I'm spendin' the night with Gold'locks. She had a fight with... No. No. Don't be like that. I got to go." He hangs up, obviously angry.

"What was that about?"

"Shaina is pissed at me. She's jealous of you." He inhales deeply then says, "She wants my heart!"

Between hiccups, I tell him, "If I had it, I—I wouldn't break your heart, M—Mack. I love you. I love all you bad boy, Bear boy... boys. If I could have all three of you, I would totally love that. I mean, I could l—love you all. I can do it. I'm—I have a lot of me—of love."

"We—we should def-n-ly go to bed." He holds up the nearly empty bottle of tequila. We laugh loud enough to hear an echo return from across the lake, which has us laughing even harder.

We stumble to the bathroom and go pee before we get glasses of water to put on our nightstands. I strip off my clothes, to which Mack hoots and hollers. We slide under the covers while laughing to near hysterics. He flops on his back and, not so elegantly, and I straddle him. We kiss and I begin to rouse his penis from its flaccid state with my hand. I don't remember anything else.

Chapter 31

My stomach lurches into my throat, startling me from a dream where I'm dancing like a crazy fool with Mack. Daylight burns my bloodshot eyes when they burst open. The realization that vomit is about to spew has me on my feet and running, banging off the doorframe along the way. Just as I lift the lid on the toilet, I empty my super-heated stomach contents with a fury.

I hear groaning behind me. The tap runs, alerting me to the fact that I have to pee. A cold rag drapes over the back of my neck just as more vomit erupts into the toilet. My stomach doesn't let up until a session of hard dry-heaving has me listless and clinging to the bowl, hoping the room will stop spinning.

"I'll make some coffee." After swaying through the doorframe, Mack disappears from the bathroom. He's still drunk too.

Several minutes later, after I'm sure my stomach won't betray me again, I slowly make my way to the living room, clutching my pounding head as I do. The brightness of the day has my eyes feeling like they've been doused with sand and lemon juice. I curl up on the sofa, pull the plaid blanket from the back onto my chest and hug it tightly.

Mack sets a coffee and a glass of orange juice on the table in front of me before pulling it closer so I can easily reach. He lifts my legs and flops, laying them across his lap.

"Thank you," I mutter before sipping the orange juice and mildly retching but managing to keep it down. "How do you feel this morning?"

"I'm seriously dreading drinking that much. Otherwise, I'm great. I see you're all peaches and daisies this morning." He rests his hand on my thigh. "I'll make breakfast as soon as the room stops spinning."

"Don't rush on my behalf." I groan, confirming my regret and pain.

***

Mack and I spend the morning recovering while watching old movies showing on a local television station the antenna pics up. By early afternoon, we don't feel much of the effects of our drunken night. When I confess I can't remember what happened after I straddled him in bed, he tells me that we started kissing, but his memory is foggy after that.

My phone has twenty-three unread text messages and six missed phone calls. Five are from Patch and one has a number I don't recognize. I start with the text messages; all of them are from Bash. Basically, he's worried about me, wants to know if I'm okay, is afraid that I might hate him, wants to know where I am, is happy that I'm safe with Mack but misses me, wants me to come back to him so we can talk it out, and other texts that simply say that he loves me. The final message was sent at five-thirteen this morning. It says only two words, *I'm sorry*.

I text back and say that I'm safe and with Mack. I ask if he worked it out with Patch and say that I'll come back when I'm ready.

He doesn't text back right away, so I listen to the voicemails from Patch.

Voicemail #1—8PM: "Goldilocks, I'm sorry you had to see that. I shouldn't have let myself fall for you, but I did. I'm going to walk away. Bash loves you, and I love him, so it's only right. Forgive me."

Voicemail #2—8:34PM: "Where are you? Are you all right? Just call me to let me know you're okay. I'm worried."

Voicemail #3—10:13PM: "I just saw the message from Mack. I'm relieved to know you're safe. He'll protect you. I'm sorry it turned out this way, but I'm not sorry that I let you into my heart. You've woken me up to realize that I need love in my life. I didn't see the unresolved issues I have. Fuck! Goldie, why won't you talk to me?"

Voicemail #4—2:05AM: "Bash and I have been discussing what happened tonight. There was a lot to talk about. I have some unresolved issues that I need to work through before I can..." There's a ten-second pause. "Listen, always know that I love you. We all love you. Bash and you belong together and by me interjecting, I've caused a rift in your relationship with him. For that, I apologize to you both." He takes a deep breath and sighs. "But I won't apologize for loving you."

Voicemail #5—2:27AM: He sounds tired as if he's been broken down. "I'm going to leave for a while. There's something I have to do. Tell Mack he can come back home with you. I won't be here. I hope you can forgive me."

The last message sounds different than the others. It's Patch's voice, but there's no soul behind his tone. My heart leaps into my throat. Is he going to be okay? Where is he going and what does he mean by unresolved issues?

I burst into the bathroom, startling Mack, who's in the shower. "Patch is leaving. Do you know where he's going?"

Mack wipes water from his eyes and looks at me through the glass shower door. "What do you mean he's leaving?"

"He left a message saying he has unresolved issues, and he's leaving."

Mack shrugs, seeming to know what it's about. "Don't worry, he won't be gone long. This is his home. He won't stay away."

Mack and I are eating tomato soup and grilled cheese sandwiches for dinner when my phone rings.

"Hello," I say into the receiver.

"Goldilocks, it's me," Patch says.

"Where are you going?"

"Babe, I'm getting on the plane soon. Listen, I'm sorry if I hurt you. I need to do something and I need you to trust that Bash loves you with all of his heart. He reacted before thinking and regrets his actions. Please talk to him. You are his whole world. Give him a chance to explain. Can you do that... for me?" He doesn't sound as soulless now. What's changed?

"Please, don't go. Stay. I don't want anyone fighting over me. This is your home, your sanctuary. I'll leave. You stay."

"Promise me you'll talk to him," he begs.

"I will when I'm ready. Did you two work it out?"

He groans as if he's coming to his feet. "We talked. Don't worry, we may have something worked out. I just have to do something first. I have to go. We'll talk soon."

He hangs up without giving me a chance to think of something to say. Mack looks at me with a concerned expression and a splotch of tomato soup on his cheek. I point, and he wipes it off with a napkin and then grins.

He asks, "Was that Patch?" I nod. "Is he okay?"

"I don't know."

My phone rings again and I immediately answer without looking at who's calling.

"Patch?"

"Um, no, it's Bash. You didn't answer an important call, so they called me. Goldie, your father's in the hospital."

My world spins and I can't breathe. Mack stands and comes to my side.

I ask, "Is he okay?"

"I don't know. They think it's his heart. You need to go there. Where are you? I'll come pick you up."

"No, Mack's here. He can drive me." I hang up and explain to Mack what I've just learned. We dress and rush to the hospital.

Chapter 32

When I arrive, the doctor is just leaving his room. He comforts me with a smile and then explains that he's going to be okay, that it was a mild cardiac event. I'm grateful.

Mack is by my side outside my father's room. I'm sure he's hooked up to machines that have beeps and chimes to alert should anything go awry. I see these machines in action on a regular basis and yet, right now, I'm terrified to know they're hooked up to my father.

Mom opens the door and steps out, stopping me from entering. "He's in a fragile state. You can't work him up. If he sees you, he might have another… Maybe you should wait out here until he's more stable." She hugs me quickly and then steps back into the room, closing the door behind her.

Tears fill my eyes. Mack holds me against his chest. A warm hand presses to my back. I turn and see the evidence of last night's battle having left Bash with a bruised eye so swollen he can barely see from it. He looks exhausted.

"Bash."

"How's your dad?" he asks, seeming too timid to attempt hugging me. With Mack having let me go, I could use his arms right now.

"He's going to be okay. I have to wait to see him." I look past him, hoping to see Patch lagging behind, but I'm let down by an empty corridor.

Mack asks Bash, "Where did Patch go?"

Bash replies, "To kindle an old flame or snuff out the embers. One or the other."

Mack nods, seeming to understand. "It's not easy to stoke an old ember when a flame burns elsewhere." Bash clenches his jaw but nods with complete understanding.

"You don't need to speak in code. He's with his ex-girlfriend trying to see if they still have the great love affair that once was. But, because he loves me, you think his trip is futile." My eyes shift from man to man. They both nod.

"Why don't we go to the cafeteria for a coffee," Bash says. "By the time we get back, maybe you'll be able to see your father. Besides, we need to talk."

Bash tells a nurse where we'll be in case my mother searches for us. I follow them and we sit at a table farthest away from other people.

"So, tell me why you flipped out yesterday," I ask Bash.

He takes a deep breath before swallowing. "I came home early to surprise you. I couldn't wait to make love to you in our bed. It would be like christening the house with our love. But, instead of me making love to you, Patch was. He was where I was supposed to be. It's my home, my woman, my bed. It should have been me telling you that I love you, not him, not in my bed, in my home. I lost it. I shouldn't have hit him, we shouldn't have fought, but that would have pissed off anyone. I felt like he was taking over my life, my hopes and dreams, and the love of my life."

"Yeah, I can see how you'd think that," Mack says.

They listen while I speak. "I'm sorry you felt that way. Anyone would be upset coming home to that. Things progressed between me and Patch, but until then, he hadn't told me he was in love with me."

"Are you in love with him?" Bash asks, his expression remaining stoic. "Please... I need you to be honest."

My eyes skip between both men. "Bash, I am in love with you. I'm also in love with Patch. I love you too, Mack, but you have Shaina, so we've kept ourselves emotionally distant. Before last night, I didn't really know you very well." I look back at Bash. "We got so drunk last night. I still feel lousy."

Bash looks at Mack, whose eyes remain puffy and bloodshot. "It's obvious."

Mack bumps him with his elbow. "You would have done it too. She needed to let off steam."

"Rightfully so." Bash's eyes drop, along with his shoulders. "So, you're in love with me and Patch."

"It wasn't supposed to be this way." I immediately bite my fingernail. Mack bumps my arm. My hand drops to my lap and I scowl at him. I nod to Bash's question. I'm ashamed of my indiscretion.

Bash puts his hands on the table, palms up. He wiggles his fingers, so I place my hands over them.

He continues, "Okay, what if we were to share you? What I mean is, we'll continue as we have been, except that you and Patch can love each other however you'd like. I'll do my best to curb my jealousy if you promise to always come home to me every night and sleep in our bed. I might not fall asleep holding you, but I want you beside me when I wake, even if Patch or Mack is sleeping on the other side of you."

My eyes close for a three-count while I breathe deeply, hoping to ease the thumping in my headache. "There will be jealousy at some point. It's human nature. What do we do if one of you wants children? What then? Whose baby do I give birth to? Or, do we throw caution to the wind and both of you spin the dice, never knowing who's the father?"

"There are a lot of questions that will need answering at some point. Why not just start off slowly and see how it goes?"

"We can try that," I whisper. My mind whirls with worry but my heart feels less burdened. Yes, I want them both. Hell, I want all three of them, but Mack has other plans and who can blame him. This lifestyle won't be easy. Who would want to share one woman's heart with two other men?

"Patch is my brother, forever. He loves you and you love him. I know this to be true. If we follow the rules and keep our communication open, we can do this."

"Mack, are you in love with Goldie too?"

I look at Mack but he doesn't meet my gaze. He's staring at his coffee cup. He finally looks at me, and I can see that he's unsure. He looks back at his cup. "Before last night, I would have said no. But now, I don't know."

"Okay," Bash sighs. He kisses each hand before brushing a lock of hair from my face. "I think we all drank the love potion. Let's go, maybe you can see your father now.

Mom allows me to see my dad. His skin looks grey, which is terrifying to me. I can't lose my father, especially when we are at odds. How could I ever forgive myself if I didn't settle things with him?

"Dad?" I whisper. His eyes are closed, but he turns his head just a little and slowly opens his lids.

"Goldilocks," he replies through short breaths. "I'm sorry for hitting you. It's hard for me to remember that you're a grown woman now. I'll try harder. Can you forgive me?"

My tears fall. The thumping in my head makes it difficult to retain a thought. "I love you, Daddy."

"I love you, Goldilocks. Now go home and get on with your life. I don't want you hanging around here. Don't worry about me."

With a kiss to his forehead, I pat the hand without the IV needle buried in a vein. He smiles weakly before closing his eyes.

"Mom," I whisper as she walks me into the hall. "Are you sure he's going to be okay? He doesn't look good."

"You're a nurse. You've seen people look horrible and come out of it unscathed." I nod, knowing she's right. "He'll be fine. Now get out of here. Nobody should be at their job site on their day off." She hugs and kisses me and I'm off with Bash and Mack in tow.

Chapter 33

Mack and Bash made dinner while I took a long, hot shower. It helped me to feel more like myself, but it hasn't been an easy day. It refreshed my memory as to why I don't drink very much or often. Hangovers suck!

It's nine o'clock, and we've been playing Gin Rummy for a few hours now. The battle between the two leading players, Bash and Mack, is getting heated. We laugh hard at times, and the name-calling has gotten out of hand, but it's all in fun.

A knock on the door startles us. Bash rises to answer it. "Don't look at my fucking cards, asshole!" He points and glares at Mack while walking toward the door. He opens it to reveal a soaking wet Patch.

"It's really coming down out here. Sorry to intrude. Mack told me about Goldilocks' father. Can I come in?"

Bash opens the door wider while Mack heads to the bathroom for a towel. Patch puts his hand out to Bash. He takes it and pulls him into a tight hug.

Mack hands Patch a towel. "Keep hugging like that and I'll assume you're in love with each other."

Bash backs up and runs his hands down his damp shirt with a grimace. "Come in. Do you want something to drink; tea, coffee, beer?"

"Whatever is readily available." He kicks off his boots and arranges them neatly beneath the bench he built. I walk toward him and smile. He nervously looks at Bash, who nods before going to the counter to make a tea for him. Mack returns to the table to give us some privacy.

"How are you? I'm sorry to hear about your father. Is he going to be okay?"

"Ah, yeah. It was a minor heart attack. He'll be home in a few days."

He hands me the towel. "That's good," he says while shoving his hands in his pants pocket. "How about you? Are you all right?"

I quickly respond. "Yes, I'm fine. I thought you left. Where did you go? And why did you leave? Was it because of me?" My arms cross over my chest to give myself comfort.

He whispers. "I didn't leave because of you. I needed to know if I was still in love with her." He reaches out for my hands and holds them in his. "It isn't her that I love."

"Then why did you leave me?"

He sinks down to his knees in front of me. "I love you, but I needed to be sure that my love for you wasn't misguided. When I got there, I couldn't leave the airport. I knew it wasn't where I was supposed to be. I bought a ticket to come home and was boarding when I got a text from Mack that your dad was sick. The plane couldn't fly fast enough. I went to the hospital first but your mom said you had left."

I step forward and wrap my arms around his head and pull it against my chest. Mack and Bash are quiet while they watch us. Bash sets a steaming mug by the empty seat and sits.

Mack gathers up the cards and begins to shuffle. "Hey, are you two done hugging? I'd like to start another game while I'm still hot. Bash, you're going down, fucker!"

To retort, Bash shoots him the middle finger. "Deal the cards, motherfucker! Let's see who's the fucking king here." As he's picking up the cards Mack flings at him, he calls out. "Hey, Patch, you in?"

"Yeah, deal me in."

Bash, with sincerity in his voice, asks, "No, Patch, are you all in?"

Patch looks up at me and asks, "It's your call, Goldilocks. Am I in?"

I pause to look at his pleading eyes. "Yes, you're in."

*** Continue Goldie's Story in Book 3 ***

If you enjoyed book two in the Naughty Goldie series, please leave a review on your favourite book purchasing site. Feel free to boast the book online and tag Pebbles Lacasse.

Goldilocks
and the Three
Bear Brothers
Book 3

Overture

Pebbles Lacasse
Amazon International Best-Selling Author

Goldilocks & The Three Bear Brothers: Overture

Book 3

The *Naughty Goldie* Series

by Pebbles Lacasse

Chapter 1

The relationship between the Bear brothers—Patch, Mack, and Bash Bear—has been copacetic.

Mack is neutral and only wants the best for everyone. He loves me, too, but differently than Bash and Patch do. After Patch announced that he's also in love with me, he and Bash fought as if they were real bears fighting over a mate, and I was that mate. It was awful! Eventually, they agreed they can all love me as long as I call Bash's bed my own and dream beside him at night, even if another brother is on the other side of me.

The bruises Patch and Bash sported for a few weeks after their slug-fest was a constant reminder that I was the reason the two came to blows. It was hard to see, even though they had settled their issues. If I didn't love all three brothers so much, I would have walked away so they could restore their bond. But my draw to them is just too strong, and none of them were willing to let me go.

Now that Bash is home from university after graduating with a degree in journalism and English, his job at the *Daily News* takes up a lot of his time. He's been filling in for the regular editor because she's off, having just had a baby.

He's also doing his regular job, which is writing obituaries. Bash believes people deserve to have the very best final sentiments written about them that are deserving of a lifetime. He's sentimental that way, despite his laughing blue eyes that make him look like he doesn't take anything seriously.

When he's not busy at the paper, he works tirelessly on writing his book, which he won't let me read yet. I've tried to sneak up behind him and read over his shoulder, but he always knows I'm there, no matter how quiet I try to be. Once, he continued typing and wrote: *Goldilocks, if you don't go do something with yourself other than hovering over me, I will call Patch over to punish you.*

I was bored and considered testing his threat, but decided I wanted to be able to sit that night without having sore butt cheeks. But sometimes I poke Patch Bear just to provoke him. His aggressive nature is something I crave. He's sure to sexually gratify me after his punishments, and he is damn good at that!

Patch has his crew that helps him cut down trees used for building log cabins and other things; furniture, barns, monuments, et cetera. He also works at the mill when they need extra help. It's physically demanding work, but he loves it. He said there's a satisfaction that comes with creating something beautiful from a chunk of wood. Patch always replaces the trees he's cut down with new sprouts to keep the forest from becoming barren.

Mack, the sweetest yet craziest of the Bear brothers, has been monitoring the build of a three-million-dollar log home he designed. He's quickly becoming one of the most sought-after architects in eastern Canada.

This design is a gorgeous six-bedroom, five-bathroom home that I can't wait to walk through when the build is completed. He said the clients are the owners of a popular fast-food franchise, but I can't remember which one. They own six-hundred acres of land surrounding the lake, making it seem like a private lake. Nobody can own a body of water, but people would have to trespass on their private property, which is illegal. It's going to be a beautiful home when it's completed.

Because the building site is four hours away by car, it isn't feasible for Mack to drive there each day. He stays with some of the construction crew during the week but comes home most weekends, and if the weather is expected to be bad for a few days and they put the build on hold, he'll come home.

He's there more often than he's here. I miss having him around. His brothers miss him, too.

Shaina, Mack's girlfriend, visits Patch now and then for a quick fuck when Mack's out of town. It's allowed because it's never kept hidden as if they're having a secret affair. She hasn't asked to be with Bash, not that we see her much these days. She works a lot, and she's still in college, which keeps her busy.

It's still hard for me to believe that Bash and I have a semi-open relationship. Sometimes I need a minute to sort through my emotions. The brothers always shared everything, including women. They're quite happy knowing I can have sex with any of them whenever I want. The guys are allowed to be with each other's girlfriends, as long as she *and* I allow it.

When I was away at college, Bash had sex with Shaina but didn't tell me right away. I was upset because Mack was the one who told me about it.

Bash hid it from me. In his defense, Bash didn't want to tell me over the phone. This was the first time he'd had sex with another woman besides me since we've been together. He wanted to wait until we were face-to-face, which would have been much better for me.

I've forgiven Bash for not having told me right away, but I think he's afraid to have sex with Shaina again, thinking I might get upset. I won't.

Am I jealous? Perhaps a little; I think it would be abnormal if I wasn't. But I know he'll always come home to me, and I don't worry about him choosing her.

Since I graduated from nursing school and moved back to my hometown, I've been working at the local hospital. Since I didn't have a vehicle of my own, Bash and I had to compare schedules to make sure we got to our destinations on time. I got a loan and picked up a used Dodge Journey, and I love it. This is the first time I've had my own car and I'm so proud of myself for taking the scary leap into financial debt.

The walls in the log house the guys built for Bash and me seem too stark, so I decided to stop at the second-hand store two towns over to pick up a few pictures to hang. When I bought some furniture here a month ago, I saw some beautiful scenic pictures of mountains and rivers that would be perfect. Hopefully, they're still available.

This store is huge and filled with everything from packaged food to clothing, furniture and pet products. My cart is nearly full of different-sized pictures when a woman walks up to me to introduce herself.

"Hi. Are you Goldilocks?" Her smile reveals crooked teeth.

I'm immediately on defense. "Um, yes."

How the hell does this woman know my name? She doesn't look familiar. Her brunette hair is cropped in a bob. She's short and tiny, aside from her wide hips. She pops her hand out toward me.

"I'm Sarah Joyeau." I take her hand and shake it. She smiles too aggressively for my comfort and then lowers her voice. "Sorry, I know you don't know me. I used to date the Bear brothers a few years ago."

Her hands rest folded together in front of her while she shifts her weight from one leg to the other. What the hell does this woman want?

My heart pounds quicker in my chest. "How do you know who I am?"

She tilts her head. "Everyone knows who you are. You're a hot topic these days." She must see the fear in my eyes and retreats. "No, no! I'm not a crazy person who's going to attack you or anything. I know what you're going through." She steps closer and lowers her voice to a whisper. "People assume you're sleeping with all of them, but they don't know how it really is. I do."

"Oh?" My eyes scan around us, fearing someone might overhear. "And how is it?"

She scratches her head and seems concerned that she's getting herself in too deep. "Um, well, the guys aren't the evil seducers of innocent females like people seem to think. They're really nice guys and wouldn't intentionally hurt a woman, ever!"

"How long ago were you with them?"

Am I prying too deeply? No. She brought it up, so I'm entitled to ask questions. Right?

"A few years ago." She bites her top lip while she looks off in the distance. She suddenly changes the subject. "Do you want help getting these to the front? They're nice pictures. New apartment? Are you decorating?"

I watch as she pulls the frames apart enough to look at each photo. "I think I can handle it. I'm decorating our new house."

She sets the pictures down without looking at the three bottom ones. "Oh, a house? Who are you living with?"

"If you must know, Bash. He's my boyfriend."

Her eyes widen. "Your boyfriend?"

"Is that weird?" I set the framed picture I'm holding back on the pile I've opted not to purchase and give her my full attention.

She waves her hand and then crosses her arms over her chest. "No, not weird. I was dating Mack for a while, but after some time, it seemed like I wasn't dating any one of them in particular. They shared me, often, but I was officially with Mack." Her fingers brush through her hair to pull it off her face, but it slips right back. "Bash was the best lover, and I thought maybe I could let myself love him, too, but he was too closed off. He said his heart belonged to someone else."

"Hmm…" I pause and wonder who the woman was that he loved. "Yeah, Bash and I live together. We don't live in the main Bear residence."

She whispers and speaks quickly. "So, you don't—you know—*play* with Patch and Mack, too? The rumors all suggest that you do, not that I really believe what people say. Well, one woman said she heard that you had sex with them in the forest." She leans close and winks. "I'll admit, I was a teensy bit jealous! I mean, if I could go back and get it on with

Bash again…" She forms her lips into an O and widens her eyes, then dances a little shimmy.

"Yeah, well," I clear my throat but don't hide my irritation in my tone. "You're not with them anymore. Since you're being so candid," I pause. "Why did you and Mack break up?"

She pulls her lips in between her crooked teeth and bites down gently while her gaze assesses me. She shrugs and runs her hand through her hair again. That must be a nervous habit.

"Patch sort of scared me." She looks to her left to see if anyone is within earshot. "He's a rough man who has strange kinks. I'm not into rough sex, at least not at his level. I told Mack that I didn't want to be with Patch anymore but still wanted to be with him and Bash. He said either I'm with Patch, too, or none of them. Then I told him that I loved him. He flat out told me he didn't love me and probably never would."

She shrugs and twists her mouth for a second. "He was kind about it, but things were different after that. I had to walk away, but I still miss him and Bash, not so much Patch." She shifts her weight and clasps her hands behind her back. "Do you find Patch to be too rough, or are you into that?"

I cut her off. "Look, what I do with Patch, or don't do, is my business. I don't know you, and I'm not going to discuss my happenings with you."

She seems surprised at my refusal to openly chat with her. "Sorry. I just thought that since we have something in common, we could become friends."

I smile but squint my eyes. "Yeah. I'm not going to start a friendship with you for the sole reason that you had sex with the Bear brothers. If that were the only requirement, I'd have an extensive friends list. Wouldn't I?"

With wide eyes and raised eyebrows, she nods. "Well, if you ever want to talk…" She clears her throat. Again, she runs a hand through her hair, not altering the style whatsoever. "When my friends found out about what I was doing … with the guys … they ostracized me. I had to move out of town to evade the cruelty. I hope that's not the case with you."

She shifts, takes a breath, and turns her attention to the paintings. "Anyway, do you need help with your pictures? I can take them to the front if you want to shop more. If you add one more, they're going to fall out of your cart." She giggles and swings her arms front and back like a child and lifts onto her toes as she does.

"No, I have all I need."

She smiles, turns, and takes a few steps, but I call out to her, not wanting to leave the conversation hanging on my rudeness.

"Hey, um—" I call out. She spins on her heel and takes a step back toward me. "I'm sorry that happened to you. People are cruel. I've had run-ins with judgemental assholes, too."

"You're stronger than me; you're still with them. I couldn't do it."

"The public's bullshit doesn't deter me, and you shouldn't let it bother you either. This is your life; live it how you want to. Fuck those gossiping assholes and their shitty existence." My smirk is met with her laugh.

She nods, laughs again, and quickly scurries away, holding her head a bit higher than she did when she approached me. As she walks away, I picture Patch fucking her while he pulls her hair and spanks her ass. Yeah, I think she's more of a love-maker than a lover of rough sex. I do wish her the best.

Chapter 2

Several sunset pictures fill the empty spaces in my bedroom. Two beach and open field pictures hang in each of the spare bedrooms. Two smaller photos of a lake dangle on nails in the bathroom. I've hung a large mountain view picture in the living room, near the kitchen.

That leaves only one more. It's my favorite; a sunset view from someone's kayak, floating on water that's smooth as glass. The kayak is bright green, a pleasant contradiction from the pink and orange mountains mirrored on the water.

I struggle to hold it up to get a better idea of where to place the nails when a knock on the door startles me and I nearly drop it. I carefully set the heavy frame on the floor.

As I near the door, I spot Patch's truck through the window. My tummy flutters and my pussy clenches. What's he doing here?

"Come on in," I yell.

The door swings open wide and in comes the mountainous man, a wooden bench perched atop his shoulder. He sets it beside the door and bends down to rearrange the shoes and boots to rest beneath it.

It's obvious he made it since it says "Goldie's Bench" along the backrest. The craftsmanship Patch puts into his works never ceases to amaze me. His talent should be featured in a magazine, but he would refuse the opportunity, not wanting to have that much attention drawn his way. He's a quiet man who prefers to stand in silence while assessing everyone in the room. If he wants to be heard, he can easily still a room with his deep voice.

"The seat lifts so you can put stuff inside." He lifts it to show me how it works and then stands tall, admiring the bench. "It looks good there. Don't you think?"

"Yes! Wow! Oh, my G… It's beautiful!" I lift the seat, look inside, then set it down and plop my ass on it while my fingertips caress the decorative backrest. "This is incredible!"

"Thanks, Goldie."

I frown. "We talked about this. I don't like you calling me Goldie. That's Bash's nickname for me, not yours."

His deviant gaze meets my scrunched-up face.

"Like I've told you before, I'll call you whatever the fuck I want." His hands rest on his hips while his brown eyes scream *danger* to me from his 6'3" stance. "Would you have preferred Slut, Whore, or my Little Cunt?"

I lean back on the bench. "Definitely not any of those."

My fingers trace the hand-carved etching of my name. I breathe in the soothing scent of wood and sigh heavily. "Thank you so much. I can't believe you built this for me; built the whole damn house! I mean, I love you guys! You spoil me."

"You deserve to be spoiled." He offers his hand to me. "Come here."

I rise from the bench and step toward him. He gathers me in his thick arms and holds me against his strong chest. His heart beats quickly beneath his khaki t-shirt.

"I love you. I do my best to give you everything…"

His embrace is calm, homey, and familiar as if I've been waiting my whole life to be this happy. My heart thumps evenly with his and it feels right, as it does when I'm with each brother.

"…including my heart," he whispers, then kisses the top of my head.

I smile and pull away from him, finger-brush my hair behind my ear, and return to the picture I sat on the floor.

"What are you up to?" he asks as he follows me around the sofa. I lift the picture, but he's quick to take it from me. "Let me help. Where are you hanging it?"

"Right there." I point to the empty space on the wall. "I think it'll be perfect beside the big window. It's too bare over here. It needs something. I thought about a cabinet but that might make the corner look too crowded."

"You're going to hang it there?" He crosses his arms over his chest and cocks his head.

"That's the plan. It'll look good there." He doesn't look convinced. "You don't think so?" I tilt my head and rethink it.

"No, not here." He draws in a long breath and scans the room. "Over there, beside the door would be better."

I turn to look at the spot. "Definitely not! I doubt it would even fit there." I step toward the spot I chose. "Nope! My mind is made up. I want it here." I gesture with both arms to frame the spot.

He scratches his freshly shaved chin. "Are you sure?"

I press my hand to my throat in frustration and lean my weight on one leg. "Why are you being an ass about this? I told you where I want it." I sigh heavily when he frowns. "I'm quite capable of hanging it myself if you're only going to pout about it. I've hung all the other ones without issue."

His eyes burn into mine. My tummy flutters and my pussy moistens. He finds my defiance arousing and usually punishes me but I like it and test the limits of his patience, often. Right now, I just want the picture hung!

His lips press together and he clears his throat. When his eyes shift to the empty wall, I look down at the bulge in his snug-fitting jeans.

"Fine. Give me the hammer!" He points his finger at me. "And drop the attitude or I'll drop it for you."

My bottom lip pinches between my teeth as I skip away to fetch the hammer and nails from the table. His eyes follow me. I hand the tools to him. His sternness never fails to ignite a flaming desire in my nether region and right now is no different. I'm heating up and my flushed cheeks prove it.

He's so powerful; two bashes and the nail didn't stand a chance. I hit the other ones at least a dozen times to get the same result. He hands me the hammer, then hangs the picture and tilts it to the right to straighten it. He steps back and assesses it before readjusting.

"Do you want a beer?" I ask as I swing the hammer beside my knee.

He leans down and relieves me of the tool. "Careful, little girl. I'd hate to see you whack your knee."

I roll my eyes and spin on my heels to fetch us each a bottle of beer. He follows and sets the hammer on the kitchen table while I lean into the fridge. I hand him a bottle and he spins off the cap with ease, while I grip mine and struggle. He hands me the open one and takes mine. He spins off the cap before he tips the bottle to swallow half of it in one gulp.

I take the caps from him and toss them while I offer him a seat at the table, to which he accepts.

"How's the job at the hospital going?" he asks.

I sit across from him and rest my feet on the chair next to me, and then take a long gulp. "The job itself is great, and most of my coworkers are nice. But there are a few that treat me like—" I roll my eyes and sip the beer. "Well, I'd be happier than a pig in a mud puddle if I never had to see them again."

"People can be assholes," he adds.

"It's not only my coworkers," I mumble.

"What's going on?" He leans toward me and rests his elbows on the table while he clutches the nearly empty beer bottle.

I tug at my earlobe. "Nothing you need to concern yourself with."

Seeming annoyed, he hisses, "Talk to me, Goldie."

I scowl at his use of the nickname. "I was told that most people know—or think they know—about my intimate relationship with all three sexually abusive Bear brothers."

He chuckles. "And that bothers you."

I shrug my shoulders but don't meet his gaze. Instead, I look at my beer label with a slight satisfaction that I got it off without tearing it. He doesn't need to know about the woman at the store or the judgemental general public who glares at me as I go about my life.

"Some of my coworkers give me a hard time." I sip from my bottle. "It's hard to tell if they're appalled or jealous. Either way, they treat me like shit whenever they can. There isn't a lot I can do about it since they have seniority." I soften my voice to seem more innocent. "I simply smile and bat my eyelashes."

"What do they do when you do that?"

I undo the ponytail from my hair and shake out my tresses. "They either pity me or glare and storm off. I think my lifestyle bothers them more than their attitude about it bothers me. I really don't care what people think. I have friends at the hospital who don't judge me, and I appreciate them. The others can go fuck themselves and probably do because who'd want to fuck a miserable bitch that's always complaining?"

He snickers and rubs his chin. "I'd grab that bitch by the hair, kiss her mouth hard, force her over a table, and fuck the hell out of her until she passed out from coming too hard. That might get her to loosen."

I lick my lips and savor the thought. "Oh?" I sip my beer, drop my feet to the floor and square my shoulders. "Well, that always loosens me up." My expression screams naughty intention.

He leans back in his chair and rests his hand on the bulge in his jeans as he sucks back the last gulp of beer. "Careful, Goldie. I'm in a mood."

I lean back in my chair and ape his position while I slug my beer until it's empty. I stifle a burp and set the bottle on the table. His gaze is locked on the hand that rests on the crotch of my dark grey yoga pants.

"And what kind of mood are you in, exactly?" I sink my hand deeper between my thighs. I don't touch my pussy but it's close enough.

He tilts his head forward and looks at me from under his brows. I'd swear his dark brown eyes turn black and sink a little deeper in his skull.

Patch rises and rounds the table while my eyes follow. My tummy flutters like a hundred bees are buzzing. He offers his hand to me and I set my much smaller hand across his giant palm.

He yanks and quickly pulls me to my feet. He hugs me to his body and lifts me off my feet. As if I'm weightless, he carries me effortlessly to the island while he kisses me. His hot tongue fills my mouth and I suck on it to arouse him further. He groans against my lips.

He spins me as he sets me on my feet but leaves his hand spanned across my shoulder blades. He presses my upper body on the countertop while his fingers reach under my shirt to hook the waistband of my yoga pants. He yanks them down to bare my ass.

"No panties." He groans his approval. "Good girl."

His massive hand glides down my back and rests on my bare ass, covering both cheeks. He weaves the other into my hair and turns my head until my cheek rests on the counter.

"Grip the other side of the counter and hang on." As I do, his voice deepens. "Don't let go."

I know better than to assume his order to be a mere suggestion. I reach up and stretch my torso over the island and grip the opposite edge.

He caresses my ass one cheek at a time. He squeezes my left buttock until I whimper and then cracks me hard with his open palm.

Fuck! That hurts!

"Your punishment is ten spanks for giving me an attitude about where to hang the picture." He caresses the sensitive, welting skin. "Don't make a sound and I'll reward you. What's your safe word?"

With a shaky voice, I reply, "Red."

He cracks me again and again until he's satisfied ten are enough. My ass is hot and tears have dripped onto the counter, but I was strong and didn't scream.

Patch stands me up when he sees my flushed, tear-soaked face. He doesn't like to see me cry so he wipes away my tears with compassion. Satisfied that no more fall, he grips my hair and pushes me onto the counter. I grip the opposite edge.

He stands behind me and kicks my feet apart until he can stand between them. My pelvic bones hold my weight painfully on the counter's edge, but I don't care to complain because I kind of like it. His fingers glide between my ass cheeks, over my asshole, and between my drenched pussy lips before delving deep into me. I wiggle, jutting my ass toward him as a plea for more. He pulls his fingers out but slips them further down between my lips until he reaches my clitoris.

I moan as his fingers tenderly rub tiny circles over my stiff button. His hand raises and he whacks my ass once more, jolting my thoughts away from my clit and back to the pain of my red-hot ass.

"I said to be quiet, didn't I?" He whispers as his fingers find my clit to continue their delicious assault. "I don't want you to make a sound until I tell you to cum. Do you understand?"

Knowing better, I say nothing; he told me not to make a sound. From past experience, to verbalize my understanding is cause for more swats. I simply nod the best I can despite my hair held in his vice-like grip. It isn't painful as much as immobilizing.

Patch pushes his fat thumb into my pussy. I tighten when he circles my clit. I try to remain calm and not cum but I'm so close, and he knows it. He won't stop until he's satisfied I obeyed his order and refused myself an orgasm.

He moves his hand and quickly fills me full of his thick, hard cock. My walls stretch and then clench as soon as he's buried deep. My breath escapes me. He holds still until I breathe.

"Don't let go of the counter, and don't lift your head."

He frees my hair and a matted wad quickly drapes over my face. I try to blow it away from my eyes but it doesn't move.

"I'm going to fuck you hard and fast; how you like. Not a sound. Don't cum until I permit it."

His pelvis rests against my ass as his hands slide along my skin and settle on my waist. He pulls back and makes good on his promise. He pounds into me. My fingertips barely hold the counter and my hip bones grate on the counter's edge.

Oh, fuck! I want to cum! It's right there. If I just let go, I'll cum so hard. Somehow, I manage to withhold the moans. At some point, I think I blackout but I can't be sure.

Oh, my God! Please let me cum!

He grabs my forearms and hisses, "Let go." When I do, he pulls them behind my back and holds my wrists tightly in one hand while his other presses on my lower back to pin me to the counter. He rams; hard, fast, incredibly fast.

"Tell me you're my slut!" he demands.

"I'm your slut!" I scream.

"My slut! My dirty little fucking slut." He slams a few more times and my pussy tightens around his cock. "Cum, whore! Fucking cum!"

A slow, steadily increasing scream builds as I let myself fall into the muscle clenching, mind-blowing euphoria of my climax. I hear him spit words at me but I have no idea what he's saying, and I don't care. My thoughts have sunk into blackness while my body floats high above the counter. I never want this to stop.

Patch wails, slams into me three more times, and then stiffens. His cock swells inside me and stretches my spasming pussy as it chokes him, desperate to keep the pulsing shaft wedged deep into me.

I'm exhausted, yet my mind is ripe with energy.

Patch's withered cock slips from me and we both groan. He releases my wrists, then grasps my hips to ensure my feet are firmly on the floor. He wraps his heavy arms over my shoulders and holds my back against his burly chest while I catch my breath.

Between breaths, he asks, "What am I going to do when you're not mine anymore; when you decide you only want Bash?"

"What do you mean? I'll always want you." I turn to look at his flushed face.

"There will come a day when you won't. When you and Bash decide to start a family, continuing what we have won't be feasible, and you know it." He sighs, then kisses my head. His eyes scan my body. "If you were mine—"

I snap at him. "You should keep in mind that I will never be yours. Bash allows us to love each other, and I'll allow you my body whenever you want, but he comes before you or Mack." I step back and look into his stoic face. "Please, don't suggest I be only yours."

"No, that's not what I was..." He groans frustratedly. "You're making a thing out of nothing. I was just saying that if you were mine—"

I raise my hand and shake my head to beg him not to continue. He holds up his hand to stop me from saying what he knows I'm about to.

He raises his voice. "Just hang on a minute, woman! Since you went there ... you know I love you. We all agreed it's okay that we love each other." He leans his back against the counter and calms his voice. "You will want something different in the future. I wasn't suggesting I was going to take you away from Bash. I was just—"

I cut him off. "You couldn't if you tried." I yank my pants up and wiggle my hips until the material slips into place.

Calmly, despite his flared nostrils, he asks, "Where is this coming from?"

I stop fussing with my pants to meet his eyes. "You said *if you were mine...*"

"Holy fuck, woman!" He groans and slaps his forehead. "Can't a man say something to you without you blowing it into something it's not? I wasn't suggesting I wanted you for myself. I was about to say that I'd never let you wear clothes if you were mine. But since you took this conversation in that direction..."

My shoulders sag. I feel like an idiot. "Well, I'm not yours," I insist. Before I can walk away, he has me by my arm. I freeze but don't turn to look at him.

"Don't walk away from me angry." His words are loud and stern. "Never walk away from me angry!"

I slowly turn my head to look at the fist wrapped tightly around my bicep. With my head tilted forward, I raise my eyes to meet his. "You'd be wise to let me go."

"Promise you won't walk away. We need to resolve this."

When my gaze falls back to the hold he has on me, he releases his grip and puts his hands in the air to surrender. I slowly walk to the fridge and lean against it with my arms crossed over my chest, and sport pursed lips.

He steps back and resumes his spot against the counter and rests the heels of his hands on the edge.

Perhaps I misunderstood him. I ask, "What did you mean when you said that thing about me not being yours anymore? When was I ever yours?"

He shakes his head and walks toward me, places his hands on my shoulders, and urges me to move aside. When I do, he opens the fridge and takes out two beers. He opens one and hands it to me, then opens the other and tosses the bent caps in the trash. We take long sips as he makes his way to the table and sits in the chair he sat in before we fucked. I take his lead and sit and attempt to peel this label too but sadly, it tears.

He slugs down a gulp from his bottle. "Every second I'm inside you, you belong to me. You're mine, and I'm yours."

I sip my beer.

He continues. "It's no secret I love you. Bash and Mack love you, too. Each of us loves you differently. When a man's inside you, at that moment, you belong to him. We all know Bash owns your heart, and if you had to choose, you'll always choose him. Nobody wants that to change. But in the moments when you do belong to us, it's nice to pretend." His gaze doesn't meet mine.

"Well, don't I look stupid?" I look down at the table and spread out the torn label. I run my fingers over it to flatten it out.

His voice softens. "You're not stupid. You simply didn't know how it is for us." He puts the bottle to his lips and tilts it until he's sucked back every drop. His eyes finally meet mine. "Well, I should get back to work. I'm sure the crew is slacking off since I'm not there to light a fire under their asses."

"Your people are excellent employees. They'll get the job done whether you're there spitting out orders or not."

He raises his brows and nods. "I know, but I should get going."

I rise and circle the table, and then flop my ass on his lap and wrap my arms around his head. "Let me assure you that I'm not considering having children any time soon. I'm sorry I flipped out. I don't know why I did that."

"Female hormones!" he says without hesitation, and I let out a harsh breath in protest. "Take it easy. Men will never understand how female hormones work, and women can't control them to no fault of their own." He laughs, then places a long kiss on my forehead. "Thanks for the memorable afternoon. Is your ass okay?"

I scoff. "Tough guy, you'd have to hit me harder than that to break me down." I run my fingers through his army-style haircut. "I belong to Bash first but I also belong to you and Mack. I'm a spoiled woman; loved by three sexy, hunky men."

"I would move Heaven and Earth for you; bring you the moon and the stars."

I cup his face in my palms and press my forehead against his. "I would never ask you to do something that extreme." I kiss his nose. "But having my very own star would be freaking awesome! Then again, I'm not sure where I'd keep it."

He lifts me to my feet as he rises. "I'll work on that."

He places one finger under my chin and lifts my face so he can plant a loving kiss on my lips. He rushes off and leaves me feeling lonely.

Chapter 3

I put the tools back in Bash's toolbox, then take a shower. Just as I'm leaving the bathroom, I hear my phone singing in the kitchen. My feet slap on the floor as I run down the hall. I turn the corner and *BAM*!

My feet slide out from beneath me and I thud to the floor. I'm sprawled out and shocked by my clumsiness but sigh with relief that I don't immediately feel any critical pain. I crawl my way to the counter. I reach up but the ringing has stopped.

I tap Bash's name and press the phone to my ear as I lean back against the cabinet. As it rings, I assess the red mark on my forearm that will surely worsen. I rub it and that seems to help.

"Hi, Goldie." I can tell he's smiling just by his tone. "What have you been up to?"

"Hi," I reply. "Patch came over and fucked the hell out of me so I had to take another shower. As I was getting out, I heard my phone ring in the kitchen. Well, I met the floor on my race to answer." I laugh.

He chuckles while he asks, "Are you hurt?"

"No, not really." I glance at my arm. "Just a bruise."

"Did you at least enjoy your time with Patch?" he asks.

"I did," I reply with a softness in my voice. We should consider putting rubber bumpers around the edge of the island. My hip bones are bruised."

He laughs. "So, do you want me to put rubber bumpers on all the counters or just the island?"

"Maybe we can get Patch to limit his play radius to the island to save on the cost of rubber." I stand and get the ice bag from the freezer and mold it around my forearm, then sit on an island stool. "So, what's up?"

"What else are you up to?" he asks.

I debate. "I was going to paint the trim on the old mirror I bought for our bedroom. Other than that, clean and catch up on the laundry."

"I ran a load through the washer but forgot to run it through the dryer." He clears his throat and says something but the phone isn't near his mouth. He returns. "Sorry, Goldie. That was my boss. I was hoping to be done so I could help Patch down some dead trees to stock for firewood but I'm going to be here for a few more hours."

He shuffles some papers and then says something away from the phone. He sighs and says, "I'm calling to suggest that I pick up some Chinese food on my way home. We can invite Patch and Mack, too—have a family night. What do you think?"

"Me, not cooking? You won't hear me complain." I celebrate with a body wiggle. "I'll text the guys to ask if they can make it. I'll ask Mack if Shaina can join us."

"Sounds great. Just text me the headcount." He pauses. "Babe, I have to let you go."

"Okay, don't work too hard."

"I'm sitting at a desk. This is not hard work. Keeping up with Patch while he downs trees is hard work," he chuckles. "Okay, text me later. Love you!"

"I love you," I say but I think he hung up too quickly to have heard it.

After I send texts to both Mack and Patch, I slip on a loose-fitting knee-length dress, put my hair in a ponytail, and start speed cleaning.

***

The guys and Shaina should all be here in fifteen minutes. I could set my clock to the brothers. They're always on time.

I don't know how they do it. I can plan with plenty of time to spare but somehow I still manage to be late.

I open the door and step aside. Bash has his hands full of food bags and his satchel hangs by his elbow and it looks heavy. He jogs through the downpouring rain while he tries to keep the food bags dry.

He rushes in and kisses me as he kicks off his shoes and kicks them under the bench. I take two of the bags and set them on the dining room table that I already pre-set. He sets his satchel on the bench, then grabs me and nestles me in his arms.

"How much time do we have?" He lifts his wrist to check his watch.

"Not enough time for what you're thinking." I wiggle from his clutches.

He pouts while his arms raise at his sides. "I can be fast!" His come-hither grin has me debating whether to lift my skirt or not. "Better yet, I bet I can get you off before they arrive."

I glance at the kitchen clock shaped like an apple. "We don't have time. They'll be here any minute." I open the sturdy paper bags and take out the cardboard containers. The smell fills my nostrils and my mouth waters. "What has you so excited?"

His eyes narrow and he pours himself a glass of water. "I kept picturing you getting fucked against this counter." He taps the island and takes a long drink, nearly emptying the glass.

"If only I had taken pictures." My eyes scan his body. "I suppose your imagination will have to suffice."

"After they leave, I'm going to make you cum on my face," he promises as he lifts my chin. "I love you, Goldie."

I whisper, "You'd better!"

Three heavy-handed knocks interrupt our moment. The solid, hand-carved door swings open. Shaina enters first; Mack and Patch follow.

Shaina leans toward me with her bright red lips and feigns a kiss on my cheek, then hands me a bottle of red wine. "Here you go, doll." She kisses Bash and wipes the lipstick from his lips. "Goldilocks, crack that shit so we can get this party going."

Bash seems unaffected by her suggestive touch but their gaze lingers. He offers to take the bottle when he notices I've been studying their silent communication.

Mack wraps his thick arms around me and tilts me back quickly. My screech quickly turns to laughter. I'm safely held in his arms. He plants a long kiss on my lips.

Patch's deep voice rings out. "Hey! Share the love, brother."

"Your lips are sweet as honey." Mack lifts me upright and hands me off to Patch. I'm still grinning from the way Mack swung me with such ease like I weigh nothing.

"It's good seeing you again," Patch says while he grins flirtatiously.

He scans my body, then his hand glides up my back and his fingers weave into my hair. He grips a wad and jerks my head to assert his dominance—like there was ever any question. My pussy clenches. He loves to be in control. When he does things like this, it turns me on as quickly as flipping on a light switch. He snickers when my lower lip quivers.

"Did you miss me?" he whispers seductively brushing his lips against mine, teasingly. I whimper and he pulls his lips away. "You fucking want more, don't you? You're an insatiable little whore." One side of his mouth lifts and he winks playfully.

My nipples are hard as marbles and my panties are damp. "Yes, but I'm *your* whore."

"If you two are done, we can sit and eat," Bash says as he walks past us with the salt and pepper in hand. "You can continue this later for the after-dinner entertainment, but right now, I'm famished. Let's do some power eating."

Patch releases my hair. I run my fingers through it to release any knots that may have formed. I'm still a little frazzled when I sit beside Bash.

He leans toward me so I lean in. He runs the back of his finger down my cheek. "You're so fucking horny right now. Aren't you?"

I swallow while my cheeks flush and a smile lights up my face. "Most definitely!"

He smirks. "Are you rethinking your decision not to let me make you cum before they arrived?"

I bite my lip and reach for the closest cardboard box, hoping it'll take my mind off my pussy's yearn for either mouth or cock.

We chit-chat and talk about what each of us did today. I love how our conversations always lead to a funny childhood story. At one point, I almost choke on a bite of General Tao Chicken because I laugh so hard.

We're stuffed but still manage to eat fortune cookies. Bash takes the conversation in a different direction. "I asked you all here so we can discuss our relationships." Everyone's attention turns to him. "We all know everyone has access to Goldie, which makes her very happy, so in turn, makes me happy. Shaina is also available to everyone, I assume."

She nods with enthusiasm.

I interrupt. "Where is this going?"

He takes my hand and continues. "Patch, you're in love with Goldie, and I'm okay with that, as you know. She has a big heart and has room for all of us. You agreed that hers and my relationship will always come first and I appreciate that, but…"

Patch glances my way. I frown and shake my head because I have no idea what he's about to say. Patch leans back in his chair and exhales heavily. His fear of losing me may be a sentence away. A muscle in his jaw twitches and his eyes drop to the tiny paper that suggests his fortune.

Bash looks at Patch. "Well, you're madly in love with her. It can't be denied. You know I love you, brother…" He pauses to examine the anticipation on everyone's faces and ends with Patch's questioning eyes. "I can't think of anyone I'd rather share my Goldie's heart with than you…" He pauses again and jokes, "Other than Mack, of course. He's a far better human than you, but his heart belongs to Shaina."

Patch takes a loud breath, then clears his throat before he looks at Mack and agrees. "A far better human indeed."

Shaina gloats and hugs Mack's arm. He leans in and pecks her forehead. She looks at me and smiles, so I return the gesture but my smile isn't aimed at her relationship with Mack; I'm more excited to know what Bash will say next.

Patch's scratchy voice breaks through the pause. "What are you getting at, brother?" He sits up and leans his elbows on the table while he folds the tiny paper.

"A proposal." Bash also leans his elbows on the table but weaves his fingers together. "Patch, move in with us. It doesn't have to be full-time. That's up to you. We can give it a try and see how it goes."

Bash and I have talked about Patch moving in but the conversations were fleeting and I didn't think he was serious. Of course, I would love to have Patch here with us.

Bash adds, "We'll have to work out the fine details like where you're going to sleep, for instance. The guest room is an option. Goldie has to be beside me at night. I don't care if you're in the bed with us but she *dreams* beside me. We can work through any issues as we come to them."

Patch's perpetually pissed-off-at-the-world expression eases into a rarely witnessed toothy smile. He stands and Bash follows his lead. They meet and embrace with slaps on the back as men often do when they hug.

Patch beams. "I love you, brother. Thank you."

Bash replies. "I love you, too, big galoot."

Shaina, in her overzealous way, asks, "Well, Goldilocks? What do you say? Do you want Patch to move in? You know he's going to fuck you raw every chance he gets." She turns back to Mack with raised eyebrows. "That boy likes to fuck hard!"

Mack agrees.

Patch and Bash separate and look at me as if anticipating whether I'm okay with this or not. Expressionless, I look at

Shaina, then Mack, who lifts his eyebrows to suggest I answer. When I look at Bash, his grin beams; he knows I'm all in. Patch, on the other hand, has never looked so vulnerable. Does he fear rejection? Would it crush him if I said no?

"Yes!" I stand, and they hug me and pin me between them with Patch facing me. "Of course, I want you here."

Shaina interrupts. "So, does that mean you're distancing yourself from Mack? I mean, if you're too exhausted with these two sexual beasts pawing at you all the time, you aren't going to have any energy left for Mack."

I turn my face but Patch's arm blocks me from meeting her eyes. "I'm sure I'll find some energy at some point..." I wiggle to get free so I can look at the two still seated at the table. "If I can ever get away from these two long enough. Don't worry, Mack, I'm not going to disown you."

Mack grins. "You'd better not forget about me! But I'm not worried. I know you'll miss having my cock in your ass."

I feel my face blush. Patch takes my hand and leads me out the front door.

"What are you doing? It's raining!" I complain.

He picks me up wedding style and carries me back through the doorway, setting me down. "I was just making it official."

Mack says, "That's how a groom carries his bride over the threshold, dumbass!"

The two men glare at each other and then laugh.

Shaina asks, "What happens if Patch finds a woman he wants to date? Is he still going to live here?"

"If he wants to," I say with a shrug. "If it comes up, he can decide then."

Patch takes his seat at the table and looks at Shaina. "I might distance myself so I can get to know her to see if it's a sure thing or not. If it becomes something more substantial, we'll sit down and vote whether she can join us as one big happy fucking family, literally."

I feel my heart sink. "If you fall in love with someone else and she refuses to join our big happy fucking family, will that be it for you and me?"

Patch bites his lip, looks down at the tiny folded paper, and tips his head to the side. "Why don't we cross that bridge if it ever comes up."

Bash calmly says, "That sounds fair. We wouldn't expect you not to be with someone else if it's what you want to do."

Mack shoots his arm in the air like a child in a classroom. "I have a question." Everyone looks at him. "What about kids? Who is going to impregnate Goldilocks when the time comes that she wants to pop out a few tiny screaming humans?"

"Wait a minute!" My arm waves at Mack. My lungs feel overly filled with excruciatingly hot air. "What if I don't want kids?"

The room falls silent. Bash looks at me and squints. "She'll have my baby first if it's what she desires."

Patch asks me, "You don't want kids?"

I shrug and laugh. "I'm twenty-three years old and nowhere near ready for shitty diapers, baby screams throughout the night, or teething." My heart pounds hard at the thought of all that responsibility.

Shaina puts her hand on mine. "Goldilocks, you'd have lots of help. It's not like you'd be doing it alone." Her kind words don't help my heart to slow to a more acceptable beat.

Bash rubs his hand on my back. "If you don't want to have children, that's okay with me. I would love to hear the sounds of children's laughs echoing off these walls but it's not a deal changer if it's not your dream, too."

"I—I do want kids *one day*. Not now! But one day." I swallow. "Maybe in about five years."

Patch stands and walks to the kitchen and collects six beers from the fridge. He walks around the table and offers each of us a bottle. Shaina seems annoyed that we have chosen to drink beer but haven't finished our glasses of wine. I didn't care for the taste but I'll empty my glass to be polite. Of course, I'll chase it with beer.

Patch remains standing at his spot at the table and holds up his beer. "To a future built on love and understanding."

Everyone clinks bottles before they shout, "Cheers!" then swig from their bottles.

The thought hits me: where the hell am I going to find the energy to keep up with two sexually charged men?

After everyone has left, I fill the sink with water and slip the plates in. Bash cleans the table, then wraps his arms around my shoulders. He kisses the top of my head and rests his cheek on it.

"Goldie, I love you so much. Are you sure you're on board with Patch living here?"

I attempt to turn but wait for him to loosen his hug. "Yes, I want him here. I love both of you so much."

He kisses me softly, scoops me in his arms, and lays me out on the island. He grabs my calf and uses it to turn me into position. He stands between my dangling calves and locks eyes with me. He slowly lifts my skirt up my thighs.

"No panties?" He watches his thumb caress my smooth pussy lips. "I like that." I giggle. "What's so funny?"

"They were damp so I took them off after dinner," I reply, then snicker. "You and Patch are so similar it's scary." He shakes his head not understanding why I think that. "I wasn't wearing panties this afternoon and Patch reacted the same way you did."

"Well, we are brothers." He smiles but it fades when his thumb delves deeper between my folds.

He slides a stool under his butt and sits. He lifts my legs and places them over his shoulders and rests his elbows on the counter. He reaches over my tummy and weaves his fingers together, essentially holding me in place. He leans in and pecks his puffy lips to each pussy lip, then glides his tongue to where his thumb was. He licks, sucks, and flicks until I've screamed through a powerful orgasm.

Bash scoops me up and takes me to the bedroom, strips me, and tucks me into bed. He undresses and slides in behind me. He didn't ask for his pleasure; his desire was my pleasure.

Sleep comes quickly.

Chapter 4

My workday felt like one of the longest days of my life. The last thing I wanted to do was cook dinner. When Mack called to suggest we meet for pizza at Fazio's Restaurant, I had mixed emotions.

We've never gone out in public together—all four of us—and I'm worried people will stare or worse, say something rude about our relationship. Most of the townsfolk have made it absolutely clear they don't approve. There are a handful of people who accept us. I wish everyone did.

Patch is already at the restaurant and seated when we arrive. This is our first family dinner in a public restaurant since our secret lifestyle hit the rumor mill and spread like wildfire. I didn't want to go but the guys insisted we stop hiding and get back to living among the masses.

As I approach the table with Mack and Bash in tow, Patch stands and pulls a chair out for me. Before I sit, he pecks a kiss on my lips.

Gasps and hushed voices fill the room. Patch's eyelids flutter and a muscle in his jaw clenches but he smiles despite them. I sit while he scans the diners for anyone staring at us. Nobody meets his eyes. He sits as do Bash and Mack who seem unaffected by the whispers followed by glances from entire tables of people.

Patch already ordered for us since he knows what we all like on our pizza and that we enjoy beer. As soon as we're seated, Bash reaches for my hand and holds it. I stare at how long his fingers are. They make my hand look so tiny and delicate.

"Are you okay?" Bash draws my attention. His head tips toward me with concern in his eyes.

"My hand looks childlike next to yours." I brush my hair behind my ear and smile while he assesses our hands.

"You do have puny hands," he snickers.

The waitress sets our bottles in front of us and disappears into the kitchen. When I look around the table at each guy, they look happy and oblivious to the whispers that contain my name and occasionally theirs. I know they can hear it but they choose to ignore it.

I don't want to be talked about. I suppose I lied to Sarah when I said I don't let other people's judgments affect me. I have to get out of here.

"Excuse me." I stand and tuck my purse under my arm. It's hard not to run when the stares follow me as I pass each table. I shove the women's washroom door open and rush inside. The moment the door closes, I take a deep breath and hold it. Slowly, I let it seep out while I look at myself in the mirror, silently giving myself courage.

A woman and small child come out of a stall. The mother is smiling until she sees me standing at the counter. She holds the child up so she can wash her hands. Her eyes dart to me when I run my fingers through my hair so I don't look like an idiot just standing in the women's washroom. She sets her down and hands her a paper towel, then turns to wash her own hands.

"Hi," the little girl bounces as she dries her hands. Her yellow dress swings and she touches mine. "You're wearing a dress, too. Mine's yellow and it's shorter than yours but I like it."

The mother hisses, "Shirley, don't bother the lady."

"She's no bother," I say while I smile at the curly-haired tot. "Your dress is much prettier than mine," I pause, "and those shoes are fancy too."

She smiles and tap dances her shiny shoes while she watches her feet. I look up at the mom and she's glaring at me.

My smile falls away and I tilt my head and brush my hair behind my ear.

"Let's go, Shirley. It's very dirty in here." She guides the tot by her shoulders and pulls the door open. With another disgusted leer at me, she walks out.

I swallow hard, then wash my hands and splash some cool water on my face. A tall, heavyset woman walks in and stops walking toward the stalls when she sees me dabbing my face with a paper towel.

"Hey, listen," she says as she nears me. "People are assholes who seem to need something to humiliate to make themselves feel good about their shitty lives." She puts her hand on my shoulder. "Before you walked in, they were whispering about how fat I've gotten this year."

I grimace. "People are assholes. I'm sorry they do that to you."

"No worries," she says with a smile. "I don't let it bother me. My thyroid went haywire and then my MS flared up. I've been riding a recliner for a while now." She laughs. "But I'm here. I'm alive, and I'm still smiling."

She takes a few steps closer. "You're a smart, grown-ass woman who can make her own life decisions. You love them and it's obvious how much they adore you, so don't let other people drag you down. This is your life, live it your way. Now let me give you a hug; you look like you can use one."

I turn and she wraps her arms around me and sways slightly. Her softness and warmth comfort me. She steps back and smiles. "There, now go live your best life and don't let the shallow-minded people bring you down."

She goes into a stall and I resume staring at myself in the mirror. I dab the water off my forehead, then clench my jaw. "You're right," I say to the woman who's now peeing. As I walk out, I call back to her, "Thank you!"

With my head held higher, I walk with purpose to three men that are pleased I've returned.

Patch leans toward me and whispers. "Are you okay?"

My smile is one-sided and I tilt my head. "I'm great, actually."

He twirls a lock of my hair as he memorizes my face. The waitress interrupts when she places a king-sized pizza in the center of the table after moving the condiments caddy.

We eat and laugh as families do. I take my cues from the guys and ignore any whispers of my name or stares meant to intimidate us. It's a much better dining experience than I thought it would be. Before we leave, I smile at the lovely woman from the washroom who showed me how to be courageous. She returns my smile, then waves. I wave, then allow Bash to usher me outside.

Mack and Patch drive back to the main house, and Bash and I go to our house.

He shuts down the engine and the headlights flick off. It's very dark but the tease of moonlight peeking around the treetops brushes Bash's face. His eyes shadow and he looks different; scarier and larger somehow.

The serenade of cicada's resume their screams and the night birds screech as they zip through the evening sky. A light breeze has the trees weaving in a slow dance. Through the clearing, tiny white caps brighten the river as it rushes over the rocks.

The back of his fingers caress down my cheek and my heart flutters. The orchestra fades into the background. He looks at me as if this is the first time he's seeing my face. He tucks a loose tuft of hair behind my ear and then kisses me with the softness of a kitten's fur.

"I'm going to make love to you tonight," he whispers.

My chest feels full. I kiss him more vigorously and put my knee on my seat. I lift my skirt and pull my panties off while he fusses with his belt, button, and zipper, and then lifts his ass to pull his jeans down to mid-thigh.

Neither of us wants to wait until we get in the house.

He wraps his hand around the back of my head and pulls my lips to his. I fling my leg over his lap and brace my shin on the door's armrest. I seem to have way more skirt than I thought, and both of us wrestle with it. I laugh and soon he laughs, too. Our lips part so I can jostle my legs while he pulls the skirt from between us.

I lift and he guides his rock-hard shaft between my slick folds. We moan against each other's lips as I slowly envelop him.

His eyes bear proof of his love for me. I lift and lower unhurriedly so I can savor every invading inch of him. I breathe in his breath—his soul—and give myself to him.

"I love you," I whisper. My pussy feels fuller as though his cock swells.

Bash moans on my lips. "You're my world, Goldie. You have my heart." I increase my pace and he moans again. "I love you so fucking much!"

His arms wrap around my back and pull me against him. He tries to hold me still but I glide my hips back and forth and press my lips just beneath his ear. It must be the hot button spot because his head tips back against the seat.

"Goldie…" He moans and holds me tighter. "Stop. Not yet. Please." He's desperate to regain control but I continue to rock my hips. "Oh, fuck!" He groans. "Don't stop! Don't stop!"

His body tenses and his arms squeeze tighter. His face contorts as if in pain as he loses himself in a powerful climax. His cock swells inside me. I savor every jerk of his muscles and twitch of his cock. I watch his expression slowly ease as he comes back to me with a long, emptying groan.

My forehead rests against his. He swallows between ragged breaths. His arms have eased their grip, but he hasn't released me. I wrap my arms around his neck.

I'll never forget his whisper in the dark. "Don't ever let go."

"Never," I reply without a voice, but he hears me nonetheless.

I have yet to free his spent penis but it's time; my knees ache. After a gentle kiss, I flop onto the passenger's seat.

He whispers, "We should go in."

I reply, "We should have a bath."

"That sounds amazing." His eyebrows raise and he grabs the door handle. "Last one in is a rotten egg!"

He flings open his door, hops out, and nearly trips when his pants drop to his calves. I whip open my door and hit the ground running. I'm halfway to the house and he's catching up quickly.

Just as I leap for the steps, he grabs my waist and yanks me back, then gently shoves me away from the porch. He leaps up the steps three at a time. He fights with his key and opens the door just as I grab hold of his shirt.

I'm laughing so hard I can barely move, let alone run. He steps into the house and turns, twisting his shirt around his waist. He trips over the bench Patch made and falls onto the seat—thankfully not the floor—but his wipeout benefits me. He grabs at the air and almost catches my skirt, which he would have used to hold me back. I screech like a teenager being chased by a horny boy.

His feet slam the floor behind me as we race to the master bathroom. I make it through the door first and leap into the tub and sprawl out on the bottom. We both gasp for breath and laugh hysterically.

He leans on the counter and pants. "You start the water and I'll go shut the front door. I'd hate to discover a raccoon wandering around and causing havoc in the kitchen."

"You have to admit that would be funny!" I climb out of the tub and sit on the ledge.

"It would, but…" He crosses the room, palms my chin, and kisses me. "But I plan on making love to you in our bed tonight and not chase a raccoon around the house."

Bash makes good on his promise to make love to me. We connected on a much deeper level than we ever have. At one point, I couldn't tell where I ended and he began. We were one. My heart was so full. I cried and I don't know why.

As I lie beside him and watch his eyes shift beneath his lids, as if he were watching a movie as he sleeps, I can't help but feel my heart break for him.

Why does he choose to love only me and yet I share my heart with two others? Why doesn't it hurt him when he sees me in the throes of passion at their doing? Why do I allow it? How can I be so cruel to him?

He's so good to me and loves me without limitation. I love him. I do.

And I love Patch. Mack also holds a special place in my heart. Each man loves me differently; no one is better than the other, just different. I desire all of them.

All I know is that I don't deserve him.

Chapter 5

It's a warm, sunny day and I'm swimming with the Bear brothers in the river. The sunlight reflects off the water like it would an immaculate diamond. I can feel their love and respect for one another.

The men look into my eyes. Each reaches into my soul, taking pieces to keep for himself. They don't realize they're breaking me. They take and take, but it's Patch who grabs the biggest piece. He smiles boastfully at his prize until it begins to crack.

Every piece of me shatters into a million tiny shards and slowly floats downstream. I pull the broken pieces of myself back together and reach for a rock. I look back and expect to see all three men, but only Mack remains.

Broken pieces of Patch and Bash float past me. I reach for them but I'm unsure which pieces I should collect. I grab at them as they float away. I open my hand and expect to see many shards, but it's empty.

I startle when my alarm rudely interrupts the bizarre dream before I can figure out the message it brings, if any. I sit up quickly and search for Bash but he's not here. He likely already left for work at the paper.

My pajama top is stuck to my sweat-soaked skin, so I pull it over my head and toss it in the hamper as I make my way to the coffee pot. I'm thankful Bash left me half a pot still hot on the burner. He must have forgotten to fill his travel mug to sip during his drive into town.

After I peek through the window to ensure nobody's outside, I take my shirtless self and my coffee onto the porch to watch the sun reflect off the lazy river a mere hundred feet from where I sit. My dream weighs heavy in my thoughts, but I tilt my face toward the sun and feel my sorrows melt away.

***

My six-hour shift at the hospital zips by. I've been in surgery most of the time, which excites me. Lizzy and I have assisted Dr. Kacey for a few weeks. He doesn't have much of a sense of humor and glares at us when we joke around. He's hard to get to know and strikes me as a lonely old man.

Lizzy is hilarious; always cracks jokes, does ridiculous things, and chooses to wear the goofiest cartoon nurse's shirts. She's wacky and I love her.

We enter the female staff locker room together. Lizzy's locker is three down from mine. She flips hers open and snatches her phone from her purse. Her fingers tap and her eyes stare at the screen, she sits but only one buttock lands on the bench. In my peripheral, I see her topple over. She lands on the hard floor on her hip and shoulder.

"Oh, my God! Are you all right?" I reach out to grab her but she doesn't accept my hand because she's still typing on her phone. Her face is red from laughter. "Why are you laughing?"

She finally looks away from her phone and bursts into uncontrollable laughter. I laugh because it's contagious. Soon, both of us drip tears on our flushed faces. I sit on the bench and cross my legs to stop myself from peeing. When I voice my struggle, Lizzy snorts and curls into a ball, hoping to alleviate the painful tummy muscle spasms.

Eventually, we settle down and Lizzy plops her entire ass on the bench. She asks, "What are you up to later?"

I swap my nursing shoes for my street shoes. "I don't have any set plans." I glance at the clock on the wall. "Mack's gone back to the worksite. Bash is working at the paper and I don't know when he'll be home. I'm going to get one of the spare rooms ready because Patch might spend the night. We asked him to move in."

"Oh, yeah? Lucky girl!" She tilts her head and bats her eyelashes. "I know what you're going to be doing later." She rocks her hips on the bench and moans. "Oh, yes! Fuck me! Harder, baby!" She clutches her breasts and throws her head back. "Make me cum! Make me c—"

She halts when Kate, a much older nurse, appears from behind the row of lockers wearing an angry expression. "That is inappropriate for the workplace! Behave yourselves, ladies."

She disappears around the corner and we bite our lips to prevent from erupting into another fit of laughter.

"That woman needs to get laid," I whisper.

Lizzy repeats her sexy bucking, silently this time. She stops when I slap her arm playfully. She feigns severe pain and rubs her arm while she playfully sulks.

"You should meet the guys, especially Patch," I suggest with a wink.

She stops humping the bench to flash me a whatever expression.

I smile and tilt my head. "He'd really like you."

She squints. "Why? I mean, not why would he like me, because, shit…" She pauses to showcase her body by waving her hands up and down her torso. "Look at this body! I'm a hot little number." She bursts into laughter. "Seriously? Why would he like me when he has you? I mean, fuck, look at you!" Her hands gesture toward my body.

"Thank you," I say as I finger-brush back a lock of hair that slipped free from my ponytail a few hours ago and has been irritating me ever since. "Patch has a thing for redheads. At least, that's what Mack told me. His ex is a redhead. I've never met her."

She stands and fusses with her bags in her locker, then shoves her phone in her purse. "And if he likes me, and I like him, then what?" She stands with her hands perched on her hips.

I shrug. "He could do a lot worse." She stands tall and smiles proudly, then tips her head to thank me. "If the feelings were mutual," I pause to make sure I mean what I'm about to say, "go for it."

Her eyes assess my face for a hint of humor but she doesn't find it. "You would be okay if I fucked him?"

I nod. "Yeah, I think so. I mean, they're allowed to have relationships with other women as long as they're upfront about it and don't hide it. Protection is a must."

She tilts her head and assesses me. "Are you hoping I'll date him or should I just fuck him? And don't you think that would put a strain on our friendship?"

I consider her question while I tuck that hair back again, but it only falls free the moment I release it. "I really like you. You're honest and upfront about everything. You're well-grounded and mature yet still a toddler." She curls her lips inward and smiles to show all of her front teeth—something a child would do. "See, you're a toddler but you're a fun toddler. You're my best friend."

"Okay, so if I hopped on his lap and started making out with that huge hunk of a man—at least, I think he's massive if I judge by your pictures—you'd be fine with it?"

"He is massive, and yeah, I think so."

She shakes her head. "Well, I'm not ready to be in a steady relationship with anyone at the moment."

"I can respect that. What are your plans for the rest of the afternoon?" I ask while I twist the loose lock and tuck it beneath the hair that's conformed to my wishes. It'll look weird but I don't care at this point.

She shrugs. "Nothing much. My mom's been on a tirade lately, so I'd rather not go home. She didn't get the promotion she was seeking. I might go shopping to burn up some time. Besides, I could use some new bras." She pulls off her shirt and jostles her bra straps. "This one's old and stretched out. My boobies are supporting the bra, not the other way around. You should come with! We can make an evening out of it."

I place my shoes in my locker, take out my purse and fling the strap over my shoulder. I'm trying not to look at her nearly nude breasts. I glance at her face but my sights drop to her bra. My tummy flutters and I jolt my eyes away. I look in my locker and collect my sweater, and then close and lock it.

"Are you embarrassed by my tits?" She scoffs and lowers her voice after realizing she said that rather loud. "You have sex with three men regularly and you're embarrassed by my bra-laden female breasts? What's wrong with you?" She scoffs again and drops her shirt.

"You're a girl." I turn toward her and bow. "You have very nice breasts." I finally meet her eyes. "Drop it, okay?"

"Fine!" she mutters and rolls her eyes. "Thanks for the compliment. I love my little titties." She gropes her breasts, and that's my cue to depart.

"See you!" I say as I fling open the door and walk through. I get halfway down the corridor and turn around. When I get back into the locker room, she's dressed in a form-fitted white camisole and a dark red zip-up hoodie. She's wiggling into a pair of faded, torn at the knee, snug-fitting jeans.

"You're back!" she says with surprise and slips her arms through the straps of her backpack and jostles it into place. "Did you change your mind and want to see my tits again?" She shakes her shoulders and they jiggle.

"No!" My eyes scan her breasts hidden beneath the white shirt. It's obvious she isn't wearing a bra because her nipples stand at attention. "Why don't you come to my house? We keep saying we're going to get together outside of work but we never do. We're both free tonight. Why not now? I mean, if your titties can bear holding up the bra for one more day."

She debates, but only for a few seconds. "Yeah, okay, but I'm not wearing the bra!" She opens the door and I walk through with her in tow. "I'll follow you. I'm parked in the back."

"Me too," I reply.

She slips her arm in mine and yammers on about how excited she is to finally see my house that I've told her all about but she's only seen in photos.

Chapter 6

Nobody's home when we pull in. Lizzy parks her burgundy Jeep beside my car and gets out while she looks in awe at the house. I gather my bag and lead the way up the porch. I love her reaction. I'm so proud of this house.

"Oh, my God! You lucky bitch! Look at this fucking place! It's like…." She turns and spots the river through the clearing. "It's fucking beautiful here. How can you stand it?"

"Come on in," I shout to get her attention before she wanders toward the river.

She ascends the stairs while admiring the exterior and the hand-carved front door. "Oh, that's it! I'm moving in!"

"You might have to share a bed with Patch since he's moving in, too."

"That might be fun!" She laughs. "He's fucking hot in your pictures. He has this naughty bad boy look about him."

I set my bag on the bench near the door and she follows suit. She slips out of her shoes but leaves them where someone might trip on them. Patch will surely scowl and place them properly if he comes home.

Lizzy follows me as I show her around the house and gush at how much I love the guys for their kindness. She's in awe of the woodwork. She claims that Patch could make a killing by selling to people. I explain that he's too humble to take more money than he thinks is fair.

After I show her the upstairs and the living room, we head to the kitchen where I pour us each a glass of white wine. I show her the rooms and conclude the tour in the master bedroom. She stands just inside the door and bites her lip while she stares at the dark red, duvet-covered, king-size bed.

She sips her wine and whispers, "So, this is where all the magic happens."

Her sideways grin and dreamy eyes have me wishing I could read her thoughts. What is she picturing? Does she imagine herself being mauled by one Bear brother or all three? Or does she see me naked and lost in the pleasures of three sinfully sexy men?

I clear my throat to get her attention. Her cheeks flush. She sips her wine and follows me into the bathroom. As soon as she enters, her face lights up. She sets her wine on the counter between the double sinks and climbs into the huge tub. She lies back as if she were soaking her weary bones.

"Would you like to take a bath? You're welcome to," I say with a smile. "Bath sheets are in the closet. Salts and multiple essential oils are over there; personally, I favor the Lavender."

She sits up and stares through the large one-way window beside the tub. "I might never leave this tub if I lived here."

"It's a good thing you don't live here then." I shrug when she looks at me questioningly. "You'd be a shriveled mess." We both laugh as she climbs out.

We sink ourselves into the Adirondack chairs on the deck and sip our refilled wine glasses. The alcohol eases away the anxieties of the workday.

The sun hovers low in the sky when Patch's truck pulls in. He parks behind my car but ogles us as he exits his truck.

As he lazily struts toward the porch with a duffle bag slung over his shoulder, he looks sexier than I've ever seen him. It's not that he looks any different than he does any other day, but the way Lizzy's breath catches has me admiring him as the sexy being I know him to be.

His faded, snug-fit jeans do nothing to hide the bulge of his groin, nor his thick, muscular thighs or firm round ass. His shirt is draped over his shoulder beneath the bag's strap. In the rare places his skin isn't smudged with dirt, he glistens with the sweat from a hard day's work. He has a five o'clock shadow that I'm sure he'll take care of soon since he prefers to be smoothly shaven.

She whispers under her breath. "Oh. My. God!" She looks wide-eyed at me before her gaze returns to him. "*That's* Patch?"

"Yes, ma'am," I reply as his worn-in steel-toed boots thump with each step up the stairs.

He tosses the bag toward the door and it lands with a thud. His eyes are fixed on Lizzy. I don't blame him; she's gorgeous and her fiery red hair glimmers in the sagging evening sun.

Despite her efforts to appear nonchalant, she clutches the armrests of her Adirondack chair and swallows hard. Her eyes follow his every step.

Patch's attention directs to me. He leans in and kisses my lips tenderly.

I ask, "Who's bike do you have in the back of your truck?"

He looks at the black and silver crotch-rocket. As if remembering something upsetting, his brow scrunches and he sighs heavily. "It's Mack's."

"I didn't know he had a bike?"

"It's been in the shed in desperate need of repairs for a few years. I didn't think he'd ever want to ride again after someone clipped him and it nearly wrote the bike off. He kept all of his skin thanks to his leathers but he broke some fingers. He was bruised all down his left side." He groans as he looks at the bike. "Anyway, since he's out of town he called to ask if I could pick it up at the shop."

I shake my head. "I don't like it."

"Me either, but he's a grown man." He sits in the chair across from Lizzy, leans back, and scans her up and down. "And who might you be?" His voice is deep with an easiness to it that has her thighs squeezed together. He crosses his feet but his knees are spread. One hand rests on his thick thigh and the other rests on the armrest.

I clear my throat. "Patch, meet my friend Lizzy. We work together at the hospital. You've heard me talk about her on more than one occasion."

"I can finally put a beautiful face to the name." He leans forward to stretch his hand toward her while his eyes blaze into hers. "Hello, Lizzy." Her name rolls off his tongue.

"Hi." She shakes his hand. He hesitates before he releases it. She clears her throat, slips her hand from his, and snuggles back into the chair. "You built an incredible home. It's fabulous."

His hand—stained with dirt from a hard day's work—strokes his thigh, drawing her eyes down toward his bulging crotch. He's testing her with subtle gestures to see if she'll show a sexual interest in him. Either that or he's simply toying with her. She's fallen right into his trap, and the twitch of his lips proves it.

He asks, "What's your favorite thing about this house, Lizzy?"

She looks up from his thigh and fixes her eyes on me. "The tub, I think." She smiles wide and her cheeks flush.

"She hopped in it. I said she could take a bath but—"

"If I did, I'd still be in it." Her smile shows off her beautiful white teeth which have Patch licking his lips.

"So, Lizzy…" He sits forward, and she looks wide-eyed at him. He takes my glass of wine and sips it while he seduces her with his dominant demeanor. "What brings you home with our Goldie?"

"I had nothing to do and considered going bra shopping but…" She pauses when she notices his eyes locked on her breasts. Her nipples are like heat-seeking missiles aimed for Patch. "As you can see, I didn't go."

His eyes jerk back to meet hers. He tips his head as if to say touché. She got one up on him and he's intrigued. There's definitely a connection between them. Any concerns I might have about jealousy are quashed by my naughty thoughts.

"Don't ever cover those gorgeous breasts. And you're welcome to visit any time. You can take a bath or sunbathe nude with Goldie, should that tickle you just right." One side of his lip twists just slightly. Fucking hell, he's sexy!

"Will it only be Goldie and I who'll be nude or will you be in your birthday suit, too?" she asks with playful innocence in her tone.

"Just say the word, little girl." He tips his head to look at her from under the shadow of his brows. His lascivious grin screams naughty thoughts and my breath catches.

She stutters, "I—I'll keep that in mind."

He snickers because he knows the effect he has on her. "I'm going to take a shower."

Patch stands and I see the bulge of his semi-hard cock from behind the denim. I tip my head back as he leans in. His face hovers above mine and his eyes are riddled with questions, especially after I wave an eyebrow. His lips press to mine more aggressively than when he first arrived.

He asks, "Have you had anything to eat or have set dinner plans?" I lift my wineglass, snicker, and then shake my head. He tilts his face toward Lizzy, who studies his every move. "You're staying for dinner."

She nods and he smiles, then collects his bag and saunters into the house.

Her mouth hangs open. She gulps the last of her second glass of wine and bursts into hushed laughter. "Holy fuck! You weren't kidding! That man is intense! No wonder you look exhausted all the time. How are you able to walk after that huge stallion humps you?" She lies back in the chair and fans herself with the hand that doesn't hold the spent wine glass.

I down mine and put my hand out to collect her glass. She hands it to me and debates on another since she plans to drive home later. She'll be here for a while longer so she accepts another refill.

While I'm in the house, Bash pulls in and parks his old truck beside Lizzy's Jeep. He hops out and strides to the porch with his long legs. He doesn't see her on the porch.

"Hi," she says. I hear her through the open window.

He stops just before he reaches the door. "Oh, hi! Sorry, I didn't see you sitting there." He approaches her with his hand out. "I'm Bash Bear. You are?"

She stands just enough to be gracious and shakes his hand before she sits back. "I'm Lizzy. I work with Goldilocks at the hospital."

I watch them through the window while I open a second bottle of wine.

He smiles. "I've heard some stories. She talks about you a lot. Only good things, I assure you." He sits on the chair Patch just vacated. "Goldie in the house?" Lizzy nods. "It's nice to put a face to the name. You're a sight to behold. Sorry if that was out of line."

She spreads her arms wide. "What woman doesn't like compliments?"

His voice lowers to where I have to listen harder to hear what he says. "I want to thank you for your kindness toward Goldie. Few people are nice to her when they learn of her relationship with us *evil* Bear brothers. We're assholes, in case you haven't heard."

"I don't listen to the masses. I'd rather go by what Goldilocks tells me." She fiddles with a lock of her hair.

"What does she tell you?" He tilts his head and crinkles his forehead in the same manner as Patch when he tries to search someone's eyes for answers.

I can't see her face. "To be honest, she's told me about her relationship with all three of you—not right away, of course. It took her a while to open up. She didn't give in-depth details but I know she's intimate with all of you and you have an open relationship."

"Semi-open," he corrects.

The sound of the wine filling her glass prevents me from hearing what she says. After I fill both glasses, I get a beer from the fridge for Bash.

"Yes, if permission is granted," I hear him say as I walk through the door.

"Thank you." He takes the beer I offer and then kisses me when I lean in.

"Permission granted?" I ask as I hand her a full wine glass.

She replies, "Bash was just explaining the rules to your relationship when it comes to other partners."

He says, "I explained that we can't just hop into bed with anyone. Its permission granted only."

"It is now," I say to him, then go on to explain to Lizzy. "Mack started dating Shaina while I was away at school. Bash had sex with her and hesitated to tell me. I found out from Mack and it went to shit. So, now it's a permission-granted thing between Bash and me. If Patch and Mack want to have sex with someone else, they can, but they have to tell us about it out of respect for us."

Lizzy gulps some wine. "I'm secretly jealous that Goldilocks has three amazing men who love her and I don't even have one." She tips her glass toward me. "You deserve them. This girl is fucking amaze-balls. Beautiful and smart!"

She points her finger at me. "I love this woman. She's deserving of only the best life can offer. I wish the whole world could see that." Lizzy is chatty from the alcohol.

"She certainly does," he says.

Lizzy leans toward me. "You're my best friend. Did you know that?"

I blow a kiss at her and notice Bash's sights are on her chest while he licks his lips.

She continues. "I mean it. I've never had a friend that doesn't judge me or get upset with me if her boyfriend checks me out. I'm small and bubbly, so sue me! I can't stop someone from looking at me. I would never get upset if my boyfriend—" She pauses and looks at Bash. "Not that I have a boyfriend. I don't. They were all assholes and I kicked them to the curb. Well, I still live with my mom and didn't actually live with the guys, but you know what I mean."

He interrupts her. "From what I can tell, you're lovely. Every woman should be adored by her man. He should put her above himself, always, and treat her with the same respect she shows him. Fuck those assholes. They don't deserve you."

"Goldilocks, if he wasn't your boyfriend I'd hop on his lap and make out with him. I totally would." She growls when Bash smiles and shows off his perfect white teeth. She waves her finger at Bash. "He's the sweetest and sexiest fucker I've seen in a long time. I mean, other than the stud in the house who's an older and more dangerous version of this one."

If he doesn't want me to catch him checking her out, he's lousy at concealing it. To fuck with him, I look at her and say, "You can hop on his lap if he says it's okay."

In my peripheral, I see his head jerk in my direction, but I'm too entertained by Lizzy's questioning eyes to look at him. She glances at him, then back at me, and bursts into laughter. I meet his squinted eyes and laugh too, then I sip my wine.

Patch steps outside wearing the low-rise faded blue jeans that look great on him. He didn't bother with a shirt or shoes. He swigs from his beer as he strolls toward us. As per typical Patch fashion, he smells great!

"I'm thinking of throwing some deer steaks on the grill. Lizzy, you like deer? I killed it myself."

"Gun?" she questions.

"Bow and arrow is my personal preference, not that I think a gun is evil or anything. I simply like the challenge of a bow."

Lizzy can hardly take her eyes off Patch's abs while he struts from the barbecue to the kitchen and back. With her distracted, Bash gets my attention. His eyebrows furrow and I wink at him, which intensifies his questioning leer.

Chapter 7

After dinner, Patch wanted to drop Mack's bike back at the main house. Lizzy wanted to tag along and Patch was more than happy for the company. They won't be gone long unless he takes her in the house to show her around where he'll likely put his moves on her—not that he'd have to work too hard at it. She looks at him like a thirsty man looks at an ice-cold beer.

Bash and I tidy the kitchen. He's quiet for a few minutes as he waves his fingers under the stream of water, waiting for it to warm up. His eyes haven't veered from me as I clear the table.

I put my hands on my hips. "Stop staring! You're creeping me out."

He smiles. "I'm glad I can still make you quiver." I scrunch my face as if undecided if that's true. "So, what was that about earlier?"

"What was what about?" I ask as I circle the table to collect the silverware.

He sets the plates into the growing suds. "You know what I'm talking about. Lizzy. Outside. You … saying it was okay if she sat on my lap and made out with me."

He straightens when I stand next to him and look up at his eyes. "Oh, that!" I jest with a smirk and a wave of my eyebrows.

"Yes, that." He licks his lips. "What were you hoping would happen?"

I shrug and turn to walk away but he grabs my arm with his sudsy hand. I yip and he pulls me close to him and holds the back of my neck to keep me in place.

He looks down at me with heavily lidded eyes and speaks slowly. "What would you have done if she had taken you up on your offer?"

"Ummmmm…" I pause to consider the possibilities and to make him wait. "I would have sat and watched."

He leans back enough that he can assess my face to see if I'm serious. "Do you think you'd like to watch me fuck your friend?"

My pussy twitches. "I might be okay with that. I mean, I really like Lizzy. She's sexy as hell, witty, intelligent and I know she doesn't have unprotected sex with anyone. When I picture you with another girl, I don't see you with Shaina even though you two did it. That's weird, right?" I don't give him a chance to answer. "I'm not going to lie; I get a little aroused when I imagine Lizzy moan as you bend her over a table and slide your massive cock into her tiny body."

He's looking over my head and wears a quirky grin as if picturing himself in that exact scenario. His smile fades. "But when it would be all said and done, you still have to work with her, she'll still be your friend and you'll never get that image of us out of your mind. What if it doesn't work out well? Are you willing to lose her as a friend?"

I'm quiet while I wet the washcloth and make my way to the table, while I consider what he's proposing. He shuts off the water and picks up the first plate and washes it, then runs it under the clean water before he sets it on the rack. I can feel his eyes on me as he waits for me to answer.

"I think our friendship is stronger than that. We both have a mature way of looking at relationships, and she's the type of person who resolves issues and doesn't let them fester. She's not shy about speaking her mind, but she'll listen to opposition and consider whether or not she's right."

With his hands sunk in the bubbles, he pauses to look at me as I lean on the fridge a few feet from him. "If I had sex with her, would you watch, or do you want to be involved…" he pauses. "Or would you like to have sex with her, too?"

He sets a plate on the rack. I point and say, "You didn't rinse that."

"What?" he asks, then discovers a wad of bubbles gliding down the plate. He rinses it and dries his hand on the towel he slung over his shoulder earlier. With one hand on the sink's edge and the other on his hip, he patiently waits for me to answer.

I flip my hands out from my sides and, with a voice higher than usual, reply. "I don't know! I—I don't know. I mean, maybe I would." My face flushes hot. "I might try it one day but what if I get down there," I gesture toward an imaginary Lizzy's vagina "and I gag? She'd be so insulted!"

"If you don't like it, you can gesture to me and I'll take over. I love eating pussy." Bash steps toward me and lifts my chin so he can look into my eyes. "You aren't ready to take that step. One step at a time, okay? There's no rush. If you decide to—and I really want you to think about it when you're sober—we can invite her to our bed. But that isn't going to happen tonight, so let's just enjoy ourselves. Shall we?"

I shake my head. "Definitely not tonight. I believe she and Patch are going at it right now."

He looks surprised. "Do you think?"

I nod emphatically. "Did you see how she was looking at him? Oh, man! That girl's hot for him." I close the distance between us. "Besides, I told her she could fuck him if she wants to."

"You did? Hmm…" He mumbles, "I'll have to ask him if she's as much of a firecracker as I imagine she would be."

"Well, fill me in after you find out." I smirk and slap his ass as I pass him to go to the washroom.

He adds, "I'm sure Patch will take the lead, and the poor girl won't stand a chance."

"He's definitely dominant."

Patch's truck pulls in and parks in the same place as earlier, less the motorcycle in the back. He hops out and jogs around the front of the truck in hopes of being a gentleman by opening her door. But before he can assist, she has both feet on the ground and the door slams shut. She's a little bouncier with each step and I catch his fleeting smile.

He likes her!

She comes through the door waving a bottle of red wine over her head. "Since we finished the last one, we brought another. Crack it open, woman!" She hands it to me with her eyes wide. She mouths the words, "Oh, my God!"

I whisper, "I thought you'd be gone longer than that." She shrugs and feigns innocence. "I figured you'd be all over him."

She sports a crooked smile. "As much as I'd like to, it would be weird. He's your man; it just seems wrong."

I roll my eyes. "It's a permission-granted situation, as you know, and I gave you permission in the locker room. Don't you remember?"

She scoffs. "That was just locker room talk. I didn't think you were serious."

"Okay," I say as I draw out the word. "Well," I pause to pick up the corkscrew. "Consider this an official permission granting conversation." I wink and she takes a step back.

She stands tall and turns at her waist to look at the boys who've perched themselves at the dining room table with their beers. Their voices are low, and I see Patch point to the picture he hung for me.

She spins back and says, "In that case, sadly, I may have missed my opportunity. He probably thinks I'm not interested because I didn't try to kiss him in the truck. I had the chance after he took the bike out of the back." Her eyes widen. "Fuck, he's strong!"

"Girl, you have no idea. If you two hook-up, he'll toss you around like you're a ragdoll." We both laugh when Lizzy waves her arms and does a little jig as if she were a floppy doll. I hand her a filled glass. "Listen, he's not shy. If he's interested, he'll let you know."

Bash breaks out a deck of cards. He assigns Patch and Lizzy to be teammates. He says it's because he wants to be across the table from me so he can look at his one true love.

Lizzy fakes a wretch and Patch snickers. I pay them no attention because I adore Bash's mushy sentiment.

After too many Euchre games to count where Patch and Lizzy kicked our asses, we're all a little intoxicated. The old clock with the crooked hands *pings* to alert us to how late it is. The sound is like a spoon tapping an empty tin can. One day I'll get a clock that chimes like a clock should.

Patch grunts. "Well, I have to turn in. Morning comes early around here." He gulps the remainder of beer from his bottle.

Bash turns his body to look at the clock, even though he could just count the number of pathetic pings. "Yeah, me too."

"Lizzy," I say while I lean my elbows on the table. Bash listens intently. "You have to spend the night. There's no way in hell I'm going to let you drive."

With a sexier voice than his already sexy voice, Patch says, "You can sleep in my bed." She tilts her head to look his way. "Don't worry, I'll climb in with Goldilocks and Bash. We can sandwich the poor girl."

"It's like sleeping between two actual bears and not just two guys bearing the name Bear," I say with a laugh that's a little over the top—thanks to the multiple glasses of wine and two beers. "Pardon the pun!"

She laughs so hard she snorts. Somehow, she manages to say, "That was so *punny!*"

It takes a few minutes before we calm down. I think the guys were laughing at our silliness but they laughed, and that's what counts.

Lizzy stands and sucks back the last swallow of wine, then hands her glass to Bash. "I'm always cold, boys!" She waves her fingers as if to suggest they warm her up. She's giddy so she can't stop giggling, which ruins the sexy suggestion—whether she meant it or not.

Patch puts his hand out to take hers. She glints and grabs it. "Come with me," he says without even a hint of a smile. "Let me take you to my bed."

I tease with a long "O" sound! She follows him while she laughs and humps her hips toward him. She looks hilarious. He doesn't see because she's behind him.

Bash runs his fingers through his thick, dark brown hair and erupts into laughter. Patch looks at him to see what's so funny. She stops humping before he sees her, and she turns her head like she's trying to find out why Bash laughed. It draws his attention from her. He discovers nothing comical and pulls her along.

Bash mumbles. "Patch isn't going to make it to our bed tonight, is he?"

I look at him with my hands clasped behind my back and a wide smile I can't seem to ease. "No, he won't."

He takes my hand and leads me through the living room and then the kitchen to shut off lights as we make our way to the bedroom. He helps me out of my dress before we reach the bed. I giggle when he undoes my bra with two fingers quicker than I ever could. I walk backward as my panties shimmy down my legs. I step out of them while he slowly saunters toward me with glassy eyes and an alcohol-induced smile. The darkened room casts shadows over his face that would have me question my decision to be alone with him if I didn't know him well.

He leans in to kiss me but before he can, I whisper, "I have to pee."

"Of course, you do." He looks toward the heavens and points to the bathroom.

When I return, he's lying on the bed with the covers pulled back. He pats the empty spot beside him. I slip in and he flips the covers over me just as my lips find his. I roll onto him and straddle his thighs. I kiss and lick from his lips down to his erection.

I take the spongy mushroom head in my hand so I can tease the slit with the tip of my tongue and taste his arousal. He moans with appreciation. His hands slip under the sheet and gather my hair gently to hold it out of my way. My head bobs under the sheet as my lips glide up and down his shaft.

"Goldie, babe," he pants. "Come up here."

My puffy lips peck at his nipples. His hands cradle my face and urge me up so he can kiss me. Our tongues dance slowly as I position myself over his shaft and slowly sink down onto him. I take every inch.

I moan into his mouth as I begin bucking forward and back, rubbing my clitoris along his tight tummy. Back and forth. Back and forth. I set the pace to ease myself toward climax. There's no need to rush. I want our bond to last.

With one of his hands on the back of my neck and the other spanned across my ass cheek, I buck above him, and rock increasingly faster as the tightness in my tummy builds as if a balloon inflates in the most deliriously mind-numbing way. I grind my body as hard as I can to take every inch of him. My slick juices allow my clit to glide easily along his flesh.

The room spins and everything tightens inside my tummy from my clit to my belly button. The room spins. My feet slide under his thighs and hold tightly. Otherwise, I'll surely float away. My lungs burn and my tits ache from bouncing...

But the balloon swells inside me and it's almost more than I can bear. Suddenly, the earth stills. My mind falls dark. My body is no longer mine. I'm afloat.

My entire body jerks as if my soul has slammed its way back in. His hand over my mouth muffles my scream. At the moment, I don't care if I never breathe again.

His hand falls away and my gasp is met with his deepthroated, lengthy groan. His body stills beneath me as his hands squeeze my ass cheeks and pin me against him. His cock swells and stretches my walls as my pussy twitches with appreciation.

Slowly, his muscles ease and I collapse against him and bury the bridge of my nose against his neck. We lie unmoved until our breathing eases. My legs ache so I lift my weary body to release his withering penis along with his spent cum.

Just as I get to my feet, movement in the shadows catches my eye and I screech. "Patch! Holy fuck! You scared me. Why are you hiding?"

He laughs as he stands from the chest he sat on. "Well, I didn't want to interrupt such a beautiful moment." I can't tell if he's being sarcastic or if he enjoyed his voyeuristic moment.

"Well, it's over now so you can climb in," Bash groans and rolls onto his side and punches the pillow to fluff it.

I say, "I'm going to take a shower."

Bash says, "I can't believe you sat there and watched. Pervert!" He throws the pillow at Patch but he bats it off course and launches it back with perfect precision.

I shut the door and shower. When I step out, Bash slips in. I dry off and slide into bed with my butt snuggled against Patch's tummy. He brushes my hair off my cheek, then kisses my neck. "I love you, Goldie."

"I know you do," I whisper. "I love you, too."

He takes a deep breath. "I like Lizzy. She's fun and she doesn't take my shit, much like someone else I know."

"Who, me?" I ask as innocently as I can manage without laughing. "No, I'm a total pushover."

"You know you push my buttons. You fucking live for that shit." He kisses just behind my ear. "Lizzy has that same defiant glint in her eye as you which is probably why you two get along so well. Your glint is more dangerous."

"Dangerous?" I question and turn my face toward the ceiling and try to look over my shoulder.

"Dangerous because it makes me fall. As great as that is, I know you could just as easily break me."

I reach down and lift his heavy arm from my waist and pull it up between my breasts. "If you want Lizzy, I already gave her the okay."

"You did?" he asks with surprise in his tone.

"She didn't tell you?" I ask but he shakes his head. "Bash and I talked about it—and it's just talk at this point—but we're considering letting her join the group. I mean, if it's okay with you and Mack, of course. I'm not sure if I'm ready to be with her—like, me, myself—but the thought of one of you fucking her while I watch is intriguing."

He yawns just as Bash opens the bathroom door and shuts out the light, returning the room to its darkened state. He slides in beside me. I reach toward him and find his hand and weave my fingers in his.

"Goodnight. I love you guys," I whisper. Both men return the sentiment and I'm quick to sink into a deep sleep.

Chapter 8

Something wakes me. A heavy arm resting over my waist has me pinned beneath the sheets. Going by the tattoo, it's Bash's arm. Patch isn't in bed in front of me where he was when I fell asleep. I use the utmost care not to wake Bash. He doesn't even stir.

I hear something. With the silence of a mouse, I make my way toward the noise. Before I arrive at the scene, something stills me. Although muffled, the sounds are obvious in nature; moans. My pussy twitches and my heart pounds faster.

I peek around the corner and hope they won't see me.

She's on her back on the island with her legs bent at the knee, spread wide and her calves dangle over the edge. Patch's huge hands have pinned her wrists to the counter beside her hips and his face is buried between her thighs.

My nipples are desperate to poke through the oversized t-shirt I tossed on before I left the bedroom. She's wearing Patch's red t-shirt. It's pulled up to her neck, exposing her breasts. They're small, perky, and perfect; much nicer than mine.

Her head flops to her right and I duck back behind the wall. If she'd seen me, she'd surely have reacted in some way, and since her moans continue to seduce my ears, I doubt she saw me.

I hear the squeal of skin scrape along the counter. I know exactly what's happening; he doesn't want her to cum until he's inside her. He'll fuck her and make her wait for her release. I peek again.

She whispers, "What the fuck, Patch?" Her breath rushes from her as if she's being manhandled. "I was almost there."

"Shush." Patch's whisper, as low and deep as it is, makes my tummy flutter and surely hers as well.

I peek again just as she asks, "What?" but doesn't protest when he lifts her up and spins her mid-air, then sets her on her feet. She grips the island while he rips a condom package with his teeth and tosses the package to the floor which is not in typical Patch OCD fashion. His jeans are in a heap on the floor beside him while he rolls the condom onto his erection.

His hand covers her mouth while he holds her back against his chest. He whispers in her ear but I can hear. "You'll cum when I allow it. Grab the edge and hold on. I'm going to fuck you how you deserve to be fucked."

She leans forward but doesn't pull his hand from her mouth. She must like to be muffled.

He pushes his cock deep into her in one thrust. If it weren't for his hand, she surely would have screamed. He pulls out and she abruptly pushes back on him. She wants more. Even though I can't see his face, Patch surely sports a wicked grin.

He pulls her head back while he presses on her lower back which forces her into an arch. She's quite flexible.

In her ear, he whispers. "You want to fuck hard, little girl?" She nods enthusiastically. "If you want me to stop, wave your hand because I'm not letting go of your mouth. I'd bet you're a screamer and I'm not about to share you tonight. You're mine! You're fucking mine!"

Patch grips her hip and continues to hold her mouth. His powerful thrusts have her at his mercy. He's rough, very rough just like when he is with me and wants to own my body. My clit twitches as I watch the mountainous man fuck Lizzy with a vengeance. Her feet aren't on the floor. He holds her by her hip and humps so hard that gravity seems to be at a loss.

She screams beneath his hand but doesn't wave to make it stop. Her muscles are flexed and her fingers are white from their death grip on the counter. She cries out when Patch's hand slips. The sound echoes about the kitchen. He covers her mouth and nose and pulls back until the back of her head rests against his chest. His hips retreat and his cock slips free.

He growls beside her ear. "No screaming!" Their heavy breaths are loud. "You scream, I stop. Do you understand?" She doesn't react. "Tell me you understand."

His hand remains in place but she tries to speak. She fails of course, but her laughter has him shaking his head; entertained by her humor. He releases her mouth.

Through her panted breaths, she says, "I understand just fine, Sir." Then curtseys.

"You're trouble! I fucking like trouble," he whispers, then grabs her hair and pulls her head back so he can kiss her mouth. She tries to turn her body but he won't allow it. He kicks her feet apart and she arches her back. He slips his cock back inside her pussy. His mouth muffles her moan. Damn, she's flexible!

To fuck her at a better angle, he pushes her head forward and bends her at her hips but continues his hold on her long red hair. His free hand slips down her tummy and finds her clitoris.

Oh, yes! My mind spins. I know exactly how she feels. He loves to get me off with his finger while he whispers naughty things and leisurely fucks me.

My fingers find my clit and begin to copycat his gentle massage, as I know is his way. I imagine him filling me, fucking me slowly so I can feel every inch of him glide along my walls. I bite my lips between my teeth to hold back my own pleasure. I want to hear her cum. She's perfectly still, as am I aside from my fingers—*his* fingers. Slowly, they rub and caress her—and me with my imagination—closer and closer to euphoria.

She covers her mouth with her palm to restrain her moan. She's coming. I want to cum too but I'm not there, yet. Her chest heaves and her legs shake as though she were supporting his weight as well as her own. She stills and her breath holds.

I step back and lean against the wall to continue my merciless assault on my own clitoris. My jaw clenches and the tingles build in my tummy until my clit numbs, but the numbness feels so perfect. I imagine how sensual she looks at the peak of her own climax. She cries out beneath her own hand and the air seems to still around me.

A thud yanks me back to reality. My knees are weak but I step forward to catch another glance. He's picked her up. Her arms and legs are wrapped around him and her back is against the refrigerator. He reaches around her ass to guide his cock into her pussy.

Patch wraps his thick forearm around her back to hold her against his chest. Their lips intertwine with a heated passion that would have Hollywood directors delirious. He carries her to the table and feels for a chair. He spins it, then turns and sits. He releases her back but quickly grips her ass with both hands to encourage her to ride him like a cowboy on a bucking bronco.

They're like wild animals. All I can do is stare at them and take notes. She's an aggressive lover, at least she is with Patch. I'm shocked the chair can withstand the severity of the assault. He reaches up and captures a lock of her red hair. She grips the back of his neck to keep her balance.

He tilts her head back and licks up her neck. She continues to ride his cock with more speed and power than I thought a woman her size could muster. Her movements become jerky, not nearly as consistent as they had been. She's coming!

"Cum on my cock. Good girl," Patch whispers against her neck. "Your cunt is fucking tight." He moans. "Oh yeah, squeeze my cock."

His erratic breaths halt, lips pull back to reveal clenched teeth. His face darkens and the veins on his forehead grow more prominent. She cries out just as he exhales with a throaty groan.

Their bodies seem to soften instantly. She cradles his face and kisses him tenderly. But only once.

"Thanks for the nightcap." She slides off his lap. "Good night, Patch."

She promenades to Patch's bedroom and leaves him seated on the chair and desperate to calm his breathing while his cock withers inside the spent condom. He snickers and sits with his hands on the back of his head. He knows he's been conquered.

I scurry quietly back to bed and slip in. I face a softly snoring Bash, who still hasn't shifted position. I want to wake him to tell him but it can wait.

Patch is nearly silent as he sneaks into the master bathroom and closes the door. A few moments pass before the sweet scent of body wash caresses my nostrils when his freshly cleansed body slides into bed behind me. His heavy arm slips beneath the sheet and flops over my waist. He pulls me back until I'm safely tucked against him.

"She's a firecracker," he whispers. "Isn't she?"

I turn my head and try to look at him but he has me too tightly against him. "How did you know I was watching?"

"I saw you."

"She's a wild woman, for sure." I can't help but smile. "I think she got the better of you."

His tummy tightens as if suppressing a laugh. "I think you're right."

I giggle louder than I should and Bash moans and rolls over. "Don't cry into a box of tissues if she doesn't call you in the morning."

"Good thing I'll be cooking her breakfast then, huh?"

Chapter 9

Morning comes too quickly. I'm woken from a dream where Mack is licking my pussy and I was so close to orgasm. For a second, I'm angry that I'm awake but then it's wonderfully clear that someone is under the covers and doing exactly what Mack was in my dream.

Not to ruin the mystery, I don't lift the sheet to see who. Instead, I close my eyes and enjoy the sensations and think only of my clit and how hot and wet the tongue and lips are as they suck and lick every awakened nerve.

It isn't more than a minute before I clutch the sheet above the mystery person's head while I lift my hips to meet their laps. They suck, lap, and spin circles around my clit.

My entire body stills as the most pleasure any woman can feel overtake every cell of my being. All too soon, I fall back into my body and twitch with each torturous flick of the magical tongue on my hypersensitive clit.

The person's head glides under the sheet like a shark about to catch its prey. It glides free. Patch's lips are puffy and slick with my arousal. He kisses me and leaves my scent on my lips. I wipe my lips as he climbs off the bed. I expected he'd be naked but he's already wearing his jeans, no shirt, no socks.

He runs his palm over his rock-hard abs. "You should get up now. I'm making breakfast." He struts to the bathroom and washes his face while I sit up and slip the oversized t-shirt I wore last night back on.

"Is Lizzy up?" My throat is dry, making my tone deeper.

He pokes his head through the doorway. His face is lathered in soap. "No, not yet." He ducks back in.

I slip my feet into my fuzzy slippers and pass Patch. I watch him look at himself in the mirror as he dries his face. He looks like he just stepped off a military base; strong, stern, and in command. He exits the bathroom and I close the door. I pee, brush my teeth, and make my way to the kitchen.

After I've sipped from the mug Patch handed me with the cost of a kiss, I set it down on the table and shuffle my feet all the way to where Lizzy sleeps. I'm too tired to lift my unusually heavy legs.

After I tap lightly on the ajar door, I push it open. Lizzy is sprawled face down under the covers with her head buried under a pillow. I flop on the bed next to her and she jolts upright.

"What the fuck, bitch? Ouch!" Her hands press over her eyes and she groans. "Too. Bright. Head. Hurts."

Slightly louder than a whisper, I agree. "Yeah, we drank too much last night. It's not bright in here; it's a rainy day. Get up, you'll feel better after a hearty breakfast and some drugs." I roll toward her and she flips to face me. I grimace at how pale she is which emphasizes the purple bags beneath her eyes. "I thought Patch would have fucked the alcoholic stupor right out of you."

Her eyes widen in surprise but she quickly grimaces at the pain her reaction caused. "You already know about that? Is nothing sacred between you people?"

"Sorry to break it to you, but I watched most of it."

Her pale face flushes to make her look almost lifelike. She presses her face into the pillow. "Oh, my God! I'm so embarrassed!"

"Don't be! You were smoking hot. Damn, girl! I could never move like that." I yawn. "You put me to shame."

She turns her head and brushes the hair off her face. "Confession: I had to learn how to use my boyfriend's bodies how I wanted because try as they might, they couldn't satisfy me." She takes a breath and releases it slowly. "That man, Patch, can fuck!"

I nod and our laughs fill the room.

"On a more serious note; are you thinking about dating him?" I ask after I cough. My throat is still dry.

"No! He's your boyfriend. Well, one of them." She snickers. "When I got into bed last night, I felt like I'd betrayed you. I don't want to hurt you in any way."

"You didn't hurt me." I roll my eyes and sigh, embarrassed to tell her. "While I was watching him rub your clit, while he fucked you slowly, I masturbated."

Her smile widens. "You did?" She rolls onto her back and looks up at the ceiling. "That's so hot!"

"The scene was hot! He's had me exactly how you were—against the counter—so I know what you were experiencing, and it was exciting." My face feels hot.

Her brows lift in the center. "So, you're okay with what happened? Like, if it were to happen again…" Her words fall away but I can tell she hopes it will.

"You can play with him any time you'd like."

"Yay!" Her smile falls away. "I know all the guys like to share their toys, so what if Bash wants to play with me? I am a shiny new toy. That's not okay, is it?"

"I love the reference, and we are toys when it comes to their dicks. But no, it's not too far. I don't think it would bother me. He and I discussed the possibility of it happening sometime in the future. But if you're going to be with Bash, I would like to be there." I waggle my eyebrows. "Maybe I'll join in, and we can tag team him. I think he'd like that."

She taps her chin as if unsure, then nods emphatically. "He'd be a fool not to!" I sit up and she copies, with a groan. "If and when you're ready for that, you let me know. If you never want me to be with Bash, I'm fine with that, too. My worst fear is losing you as my best friend."

She stands and stretches as I make my way toward the door. "I'm not going anywhere. As long as you abide by the rules and don't lie about anything, I can't see there being a problem." I turn and point at her. "And don't get pregnant!"

"Ew!" She reacts as if I asked her to eat poop; she shivers clear into her soul. She follows me. "I don't want kids! No, thank you!"

"Never?" I ask and she emphatically shakes her head.

Before we enter the hallway, she lowers her voice. "*If* I ever were to have sex with Bash, and you don't want it to happen again, you'll tell me, right?"

"Of course!"

She yawns. "I have yet to meet Mack. In pictures, he's the cutest of the three. Sorry! That isn't to say Patch and Bash aren't hot as fuck because..." She raises her eyebrows and waves her arms as if to showcase them like they're right in front of her. "Fuck!"

"I know, Mack's *GQ* pretty," I say with a smile.

We enter the kitchen together and Patch takes notice. He whistles. "If you two aren't the most beautiful creatures I've ever seen..." He pauses to look us up and down. "Ladies, you're a sight to behold."

We both grimace and mumble about how awful we look and how hungover we are. I reach for the pill bottle while she takes the full mug from Patch. He doesn't lean in to kiss her but the way he looks at her commands submission. She glances at his strong abs and then winks at him but doesn't let him kiss her when he finally does lean in. She challenges his dominance and I try to hide my entertainment.

"Where's Bash?" she asks as she turns her back to Patch. She sips her coffee and sighs happily.

Patch lifts his shoulders in a half shrug then rubs his chin. "He left for work almost an hour ago."

Chapter 10

It's been a few days since Lizzy spent the night. We're getting along superbly, and our dynamic at work is excellent. Neither of us feels awkward about her wild night with Patch. The only change is that we can talk on a more intimate level than before. I don't have to hold things back from her anymore.

When I asked her if she was going to call him and maybe go on a date, she told me that she doesn't want to get serious with anyone. She wants to fuck him again but keep it casual. I'm sure he'll be okay with that.

We discussed her having sex with Bash and decided to let the idea float around for a while. If the right moment hits, it'll be up to me to act upon it. If it never does that's okay too.

Lizzy and I have Friday off so I invite her to go to the mall with me to do some lingerie shopping and then to come over for some day drinking. She accepted with great enthusiasm.

My arm stretches along the cool sheet in search of Bash's hot body but the vacancy has me painfully aware of how much I miss him.

There's a note next to the half-full pot of coffee still perched on the burner. After I pour myself a steaming mug, I read the note.

Goldie, I had a meeting with Garrett at the Daily News, *then I'm going to meet up with Patch for some brother time. He wants to walk the forest to find the perfect tree for his projects. We might not be home until late. Mack is expected back from the site and promised to check in on you later. Have fun!*

P. S. I'm your most cherishing admirer!

I take my book and head outside to read on the porch. The sun is low on the horizon, promising to be a hot day. The sky is powder blue with cotton ball clouds. It's hard to believe they're calling for a heavy storm.

After two mugs of coffee, the sky darkens, and the wind whips. Time to head inside and do some housework. I shower, sweep the floor, do some dusting and start some laundry. It's only eleven o'clock and I'm already bored.

I should text Mack to invite him over for lunch. He should be back from the build site by now.

Me: Are you back yet? Want to come over for lunch?

I fill a glass with water from the jug in the fridge, gulp down half of it, and let a burp roar. It echoes off the walls and I giggle like a five-year-old boy.

Mack: I just got to Shaina's. We're heading to Rosie's diner in about twenty minutes. Join us. I'm sure she would love to see you.

Me: I don't want to intrude on your date.

Mack: Don't be ridiculous. Meet us!

Me: Do you think it'll be crowded?

Mack: It will be lunchtime so I imagine it will be.

I gulp the rest of the water. Eventually, people will get used to seeing us in public together ... won't they?

Me: Okay, I'll meet you.

Mack: Excellent! Drive safely.

Me: You too!

I rush to throw my hair into a ponytail, slip into my lightweight pale blue dress and sandals, and then dig my tiny clutch purse from the box at the back of the walk-in closet I have yet to unpack.

I arrive before they do despite the sheets of rain that make it damn near impossible to see the road at times. I run into the restaurant and stop just inside. My hair is stuck to my face after the rain and whirlwind I just sprinted through. I do my best to put it back in order. Nobody gives me a sideways glance which has me at ease. Maybe they don't care that the town's harlot is in the room. Good!

Luckily, there's a table at the back of the restaurant where we'll less likely be ogled while we eat. I recognize the waitress to be Alicia, daughter of Larry and Wendy Gibson. I used to babysit her when she was seven. She smiles and addresses me by my name. We exchange pleasant greetings before I order a coffee and tell her I'm expecting guests.

She sets the mug of coffee in front of me just as Mack and Shaina arrive. Shaina wraps her arms around me and then quickly pulls back to give me a wet kiss on my lips. I scan the room for critics but no one's paying us any attention.

"I missed you so much!" she says as she slides onto the booth across the table from me.

"It's been a while, hasn't it?" I reply and wipe her burgundy lipstick off my lips.

"Goldilocks, you look beautiful as always." Mack gives me a quick peck on the lips before he sits beside his girlfriend.

It's strange but they don't look right together. Some couples suit one another; these two don't. It's not because she's Black and he's white; she's a city girl who wears lots of make-up, always has her hair styled—which is odd considering the weather outside. Unlike mine, her nails are long and painted, and she always wears fashionable clothing. She's fun and pretty, but high maintenance; not the kind of woman I would expect Mack to be interested in.

Mack's long hair fans over the flannel, grey and black plaid shirt he left unbuttoned to reveal a snug black t-shirt. He's usually in well-worn blue jeans that accentuate his thick thighs and tight ass, and I've only ever seen him in running shoes or hiking boots. He's a woodsman through and through.

The waitress takes their drink orders and scurries away. Shaina still seems overly excited to see me. "I'm so happy you called. It's always so great to see you." She leans forward and taps her nails on the menu. "So, what have you been up to lately?"

"I've been getting the house together, trying to figure out where things need to be situated. I just hung a bunch of pictures I got from the second-hand store. They'll do for now." She's put off from the mention of the second-hand store.

She relaxes her scrunched nose. "I'm sure they're lovely; vintage, as they say. We all have to start somewhere," she says while scanning the menu.

Her tone seemed condescending. She may very well feel more superior than me but it's rude to point it out.

The waitress brings their drinks and with a click of her pen, she's prepared to take our orders. Shaina fusses with her thick gold necklace when she asks to exchange a garden salad for a Caesar to go with her tuna-melt sandwich. When the waitress informs her of the price difference, she complains but still wants the exchange.

Mack rubs his hands together. "So, Patch and Bash met your friend, Lizzy." He smirks and waves his eyebrows. "I hear Patch is especially fond of her."

"He, ah…" I feel like I'm gossiping. "He *really* liked her."

Shaina looks annoyed. "Did Patch fuck a friend of yours?" I nod and she glares at Mack. "When did this happen and why am I only hearing about it now?" He shrugs as if to say he doesn't know.

To save him from her inquisition, I say, "It only happened a few days ago, and Mack's been at the site…" I pause when she purses her lips. I can't tell if she's angry, jealous, or anxious to hear more? I look at Mack who pays her no attention.

Mack leans forward. "He told me he wants to see her again. Said she challenged him, much like someone else I know." He squints his eyes at me. "He said you enjoyed watching them."

I simply smile innocently. He wants to hear the dirty details but I sip coffee to make him wait. I whisper so no one will overhear. "She rode him like he was a bucking bronco. Afterward, she thanked him, said it was fun, and then walked away as if she were done with him. His reaction was priceless. He's used to women fawning over him, especially after sex."

Mack grins widely and runs his fingers through his long hair. He's pleased that someone put Patch in his place. "He probably felt rejected."

Officer Grant Callan, an old high school acquaintance, enters and tips his head to let the water drip from his hat. He looks around and then advances toward us. He doesn't sit at the vacant bench before ours like I thought he would; he continues and stops beside Mack.

"Hello, Mack," he says and tips his hat toward me, then Shaina. "Goldilocks. Ma'am. It's been a while, hasn't it?" I nod and smile.

"Callan," Mack juts his hand out and the two greet one another. "How the hell are you? I haven't seen you since high school graduation."

It's strange to see Grant dressed in a cop's uniform. When we were teenagers, he was the biggest pot smoker in town. I don't know what happened for him to turn his life around the way he did, but the uniform suits him.

"You're probably right." He shifts his weight to the other leg. "One of these days I'm going to have to come over to see the new house. I hear it's really something to see."

Mack turns his face to look at the cop. "It's a great house. It's not spectacular but you'll like it." He looks at me.

"I love it and it is spectacular," I reply.

Grant takes off his hat to run his fingers through his thick red hair before he puts it back on. He glances at the officer that sat at the empty table, who's busy reading the menu. "Well, I don't want to interrupt your lunch," he pauses to shake his head. "I'll never forget that time we went to the quarry and you jumped but didn't get a running start and hit a few rocks on the way down. Shit, I thought you were a goner!"

Mack takes a sip of his soda. "I have a scar on my leg from that."

The cop laughs, "You should have had stitches."

"Nah!" Mack waves his hand. "It healed—took a while but it healed."

"Patch was so mad at you for that." He looks at me and then Shaina. "He chased Mack around the yard but he couldn't catch him. Even with a split leg and multiple scrapes and bruises, he was fast as hell."

"I ran faster scared than he did angry," Mack laughs.

Callan snickers and rests his hands on his hips. "Well, I'll never forget it." His shoulders lift and he presses his lips into a thin line. "All right," he says then pats the table. "Good seeing you. Give me a call some time." They shake hands. He nods toward us ladies. "Goldilocks. Ma'am."

Callan walks away and Shaina huffs and rolls her eyes.

"What's wrong with you?" Mack sighs heavily and picks up his menu and begins reading it. I hold my menu up but look over it to watch the show.

She turns her head to look him up and down while her lips twist. "Are you ashamed to have me as your girlfriend?"

He drops his menu and folds his hands over it. "What makes you think that?"

Her arms cross over her chest. "You didn't introduce me." Mack looks at me. "Goldilocks isn't going to answer for you?" she says with arrogance.

He shakes his head. "I didn't think about it, that's all." He snickers. "And no, I'm not ashamed of you. Not at all." He pecks a kiss on her lips and she seems to soften.

"All right, then. Don't do it again."

He places his hand over his heart. "I'll never not introduce you again."

Our conversation is casual as we eat; mostly we talk about the mansion being built that Mack designed.

The waitress takes our plates and sets the bill on the table. I pick it up but Mack yanks it from my fingers. He insists, "I'll take that."

"No! At least let me pay for my own," I argue.

He squares his shoulders and shakes his head. "Not going to happen!"

I point my finger at him. "Fine, but I'm getting it next time."

Shaina looks at her pinky fingernail with a frown. "You should know you can't argue with this man when it comes to paying for shit."

With my elbows resting on the table, I form a steeple with my fingers and rest my chin atop. "We don't often go out in public."

Mack reaches across the table and strokes my forearm. "No," he whispers and waves his brows over hooded eyes. "We find ways to entertain ourselves at home." He winks.

My face heats up. I meet Shaina's quirky smile. My eyes widen as my brows lift and I inhale deeply. "You know what he's like. He can be very entertaining."

"Mhm," she agrees. "It's true; he loves to shove his cock up the asses of willing women. And you're about as willing as they come." She grins, then nips at her fingernail.

"Hey, now!" Mack leans away from Shaina but turns to look at her. "Don't slut-shame! We don't do that. Besides, you have never denied having my cock deep inside your ass."

She rests her hand on his thigh. "I wasn't shaming her. I'm just as much of a slut as she is. I fuck you and your brothers just like she does."

She shocks me when she insinuates that she's presently fucking all of them including Bash. "Have you been with Bash lately?"

She shrugs one shoulder and waves her hand at me dismissively. "Don't you talk to your man?"

Mack can sense my irritation. His hand pats mine, which are folded on the table in front of me. "She hasn't been with Bash in a long time. We have no secrets in this family." He pauses and looks at Shaina. "Do we?"

She shrugs again. "No. No secrets."

He pats her shoulder then stands. "I'll be back." He struts toward the cash register and I nearly burst into laughter when two women in their forties stop their conversation and follow him with their eyes. They whisper and giggle.

"I'm not fucking your man," Shaina says, breaking the silence between us.

I sit back and fold my hands on my lap. "That's what Mack said."

"Since you freaked out when you found out he fucked me that one time, he won't touch me." She crosses her arms in front of her and rests her forearms on the table. "Pity because he's a great fuck. That man's cock had me screaming."

I hide my irritation as best I can. "He does have an exceptional cock."

She's glaring at me. "Listen," she whispers, then turns and sees Mack is still at the cash-out and is flirting with the cashier. "Since I can't touch your man, you can't touch mine."

"What?" I lean in, unsure if I heard her right. "Do you have a problem with me?"

Her shoulders lift. "Since you asked..." She sits tall but keeps her arms crossed over her chest. "I don't like it when you call Mack and he goes running. Until Bash wants to fuck me again, I think you should keep your hands to yourself."

"Oh, wow!" I pause to take a deep breath so I don't make a scene. I lean toward her with my clenched fists. I whisper, "If you have an issue with me and Mack, you should have said so right from the beginning." I sigh heavily. "I don't want to get into this here. We can discuss this another time and in a more suitable location."

I scan the other patrons who aren't paying us any attention. Mack is leaning on the counter while he slips his wallet into his back pocket. He's smiling at the woman and she's obviously smitten.

She leans back. "At least I know where my man is all the time."

My eyes shoot back to her smug face. "What the fuck does that mean? I don't need to know to keep tabs on Bash because I trust him."

She smirks. "Mhm."

"Why didn't you want to talk about this when Mack was sitting here? Are you afraid he'll dump you?"

She spits, "Fuck no! The man loves me."

I roll my eyes and decide to play dirty. "Did he actually tell you that? He tells me he loves me all the time." Her lips purse and her eyes shift. "I take that as a no."

Without another word—because I won that argument—I pick up my purse and weave through the tables toward Mack. He spots me and then winks at the cashier, who's flushed. She sees me and scurries away.

"I have to get going." He lifts his arm over my shoulder and pulls me in for a lengthy hug. "Thank you for lunch."

He eases his grip and kisses me before he releases me. "I'm glad you came." He looks over my shoulder at Shaina who's standing behind me. His bright blue eyes burn into mine. "Maybe we can meet up later? Dinner at the main house, perhaps." He lifts my hand and kisses the back of it.

"I'm not sure what Bash has planned if anything. One of us will call you," I say, then kiss him once more for good measure because I know it bothers her. "Love you."

"I love you, too, beauty," he whispers and runs his finger down my nose. "Drive safely."

I leave and say nothing else to her.

I'm huffing mad and regret not tossing my half-full glass of ice water in her face. I slam the car door and scream. When I attempt to throw my purse on the passenger's seat, some of its contents spill onto my lap and the floor. The strap is stuck in the door. I free it and slam it a second time and then growl as I grip the wheel and yank and push until my arms are tired.

Mack looks for my car as they're walking out. He waves so I smile and wave back. She waves, too. I ram the key in the ignition and start the engine.

I drive calmly despite my mood. How did this day veer so badly off course? It started off so well and then *her!* Should I tell Mack his girlfriend has staked her claim on him and wants me out of the picture? I know Mack to be a free spirit. If she holds him tightly, she'll lose him. I'll talk to him about it but I'll do it when we're alone.

Did Bash step out on me, as she insinuated? Is there another woman? What reason would he have to lie about something like that? He wouldn't. She's just trying to stir the pot; unless he's having sex with her but afraid to tell me because I got upset the last time. What if Mack doesn't know? I can't think like that.

Why am I doubting Bash?

He *has* been working a lot of hours, and he's distracted when he's home. Too often, I see him stare at the wall and deep in thought. When I ask, he says he's just thinking about his book.

Chapter 11

The four of us have dinner at the main house. Patch cooked his delicious rabbit stew. Even though there are times I could mention the conversation I had with Shaina, I don't. We're having such a great time, and I don't want to ruin it.

I brought a chocolate cheesecake with me for dessert and the guys praised me for it. It was a big cake but there's nothing left after they have seconds. I help Patch clean the kitchen while Bash and Mack sit on the deck with a beer and a cigar.

After he tells me about his worker having a near miss when they downed a tree earlier today, I beg him to be safe. He kisses my forehead.

"We're as careful as we can be," he says as he dries his hands on the dishtowel I'm using. "So," he pauses to bite his lip as he leans against the counter with his hands on his hips. "What's Lizzy been up to? I haven't heard from her."

A smile creeps onto my face. "She doesn't want to be in a relationship, so she probably won't call you." I hang the towel over the oven handle, slide my arms around his waist, and look up at him as he looks down his nose. "She does want to fuck you again."

His face lights up. "Well, that sounds like fun. When?"

"Look at you," I tease. "You're smitten with her."

"Maybe I am." His chin lifts and his hands rub my back. "She's funny, intelligent, fucking hot as a demon straight out of hell, and she fucks like a wild cat. Of course, I like her."

"And she challenged you," I say and step away from him. I do a little dance. "You like her! You like her! She's sexy and you like her!"

His eyebrows lower but he laughs. "You're so fucking weird." He takes a beer from the fridge and offers me one but I turn it down and point to my glass of water. "But I love your weird."

We join the guys on the porch to share more laughs. A while later, Bash says, "Well, Goldie, it's getting late and you have to get up for work. We all know how much you love to sleep."

The brothers nod and chuckle.

"She's just getting her beauty sleep," Mack sticks up for me. I blow him a kiss as I stand.

Patch adds, "It's working, so who are we to criticize." He stands with his empty beer bottle and offers to take Bash's.

Mack waves his eyelashes and lifts his eyebrows to entice me with his boyish charm. "I'm going to kiss you." He pauses to gaze up and down my body. "Ready?"

I nod, and he springs from his chair, wraps an arm around my back and plants a sensual kiss on my lips, and then dips me. He's a lover of old movies and I think that's where he gets his tips for seduction.

After I'm righted, I glide over to Patch and brush my fingernails down his bare muscular forearm. He sets the empty bottles on the table. Before I can react, his strong hand is weaved in my hair and he's kissing me firmly. If Mack's kiss hadn't aroused me, this one sure as hell will do the trick. He releases me and immediately collects the bottles and heads into the house as if he didn't just make my pussy damp. I'm flushed and trembling.

I go inside and get my purse. As I'm heading to the kitchen, Patch steps in front of me. I hear the door open and Mack and Bash enter while they're laughing about something. Patch's palm glides along my jaw until it rests on the side of my neck. He leans in and presses his lips to the other side of my neck, and then breathes in my scent. He moans and kisses softly along my jaw to my lips. He leans back and looks into my eyes.

What is he thinking? I can't read him. The corner of his lip lifts. "I love you, Goldie."

I grimace. "Stop calling me Goldie. That's Bash's nickname for me." He chuckles as he walks over to Bash. They shake hands and bump chests.

Bash asks, "Patch, are you coming back to the house or staying here tonight?"

He replies, "I'm staying here. Mack and I are going to shoot the shit like brothers do." Patch grabs Mack in a headlock. "We might even get drunk."

I stomp my foot like a child. "I want to stay!"

With his arm wrapped around my shoulder, Bash looks down at me. "Not this time, Goldie. You have to work in the morning."

Mack wrestles with Patch and manages to slip from his grasp. He nearly knocks Patch on his ass in the process. Both men laugh like young boys.

Despite all the excitement and Patch ready to charge, Mack says, "Yeah, but *you* don't have to work tomorrow, little brother." Bash looks at me questioningly.

I roll my eyes. "Fine! Go ahead. I'll drive myself home." I pop my bottom lip out to exaggerate my pout.

Mack laughs. "Thank you, Goldie."

"I love you, Goldie," Patch says as Mack rushes him.

"Don't destroy the place before I get back," Bash says, then opens the door to usher me to my car. He opens the car door for me and we both cringe when we hear a kitchen chair topple.

I sit in the car and toss my purse on the passenger's seat. "Hey, I keep forgetting to ask you about someone, and since she just popped into my head again…"

"Who?"

"Sarah Joyeau." He closes my car door and I put the window down after I turn the key to auxiliary.

He rubs his forehead. "Yeah, she's a sore spot with us."

Curious, I ask, "Why's that? She seemed nice; a bit twitchy, but nice."

"Where did you meet her?" he asks as he places his hands on the roof.

"The place I bought the pictures from. She works there."

"Do you want the whole story?" I nod with wide eyes. "Mack started dating her. So, with her permission, we started fucking her." He clears his throat. "She started coming over when she knew I'd be home alone. It quickly became apparent that she favored me sexually. As you can imagine, Mack wasn't thrilled. After a while, she refused to spend any time alone with Patch because she said he scared her."

He bends down to lean his elbows on the driver's door. "But the final straw was when she told Mack she didn't want him anymore because she fell in love with me." He taps his fingers on the door.

"Yeah, she said you told her your heart belonged to someone else." I tilt my head like I'm an overzealous teenager. "Do tell who?"

He furrows his brow. "Seriously? You don't know?" I shake my head. "You! My heart was yours the first time I set eyes on you, way back when girls were still yucky."

My heart melts and I can't think of anything to say that would do justice to his confession. He leans in, looks lovingly into my eyes, and kisses me softly. If I wasn't already in love with him, that kiss would have me swooning.

"Does that happen a lot?" I ask. "Do women start dating one of you but lean more toward another?"

He drops his head and clears his throat. "From time to time." He pauses. "It happened with you, too; well, sort of."

I jerk my head and look at him, shocked and confused. "What are you talking about?"

He rubs his chin and looks everywhere but at me. "You're with me and you love me, but you're in love with Patch, too." He shrugs. "Like I said, it happens."

What the fuck do I say? He's right; I love Patch. Yes, I'm in love with both of them and I never thought it possible. If I had to choose, would I choose Bash? Yes, I'm sure I would.

"I love you! You know I love you. I mean, I do—"

"Listen," he interrupts, then pauses to clear his throat. "I'm happy that you love Patch and Mack. I'm okay with you being in love with Patch. I know you love me, too. Hopefully more than him. But if not, never tell me. Okay?"

"I do. I'm not—" I shake my head and for whatever unknown reason, maybe deep-rooted guilt, I can't maintain eye contact. "I'm … I love you both."

"Yeah," he smiles but the corners of his eyes don't crease. "I know. It's good."

Bash leans in and kisses me with a tenderness that has me wishing I could wrap myself around him. He pats the door as he steps back.

He points at me and insists, "Text me when you get home and the doors are locked."

"I will. Now go play with your brothers." I drive away and watch him through the rear-view mirror until the driveway arches. This conversation might need more discussion.

***

After a long, hot shower, I blow dry my hair and expect he'll be home soon.

Did I leave with a huge question mark between us? I keep running the conversation through my head. Does he feel pushed aside? If he can't be honest about his feelings this early in our relationship, how can we possibly survive a full year let alone a lifetime?

At 12:30, he's still not home. I close my book and snuggle under the covers.

I startle awake when something thuds in the living room. My ears strain and my heart pounds. I hear another thump and boots shuffle on the hardwood floor. Two men shush each other but fail to muffle their laughter. It's Bash and Mack, and they're drunk.

It's 2:30! Should I be angry? The guys like to drink but I've never seen any of them full-on drunk. Happy, yes. Drunk, no.

"Shh, you'll wake her," one voice whispers.

"We should wake her and maybe we can…" the other says but stops to sing some porn music. I laugh but fight to keep quiet. "We could rock her world because we know how to, and we can, we can do it."

I think that's Bash's voice and he's sloshed.

I'm sure their alcohol-induced limp dicks would overrule any desire they may have to rock my world. I clamp my lips between my teeth to prevent my laughter from being heard. What a couple of clowns!

Mack whispers. "Okay, now!" Laughter. "Now sneak in there and—" More laughter from both men. "And slide in really quiet-like." Both giggle like happy drunk men.

"Yeah, I'm gonna! Yeah."

"Just, you gotta be, like, um…" More giggles and then both men shush each other rather loudly. "Be very quiet. Like a quiet tiptoeing mouse. Like that quiet. Okay?"

"Yeah! What? You don't think I'm quiet? I'm a—I can be a quiet guy. Like, I'm a mouse. A really big fucking mouse!"

Loud laughter, then shushes.

I'm about to burst. This is hysterical! Tears spill from the corners of my eyes and onto my pillow. My hands cover my mouth to hold in my laughter.

"Hey, middle brother?"

"What's up, baby brother?" Mack whispers and then laughs.

Bash says, almost low enough to be a whisper, but not quite, "You're my favorite brother because you didn't fall in love with my Goldie."

"Nah, man! Come on! I am in lo—I mean, I love her too, but like, um, I mean, there's Shaina, but I don't think I love her."

I hear a thump and a shush followed by another thump.

Mack says, "Dude, you're too loud."

"Well, I can't go to bed with my boots on."

The door slowly opens wide, allowing their hushed banter into the room unobstructed. It's like their drunken stupor had them believing it was a magical door that kept out all sound. There's a distant sound of footsteps in the living room, and then the front door shuts.

Bash is quiet aside from his clothing landing on the floor as he strips. The bed jerks and he stifles a laugh. The covers lift and he slides in up against my back and flops his arm over my waist. He pulls me so my butt presses against his belly. He reeks of beer and whiskey.

His whisper is faint, but I'm sure it's louder than he hoped it to be. "I love you, my Goldie girl, and I've never been more afraid."

In a few seconds, he's snoring, and I'm left to wonder why loving me scares him.

Chapter 12

I wake to the scent of bacon cooking. My arm stretches to the other side of the bed in search of the warm body who passed out next to me, but he's not here. I stuff my face in his pillow and breathe in his scent. A waft of his cologne lingers.

How the hell is he up and able to make breakfast when he's likely still drunk?

Plates click together, and that's the signal I should get up. He'll soon come to fetch me and tease me for being a late sleeper, even though it's only 7:30am. All three boys wake before 6am every day, no matter what. They referred to me as Rumpelstiltskin for a week after I slept past 8:30am.

The door slowly opens with whisper silence. I quickly fling my legs over the edge of the bed and raise my arms over my head to stretch as my jaw gapes from a lengthy yawn.

"You didn't sleep well last night?" he says as more of a question.

I reply, "It's hard to sleep next to someone who snored as loudly as you did."

He carries in a full tray: two plates full of food, two coffee mugs, a bowl of fruit, and a small vase that holds a fat white rose. "Get back in bed. You're ruining the whole breakfast in bed stereotypical romantic moment."

"Sorry, I was unaware of the protocol for etiquette pertaining to the breakfast in bed scenario. I'll study up on the acceptable reactions for future loving or apologetic gestures."

He grimaces. "Sorry about snoring."

My eyes lock on the beautiful pink-tipped white rose. "Where'd you get this? It's too early for the flower shops to be open."

He sits on his side of the bed, holds up the tray, and gestures to its legs. "Would you be so kind?"

I adjust them and he sets it between us. As he tries to find a level spot amid the tousled comforter, I pick up the rose and stick it under my nose. My eyes close as I sniff in until my lungs are full.

I'm reminded of a hot summer day when I was a child. I sat among the rose bushes and Mom was taking pictures. I was maybe three-years-old. My father told me to look at her, to smile, and not to squint. But the sun peeked under the brim of my hat when I'd look up. Mom warned me about the thorns and it scared me. I stood up and fell. I remember the red blood on the white petals. I open my palm to admire the scar left from a thorn.

"Do you like it?" His voice pulls me back from my memory.

I close my eyes, and the edges of my lips lift. I moan my approval and open my eyes just as he tucks a tress of tangled hair behind my ear.

I breathe in the rose's scent one more time. "I'm keeping it forever," I say as I set it back on the tray.

"I woke up and you were having a bad dream," he says with a questioning expression. "Want to talk about it?"

"I don't remember it. Why didn't you wake me?"

He quickly looks down at the tray. "Here, eat. It'll help give your sleepy ass some energy," he teases and hands me a plate and fork. He leans against the headrest with a plate of his own.

I ask, "Was I saying anything?"

His eyes don't meet mine. He shoves food around his plate before he stabs a chunk of egg and stuffs it in his mouth. He glances at my plate as he chews.

He waves his fork. "Eat. It's good for you," he says between chews.

"You're being evasive." I set the plate on my lap. "Did I say something you didn't like?"

He sets his fork on his plate but takes too long to swallow the bite of egg. "Yes, you were mumbling." His eyes meet mine. "Specifically, you were saying Patch's name, a lot. The words *I love you* came up more than once." He shrugs, then shoves a whole piece of bacon in his mouth.

"I'm sorry. I was asleep. I don't remember the dream. I have no control over what I—" I stop talking when he smiles and winks.

He covers his mouth. "I know you love him, and I'm happy you do." He pauses to chew and swallow. "The relationship you have with him is different than it is with me. I understand that. Even though we're brothers, Patch and I are not the same. I wouldn't expect your experiences with him to parallel ours." He runs his fingers down my cheek. His eyes plead with me. "Just, please, let me love you more."

My heart aches. I slice through my egg with my fork and stab it. "I heard what you said when you got into bed last night." I shove the fork in my mouth and moan at how delicious it tastes.

He nods and looks back at his plate. "I figured as much. Sorry, I was drunk. People say things when they're drunk and—"

"People tend to say what they mean when they've lost their inhibitions from an alcohol-induced stupor." I stab another chunk of egg. "And don't worry. I love you and I'm not going anywhere."

"I know. But," he pauses to clear his throat. He fiddles with his fork. "You had a lot of time alone with Patch while I was at school. Mack was away at the build more often than he was home. Patch took great care of you, so of course, you love him. I'm happy you do, I really am. I gave you my heart with no regrets."

He tips his head back against the headrest and looks at me. "Much like you never having been in a sexually explorative relationship, I've never given my heart to anyone before. This

is new territory for me. As much as I don't want to admit it …
it scares me."

He continues to eat as if he didn't just beg me not to tear
him to pieces. Nothing more is said about it. I eat more than
my share before I shower and get ready for work while he
makes the bed and tidies the kitchen.

I love him. I really, really love him. What the fuck is wrong
with me?

Why won't I let Patch fall to the wayside and focus all of
my energy on Bash, which is what I've wanted since the day
we met back in grade school? He said he loves to share me
with his brothers. Maybe I should stop reading so much into it
and freely love them all, just differently, as Bash suggested.

***

They're short-staffed in the surgical preparation wing so
Laura, my supervisor, has me work there for the day. I have
the least amount of seniority and expect to be shuffled around
but I prefer to be in the operating room.

An elderly, fragile woman aided with a cane slowly makes
her way toward the check-in desk where I sit.

"Hello," I say with a welcoming smile.

She returns the gesture, and her wrinkles deepen. "Hello.
Is this where I need to check in?"

"If you're here for day surgery, you're in the right place."
I point to the chair next to the desk. "Please, have a seat, and
let me get some information from you."

She tells me her name is Marianna Colt, and she was born
on November 3, 1935.

I take a moment to study her face and then lie to her. "You
don't look a day over sixty-five."

She bursts into laughter. "Oh, dear! I appreciate that but
I'm old, not blind." She pats my hand. "You're a young, pretty
girl. Do you have a man in your life?"

Actually, I have three!

"Yes, I do."

She smiles as grandmothers do. "Good! Marry the man and have lots of sex. It'll keep you young and put a bounce in your step."

I nod but quickly change the subject. "Looks like you're scheduled for a minor procedure. I'll have to give you an I.V."

She shrugs as though she hasn't a care in the world. I prepare the smallest needle we have and try to find a viable vein which isn't easy in a woman of her age. After two failed attempts, the woman's obviously irritated.

"What's your name, dear?" she asks.

"Goldilocks," I say while I search for a worthy vein. I've never had to poke three times, and I'm beginning to doubt myself.

She's quiet which is unlike her. I look at her to make sure she isn't about to pass out. She's expressionless as she studies my face. I press the button on the blood pressure monitor and she rolls her eyes, irritated that the cuff will soon squeeze her arm for the third time.

She says, "I suppose telling *you* to have lots of sex wasn't warranted. You're the woman living with those hoodlums; the Bear boys." She points her shaky finger at me. "I've heard all about you."

Has all the blood left my face? I think it has. Back in her day, I would have been considered a societal leper and cast out of town as a Jezebel and forever disrespected.

"Is there another nurse who can tend to me?" She glances down the hall with hopes a nurse will magically appear.

I clear my throat and release the pressure cuff before I pick up the phone. I call my supervisor, Laura.

The lull of uncomfortable silence fills the room for several minutes before the familiar heavyset woman with the brown hair twisted into a bun stomps around the corner wearing a friendly smile.

"Hello," Laura says with a strong southern accent. "Goldilocks, how can I help?"

Before I can explain, the woman speaks. "I don't want this harlot poking me again. She tried twice already and well—"

Her tone is demeaning. She leans closer to Laura and fails in her attempt to whisper. "She's obviously unqualified to work with someone my age. Besides, how can I be sure she doesn't have one of those new diseases she might give me?"

Laura scratches her head. I shake my head and nervously chew on my cuticle. She nods to suggest I leave. I'm grateful for the dismissal.

I barely make it to the employee restroom before I erupt into a crying fit. How can someone be so rude? I know she's elderly but that doesn't give her the right to be an asshole. My personal life is my own. Isn't it?

After ten minutes and a splash of cold water on my face, I'm composed. I'm relieved to see a different woman seated just down the hall. I force a smile and wave her over.

The rest of my shift was uneventful. I doubt I could have survived another difficult patient. But before I go, I check in with Laura to apologize for earlier. When I tap on her door frame, she calls me into her office and waves her hand for me to close the door.

"Goldilocks, please don't think I'm passing judgment on your lifestyle because I'm not. My religion has taught me that it's not my place to judge anyone. I am, however, going to suggest you keep your personal life personal. In other words, don't bring your drama into my department."

Thankfully, she doesn't raise her voice. With a nod, I reach for the door handle.

"Goldilocks," she calls to me and waits until I look at her. "If you ever need to talk, I'm a good listener and I don't flap my gums. My door is always open." She smiles and it's believable.

"Thanks. I'll keep that in mind." I hastily retreat.

I'm torn between tears, pity, and a raging anger by the time I get to my car. I start the engine and push the buttons to drop the windows.

Before I drive, I call Mom and Dad's house. Although my dad said he'd try to come to grips with my relationship with the Bear brothers, he hasn't given much effort. I've invited them over for dinner a few times but there's always an excuse why Dad can't make it. Mom comes over often but Dad has visited only once and didn't stay an hour.

The ringer sounds loud in my small car. It rings three times before someone answers.

"Hello?" It's more a question than a greeting. "Hello? Mom?" More silence. "Dad?"

"Mom's not home." Dad's voice is vacant of emotion. "Do you need something?"

"Um, no," I reply. "I was just looking to chat with Mom. I had an awful day at work. This one patient gave me a hard time and—"

"Listen, Goldilocks, Mom isn't home and I'm on my way out. I can write her a note or you can call her cell phone. Although, I doubt she'll answer; she's at the legion jarring pickles with the ladies."

"Oh, right." I recall the conversation where she invited me to join her. "Okay, I'll try her later."

"Good-bye, Goldilocks."

He hangs up quickly. My dad didn't give ten minutes of his time to listen to his daughter talk about her shitty day at work. He's a tough-hearted man. We used to chat for hours but that was before I gave myself to the town's evil spawn.

When I stopped at a light, I look for Lizzy's address in my phone. If her car's there, I'll stop. She always lifts my mood and I could use that right about now.

I rap at the screen door and see her rush toward me. "Hey, hey!" She opens the door. "Come on in! I was just burning cookies. I mean, baking cookies." She giggles.

The smell of burnt food stings my nostrils. She wasn't kidding when she said she was burning cookies. I follow her through the living room. It could use some upgrades. The dining room as well. The old table hasn't weathered the years well enough to be referred to as vintage.

We enter the kitchen through a small archway and the smell intensifies. A wood-framed window above the sink is propped open with a wooden ladle. The back door is held wide open by an old metal-framed kitchen chair with rips in the plastic backrest and seat.

She points to a tray of blackened cookies. "Like I said." She pulls out a chair that looks just as worn as the other. "Have a seat. So, what brings you here?"

While we talk, I watch her scrape the burnt pucks from the metal sheet and then plop fresh balls of dough in four rows of three. She sets them in the oven and adjusts the timer shaped like an egg.

"I had an awful day," I pout.

She wrestles the chair from the door then sits kitty-corner to me. "Of course, you did!" She gloats, "I wasn't there to keep you entertained."

"Well, that's one reason," I say with a nod.

"What happened?"

I roll my eyes and take a deep breath. "I was in receiving today," I say and she scrunches her face to show her distaste for the position. "Some old woman… She was fine with letting me try a third time for her I.V. but refused after I told her my name. She recognized me as being the sinner living with three men."

"Did it cross your mind that she didn't want you to stab and miss a third time? Maybe it had nothing to do with you personally."

I lean back and the chair wobbles on its uneven legs. "No, she wasn't coy about it. She even told Laura that she thought I might give her a disease. It was humiliating! I cried in the bathroom." I shake my head and raise my palms. "It wasn't the first time I've been degraded and it won't be the last."

"Eventually, you'll get used to it. Either that," she leans in and whispers, "or you'll have to start telling people to fuck off."

"I heard that!" A red-haired woman strolls in from the other room. She dons a fluffy purple robe and a smile. Her red nose and droopy eyes are evidence she doesn't feel well. "A lady doesn't swear," she pauses. "In public."

Lizzy lowers her face but not her eyes. "We're not in public."

"Oh, then go ahead." The woman, who's likely her mother, pats her on the shoulder before she notices me. "I'm sorry. I'm not dressed for company." She fusses with her robe. "I'd shake your hand but you'll appreciate it more if I don't. I'm sick." She lifts her hand to reveal a crumpled tissue.

Lizzy waves her hand between us. "Mom, this is Goldilocks. Goldilocks—Ginger, AKA my mother."

The woman's smile drops quickly and what little color she had in her cheeks has washed away, leaving her very pale. It suddenly dawns on me where I've heard that name before. Ginger is the woman who saw me bound to a tree and getting fucked by all three brothers in the woods.

She told one person and it spread like wildfire. Soon, the whole town knew about it. Worst was my parents heard, which is why my dad has been so short with me. Mom accepted my choice to be with them but Dad just can't. Because of her big mouth, I went from being known as the good girl who does everything right to a disgrace who spreads her legs for three brothers in the most deplorable ways.

She nearly ruined my life. If the guys weren't there to support me through all of that, I would have left town and never returned. The look on her face carries fear, embarrassment, and a plea for forgiveness. She waits for me to react.

Lizzy looks from her mom to me and back. "What's going on?"

As if snapped out of a trance, I look at a curious Lizzy and wonder how she doesn't know what her mother did. "Nothing. I thought I recognized her name."

Lizzy hops up to look in the oven at the cookies. "She works at the Mill Street bank. You probably saw her there."

"It's nice to meet you," I say to the short, thin woman.

She looks relieved that I haven't shoved my fist down her throat. "And you."

She reaches in the newer stainless-steel refrigerator to collect a bottle of orange juice, then retreats back to where she originated after she steals another wide-eyed glance at me. I want to punch her in the face and scream humiliating things at her so she can have a taste of how much she hurt me, but it won't fix anything. The truth about the brothers and me would have come out eventually. I would have preferred it to happen on my terms and with a bit more discretion.

I stand and the chair squeaks. "I should go."

Lizzy opens the oven and glares at me while she slips on an oven mitt. "You just got here!" She removes the tray of cookies which are baked to perfection. "At least stay for some cookies."

I sit back down and her little dance proves her excitement. A cookie drops from the tray, halting her dance moves. She pouts as if mourning its death and I laugh.

By the time I leave, I've eaten three delicious cookies and had a few laughs. We discussed what we could about our secrets but with her mom in the next room, we had to keep the conversation to more appropriate topics. Although she's put me in a much better mood, I know my woes will continue to haunt me.

***

Bash's truck isn't home when I arrive. With my forehead resting on the steering wheel, I turn the key to stall the engine. My arms hug the wheel and turn my head to look down at the river. The heavy downpours we've had over the past week have it rushing past.

After I lock my purse in the car, I head down the path toward my favorite place; the rock. Strangely, I doubted it would be there since my day has been shit. I roll my eyes at the ridiculous thought. It's a boulder. Boulders rarely move.

I stretch out on my tummy so I can watch the water rush past while the minnows huddle in the shallows to remain protected from predators. I feel akin to the minnows as I rest on this rock and hide from those who would cause me pain.

The sun is warm on my back, soothing, exactly what I need to ease tense muscles. The low-hanging sun reflects off the tiny waves like millions of sparkling diamonds. It's sedating.

Chapter 13

"Goldie."

I'm annoyed.

"Goldilocks! Goldie…"

I jolt awake. Judging by the pain in my lower back and the darkness that surrounds me, I fell asleep on the rock some time ago. How long was I asleep?

"Goldilocks!"

Is that Patches voice?

"Goldie…" Bash? "Baby, where are you?"

"Guys?" I yell but my voice is hoarse and scratchy. I clear my throat and yell again as I peel myself off the rock with a groan. I stretch my arms over my head and bend to the left, then the right. "I'm here!"

"I hear her!" Patch yells.

He's close but I can't see him through the ebony shadows cast down from the trees. His boots thump the ground as he rushes toward me, but from which direction? I turn just in time for him to wrap his arms around me and hold me in a hug that's way too tight and I can feel him shake.

I squirm and he releases me but holds my shoulders to assess me for injury.

"I'm fine," I say after he turns me so the moon's light will void the shadows. "Seriously, I'm okay."

"What the fuck, Goldilocks? You scared me." He corrects, "You scared us."

"Sorry. I had a shit day at work and came here to decompress. I fell asleep so mission accomplished." I joke but he doesn't see the humor in the situation.

He picks me up wedding style and stares down at my face. "Don't fucking scare me like that again." His tone is threatening but I hear the fear behind the words and that hurts me more than anything. He carries me down the path.

"I'm capable of walking on my own. I'm not injured."

He huffs. "I don't care. I'm not ready to let you go."

"Did you think I ran away?" I joke and struggle against his grip. "Seriously, put me down!"

Patch sets me on my feet just as Bash storms toward us. You'd think I was gone for a week by how hard he hugs me.

"Dammit, Goldie," Bash hisses. "Your purse and phone were in your car and it was locked. You were nowhere! Fuck, Goldie!" His hands cradle my face. I must look annoyed because his head tilts and he speaks calmly. "Forgive us, we were scared for you. We thought something happened."

Okay, so my workday was shit and the woman was rude, but the love these men have for me can't be denied. They love me and I them.

Patch looks at the rock and rubs his chin. "Why were you out here sleeping on a rock?"

Bash holds my hand on the walk back to our house. Patch strolls silently behind as I tell them about the woman who upset me and how I met Ginger but kept a cool head. They were proud of me for that.

Will I ever get used to the stares, whispers, rumors, and blatant insults? Will it always be so hard or will our relationship eventually become old news where nobody cares anymore?

When we get back to the house, Bash hands me a glass of water and a granola bar. "Eat. Drink. Later, I'm going to fuck you so hard! I'm angry because you scared me and I need to work through that."

I laugh and stretch my back again. "You won't hear me argue."

He continues, "Eat. Drink. We have to go."

"Go? Go where?" I shake my head and toss the bar on the table. "I just got home and my back aches. The only place I'm going is in a bathtub filled with steaming hot water."

Patch, who stands beside the open front door, says, "Mack's in the hospital."

"What? Why? What happened? Oh, my God! Is he going to be okay?"

Panic! Fear!

Bash grips my shoulders and looks into my eyes. "He's going to be okay. He's been hurt worse. He took the bike out knowing the roads might still be slick from the rain this morning. He wiped out but he wore a helmet and his leathers so there's no road rash."

"Okay, but..." My words fall away.

Bash brushes hair off my cheek and cups my chin. "He'll be fine in a few weeks. We have to go." He tries to smile but I can see the concern in his eyes. He looks at Patch who's rocking from leg to leg. "He'll be so pissed about the bike having to go back in the shop."

"What?" I shake my head. "No fucking way is he getting back on that bike! One accident, okay. Two and there's a curse on that bike. It's gone! I will burn that fucking thing before I let him ride it again!"

Patch laughs and I turn to glare at him. "You'll have to take that up with him, little lady. He won't take too kindly to your suggestion."

I grab my purse and rush to the door. "It's not a suggestion!" I run past him and toss my car keys to Bash. "My car's faster."

A typical half-hour drive to the hospital took only ten minutes with Bash behind the wheel. The nurse won't tell us where he is. Instead, she directs us to a waiting room.

My heart pounds rapidly and I feel faint. I sit and my leg bounces to expel some of my nervous energy. Patch sits beside me and takes my hand. Is he looking for comfort or is this for my benefit? His hand still shakes. Bash paces but stops to look down the hall each time he passes the doorway.

The half-hour wait drags. Finally, a nurse comes. We all stand in anticipation and our hearts pound wildly.

"Are you Mack Bear's family?" he asks and we all nod. The tall, forty-something man puts his hands on his waist. "If you want to see him, follow me."

He leads us down the hall, around the corner, and down another hall before we enter a dimmed room. Mack is lying on the gurney with his hand on his forehead, the other arm propped on pillows.

He sees us and smiles but his eyes dance back and forth. "Sorry, I'm dizzy." He groans in frustration. "Quit moving, will you?" he jokes.

Patch in his typical fatherly tone, says, "So, you still have your sense of humor. That's a good sign. Now quit joking around. I'm pissed at you."

"Give me a break; I'm damaged," Mack smiles wide with his eyes barely open.

Bash stands on the other side of the bed and sizes him up. "Damn, brother, did you flip through the air and land on your face because you're fucking ugly! No! Wait! That's how you always look."

They chat while I attempt to straighten his matted hair but it's stiff. It's now that I see the line of stitches on his neck. My stomach leaps into my throat. I'm a nurse! This shouldn't bother me but it does. A slice like that could have killed him.

My words are faint. "Your neck…"

Bash and Patch groan and lean in for a better look while they wear disgusted expressions.

He snickers. "It could have been worse."

I snap at him. "Yes, you could have bled out."

He reaches over his belly so I take his hand which is scraped along the top. I try not to touch the wound. "I'm okay." He sighs. "Beauty, don't worry. Fuck, you're pretty! She's fucking gorgeous, isn't she?"

"Do they have you on pain killers?" Patch asks.

Mack snickers and raises his eyebrows. "Fuck, yeah! I'm floating, man. I asked if I can take some of this shit home but they said no. I'm still working on the nurse with the red top. I think I can sway her." He laughs hard, grimaces, and releases my hand to hold his ribs.

I wet some paper towels and start wiping the blood from his hair while Mack tells us how the bike started fishtailing and hit the loose gravel. He was thrown and landed on the other side of the small ditch, on a dead tree.

He said it hurt right away and there were a few minutes when he couldn't catch his breath. He thought his ribs were busted and puncturing his lungs. He said his life flashed before his eyes and all he saw was me beneath him while he slid into my ass that first time. Of course, he smiles at me and waves his brows.

"You're such a damn flirt," I whisper and twist my mouth.

"I love you, Goldie. You know that, right, baby?" Mack hooks his finger in the collar of my shirt when I bend over to look for any blood that I may have missed. He looks down my shirt. "You have the prettiest titties. Do you know that?"

A tall doctor I recognize but haven't been formally introduced to, walks in holding an iPad at his waist. He stops at the door when he sees all of us in the tiny room. He sees Mack's looking down my shirt while I argue with him to let go. He's kind enough to look away.

"Hey, doc! This is my family; my brothers and our girlfriend, Goldilocks." He sings "our girlfriend." Either Mack doesn't realize he just outed us or he doesn't care.

Patch and Bash try to get him to shut up but their efforts are futile. I hope the doctor doesn't recognize me and tries discussing it when I'm working. But he looks at me and nods as if we're old friends. Patch shakes his hand then Bash rounds the bed to greet him.

Damn this day!

Bash continues. "I was just saying how perfect her nipples are because they stiffen like pencil erasers. I could suck on them all day and never get bored."

The doctor pinches his lips together to ward off a grin. He looks at me and blinks several times before he looks down at his tablet.

"He was conscious when he arrived but he has a slight concussion. Other than some dizziness, he should be fine." I meet his tired eyes and he asks, "Are you his girlfriend?" I look at Bash and he nods so I confirm it. "You're a nurse?" I nod again. "I thought I recognized you."

I smile and try to think of something to say, but it's Patch that asks a question. "And his other injuries?"

The doctor clears his throat. "He broke his Ulna but it's still aligned so he won't require surgery. He has a fractured Clavicle, bruised Scapula, and some bruised ribs. He'll have to support his arm with a sling. Unfortunately, the paramedics said he landed in a dead tree and was cut up by some branches. He has some stitches in his neck. He's lucky it wasn't deeper."

Bash sighs and asks, "He'll be okay then?"

The doctor nods. "He'll be sore for a while but he'll recover. With a head injury, you'll need to wake him every hour to make sure he's coherent."

Patch pats the man on the shoulder and offers him his hand. "Thanks, doc."

The nurse comes in with bandages and sets them beside him before he gets some gloves. He bandages while I watch.

The doctor shakes Patch's hand then gives him a prescription. "You can take him home after his neck is bandaged. Fill this prescription downstairs before you leave." Bash leans in and shakes the doctor's hand and thanks him to which the doctor nods. "At eleven o'clock give him two tablets; they'll help with the pain. Tomorrow morning, he can start with one pill every six hours as needed. There's enough to get him through three days. He should be fine with acetaminophen after that."

I push past Patch. "Can I see the x-rays?" The doctor looks at me wide-eyed. "I'll be caring for Mack when we get him home so I'd like to know the extent of the injuries."

He brings the x-rays up on his tablet to show me. The nurse finishes. Bash helps Mack sit up while Patch takes a cut and bloody shirt from the bag of the clothes he wore when the paramedics brought him in. He cusses and stuffs it back in the bag, unbuttons his red checkered fleece shirt, and takes it off.

He's wearing a simple white t-shirt beneath and it's snug-fitting, which emphasizes his muscles. I notice the doctor check him out with a sideways glance while the guys help Mack dress. Occasionally, Mack cusses louder than what's appropriate in a hospital setting.

We drive much slower on the way home. Mack lies across the backseat with his head on my lap. I'm doing the best I can to hold his casted arm still but the potholes in the road make that a challenge.

We insist he eat a sandwich before we put him to bed. He falls asleep right away. He can thank the drugs for that. After his arm is propped up on pillows, the guys leave the room and shut the light out.

"Goldie?" Bash calls to me.

I whisper, "Give me a minute."

I lift Mack's head to free his hair from beneath his shoulder and it wakes him. "Hi, beauty. Don't be mad at me."

"I'm not angry. You're going to be fine, but your motorcycling days are over."

"Do I have a say in that?" he asks. I sternly shake my head. "Fine, I'll sell it."

"Thank you," I whisper, then lean in and kiss him. "How's your pain?"

"I'm okay." His eyelids seem heavy. "Did anyone call Shaina? She might like to know."

I tuck my hair behind my ear. "Yeah, I did. She's working; said she'll call you tomorrow."

He frowns. "Did she seem at all concerned?"

"Yeah," I say, but recall how cold she seemed when I talked to her. Maybe it was just because I was the one to call her. If it had been anyone else, she might have been more receptive. "She was working and could hardly hear me over the music. She'll call tomorrow."

His eyes close and his whisper is faint. "I love you."

"I love you, too."

Chapter 14

I offer to stay at the main house in case Mack needs anything through the night and to wake him every hour, but Patch insists he'll tend to him.

When Bash and I get home, I fill the tub with hot water and swap my work clothes for a robe. I pour a glass of pinot grigio, illuminate the bathroom with the flicker of a candle flame, and then slip my weary body into the hot bath. My back still aches from lying on that huge rock. I used to love sleeping on it but there are consequences now that I'm a grown woman.

Bash taps on the door. "Can I come in?"

"Of course."

He closes the door behind him to hold the heat in the room. I wave for him to come in with me. He takes off his shirt as he kneels beside the tub. He dunks the sponge, then holds it over my left shoulder to allow the water to warm my exposed skin as it drains.

"I've been a bit off lately," he says. I shake my head but he insists. "Yes, I have. Please know I love that you enjoy my brothers. We've always shared everything and it's never bothered me." He pauses. "But I've never been in a steady relationship with someone I cared this much about, and I'm afraid to lose you. I want to be with you forever. I want you to carry my babies if you choose to, and I want to grow old with you."

"I want that, too. All of it." I insist he joins me.

He strips and slips in behind me. I rest against him. After he uses the sponge to dribble water on my chest, he lets it float and wraps his arms around my shoulders. We enjoy the silence, each of us lost in our own thoughts. I wonder if he thinks the same thoughts as me. The water has cooled and my fingers are wrinkled, so I sit up and pull the plug.

I stand and reach for my towel but he takes it from me, then helps me out of the tub. He dries every inch of me. I watch him dry himself and how his muscles flex through such a mundane task. He hangs the towels and takes my hand.

He stops halfway to the bed and spins us like a dancing couple. He weaves his fingers in my hair and pulls until my head tilts so his lips meet mine. His kiss is delicate, contradicting the tension he inflicts on my scalp.

Bash releases my hair and spins me again but stops me when I face away from him at the end of the bed. I giggle like a schoolgirl with a crush. He pushes on my upper back until I bend over the bed and he has my chest pinned to the comforter.

His fingers glide down between my ass cheeks and further until they're between my saturated pussy lips. They leave me and he moans. "You taste so fucking good, Goldie." His wet fingers glide between my folds.

In one swift movement, he's buried deep inside of me. The shock of his size has me unable to breathe. He holds still. With conviction, he says, "I said I was going to fuck you hard."

His hips pound against my rear, over and over until I'm drenched in sweat and gripping the comforter. I couldn't say my name if he insisted upon it.

Bash breathes fast as he wraps his hand around my bicep and pulls me off the bed, then flips me onto my back. He pushes my thighs up to my chest. His mouth envelops my dripping wet vagina.

Holy hell!

My pussy spasms with each flick of his tongue as he urges me closer to the most wonderful orgasm a woman can have—clitoral. My arms stretch out to my sides and grasp a fistful of the comforter. I have to hold myself down otherwise I'm sure I'd float away. I'm light, so damn light like I'm not made of flesh and bone but of only a soul.

Have I left my body? No, the physical pleasure is too great.

I spin and float as I fall into darkness. My clitoris is all of me and he licks every bit. He sucks and I let go—let go of every thought, every fear, everything that makes me *me*. I just am, and for a moment, I am unrecoverable.

I'm spun like a ragdoll onto my tummy with no help from me. I can't move, still lost in my euphoria. He straddles the back of my thighs and aims the head of his cock and pushes forward. Despite the tight spasms of my orgasmic walls, he slides right in and pushes my mind even further from reality.

His legs stretch alongside mine and hold my thighs together. With his forearms slid beneath my armpits, I pull my arms in to hug his. My fingers weave into his and hold on. His weight pins me to the bed.

He glides his cock into my pussy in a steady rhythm. My thoughts slowly return but not enough to stop myself from moaning each time he sinks into me. He pants against my shoulder.

I tense; I want more. There's pain on my shoulder but I give it no concern. I bounce under his powerful thrusts. I'm unable to think, move, or stop myself from grunting like a wild animal on the verge of its death—pure ecstasy.

Bash cries out. "You're mine! You're fucking mine!"

His lengthy scream signals the end of all things wonderful. He collapses beside me and I suddenly feel lonely, cold, and wrought with emotion.

I haven't moved; can't move, don't want to move. Tears gush onto the comforter and I fail to silence my gasps.

"Baby?"

Bash quickly sits up. He scoops his arms beneath me and, as if I were light as a feather, cradles me in his arms. He holds me and rocks but doesn't say a word. He gives me all the time I need to work through my emotions.

I don't know how long he holds me but I feel safe from every cruelty the world has to offer. I gather myself enough to sit up. He brushes the hair off my shoulder as I wipe my tear-soaked cheeks.

I whisper, "I'm sorry. I don't know why…" My words fall away.

He whispers, "Goldie, it's okay."

He doesn't ask me why I cried. He seems to know, even though I don't. He lifts me onto the bathroom counter and wets a washcloth with cool water and wrings it out. As he cleans my face, he seems to understand me better than I understand myself. I watch his eyes and see the depth of his love for me. And that's enough to make me want to cry again.

He sets the cloth in the sink. While his eyes gaze into mine his hands caress down my arms. He takes my hands in his and lifts them to his lips, one at a time, to kiss each tenderly.

"Why did I cry?" I whisper.

"Because you let me in."

Chapter 15

My alarm screams and I jolt. My dream has left me feeling safe and loved but I can't recall what it was about. I slap the alarm and sit up with a groan. Bash isn't in the bed; he's likely at work already.

There's no coffee made so I start half a pot and stand like a mindless statue as I watch the stream slowly pour. The delicious aroma wakes my mind. I recall how Bash took charge of my body. Damn, that was so hot!

I fill my mug and sip it twice before I do anything. Must. Have. Caffeine. After a quick shower, I dry my hair and apply a little make-up—mostly to draw attention away from the purple bags beneath my eyes.

I hear the front door open and wonder if Bash forgot something.

"Bash?"

Patch's deep voice replies from the bedroom doorway and approaches. "Not Bash. I hope you aren't disappointed." He leans against the doorframe. The way he looks down at me is meant to intimidate me. "Looks like I arrived at the right time."

I'm naked because…

Well, why not? I'm in my bathroom and I was alone. "I wasn't expecting *you* but it's not a bad surprise." I wink. "Aren't you supposed to be tending to Mack?"

"He's a big boy." His eyes take in my nudity. "He fell asleep on the sofa watching television, so I left." He licks his lips. "And I have no regrets."

"Easy, cowboy," I say as I swipe the mascara bristles along my lashes.

"You're putting on make-up." He sighs. "That means you're getting ready for work and probably short on time."

I look over my mascara brush to meet his eyes. "I'm shocked my nudity hasn't clouded your rational thought."

He stands behind me. He isn't coy about where his eyes go. "Oh, don't you worry your pretty little head." His hand glides down my ass cheek and gives it a squeeze. "Nothing's clouding my thinking and my rationality has always been questionable at best." He leans in closer to my shoulder. "Seems you've been marked."

"What? Marked?" I turn to look at my back in the mirror and see a large bite mark. It's tender when I touch it. Under my breath, I whisper, "Now I know what that pain was."

"Bash bit you."

I twist my mouth, unsure if I'm okay with the bite mark or disturbed by it. I open the cabinet and hand a tube of antibiotic cream to Patch. He opens it and puts a glob on his finger. He hands me the tube. With great care, he applies the cream.

He explains, "Maybe he marked you so others will know you're his." Our gaze meets through the mirror and we're both expressionless.

I laugh. "Do you think that's why he bit me; to stake his claim on me?"

His arms wrap around my shoulders until his right-hand cups the left breast and vice versa. He fondles me and I don't stop him. "It doesn't scare me off. If I bite the other shoulder does that mean I own you, too? Maybe Mack should bite you as well. Since both shoulders will have been claimed, I wonder where he'd choose to leave his mark?"

"He'd bite my ass. I'm sure of it." I point through the mirror at him. "You're not biting me so get that out of your head!" I purse my lips and glare at him.

He laughs and shows his teeth as a vampire would. "I'll bite you if I want to." He winks.

"Red."

His smile drops and he frowns. "Fine! No biting." He releases my breasts and slaps my right ass cheek. "I could spank the hell out of you instead."

My pussy twitches. "You could, but I have to go to work."

I brush my hair and pull it into a ponytail. Before I can turn around, Patch has my thighs pressed to the counter with his. He cocks his head and stares at me through the mirror.

"What?" I shake my head and shrug. "Why are you staring at me like that?"

Patch lifts his hands over my shoulders and dangles something in front of me. It's a thin gold necklace. A sparkling white diamond sits in the middle of the star-shaped pendant and catches the light as it swings. He wraps it around my neck and fastens the clasp.

I brush my fingers over it, then lift it to feel its weight. I find his gaze through the mirror. He doesn't wear his familiar rough around the edges expression. Instead, he looks softer somehow.

"Patch, it's beautiful. But why?"

"Because you said having your own star would be awesome and I told you I'd work on it." He kisses the top of my head. "And so you never forget that I love you."

I spin and wrap my arms around his chest. He hugs my head to his chest while his hand rubs my back.

"Thank you. I love it," I whisper and tip my head back to look up at him. "And I love you."

He leans in and kisses me as if it were our first. He's gentle, loving, and yet eager for more. He palms my ass cheeks. Just as he's about to lift me, I break away. I lean against the counter with my arm extended between us.

"As much as I love where this is leading, I have to get ready for work so please stop."

Patch steps back with his hands up in surrender. "Yes, ma'am. I have something to do anyway."

"Good, then leave me be," I say as I shoo him from the bathroom. My fingers graze the pendent once more. I call out,

"And if you drink the rest of the coffee, you'd better make more."

As my shirt slips over my head, Patch grunts in the living room. I pick up my empty mug and rush to see what he's up to. It'd be awesome if he's fucking Lizzy in the kitchen again. It's not likely but a girl can wish, can't she?

The picture Patch hung beside the bay window is now lying on the island. Patch holds a large wooden clock made from the cut slab taken from a wide tree. It's shiny, polished, and beautiful. I set my cup on the island beside the painting and cross the room to get a better look.

He notices me and groans. "You weren't supposed to see it until it was hung."

"Oh, my God! It's so … so … wow!" I say excitedly. He struggles while it slides up and down the wall seeking an anchor. "Can I help?"

"Yeah," he says sharply. "Look behind and find the hook in the wall."

"When did you put that there? It's definitely stronger than the nail was." I hook my finger over it to test its strength and momentarily forget the direness of the situation.

"You were at work." He shifts the heavy clock in his arms. "See the hole in the back of the clock?" I nod. He pants. "Help me line it up."

"Higher," I instruct.

The clock slips onto the hook with ease, much to Patch's relief. I can see the indented red marks from where its weight sat on his arm. He spins the hands to the correct time while I admire his craftsmanship.

He turns and I leap at him. My arms wrap around his neck, my legs around his waist, and I hold on. He grips my ass and his kiss meets my lips with vigor. He's rough with passion and a heady desire. He carries me to the dining room table and sits my ass down. His hand glides up my shirt and cups my breast over my bra.

"How much time do you have?" he asks as he pecks kisses on my neck.

I reply with a breathy whisper. "Less than fifteen minutes."

He jests, "Plenty of time and we can cuddle after."

He yanks me off the table and onto my feet. His fingers find my waistband and tug but the little bow holds them in place.

"No, I don't have time for that," I say, then wave my eyebrows. "Come outside."

Patch wiggles and shifts his semi-erect cock to better position it before he follows me out of the door. I walk to the porch railing and turn around. His questioning leer has me giggling.

"Come here." I glance at my watch. He gets to arm's length and I stop him, unzip his pants and flip the button. The corner of his lip lifts. "You look too happy and that's not doing it for me. Where's the angry man I love to hate?"

"Maybe love to fuck but not hate." He clears his throat and suddenly looks like the familiar, confident man with a dangerous determination to get what he wants. He grips my ponytail and pulls my head back so he can lick my neck and kiss me hard. His fat, strong tongue delves into my mouth to dance with mine.

Our kiss stops and I take in a breath. His face hovers above mine. He whispers with confidence. "You're going to suck my cock." I bite my lip and slink to my knees. He demands, "Take it out."

I slip my hand in his pants and shift his hard cock until it pops free of his black boxer briefs. He's rock-hard. I ask, "May I suck it?"

"I already told you to suck it, don't make me repeat myself."

I wink. "I just wanted to hear you say it again."

He hides his entertainment behind his bad boy expression and watches me take the mushroom head between my lips and roll my tongue over the slit. His nostrils flare and his blink is a few seconds longer.

"Take all of it," he demands.

I take his entire cock down my throat and he rewards me with a moan. I slowly glide my lips to the tip and look up to see him looking out at the forest and not me. When I pause, he glances down. I smile to let him know I want him to watch me pleasure him.

With a crooked smile, his fingers weave into my hair. He pulls and pushes my head how he wants me to suck his cock. He's good not to choke me but sometimes he holds himself down my throat a few seconds too long and I gag. He pulls me back, lets me recover, and does it again. He repeats this eight times.

"You're a very good cock-sucker." He forces me to take him faster into my mouth but doesn't push down my throat. I grab his thighs for assurance. "Put your hands behind your back."

I do what he says and weave my fingers together at my lower back. A sense of helplessness has my heart pounding. I can make it stop if I choose but I pretend I can't and it enhances my fear level.

"That's right. Just like that." He moans. "Be a good whore and make your Master cum."

I hold my throat open and he fucks my mouth deeper.

Surely my mascara has smeared down my cheeks and saliva drips off my chin. I wipe it and hope I won't get any on my uniform.

He breathes erratically and his moan is sharp; he's going to cum. I take a breath and slide him all the way down my throat until my nose presses to his tummy. He cries out as hot jizz shoots down my throat. I gag but try to relax my throat. Slowly, I let his cock ease from my throat but his seed still spits onto my tongue. I suck hard and he grabs my head. I suck and release repeatedly until his body jerks, followed by a lengthy exhale.

Patch looks at me with a flushed face and a gaping mouth. He takes my hand and helps me to my feet. His thumbs wipe my cheeks to rid the spilled tears but his grimace tells me I need to fix my make-up.

He kisses me tenderly. "Too rough?"

I shake my head. "A bit but I liked the control you had over me, Master."

"I could get used to you calling me Master and sucking my cock outside."

I wink and slip from his clutches. "Think of it as payment for my star necklace and the fucking amazing clock. They're both beautiful, by the way."

"You once said you loved the clock we have at the main house so I wanted to build one for you, too."

"You're so damn talented!" I kiss him once more, then disappear into the house. His truck drives away before I've made it to the bathroom.

Chapter 16

The patients seem to come and go through the operating room as if on a conveyor belt. The surgeries today are quick and repetitive, which means nothing of interest like a knife to the chest, for instance. Not that I'd want anyone to go through that, but it would make for an interesting day.

Today, eighty-seven-year-old Mr. Lennysman will have a lump removed from his throat. Surgery at his age holds higher risks but it's beginning to impede his trachea so it's necessary. I check him in while he chats with me about how nosy the townsfolk are and how they should stay out of my love life. He told me that some time ago when the shit first hit the fan, so to speak. He told me to enjoy my life and do what makes me happy. He's a sweet man and I hope he recovers from this.

An hour passes quickly as I tend to more patients. Lizzy, who's been assisting in surgery today, strolls up to the desk with a sucker wedged between her puffy, pink lips.

"Hey, sexy baby!" she jests with a swing of her hips. "Mr. Lennysman is out of surgery. Before we put him under, he asked me to relay a message." She tilts her head. "He said, 'They can either accept you or they can fuck off.' Then he apologized for the vulgar language. I'm not even going to ask what the hell that's all about but I'm sure it's an interesting story."

I chuckle. "Private joke. How did his surgery go?" I ask while I tidy the desk.

She shrugs and scrunches her face. "It looks like cancer."

"Oh, shit!" I sag. "I'll have to stop in to see him before I go home." I groan and lean back in the chair and rest my forearms over my eyes.

She slides her ass onto the desk and pulls the sucker from her mouth with a pop. "Okay, fill me in. What's up with you today?"

I sigh, drop my arms, and spin my chair left to right to rock myself. "I'm sexually frustrated thanks to Patch."

"Patch left you sexually frustrated? That doesn't sound like him." She wiggles on the desk until she's further back so she can use the faded pink wall as a backrest.

I giggle and roll my chair forward and rest my elbows on the desk and my chin on my fists. "Patch came over this morning. Bash had already left for work. Patch gave me this necklace." She leans in to get a closer look and then frowns as if to ask why. "Something he said about giving me everything, even a star if I asked for it."

"Ah," she says with a tilted head. "That's so sweet." She tastes the lollipop, then pulls it from her lips. "Patch. Hot, sexy Patch left you sexually frustrated."

"I wasn't in the mood for a quick fuck." I half-shrug. "So I sucked his cock on the porch."

Her eyelids droop and she licks her lips. "So, you have a belly full of cum and a dripping wet pussy that aches for cock. You poor thing!"

"Oh!" I sit straight up. "I completely forgot! Mack had an accident last night."

Her face scrunches and she swats my arm. "Why wouldn't you lead with that?"

I feign severe pain. "He's okay but he broke his arm and fractured his clavicle, a gash, bruised ribs. Patch's playing nurse to make sure he takes his pills. We have yet to compare schedules so he isn't left alone for any length of time, at least for the next few days."

"Well, if you can use me, call me."

I shake my head. "I can't ask you to do that."

She scowls. "You aren't asking, I'm offering." She glances at her watch and slides off the desk. "Besides, I want to meet the pretty-boy with the long hair and seductive blue eyes." She waves her eyebrows.

"He's a beautiful man," I moan. "And he loves anal."

She looks around but the hall is empty. She grabs her ass and humps backward. She whispers, "Fuck my ass! Give it to me, pretty boy!"

I burst into laughter but slap my hand over my mouth to regain some control. She laughs and waves as she retreats down the hallway and reminds me to call her just as she rounds the corner.

After my shift ends, I stop in to see Mr. Lennysman. They'd moved him from recovery to intensive care. The nurse said he's not doing well. He still hasn't awakened and isn't responding to stimuli. I know he might not survive through the night.

I hold his hand and whisper in his ear. "Mr. Lennysman, I got your message and I agree; they can either accept us or fuck off." I snicker. "Thank you for being kind to me. I wish you happiness and peace."

Chapter 17

Bash isn't home when I arrive. He called to say he'll be working late at the *Daily News*. Ever since they promoted him to an editor's position, his workdays are getting longer and longer and he doesn't have as much freedom to work from home.

Patch is working at the mill until late tonight. Shaina said she'd stay the night to care for Mack. I sent her a text but she hasn't gotten back to me. I had doubts she would but I need to know if I'm still supposed to bring dinner over, which were the arrangements.

I take the chicken breasts from the fridge and prepare them so they'll have a spicy, crunchy coating, then space them out on a baking sheet. After I peel potatoes, I check my phone. Still no reply from her. After the chicken and cheesy potatoes are in the oven, I wash the dishes then take a quick shower and slip into yoga pants, a white t-shirt, and a long button-up sweater that I leave unbuttoned. I put everything in my car and drive to the main house.

I carry the potatoes first and knock on the door but quickly push it open. They're so hot! I rush to the stove and put it down. I turn and rush back out the door to get the chicken. Shaina comes out of the bathroom just as I close the door.

She stands with her hands on her waist, hip jutted out and glowering. "What are you doing here?" she whispers condescendingly.

"I brought dinner," I reply and refrain from including the sarcastic comments that whirl around in my thoughts. "We agreed to it last night."

"*We,*" she says with great emphasis, "did not. I can cook for my man."

"And you can afford to buy his lunch. I get it. This isn't a pissing contest. Bash had to stay late at work. Patch is at the mill until later and since it was already arranged that I would cook dinner and nobody called to change the plans, I assumed I still would be. You obviously didn't get my text, otherwise, you could have let me know you'd be here to feed and tend to him."

We stand in silence for several seconds while she scans me top to bottom. Her lip quirks. "I already ordered a pizza. It should be here in about half an hour. But thanks anyway."

"I'm going to check in on him," I say, not giving her a chance to deny me.

"He's asleep," she says as I pass by her.

I peek into his room, and it's dark and I can hear his light snores. Damn, he is asleep. I was going to ask him what he prefers to eat for dinner. If he chose pizza, I'd be okay with that, as long as it's his choice.

I make my way back to the kitchen island where she set the food to wait for me to take home. I ask, "Did you order enough for Patch or should I wrap some chicken up for him?"

"Oh, I plan to stay all night so Patch can stay here with me or go be with you. I don't care either way."

Laughter escapes me. "That's not what I asked. Patch often comes here to eat and then comes home to us. I just need to know if I should leave food for him or not."

"I ordered a king-sized pizza, fully loaded. There will be plenty," she insists.

I pick up the food and walk to the door. She opens it for me. As I step out, I pause to look at her with a pitiful expression because I know it'll piss her off. "You have problems, lady."

"Oh, *I* have problems?" She hisses as she follows me out to my car.

Over my shoulder, I reply, "Obviously! When you first started dating Mack, he told you he fucks around with other women. You said you were okay with it but now you aren't? Or is it just me you don't like?"

As I set the food on the roof and open my car door then put the food on the passenger's seat, she yells, "You weren't satisfied with the man you already have, so you take another man's heart. And the greedy bitch you are, you want my man's heart, too. Even after I asked you to back off, you still come around and want to play nursemaid."

I really want to punch her lights out! Instead, I lean on the driver's seat and set the food on the floor in case something leaks. "He's broken! Forgive me for checking in on him. I AM A NURSE!"

She points her finger at me as she nears me. "He doesn't need you for anything. He has me. I ... will take care ... of *my* man. No more hugs, no more loving kisses, and don't even think about fucking him."

"Didn't we already go through this in the restaurant? You want me to leave Mack alone? Fine! When he tells me to stay away from him, I will, but—"

She hisses, "I don't need you spreading your bad boojoo all over my man, too. You've already got Patch and Bash twirling around your little finger, dancing like puppets at your beck and call. Do you really want to turn the third brother into a sucker, too?"

"SHAINA!" Mack shouts from ten feet behind her. We both startle. She spins and I bump my head on the doorframe. "What the hell is wrong with you?"

"I'm just suggesting she—"

He doesn't let her finish. "You should go now."

Stunned, she takes a step back. Calmly, she asks, "What? You want *me* to leave?"

Mack slowly nods. "Yes, I think you should." He walks toward her. "When we started dating, I explained in detail that Goldilocks will be in my life and my bed forever, and you will need to accept that or walk away. You chose to accept my lifestyle and this is how I catch you speaking to her."

With wide eyes, she walks to him and starts to explain. "I only meant that she—"

"No woman of mine will insult or threaten Goldilocks. She belongs here." With little expression, he dismisses her. "You can go."

She storms into the house; the screen door slams behind her and I can hear her stomps in the house. A few seconds later, she rushes out while she mumbles to herself. She spits a few choice words loud enough for us to hear and throws her purse in her car.

Before she gets in she yells at Mack. "What are you going to do when she chooses Bash, leaving you and Patch to pine over that little twat? Huh? I know, you're going to become hard and numb like Patch already is. Enjoy your misery! And, *Goldilocks*," she says my name with the sarcasm of a teenager. "Fuck you, cunt!"

I yell back, "I've been called worse by Patch. You've only succeeded in turning me on."

She screeches at me and shoots me the middle finger. Her car whips down the driveway and around the bend so quickly Mack and I wince and wait to hear the crunch of her fender against a tree. Surprisingly, she doesn't hit it.

"I'm sorry, Goldilocks. I didn't know she was like that." He wraps an arm around my shoulders. "Why didn't you tell me she confronted you at the diner? And when did this happen?"

I lift my face and kiss him just once. "You were paying. Mack, I'm a big girl and can handle my own battles. I thought she'd calm down at some point."

"It's not only your battle though, Goldilocks. It's mine too; I brought her into our lives. It's only right that you should have talked to me when she became a problem." He brushes a lock of my blonde hair behind my ear. "I'm starving."

"Oh, I made chicken and cheesy potatoes but Shaina said—"

He shakes his head. "I don't care what she said, I care about my growling stomach." He leans to smell the food and sighs his approval.

Just as I pick up the container and the toweled glass dish, a car rounds the bend and stops beside us. A teenager climbs out, opens the back door, and takes a king-sized pizza from the warming bag.

He says, "Whoever just left here nearly hit me."

"Oh, sorry about that." I apologize on her behalf and then look at Mack who doesn't know why the kid is here. "Shaina ordered pizza. She didn't know I was cooking."

"She knew! I heard Patch tell her." He looks at the kid who holds the large box. "Can I refuse that pizza and have it sent elsewhere? I'll give you a tip for your trouble but I'm not paying for a pizza I didn't ask for."

The scruffy kid looks confused. "It's already paid for." He looks at the name written on the receipt. "Someone named Shaina paid for it with a credit card." He shrugs. "Do you still want me to take it somewhere else?"

"Well, since it's already paid for!" I set the food on the hood of my car and then take the pizza from the kid. My smile isn't for the free pizza. I wear it because accepting it is a little *fuck you* to Shaina.

Mack snickers and gives the kid a tip. He thanks him and hops back in the tiny car and speeds away; not nearly as fast as Shaina.

We eat both my dinner and some of the pizza while we discuss topics that range from our high school days, past relationships, and even touch on politics. Mack's eyelids weigh heavily. Despite his denial, I know he's tired so I insist he gets into bed.

"Lie with me?" he asks as I pull the comforter up to his chin and tuck it around the cast as best I can.

I reply, "If I do, I'll end up falling asleep and Bash won't appreciate me spending the night with you; it's one of the rules. Do you have everything you need?"

His eyebrows raise, then he lifts the sheet and looks down. "I have a … small problem."

I look under the sheet and see that his erection tents his pale blue pajama bottoms.

"That does look like a problem, but it's not small."

I flop the blankets back and pull down on the waistband until his hard prick pops free. It stands at attention before me. I wrap my lips around the head and glide as far down as I can. He moans appreciatively.

His cock is longer but thinner than both Bash and Patch which is perfect for anal sex, which is his kink. He took my anal cherry so to speak.

I bob on his prick and suck and swirl the head.

"Take your clothes off and sit on my face." He moans. "Let me taste your pussy. Please?" he begs between pants.

I shake my head and continue my delicious assault. I cup and squeeze his balls just right. I grip the base of his cock in my other hand. He moans out and his hips lift.

"Oh, fuck! Goldilocks…" He wails while his body jerks and he fills my mouth with his seed. I swallow and continue to glide up and down as he twitches and whimpers. "I fucking love your mouth! I love you!"

I wipe my mouth as I tuck him back in. His eyelids hang and his blinks are progressively becoming longer. I kiss his forehead and whisper, "I love you, too, and I'm sorry about Shaina." He shakes his head so I grow a half-smile. "Go to sleep."

His smile fades as his eyelids close.

After I text Patch to see when I should expect his arrival, he immediately writes back and says he'll be here shortly. I let him know I'm going home and there's food in the fridge. He begs me to stay so he can repay me for this morning but I kindly decline.

I lock up and drive home. Bash is eating the food I left in the fridge for him in the living room while he watches television.

As I set my purse on the bench by the door, I snicker. "I'd come to kiss you but I need to brush my teeth first."

A potato wedge hangs off his fork and he gives me a sideways glance. "Patch?" He shoves the fork in his mouth.

"I blew Patch this morning," I confess with a shrug. "But Mack felt a little lonely so I blew him, too." Bash snickers. I progress toward him with my arms crossed over my chest. "I think him and Shaina are finished."

He looks surprised. "That's too bad. Do you know what happened?"

Mack overheard her yelling at me. She's been a bitch to me lately. I thought she'd work past it but…" I shrug.

His forehead crinkles. "How come you didn't tell me?"

I shrug to blow it off. "Like I said, I figured we'd work it out."

"Mhm." He doesn't look satisfied with my answer. "If you have a problem with someone we bring into our circle, you have to speak up. Promise me."

After a long sigh, I reply, "Deal."

He tilts his head and raises his eyebrows. "So you sucked two cocks today, huh?" He lifts his plate and I can see the bulge tucked away in his jeans. "Want to try for three?"

"Can I brush my teeth first?" I tease. "Unless you want me to kiss you with Mack's cum in my teeth."

He grimaces. "You don't have to kiss me if you're just going to blow me, but … EWW!" He stabs a piece of chicken. "Mouthwash twice, okay?"

I laugh as I walk through the kitchen and down the hall to the master bathroom. After a shower and hearty mouth cleansing—as requested—I slip on matching red stockings, garter belt, bra, and black high-heels, and then send him a text to ask if he can help me with a box in the bedroom.

He enters and his eyes light up. He immediately strips off his clothes with lightning speed. He bites his lip as he struts toward me; his huge, steel-hard cock swings as he does. He grips it and slowly strokes as his eyes drink me in. "So, you have a box that you need help with?" Before he scoops me up and tosses me onto the bed, he whispers, "Girl, you are in for it tonight."

He's on me quickly and kisses me while his hands grope my body. Bash moans and slips down. He jiggles my bra cup until my nipple pops free below the underwire. He sucks and laps on it while he frees the other. He nips and sucks my nipples and my pussy clenches, eager to feel the heat of his mouth. Slowly, he kisses down my tummy while his beautiful blue eyes burn into mine.

His hands glide along my thighs then spread them wide. He kisses my panties before he gently pulls them aside. With a flat tongue, he licks from asshole to clit and sucks my swelling button before he laps at it with a fury. I grip the light grey comforter and hang on as I fall deeper and deeper into my body; into the mind-numbing deliciousness of orgasm.

No thoughts. No control. Stupendous pleasure.

I revel in the aftermath of so much pleasure. He tenderly pecks kisses on my twitching clit while it sends shockwaves through my entire body. It's both wonderful and painful.

Bash rushes up my body and fills me with his thick, hard cock. My nails dig into his waist to pull him in. My cries are met with his lips. His hips pound against me. My legs, as if having a mind of their own, wrap around his waist so my pussy can pull him in further, so the tip of his cock can torture my cervix.

He lifts himself up and grabs my panties and yanks them down my legs and tosses them aimlessly. He's inside me again and pounding himself deep into me as he watches the action.

He groans, "Fuck, you're so beautiful."

Before I can react, he's up on his knees. He has my right leg on the bed between his legs, and my left leg bent at the knee and pressed against my chest. He turns me so my left leg crosses my body and then slams deeper into me than I've ever had anyone. At first, I'm shocked by the pain of the depth but my body surprises me and spins me into a screaming orgasm, and then another, and another.

I have no idea how much time passes or how many orgasms I've screamed through, but I've found my new favorite position. Bash pulls out of me, grips his cock, and begins to jerk himself off.

"No, please," I beg. "I want you in my mouth."

He grips the leg lying straight on the bed and my shoulder and spins me so I'm on my tummy facing him. I lift myself on my arms and open my mouth. He holds my head and fucks my mouth but refrains from pushing into my throat. I push myself onto him to take more.

"Shit! I'm going to cum, baby," he mutters, then his tummy muscles lock tight to reveal washboard abs.

I pull my legs beneath me and grip the base of his cock tightly while I suck and bob. His wail cuts short as his body seizes and jerks. Seed fills my mouth for the third time today. I wonder if people would refer to me as a cum-guzzling whore if they ever found out. I don't care, my men are satisfied and they don't disrespect me for my whorish behavior.

Bash falls to the bed and pulls me with him. I land with my head on his shoulder. Slowly our gasps ease and the brightly lit room is quiet.

"Goddamn, Goldie," he pauses. "You drive me fucking nuts because you're perfect in every way."

"I'm not perfect; I have flaws," I retort.

"I don't care about your damn flaws." He turns his head to look into my eyes. He kisses me with velvety softness. "My love for you is infinite. And my brothers love you, too. One day, you'll really be ours."

My eyebrows lift. "What does that mean?"

"It means I'm going to marry you one day."

I smile, kiss him quickly, then slide out of bed. "Yeah, we'll see," I tease as my wobbly legs carry me to the bathroom.

He calls after me. "Yeah, we'll see! You'll see." In a whisper so quiet I'm sure it wasn't meant for me to hear, he says, "Sooner than later."

GTB

Chapter 18

Getting to work with ten minutes to spare is a windfall for me; I usually run in at the last minute. I go to check on Mr. Lennysman but I'm told he passed away during the night, having never woke from surgery.

Maybe I should have stayed and talked to him to give him some comfort. He died alone in a cold, bright, sterile room. Surely he deserved better than that.

Between my first and second surgery, I text Bash to let him know about Mr. Lennysman. He writes back immediately that he's sad to hear and how he really liked the old dude; his words, not mine.

Lizzy is nothing if not a woman who isn't afraid to do silly shit simply to lift my spirits. She's quickly become one of my favorite people.

For the first surgery, she drew a goofy smile on her surgical mask but it was missing a few teeth. The fourth surgery had her smoking a cigar. The sixth, she was puckering up for a kiss. It kept me entertained but Dr. Kacey didn't seem all too amused. He sensed I was upset about something and was kind-hearted enough not to ask her to cut it out.

"Lizzy?"

She replies, "Yes, dear Goldilocks."

"Are you busy tonight? Any grand plans?"

She replies in a high pitch, Alabama accent, "No, ma'am. I am free as a jaybird. Why? Do you want to get drunk tonight and have your way with me?"

Dr. Kacey looks at her and clears his throat and then glances at me.

I stutter, "She's kidding. We, we don't … do that." His eyes drop to my chest and to the patient to continue the surgery.

Her eyebrows dance and she giggles. "Do you want to do something tonight?"

I can smell the stench from the cauterization. "Actually, I thought I could introduce you to Mack."

Just by her tone, I can tell she's smiling. "I'm finally going to meet that stud-muffin? I. Am. In!"

"Okay, pick me up at my place at six and we can go together."

She enthusiastically asks, "Where's Patch going to be?"

I giggle. "He'll be at the mill, and I don't know what time he'll be done."

She pouts. "Damn, I was hoping to *see* him again."

***

Lizzy parks her burgundy Jeep beside my car. She's wearing snug black jeans and a white V-neck cashmere sweater. Her hair is wavy with perfect curls and her make-up looks freshly applied.

I lean on the open-door frame and whistle as she ascends the stairs. "Damn, woman! You're gorgeous!" I whistle again and she does a little twirl and flips her hair.

"Thank you," she says, then looks past me into the house. "Bash home?"

A smile grows on my face. I sing, "You want him. You want him. Hell yeah, you want him."

Her palms lift. "You make it sound like I'm going to hop on his cock before we say hello. Although that sounds like fun, I'd like to meet Mack."

I shut the door and start down the stairs while she follows. "That's too bad. I'm sure he'd love to *say hello* to you, too."

I direct her as she drives to the main house. She follows me inside while she compliments on how quaint and relaxing the setting is. Mack is in the kitchen munching on potato chips. They're scattered on the counter, floor, and table.

"Jeeze, Mack! Did you get any in your mouth?" I tease and start to pick them off the floor.

"I couldn't open the bag so I used my teeth." His toothy smile has his face even more handsome than it already was.

I hear Lizzy whisper under her breath. "Goddamn. Not an ugly brother in the bunch."

"How rude of me," I say and step to the side as Lizzy nears us. Mack licks his lips and doesn't blink. "Mack, this is Lizzy. Lizzy, meet Mack."

Mack whispers, "Patch wasn't bullshitting. You are gorgeous!" He looks at me as if to give me shit for not having introduced them months ago. "I'd shake your hand, but…" He points to his cast held against his bare chest by a dark-blue sling. His loose-fitting black pajama pants flow as he walks to the fridge and it's obvious he's going commando. "Can I get anyone a beer?"

"I'll take one," I say and look at Lizzy who has yet to avert her eyes from Mack's body. "Make it two." He takes three out. "None for you. You're medicated."

Lizzy sees his sexy glare and whimpers but quickly recovers by clearing her throat. "You have a great house, Mack." She slowly walks away as she turns to admire the room.

"Thank you. It keeps the rain off." Mack admires her breasts, but when she walks away, he tilts his head and sways his hips. His gaze meets mine and he silently mouths *great ass!* "Would you like me to show you around?"

I open his bottle of water and hand it to him. He takes a gulp and pouts when I lift my beer and sip it.

She takes a beer and follows him around the house. I stay in the kitchen to sweep up the chip crumbs and then prepare a couple of ham sandwiches for Mack. When they return, it's obvious both are smitten with each other. I refill Mack's water bottle, then we all sit and watch him eat while we chit chat.

An hour later, when Lizzy's in the washroom, Mack tilts his head toward the ceiling. "That fucking chick could be the death of me and I'd welcome it. Fuckin' Patch got to her first." His mouth sets in a hard line.

"I'm sure if you asked nicely, he'd be willing to share the shiny new toy but it's up to her, of course."

"Of course," he repeats and his eyes narrow as he surveys me. "And you, too."

"Me?" My forehead furrows.

He looks down at his bottle. "How would you feel about it if we hooked up?"

"She can do anything she likes because I trust her." I take a long gulp of beer while my eyes remain fixed on his. "She's fucking hot! I would fuck her if I had a cock and if I were into pussy. I just might be willing to hop the fence for a little ménage."

"I'd pay a hefty price to sit in the corner and watch that." He looks vacantly past me as if watching it play out in his mind. He rests his casted arm on the table. "So...?" he questions with round eyes.

I laugh. "So, go for it! I'm sure Patch wouldn't mind. I'll text him if it'll make you feel better."

He says, "It would."

I pick up my phone while Mack hums a happy tune with a smile plastered on his face. I set my phone down and laugh at his silly display of excitement.

He asks, "What about you and Bash? Have you two considered taking her to bed?"

"I've been thinking a lot about it and I want to see Bash and her in a sweaty heap; moaning, licking, and fucking each other. Just thinking about it revs me up. But I'm not sure I have the courage to get in on something like that just yet."

"Goldie-girl," she says as she crosses the room toward the table and does a little hop before she sits. My phone chimes when she says, "We should give Patch a night off from babysitting Mack. Why don't I," her gaze falls to Mack "stay here with Mack, so Patch can spend the night with you and

Bash?" Faking innocence, she adds, "I can sleep on the couch."

Mack looks at me to judge my reaction to the text message. I meet his gaze and the corners of my lips lift. We simultaneously agree that she should stay. I think we're all going to win tonight! Half-hour later, I take a flashlight and head off into the woods and leave the two of them to whatever mischief they can get into.

I'm immersed in the darkness of the night. The shadows cast from the roots of the fallen trees resemble bears or wolves ready to attack. It's hard to keep myself calm even though I've grown up in these woods and have yet to hear of a bear or wolf attack on a human. Lizzy offered to drive me home but I refused it. I love the forest; day or night.

When I arrive home, Bash tells me Patch just got in the shower in his ensuite bathroom.

With wide eyes, I say, "I haven't showered in there yet. Have you?"

"Nope." Bash tilts his head away from the television as he tosses a peanut in his mouth. "Well, I think it's about time you do. Don't you?"

"We aren't going to fuck," I say and he gives me a confused look. "I don't want to tire him out. I plan to take you both to bed tonight if that's okay with you."

"Patch said he was going to the main house tonight to help Mack."

I wave my eyebrows. "No need. Lizzy's there and I think they're going to get along swimmingly."

"Oh!" he says with a naughty grin. "That means you get both of us tonight. I hope you had a nap today; you're going to need it."

My pussy clenches at the image of me sandwiched between them while they kiss me everywhere and drown me in euphoria. "I'm going to go join Patch and then I'm going to get into bed to wait for my two studs."

"I'll be there," he promises. I kiss him, then rush to join Patch.

Patch washes every inch of my skin, then my hair. I do absolutely nothing to help, as per his wishes. He takes extra care to ensure my vagina and nipples are well washed, he even drops to his knees to taste me just to make sure I'm clean. He dries me and wraps me in a fluffy yellow towel. He dries himself then takes my hand to lead me through the house to the master bathroom where Bash showers. He has me sit on the stool while he blow-dries my hair and Bash rinses off.

The two stand behind me with towels around their waists. My eyes shift between their well-formed arms, chests, abs, and bulges. My legs squeeze together to stifle my pussy's hunger.

Bash watches Patch work the hairdryer as best he can for a man whose hair has always been cropped army short. As he puts away the dryer, Bash brushes out the knots.

"Would you like me to put it in a ponytail?" I look from man to man.

Patch's mouth twists as he considers. Bash asks, "Can you braid it?"

They have identical deep creases on their foreheads as they watch my hands flip tresses of hair this way and that.

I stand and turn to face them. I am a lucky woman!

PTB

Chapter 19

Bash takes my hand. I stand and follow him as he walks backward toward the bed. He stops a few feet from it. Patch slides my towel from my body. He stands so close behind me I can feel his heat. His lips press feathery soft to the back of my neck and I shutter. Bash kisses my lips just as tenderly. My knees weaken.

Patch whispers just behind my left ear. "We're going to bind you in rope. You won't be able to use your hands or arms. We will do everything for you." He kisses me again. "Do you trust us to keep you safe?"

"Yes." My whisper is barely audible.

Bash sits on the bed. A brown rope with a scent I'm not familiar with is held in front of me by Patch. I watch him undo the tan-colored rope and run his hands along it as if he treasures it.

He moans softly. "There's nothing sexier than a woman bound in rope, giving herself to me and entrusting me to protect her."

Patch loops the rope over my neck and begins tying the two ropes together with small knots about four inches apart. Each line of rope runs between my legs, up my back, and through the loop at the back of my neck. The ropes are separated and fed under my armpits and then looped through one of the four-inch sections before it returns under my arms to loop around the rope lining my spine.

He repeats once more but has me hold one rope end in my mouth while he wraps my left arm three times, then knots it somehow. He relieves me of the rope and repeats with my right arm. He continues to wrap my torso but stops twice more to incorporate my arms in the binds. As he continues, the two ropes that run through my pussy pull tighter and tighter.

When I wiggle, Patch has concerns. "Are you in pain?"

I shake my head. "It's pressing on my pussy."

Bash asks, "Do you like the way it feels?"

I wiggle again. "Yes, but the placement is off."

He sinks to his knees and guides the ropes until they each lie in the leg's crease on either side of my pussy. Now they squeeze my labia together. I moan and Bash's lip lifts at the corner as his eyes burn into mine.

Bash sits back on the bed to watch Patch enjoy his rope-play as if to bind me is his most intimate way for us to connect. He stands before me to tie the final knot. His face isn't rough and angry as is his usual expression; he seems softer somehow as though his mind has quieted. He could say he loves me a hundred times but at this moment, the way his fingers trace the ropes that line my skin, he's not just watching me; his soul watches mine. The peaceful silence screams love.

He slips a finger under the knot between my breasts and leads me. Their towels fall to the floor as they crawl onto the bed. Bash lies on his back and Patch maneuvers me so I kneel on either side of Bash's head, my pussy hovers above his lips. Bash's hands pull down on my hips until my labia presses to his mouth. The restriction from the ropes and the way his tongue fishes between my lips has me edged so close to orgasm in an instant. Perhaps ropes are my kink, too.

Patch instructs me. "Don't cum."

This will not be easy. I wince when he pinches my nipples with wooden clothespins. He kisses me tenderly, then his tongue glides along my upper lip.

He whispers, "You are so fucking beautiful."

Patch stands on either side of Bash's waist and grips my braid to guide my mouth around his rock-hard cock. I lick and suck him while Bash does the same to me. It feels so good that I get lost in it and forget about Patch.

He steps aside and grasps the rope on my back. He slowly lowers me until my mouth lines up with Bash's cock. Patch releases the ropes.

I do my best to mouth the huge cock but without the ability to raise my chest, it's a rather pathetic attempt at oral copulation. Bash lifts me by my ribs and rests his elbows on the bed at his waist. It's a little easier this way.

I fight the urge to orgasm by lifting my pussy off his face for a few seconds until the tension eases. Patch steps up on the bed and slips his fingers under the crisscrossed ropes by my shoulder blades and down at my lower back. He lifts me using the ropes. I hover, suspended over Bash, who slides up the bed and stops.

Patch lowers me and Bash spreads my knees, then uses my hips to guide my pussy over his cock. Patch lowers me slowly and releases me only when I've enveloped every inch of Bash's erection. With the aid of the ropes, Bash guides my movements so I rock on his cock how he wants me to move.

This is so fucking sexy, but I wish I wasn't backward because I want to watch Bash's face as I ride him. Does he love the ropes as much as I do?

Patch stands over Bash's legs and again grips my braid to aim my mouth so I can suck him. He's more forceful this time and holds himself in my throat a few seconds longer than I desire but I trust in him not to hurt me.

An orgasm rolls through me. I couldn't hold it off any longer, and I couldn't ask permission because of the cock in my throat. Bash holds himself inside me. His moans prove he favors my vaginal spasms as my orgasm slowly concludes.

Patch feeds his fingers beneath the ropes at my shoulder blades and tailbone and lifts. I'm suspended again, aside from my feet that hope to find their footing on the bed. He steps off the bed and I swing and scream, then laugh. It looks like I'm going to hit the floor face first but he has me safely in his clutches.

I laugh again but I don't know why. Is it because I didn't die just now or because I love the thrill of it all?

A waist-high A-frame bench with a leather padded top has me curious where it came from. I would have noticed it there when I came into the room. Patch sets me so that I lie over it, face down. My chest hangs over one end and my legs the other. I look under the bench and see Patch squatted behind me.

Using three leather straps on each leg, he binds my legs securely to the A-frame. Two more straps wrap over my torso and arms like seatbelts and fasten tightly. I can barely move.

I'm scared and yet more aroused than I've ever been. What will they do to me? Will I like it? My chest has limited movement but the rest of me is locked down and at their mercy.

"What's your safeword, Goldie?" Bash stands a few inches in front of my face while he strokes his heavy cock. Patch's hands slap down on my ass and I jolt.

"Red," I reply while I twist my upper body and neck, attempting to look at his face. I smile when I understand my limitations and then relax back into position.

Patch fiddles with my braid but Bash's hand gliding up and down his cock holds my interest. The ropes that lead between my ass cheeks are yanked and then yanked again until they slip over my buttocks and are no longer wedged between the globes. The ropes hold my pussy lips apart and the air feels icy as it teases my superheated flesh.

Patch slides his cock into my pussy and holds himself inside while he fiddles with the knotted rope near my ass. My braid pulls and my head tilts until my mouth is perfectly lined up to take a penis. He ties it, then fucks me; hard and fast.

Bash slips the fat mushroom head between my lips and I suck like there's no tomorrow. I want him in my throat. I want my whole body full of them.

Take me! Take all of me!

He slowly fucks my mouth but not nearly as hard, fast, or deep as Patch takes my pussy. I can't move and the weight of my torso pressing into the bench makes it that much harder to breathe, but I love the restriction. Patch slows and something cold drips on my asshole. His finger slips in while he continues to fuck me but with an easier rhythm.

Bash eases his cock from my lips and bends to kiss me with vigor. His hand wraps around my throat and applies a little pressure on either side of my trachea to slow my blood flow to my brain. I'm lightheaded but I'm not afraid; I like it. Patch stretches my asshole while my pussy clenches his cock and my mind whirls.

The tip of Patch's cock presses into my ass and it welcomes him. Bash's grip eases as his lips and tongue assault my mouth. Patch eases into me and I moan. My throat is set free and Bash stands and then pushes the head of his cock in my mouth. I suck while Patch slowly fucks my ass. His cock is thicker than Mack's, and I can definitely feel the difference but it's wonderful.

The rope that held my braid is removed. My head hangs while Patch slowly glides in and out of my asshole while Bash frees my legs and then my torso. Patch slips out of my ass and lifts me by the ropes. He carries me to the bed like a sack of potatoes with legs and I giggle.

Bash lies on his back on the bed. Patch sets me on my knees on the bed and Bash grips my chest ropes and guides me until I can straddle him. His prick is quickly devoured by my wanton pussy. I immediately slide back and forth greedily. Patch moves in behind me and slips his knees between my calves and Bash's thighs. My knees are spread very wide.

Using the ropes bound over my chest, Bash pulls me down on him but stops me just before our faces collide. He holds me in place and kisses me softly, seductively. Patch gently slips his cock back into my ass and pauses to give my body time to adjust to the overwhelming fullness.

I can't kiss. I can't moan. I can barely breathe. I've never been this full in my entire life. The skin on my back beneath Patch's kisses prickles in the wake of his hot breath.

Beneath me, Bash lifts his hips to press himself deeper into me while Patch gradually retreats, then eases all the way back in again. They mold into me with a slow passion and it's deliriously marvelous.

My hips are lifted an inch or so, and then I'm lowered. Something cold is placed between me and Bash, up against my clit. It suddenly springs to life with mild vibration.

I might be drooling. I can't be sure. "Oh, God! Please…"

As they continue to fuck me, the vibration increases and my body stiffens. The tightness in my tummy is so immense, like an expanded balloon. If I cum it might be too much and I may die but I don't care.

They fuck faster and the vibration revs into warp speed. I jerk and mumble sounds that don't form words. I fall further and further into a black hole, yet somehow I'm afloat near the ceiling. My entire being twitches and the vibrator slips to the exact spot on my clit and I'm drowning in the peacefulness of euphoria.

I'm lost. My soul is gone, or maybe I am only a soul now and I've left my body. I feel nothing except immense pleasure that can't be measured or explained. It just is…

Someone screams and I fall back into my body. It was me; I screamed. Both men use me like an old whore and I can't get enough.

"Yes! Fuck me!" I yell as the sweat between our bodies builds. "Ah, gaaa! Fu…" My thoughts spin wildly until they no longer exist. I don't exist. Nothing does. Absolutely nothing.

A barbaric groan vibrates my back and prickles my skin with its heat. Patch wails again, then quickly pulls himself from my ass and sinks to the end of the bed. His grunt echoes about the room. His breath holds—he's coming, hard!

Bash wraps his arm around me and rolls us both. I'm below him and try to see his features through blurred vision. He lifts my knees and spreads them, then sinks his thick cock into my pussy. He leans forward to rest his weight on his forearms. His lips press to mine and hold. He's not delving his tongue or trying to advance our kiss. He fucks me and he's lost.

He whispers, "I love you. I love you. I love you. I love y—
"

Bash's breath holds and his body stills, and then jerks. His cock throbs inside me as he fills me with his seed. His exasperated exhale has his tension slowly easing.

His eyes remain closed and he drops his forehead to my shoulder. He whispers, "I love you so much." He shutters, whimpers, and then swallows hard. His exhale is long and hot on my neck.

My breath slowly calms. I want to hold him, but my arms are still bound by my sides. I settle for resting my cheek against his forehead. His softened penis slips from me and we both groan from the disappointment. He lifts his face to kiss me.

"Let's get her untied," Patch interrupts our moment with as soft a voice as he can manage.

Bash smiles then kisses me before he helps me onto my feet. My knees are weak and my entire existence is spent. If I could see my soul, it would look disheveled and exhausted but smiling and utterly satisfied.

I'm silent as the ropes glide against my skin. Patch's eyes lock on mine when they can, and I miss them when he's behind me. The love I see in his eyes screams volumes. Even the world's best poets couldn't put into words the love these men have shown me tonight.

As the ropes glide and edge me toward freedom, I understand why Patch has a bondage fetish. My trust in him means everything to him and I can feel that through the ropes as they caress my flesh.

The rope lifts from around my neck, and I'm freed. Patch looks at my face as if to memorize my features. "Goldilocks, you own my heart. I will always be here for you. Even when I'm not, I'm still here." He lifts my hand and sets my palm over his heart. "It beats for you."

Bash stands next to Patch. He lifts my other hand, tips his head toward me, and sets my hand on it. "You already know you own me ... you own all of me."

I look at him and laugh. He can really ruin a romantic moment! Patch slaps the back of Bash's head and they both laugh.

We shower, eat ice cream, and discuss the magic of what just happened. All in all, we want to do it again soon. We snuggle into bed, me in the middle, and quickly drift to sleep.

Chapter 20

It's early when I feel Patch slip out of bed. Instead of using the master bathroom, he leaves the bedroom and closes the door behind him. I turn my head and see Bash asleep with the blankets at rest about his waist. His hand holds his cock the same way Patch does as if to protect the most valued part of their bodies from danger while they sleep.

I slide close enough to trail my fingers down his arm. He scratches the spot. I tickle again and he scratches harder. His eyes open with a growling expression until he sees me lying next to him, watching him.

"Hello, handsome," I say, then repeat the tickle.

He reaches for my hand and lays it on his chest. "Good morning. Since when does Miss Sleepyhead wake before me?" I shrug. He says, "I could get used to it."

"It's a one-time thing so don't rely on me to get you up in time to go to work unless you enjoy being late."

Bash lifts his head to look over me at the empty spot. "Patch gone to his room?"

"He just left. I'm not sure where he went, but I assume so." I roll toward him and kiss his chest. "Last one up is a rotten egg." He jerks and I leap off the bed only to realize how achy my body is.

He snickers. "Ropes are a bitch, aren't they?"

"I don't think it was the ropes themselves so much as how hard I fought against them." I wave my eyebrows. "I'm beginning to think being bound is my guilty pleasure."

After a few stretches, I toss on a purple nightgown with a cartoon bear on the front and head to the bathroom to freshen up before I go to the kitchen.

"Hello, beautiful," Patch says as my feet slap the cool wood floor with each step. He waits for a kiss before he hands me the mug of coffee he readied for me.

"Thank you," I say with a smile. I groan. "I'm so sore today. You guys really gave it to me last night."

He stops taking things out of the freezer to look at me. "If you're rather us take it easy on you from now on—"

"Ha!" I yelp. "Hell, no!" I sip the liquid of the gods. "Totally worth every ache and pain."

"I'll have you know my knee is giving me shit today," he says as he swings his right calf and grumbles.

"Hey, I was thinking," I say just before Bash walks in the kitchen.

"Good morning, brother!" Bash says and takes a mug from the cupboard, then heads toward the coffee pot. "Yes! Mm, breakfast!"

"As I was saying," I continue. "We should pack up the ingredients and bring everything to the main house."

They both agree but Patch says, "We can check in on the lovely couple to see how their evening went."

After we shower and dress, we pack everything in a cooler and climb into my car. I sit in the back to let the boys chat. Bash zips down the driveway and speeds down the highway that leads to the driveway of the main house. He stops so Patch can collect the mail from the flag risen box.

He reaches for the handle but Bash jerks the car forward a few feet. Patch scowls as he reaches for it again. Bash jerks the car forward just enough that he has to reach further. Patch whips open the door then drops into the car and throws his body weight against Bash and pins him to the door.

Bash grunts breathlessly and can only manage to whisper. "Get the fuck off me, cow!" They both laugh like brothers do all the way to the main house.

We walk in and expect them to be awake but it's quiet. Mack's bedroom door is slightly ajar so I slowly push it open. The sliver of sunlight seeping through the gap in the drapes does not reveal a sleeping Mack.

Lizzy's straddled over his face with a strong grip on the wooden headboard. I can see Mack's chin move beneath her as she slowly sways her hips. Her red hair flows down her pale shoulders with messy disregard. She's shockingly beautiful and she nears orgasm. Her ribs widen her back as she sucks in her breaths.

Her head whips around and her eyes dart to mine. I should retreat from the room but when she doesn't startle, my feet seem to cement themselves to the floor. I can't look away, neither can she. Her whimpers are like soft, sexy music. She moans and her eyelids droop. Her chin drops to her chest as her body quivers. She gasps and pants before her shoulders slump forward.

She shivers then lifts off his face. Her hair blocks me from seeing their kiss. I should walk away and close the door. I should. Why can't I leave?

Lizzy whispers something to Mack before she stands. He looks at me and grins. "Are you next?" He reaches his hand out to me and waves his fingers to urge me to go to him.

I snicker while I lean against the doorframe and cross my arms over my chest. "I don't think I could if I wanted to." They both look at me as if waiting for me to continue. "Patch bound me in rope and they dual fucked me. I'm exhausted and every muscle in my body aches."

Lizzy pulls a black t-shirt over her head and rams her arms in, pulling the snug fit shirt over her perky tits. "You're a lucky girl!" She slips her legs in her panties. "That's something I've always wanted to do—two guys at once."

"Put it on your bucket list," I say with a grin.

She laughs and pulls on a pair of yoga pants. She fluffs her tangled hair as she crosses the room toward me and a naked Mack sits on the edge of the bed.

She whispers, "He is really good at that." I nod and she kisses me as friends do. "Are you okay?" Again, I nod but this time my lip is pinched between my teeth. She smiles and winks as she leaves the room.

I remain to make sure Mack is able to manage his pajama pants. He asks, "Are you okay with what you saw?" He stands and pulls them up.

I nod. "Yeah! Absolutely." He stands and we take a few steps toward each other. "That was," pause in search of the words, "fucking beautiful. I hadn't expected to see that, but I'm glad I did."

He tilts his head and brushes a stray lock of hair behind my ear. "Why is that?"

"Because of how I feel about it. It's confirmation that I like her being with you guys. I'm not jealous at all. I'm no longer nervous about her being with Bash, should that situation arise." He kisses me and I can smell her on his face. I crinkle my nose. "Um, you should wash your face." He smiles apologetically and I shrug as I turn to walk out of his bedroom. "It's okay, I didn't hate it."

Lizzy has to leave almost right away. Her shift at the hospital starts in less than an hour from now and she still needs to get home to shower and change.

The guys and I eat and talk about what we all did the night before. Mack tells us that she came in through the night to ask if he needed anything. He said he didn't say anything, he just looked up and down her body. She stripped, and it went from there.

He said he felt useless since he can't move around very much. She rode him slowly because the pain from his bruised ribs was too unbearable when she bucked hard.

Mack likes her. Patch likes her. I'm sure Bash will, too.

***

Bash and Patch had to work this morning so I stayed to help Mack; who can mostly care for himself other than bathing and tasks that require two hands.

I love my time alone with Mack. He's very sweet, funny, and he loves to talk, so I don't have to hold up the conversation. After I've prepared his lunch, he insists he'll be fine alone. I try to argue but he's persistent.

The walk home through the woods is peaceful and quiet aside from the sounds of the forest. The smell of moss tickles my nostrils and I savor it. Nothing reminds me more of my happy childhood more than the smell of damp moss.

At two o'clock, Mack calls me and sounds distressed. "Goldie, are you busy?"

I set my book down and sense something's wrong. "Are you okay?"

He grumbles. "I'm fine, but I could use some help."

I walk into the house and set my book on the end table. "What's the matter?"

As I sling my purse strap over my shoulder he explains. "Well, I tried to make a coffee and dropped the container."

"Oh, shit! Let me guess," I say while I walk to my car. "Coffee grounds are all over the floor."

"Ah, well," he pauses and I can picture him peering down at the floor and shrugging his healthy shoulder. "There's a lot going on over here."

"I'm in the car. I'll be there in a few minutes. Go sit down somewhere and try not to make more of a mess." I laugh as I hang up.

I walk into the house and toss my purse on the table by the door and stride toward the kitchen. "Where's the mess? Mack?" I make my way around the island and look at the floor expecting a mess. "Mack, where did you drop the coffee? Did you already clean…" My words catch in my throat and I can't believe my eyes.

All three men are dressed in tuxedos. Patch and Mack are side by side, each holding a dozen red roses. Mack's jacket is draped over his casted arm. Bash is down on one knee and a single white rose lies beside his foot. He holds a small open box.

Patch waves me over and it's what I needed to snap me out of my trance. My feet weigh a ton and yet I think I hover above the floor. I stand before Bash and take a breath. I think it's my first one since I noticed them.

Bash swallows. "Goldilocks, I've loved you since the day I walked into that classroom a shy little boy. Our eyes met and you smiled at me. My tummy felt funny; nauseous but in a good way. I didn't know it then, but as we aged my desire to be yours never wavered even though I doubted the probability of our union. And now, as you stand before me... before us," he pauses to swallow.

His voice cracks. "It's been a lifetime in the making. I kneel before you, as vulnerable as that little boy who first met your eyes." He fights back tears. "I want to fall in love with you every single day." He blinks and tears spill. "Will you marry me?"

I'm a blubbering mess and can barely speak when he plucks the ring from the box and holds it before me, hoping I'll slip my finger into it. "Yes, of course, I'll marry you."

I lift my hand and spread my fingers. The ring is a perfect fit and absolutely gorgeous.

He stands, holding my cheeks in his palms, and kisses me three times before he hugs me. Patch taps Bash and he steps back but continues to hold my newly ringed hand.

Patch hands me the roses before he kisses me. "Congratulations, Goldilocks." He grabs Bash's shoulder and pulls him into a hug and mumbles something into his tuxedo-clad shoulder.

Mack kisses me softly, then brushes his thumb on my chin as his eyes shine with tears. "Welcome to the family." He places his roses over my arm atop Patch's. He wraps his arms around Bash and they hug while I blink and try to see the ring through the pools of tears.

The setting is small. It contains two small pearls that rest on either side of a much larger pearl. They're off-white and set on a silver band. It's beautiful, small and showy. It's perfectly suited for my personality.

"It was our mother's ring," Bash says as he takes my hand, allowing my fingers to drape between his thumb and forefinger. They all stare at it as if seeing it on my finger brings back happier memories of their mother. "She would have loved to know you and I are together, and she'd want you to have it."

Patch cuts in. "Bash wanted to add to it to include Mack and me."

Mack cuts him off. "The little pearls represent us."

Bash clears his throat rather loudly and they take a step back. "Patch and Mack love you, too. Although you'll be saying yes to me, they'll always be—I mean, they'll be there—"

I interrupt him. "I know what the ring represents to you," I pause to look at Patch and Mack then back at Bash. "To all of you. I'm not just giving myself and my heart to you, Bash." My smile grows. "You come as a package deal. I know what I'm getting into."

With a smile plastered on his face, Bash asks, "So when do you want to do this thing?"

"First I have to ask Lizzy if she'll be my maid of honor."

The corners of Patch's mouth turn up. "We're sharing the role of best man so I guess that means…"

Mack thrusts his fist in the air. "Two-on-one sex at your wedding in the coat closet with the maid of honor!"

*** Continue Goldie's Story in Book 4 ***

If you enjoyed book three in the Naughty Goldie series, please leave a review on your favourite book purchasing site. Feel free to boast the book online and tag Pebbles Lacasse.

Goldilocks
and the Three
Bear Brothers
Book 4
Liberated

Pebbles Lacasse
International Best-Selling Author

Goldilocks & The Three Bear Brothers: Liberated

Book 4

The *Naughty Goldie* Series

by Pebbles Lacasse

Chapter 1

My best friend Lizzy is supposed to pick me up for an afternoon of wedding dress shopping, and she's late. Her tardiness has given me time to buzz through the wedding magazine I stole from the lobby at the hospital after my shift.

Until this morning, I wasn't sure what style of dress I wanted, and I didn't know there were so *many* styles. The mermaid looks about right for my hips and small waist, so I'll try on some of those.

I'm not just marrying Bash. Well, I am. But in marrying one, I'm accepting his two brothers as well. They all love me, but Bash owns the majority of my heart. For this reason, I have to think of a way to represent my love for Patch and Mack either in my bouquet or on my dress. But how?

Mack's eyes are pale blue, and Patch's are dangerously deep brown. Blue flowers in a bouquet are beautiful, but brown flowers? Maybe not.

Several pages I tore from the magazine are folded in my purse to use as a reference for the shop owner. Picking out a dress for the most important day of my life—my wedding day—is more stressful than arranging everything else pertaining to the wedding. I've heard so many horror stories that my stomach has been on a continuous rollercoaster ride for weeks.

Lizzy's my best friend and maid of honor. Thankfully, she's been helping with most of the arrangements. Bash, my fiancé, voices his opinion now and then to make it look like he's interested in helping, but he doesn't have the feminine touch needed to arrange a wedding. But he earns points for his efforts.

Patch, Bash's oldest brother, is no use at all and insists we should just go to a church one day, say the *I do's,* go home and get drunk, and then get on with it—no fuss, no muss.

Out of all three brothers, Mack is the most helpful. There's a delicateness to him that the others don't possess. He's not feminine; he's a wild man at heart, but he's more in touch with his emotions than his brothers. He and Lizzy chose the flowers and designed the bouquets. I've asked them to describe the flower arrangements, but neither will spill the details. I could ask her to include a red ribbon to represent her fiery red hair.

Lizzy and Mack are beyond smitten with each other. They spend a lot of time together, but Lizzy sometimes needs her space and goes to her place for the night. We all need our space sometimes. She's been intimate with Patch and Mack but has yet to savor the likes of Bash. I honestly can't wait to watch Bash and Lizzy in a sexy tryst.

The way the brothers share us is beautiful. I'm in love with all of them but the man who holds my heart the deepest is Bash. We didn't know it at the time, but all through our school years, we shared a mutual pull toward each other. He was considered to be a bad boy and someone my parents forbid me to be seen with. I always thought that was the reason I liked him so much: we always want what we can't have. But forbidden or not, we were destined to be together.

Now he and I are getting married soon. We already live together in our house the brothers built especially for us. Patch has his own room because we asked him to join our relationship, but he rarely sleeps there. Instead, he sleeps on the left of me with Bash on my right. Patch often brings Lizzy to his bed when Mack's off on a build and not home for a few days or longer.

We never hide the fact that they share Lizzy and me. We love all three of them. Lizzy and I haven't been intimate with each other and have yet to share one of the guys in a threesome. Every time we've tried to set that up, our plans have fallen through.

Lizzy's Jeep speeds up the driveway and she locks up the tires, brushing a cloud of dust from her wheels. She hops out and jogs up to the porch while I get my purse.

Her long hair is pulled back into a ponytail and her tiny body swims in an orange jumper. The sleeves and collar of her white t-shirt peek from beneath the bib. The legs are cropped to reveal her folded-down white socks. The ensemble is completed with high-top white runners. She looks adorable.

Exasperated, she flops her arms at her sides. "Sorry I'm late. I had an argument with Mom."

I snicker. "When do you *not* argue with your mom? Seems like you two have been fighting more lately."

"Yeah, we are." She shrugs and holds the screen door.

I lock the thick wooden door and then glide my fingertips over Mack's name carved in it.

She continues as we make our way to the Jeep. "Mom's upset that I've been spending so much time with Mack, and she doesn't believe me when I tell her it's only him I'm interested in being with. She doesn't need to know the truth."

"No. She doesn't need to know you're fucking Patch, too. That would open a whole new discussion."

Lizzy opens her door as I round the hood. "I can't tell her. Can you imagine how that would go?" Mimicking her mom's high-pitched voice, she says, *"You're what? Sleeping with Patch, too? That huge beast with the deep voice and humongous body? How the hell does he not squash you?* Blah, blah, blah."

I laugh as my seatbelt clicks. "She wouldn't say that! She'd be pissed at you and probably call you a slut or something. We all know you're a slut, but we love you for it!"

Her shoulder lifts as her mouth twists. "Yup! And I love being a slut." She gyrates on the seat and revs up the engine. "Oh yeah, big boy! Fuck my pussy. Fuck it good!" She moans.

"You're such a whore!" I tease and open the map on my phone. "Okay. So, I'm thinking we should hit up the bridal shop in town first. If we find nothing there, we'll have to drive to the city, here." I point to the screen.

She takes the phone from me and types the address of the second shop into the Jeep's GPS. "It'll take almost an hour to get there, but our small-town bridal shop offers little wedding garments and arrangements. I went there when my friend's sister was getting married. We'll skip it and go right to the city."

On the drive, Lizzy talks about the female patient we assisted the doctor in pulling a gallbladder from yesterday. According to Lizzy, every twenty minutes, the woman would push the call button to complain about her pain. She wanted to tell the woman to put on her big-girl panties, but she thought better of it and instead faked sympathy.

When there's a pause between conversations, I say, "So, I was thinking—"

Her curious eyes meet mine. "Did it hurt?"

"So much! My brain almost melted!" I sigh as if exhausted. "Watch the road, woman!"

Lizzy turns her face as she rolls her eyes.

This is as good a time as any.

Shyly, I ask, "Would you like to spend a night with Bash and me? It's time. Don't you think?"

Her head turns twice before focusing her attention back on the road, and she's quiet as she merges onto the highway.

She finally frees her lip from between her teeth. "Yes. But only if you really want me to. I mean, you two will be married soon. If you don't want to share him, it's okay. I don't have to join you."

"Honey, I wouldn't have asked if I didn't want you with us. The thought of you and Bash naked, skin glistening under faint light as you ride his big cock while he holds your hips and guides you... The sounds you two will make will be hot as fuck!"

"You paint one hell of a picture!" She sighs and bites her bottom lip and then looks at me and smiles. "I really want that. I mean, I want to be with the *two* of you. Like with you, too. What do you think about that?"

After watching a small red car zip past us, driving way over the speed limit, I say, "We could test those waters. The only concern I have is... What if I hate the taste of pussy? What if it grosses me out? What if one of us loves it but the other is turned off? And what if it doesn't go well?"

"Take a breath, woman!" she says with a snicker, and then slaps my thigh. "We're best friends. If we don't like something, we can talk about it. It's not like you'll hate me if I gag when my tongue touches your clit."

I sharply say, "No! I could never hate you."

Her hand leaves my thigh as she tucks a tress of her red hair behind her ear. "I'm looking forward to it. You worry too much about things you needn't worry about. If you don't like something we're doing, don't do it. You know how it is: you can tap out if you're uncomfortable."

She meets my eyes and smiles sweetly, easing my nervousness.

My tongue moistens my lips before I confess my desire. "Having you naked against Bash is my hottest fantasy." A smile sneaks up on me, and my cheeks burn.

We're quiet when she stops at a light. I'd bet my house she's picturing the steamy scenario as we watch the cars pass in front of us. I sure am.

I add, "When I walked in on you riding Mack's face, and you orgasmed after looking at me... That was so fucking hot."

"Agreed! Okay. So, it's settled; we're going to be all over your hot stud of a fiancé." She pauses when the light turns green and then she proceeds through it. "When?"

My tummy flutters as I suggest, "How about tonight?"

She bounces on her seat and moans. "Oh, yes! Bash! Fuck me, big boy! Let me ride that hard cock of yours and kiss your gorgeous fiancé while she rides your sexy mouth!"

"That's masturbation material. I'm going to store it away in my spank-bank." My hand waves before my face to fan myself. "We have to do that. Bash is going to love it!"

"Don't tell him. If we wait until you're both in bed and having sex—when he's totally into it and beyond aroused—

you can sit on his face, reversed. I'll come in and sit on his cock. He won't be able to see me, but he'll feel me."

"Girlfriend, you're so wicked! I love how you think." My pussy twitches and I swear my temperature just rose ten degrees. "We can discuss the specifics later."

She bites her bottom lip and nods. After a breathy giggle, she says, "There's only one problem I can think of that might prevent us from playing. If I hide in Patch's room until you and Bash are in bed, the man won't let me leave."

"I'll threaten his life." My fist waves in the air. "He'll be fine. If I tell him we want to surprise Bash with a threesome, he'll keep his hands off you."

Lizzy yells at the guy who cut her off even though he can't hear her. "Fucking asshole! Learn how to drive!" She growls wickedly and then returns to our conversation as if that didn't just happen. "Maybe I'll blow Patch before I come visit you two. He'll be satiated, and I'll get to play with his cock, which I love, by the way. That man knows how to fuck hard. Is Bash a gentle lover or rough?"

"He can go either way. He's the sweetest, most loving lover when he wants to be. But when he's in a mood to fuck, he's a goddamn animal."

Lizzy hasn't seen Bash naked and doesn't know what he holds in his pants. She's in for a surprise.

"Not that it matters, but his cock's bigger than both of his brothers'."

Her head whips around to look at me with wide eyes. "No! *Really?* Bigger than Patch?" She mouths the word, *"Wow!"*

"We're going to have so much fun!" I wiggle in my seat as we both giggle like immature high school girls.

All too quickly, we switch back to adulting when I say, "Okay. Get off just up here. We're almost there."

FTBA

Chapter 2

The fragile-sounding bell dings to alert the staff of our arrival at Lacey's Dress Shop. I'm immediately overwhelmed by a sea of white. My heart pounds wildly, and the air suddenly feels heavier than I know it to be. Is this what a panic attack feels like?

My feet won't move, but my eyes frantically shift from dress to dress, taking in the white fluff, sparkles, pearls, and lace. My legs weaken, and I drop onto the bench beside the main glass door. I rub my thighs to ease my fingertips of their tingles.

Lizzy's eyes widen with concern as she leans toward me. Her long red ponytail frames her neck as she rubs my arm.

"Deep breaths. In. Out. In. Out." Lizzy giggles, no longer worried for my welfare. "Wow! I didn't think anyone could lose *all* the blood from their face, but you managed to. Damn, girl. You're as white as the dresses."

I stutter, "It—it's a lot of white."

Now I'm lightheaded. Outstanding! As I breathe in through my nose and out of my mouth, my hands slide down my face but remain on my cheeks.

My whisper is meant for me. "How will I ever find my dress among all these?"

A tall woman approaches. Her short, mousy-brown hair bounces. She's wearing a tight burgundy dress to accentuate her slim figure.

While she emphasizes certain words through her wide, forced smile, she says, "Your reaction isn't uncommon. The bench is there for exactly that reason. You must be the bride-to-be. My name is Carol, and it's my job to help you find the perfect dress to suit your body that will have your groom drooling at the altar. And I haven't failed yet."

How would she know if she had? Would a bride waste her time returning to demand her money back because she didn't think the groom looked pleased enough? Not likely.

My smile isn't easily maintained because my heart continues pounding like a drum.

She turns to greet Lizzy, and Lizzy quickly introduces us before going into great detail about the dress styles she and I discussed. Her hands wave to add to her descriptive words.

After several minutes, I'm able to stand and follow the women's voices through the aisles of chiffon and lace. Who knew there were so many different shades of white?

Four dresses hang on a rolling rack Carol pulls behind her. Lizzy has a bounce in her step as she follows, her hands laced together behind her back. She doesn't notice me until my heavy sigh alerts her.

Her excitement radiating, she says, "There you are! Are you feeling better?"

With my hand pressed to my queasy tummy, I take a deep breath and release it with a quiet chuckle. "Yes. I'm okay. I was a bit, ah… Overwhelmed isn't a strong enough word to describe how I felt."

Her arm slips around my elbow. She whispers so the woman won't hear. "I like the second dress on the rack. The others are nice, but that one's gorgeous. But we won't know for sure until you slide your sexy self into it."

Carol chooses another dress from the assortment and hangs it among the four already on the rack. "These should be a great start." A sincere smile softens her sharp features. "You look much better. How about I get you a bottle of water? Or would you prefer wine or champagne?"

Lizzy's hand shoots up like she's in a classroom. "Champagne? I'll take one of those. Goldilocks?"

"Champagne might ease the drumming in my chest." My laugh sounds strangely obnoxious, but the woman finds it humorous.

***

Lizzy and I follow the five dresses into the large changing room. Carol closes the door but remains inside with us. She hangs the first dress on a wall hook, unlaces the bodice, and asks me to undress down to my bra and panties.

Reluctantly, I remove my shirt and hand it to Lizzy. She folds it as I remove my shoes, socks, and jeans. I pull my hair into a bun atop my head and bind it with the elastic on my wrist and then walk toward the puff of white lace.

Carol holds the opening to the dress low enough for me to step into and lifts it so the corseted body with molded breast cups is positioned. She holds the back closed and asks me to step up onto a small platform. The reflection takes my breath away.

Oddly, I'm calm. I whisper to nobody, "Holy shit! I'm getting married. I'm going to be someone's wife."

Lizzy's fingers graze the pearls on the bodice as her smile lights up her porcelain skin. "Yes, and what a beautiful bride you'll be." She admires my reflection and then tips her head to the right. "Can she try on the second one you picked out?"

Carol looks up at me as she fluffs the skirt of the dress. "Would you like to try on another one?"

"Yes. Thank you. This one's nice, but I don't like the way it flares so high at the waist. I'd like it to be fitted to my hips."

"Let's get you out of it. We'll try you in the second gown." Carol helps me off the platform and behind the curtain before she allows the dress to sag at my feet, and I step out.

Lizzy and I are quiet as we sip from our champagne flutes and watch the woman arrange the second dress. I step into it and she holds the back closed as I ascend the platform.

I'm immediately taken by how comfortable it feels against my skin. This dress is softer than the first. Carol holds the bodice closed in the back as she slides the curtain back. Lizzy stands beside the mirror staring at me. I have yet to look at myself because I don't think it's necessary. If I were to judge by her awed expression, *this* is the dress.

"Can you lace up the back?" I ask and hold the bodice under my breasts, snug to my ribs.

"You are so—" Lizzy's lips curl in and she bites them as her palms press together before her chin. "What do you think?"

As soon as I allow myself to look in the mirror, warmth eases through me from my head to my feet. All the anxiety I felt walking into the store is gone. This is the dress. But how could I have found it so easily? I've read horror stories in wedding magazines about women searching for months and trying on hundreds of dresses before they settled.

"This dress is the perfect dress, but I'd like to add something." The woman's eyes meet my reflection. "Can two red bows be sewn onto the back of the dress?"

"Red?" she asks while her mouth twists from curiosity. "May I ask, why red?"

My face flushes, and I shrug. Telling her the real reason is a bad idea. "It's my favorite color."

She tilts her head. "Red is lovely, but wouldn't one bow suffice?"

How beautiful will the back look with two crimson bows drawing our guests' attention as I stride past each pew? Thoughtlessly I say, "They represent—"

Lizzy clears her throat, snapping me back from my fairy tale thoughts of a dream wedding with bows for Mack and Patch.

A frail voice comes from behind me. "They represent Patch and Mack, or have I incorrectly assumed Bash is the wrong groom?"

Sara Joyeau appears in the mirror, wearing a pale blue dress and a smile tarnished by crooked teeth that could benefit from whitening strips. When did she enter the room, and why is she here? She works at the second-hand store at the opposite end of town, not here that I know of. Is she getting married?

She rocks from her toes to her heels with her hands perched on her hips. "You're marrying Bash, right?" Her tone reeks of jealousy, but her expression says otherwise.

"Yes. I'm marrying Bash." My eyes don't leave Sara's reflection as she admires the dress while the bodice is being laced. "Are you still working at the second-hand store?"

"I'm still there, but I've been here a while, too. So... Bash, huh?" She clears her throat. "Well, aren't you the luckiest woman?"

Lizzy must feel the weight of the air in the room because she approaches Sara with her hand extended. In a sweet voice, she says, "Hi! I'm Goldilocks's best friend and maid of honor. How do you know my girl?"

They shake hands and Sara, just as pleasantly, replies, "I met her not too long ago when she was buying pictures for her and Bash's house. We have a commonality between us." Her attention turns back to me. "Don't we, Goldilocks?"

Naïve to the insinuations floating about the room, Carol interrupts, "You two know each other? What do you have in common?"

Before Lizzy or I can stop her, Sara says, "The Bear brothers: Patch, Mack, and Bash."

Sensing the tension building, Carol says, "Sara, can you find two red bows about three inches wide? Bring all the red ones that size so the bride can choose a shade."

Unenthusiastically, Sara replies, "Absolutely. I'd love to."

Why would Sara be so cruel? Is she so jealous she'd purposely shit on my parade by embarrassing me in front of the store owner? I want to cry, but I won't give her the satisfaction.

Deep breaths.

Sara rushes from the dressing room, and the woman pauses her lacing to meet my glassy eyes. "What you do is *your* business. I'm not here to judge anyone. Sara was out of line, and I apologize on her behalf. Don't worry; I don't gossip." She continues feeding the lace through the eyelets. "The things that come out of the mouths of some brides would make you blush. I've often thought I should write a book. I'd change the names, of course, and write under a pseudonym so people can't trace it back to me." She steps away and sighs as she admires me, and smiles. "There you are. What do you think?"

Tears pool in Lizzy's eyes before a blink releases them. "That's your dress."

The soft white, off-the-shoulder mermaid-style dress has elegantly crocheted roses and swirls covering the satin material over the breasts and waist. Sheer lace sleeves have a crocheted, tattooed effect to match the bodice, less the satin. Over the white satin skirt and down almost to my hips in no discernible pattern, the weave continues. Although intricate and decorative, it isn't overdone.

The silkiest material I've ever felt on my skin drapes in a perfectly straight line from just below the hips to the floor. A gathering of material at the back starts high on my thighs and flows in a gentle wave down the platform step. The crocheted weave accents from just below my knee at the front and dwindles around the delicate scallop-edged train. At the back, a match to the sleeves leaves a seductive sheerness in an upside-down V to allow the eyes to catch a teasing glance of my calves should it spread just right.

My voice cracks as the lump in my throat reaches my eyes and tears overflow. "I love this dress."

Carol walks around me and admires the fit. "It doesn't look to need any alterations. It fits you like a glove. Even the length should be perfect. Did you bring your shoes?"

"Shoes?" I ask as a pang of anxiety halts my tears. "No. I was going to wait until I had the dress. Was I supposed to get the shoes first?"

She smiles and shakes her head. "No, Goldilocks." Her head tilts and her eyes squint. "What size are your feet? I think I have the perfect shoes."

"I'm usually an eight."

Sara enters, holding a white box full of an assortment of red bows. Carol whispers something as she passes.

A pouty Sara sets the box on the table beside my champagne glass. "I'm sorry if I was out of line." Her fingers comb through her hair in an automatic motion, but it falls back into its original disorderly place. "My envy took hold and, um, well—" She shrugs. "So, this is the dress? It looks great on you."

Her back straightens and her lips pinch tightly together like the compliment physically hurts her to say.

Lizzy's arms are at her sides, hands fisted like she's ready to pounce on the woman. I'd better handle this before there's a punch thrown.

"Envy? You have no right to be envious. You walked away from them." I watch Sara swallow hard. "Never again offer innuendos about my personal life to anyone, ever! Do it again, and you'll likely eat my knuckles. Do you understand?"

She nods quickly and changes the subject. "Were you hoping for bright red, or are you leaning more toward a deep crimson?"

"Deeper, but not too dark; sort of like blood. They're brothers, so blood red would suit, I suppose."

Sara digs into the box of bows. Lizzy's assessing Sara while her lips quirk to the left.

My hand waves in her direction to get her attention. "What do you think of the bow idea?"

Lizzy straightens her back, smiles, and then spreads my train down the stairs. "Red bows... I love it. Nobody will understand the gesture, but the guys will. You're not only marrying Bash, you know. As the saying goes, *you're marrying the family, too!*" She steps back and takes several photos. "Besides, the red will add a touch of elegance."

Sara holds two bows in the perfect shade of red. She sets them on the gown in a few different spots while Lizzy snaps photos for me to decide on their permanent placement.

Carol returns, sporting a wide smile, her shoulders waving as she holds a pair of white stiletto shoes. "Are you opposed to three-inch heels? After the ceremony and photos, most women switch them out for a lower heel."

She holds them up for me to admire. They're bright white, sleek in their design with a silver-tipped, pencil-thin heel. Along the outer sides and gracing part of the toe is a lacy design that matches the dress almost perfectly.

How is it possible to have everything going so smoothly and easily? Something awful is bound to happen because wedding planning shouldn't be this easy—

No! Nothing bad is going to happen. All is good in the world.

"Heels are fine. Those are beautiful."

She sings as she dances toward me. "And they're your size."

Sara lifts the front of the dress, and Carol guides the shoes onto my feet. They fit so well and are surprisingly comfortable for having such a sharp toe. Hours of wear might change my opinion and have me cursing them, but I can survive for a few hours.

Carol stands before me and spreads her arms wide. "Would you look at that? We won't have to alter the length. It's as if this dress and the shoes were made for you, Goldilocks."

"I agree." My cheek tucks between my teeth and releases only after my brows lift in their center because I know the answer is going to cut deeply. "How much?"

Just the way Carol tilts her head and smiles has my stomach sinking.

Lizzy says, "Don't worry about the price. You have the rest of your life to pay for it. Maybe your parents will chip in."

My head tips toward her as my face twists. "I don't think my father's even coming to the wedding. He's cordial with Bash, but that's the best he can manage."

Lizzy snaps another photo. "What about your mom?"

"She'll be there." My reflection screams perfection, but it might not happen. "They don't have much money. I won't ask them." My lungs fill with air and my hand holds my tummy to ease the sinking feeling. Regretfully, I ask again, "So, how much?"

Sara hands the bows to Carol before she leaves the dressing room to see to the delicate doorbell.

"The dress is $3,282.00 and the shoes are $79.00. You don't have to pay all at once. We can arrange a payment plan." My reluctant smile has her lips lifting at their edges. "When you're ready, I'll help you out of the dress?"

My mediocre nod has her untying the lacy back while Lizzy snaps picture after picture. She might be more excited about this dress than I am, and that's quite a feat.

"I'd like to arrange that payment plan. I can manage a down payment of almost half."

Not to be overshadowed by Lizzy's ridiculously huge smile, I stick my tongue out and to the side, cross my eyes, and scrunch my nose. She snaps a picture.

She looks at her phone and laughs. "That's one for the wedding album!"

After filling out more paperwork than I did to buy my car, Lizzy drives us back to my house. We hide my shoes in my closet behind a bin of my old textbooks from college. Bash doesn't go into my closet unless I ask him to, but just in case he's in the mood to snoop, he'll have to work to get at the box.

Mack's been away at a building site and won't be home for a few more days, so Lizzy's had more time to spend at our house, and with Patch. She's spent the last two nights in his bed. Bash and I heard her wailing through one of his hard fucking sessions from across the house. He bound her in rope the night before last, and she said she loved it. Maybe one day he can bind both her and me while all three men play with us. My pussy twitches at the thought.

Lizzy reluctantly picks up her purse and keys. "I have to go home and smooth things over with my mom."

"Does she really think you're sleeping with all the brothers? I mean, you have the intention to, but you've only been with Mack and Patch." I pause, squint one eye, and rock side to side with my arms crossed over my chest. "Okay. Now that I've said it out loud, she'd be upset if she knew."

Her eyes roll and she huffs a breath. "I think she's mostly upset that I've been here instead of at home in my bed. She insisted I tell her what I've been up to. She pushed and pushed and wouldn't let it go. So, with sarcasm, I told her, 'I'm giving my body to Patch every night, and Mack encourages it,' and then I added that you and Bash are cool with it, too. I'm not so sure she believed me, judging by my tone."

"What? Why bring me into this? She already thinks I'm a slut."

Her head bobs as her chin pulls in. "Well, you are. Aren't you?" She laughs when I nod and roll my eyes. "She did see you getting fucked by all three Bear brothers in the forest on one of her runs. She wishes she hadn't and, even more so, regrets telling her friend, who has the biggest mouth in town."

The whole town knew I was bound over the trunk of a fallen tree while each brother took a turn and fucked me. Because Lizzy's mom told her friend, who hasn't a clue how to keep a secret, my parents confronted me. That didn't go well, and I can almost still feel my father's palm print on my cheek.

Her shoulders lift, and her voice softens. "She truly regrets saying anything. You know she does."

My hand brushes over my cheek to rid the awful memory. "I know. It's in the past. I've moved on."

Lizzy leans in and hugs me. "Okay. I'll be back later tonight, and then we can turn your fiancé into the luckiest man alive!"

As she leaves the house, she humps the air and dances her way to her Jeep, and then fist bumps the air. That woman can make my worst days seem bright.

Chapter 3

Patch called to say he'd be working late and asked for the grocery list. He plans to stop on his way home, but he won't be here before nine o'clock.

Bash has been working at the newspaper past ten almost every night for over a week. Most of my shifts start early in the morning, so he and I have had little time together. Often, I'm asleep when he gets home. He always pulls me against him when he comes to bed. I love the comfort of his warmth, but I miss him. Tonight, he promised not to come home late.

Having Lizzy over to join Bash and me will work out perfectly because none of us has to wake early. We can spend hours enjoying each other's bodies late into the night.

This will be my first time with a woman. I'm nervous and excited but scared I'll do something wrong or look foolish. Lizzy's been with a woman once and said she had fun. There were also two men there who were their primary focus and not each other, but they played with each other a little.

While I sup on the roast, cubed potatoes, carrots, and celery I slow-cooked today, my laptop plays a comedy movie. It's a great way to distract my thoughts. After dinner, I make a plate for each man and tuck them in the oven on low to keep warm. After changing the sheets to make the bed fresh, I tidy the house. A long, hot bath with lavender essential oil and Epsom salts to ease away my concerns is my reward.

Patch arrives home before Bash and sits at the table with his plate and a beer. He sees me come into the kitchen wearing my knee-length red nightshirt and chuckles. "That's the most unsexy shirt you own."

I stop and look down at my body. "What does it matter? It's just a long t-shirt and not meant to be sexy. Would you rather I put on a corset with garters, stockings, and four-inch heels to go to bed?"

His brows wave as he nods and chews.

I grumble, "Not going to happen."

Patch swallows as he stabs another good-sized chunk of beef. "Damn. Maybe you can visit me tomorrow night wearing what you just described."

"Sorry, I'm working a double tomorrow, and I'll be too tired to settle your exhaustive sexual appetite." I sit on the chair opposite him with a glass of water. "So, tonight, Lizzy's coming over—"

His voice rises as he talks. "This night is looking up. That woman has endless energy."

My mouth turns down at its edges. "Sorry again. She's going to join Bash and me in a threesome." He stops chewing to study my flushing cheeks. "Her and I are going to entertain Bash... and each other. Maybe. Hopefully. I'm nervous. Have you been in a threesome with two women? What did they do to each other? I mean, I don't need details. Then again, yes, I do. Please. I'm sorry, I'm rambling. Can you tell I'm nervous?"

My cheeks are so hot they could light a cigarette.

Having expected him to poke fun at me, I'm relieved when he sets his fork down and reaches for my hand. "You don't have to do anything you don't want to do. But, if you push yourself to try something new, you might discover you enjoy it. If you don't push yourself, you'll never know either way."

"Don't laugh at me, but I'm hoping for suggestions on technique."

Patch restrains his smile. "Just do to her what you'd like her to do to you. Women should know what feels good on other women. Do that."

He isn't great at going into detail, but what little he said helps.

"Have you ever been with a man? I mean," my voice lowers and my brows wave, "*been with a man?*"

"No. Not my thing. I enjoy the spoils of women too much to hop the fence to sample cock. I've had sex with women simultaneously with other men. Our cocks touch if one pops out. It happens more often than you'd think. When Bash and I fucked you, it happened."

"I love being between two men while they penetrate me: one in my pussy, the other in my ass. It's awesome!"

Patch grins. "Feels great on our end, too. Any time you want to give it a go, you just let us know."

"How very selfless of you!"

He shrugs and waves his fork. "That's how I roll, Goldie."

"Don't call me that. Why must I repeat myself?"

I hate when he calls me by Bash's nickname for me, but he does it to tease me.

My elbows lean on the table. "Bash doesn't know she'll be joining us. Please say nothing."

His eyes study me through slivers as he sips from his bottle. "I think he'll figure it out when she strolls into the bedroom naked."

"We have it all planned. He won't see her coming," I say, and bite my bottom lip.

"I won't say anything, and don't beat yourself up if you don't enjoy eating cunt. You'll have fun watching Bash enjoy Lizzy's pussy."

"Eating cunt?" My nose scrunches. "You're so classy."

He grins. "A gentleman I'm not. Want to find out how much of a barbarian I am?"

The distinct sound of Bash's truck interrupts the silence of the yard as he pulls up in front of the house.

"Put a pin in it for another day," I say with a wink. "I'll need my strength for later."

"Sorry I'm late," Bash says as he rushes through the door, kicks off his shoes, and offers me a kiss before setting his lunch box on the counter by the sink. He washes his hands before he sits, and I set his plate in front of him. "Greg's article needed serious rewrites, so we stayed late to work on it. How are you, big bro?"

Patch pushes his empty plate away and wipes his mouth with his napkin as he eyes Bash's dinner. "Good. Worked late, too. I stopped at the grocery and grabbed you some of the pink marshmallow things you like so much. Those things are full of chemicals and shit."

Bash forks a carrot. "Yeah, and those chemicals are fucking delicious!"

Patch cringes, and Bash laughs.

Bash sprinkles salt over his plate and asks me, "How was your day, my dear fiancé? Was dress shopping productive or disappointing?"

With my hands folded on the table in front of me, elbows pointed outward, a smile illuminates my face. "Definitely productive. I bought my dress." My head bobs from side to side. "Well, I put a down payment on it. And I have the perfect shoes to go with it. It couldn't have gone any better unless Sara Joyeau didn't shit on my happiness."

Both brothers tip their heads when they look at me.

I add, "Yeah! She works in a few places, apparently. Anyway, she was surprised to see me trying on a wedding dress and let it slip about my relationship with *the Bear brothers*. What is it with that chick?"

"There's a name I haven't heard in a long time." Patch groans and sets his plate in the sink before getting himself another beer. "Little twat accused me of being forceful." He twists off the cap and grimaces. "I wasn't. I was aggressive, but she was familiar with my nature. In the beginning, she liked it. She knew she could say 'red,' but she didn't. The accusations weren't favorable. Thankfully, she didn't have me arrested for doing exactly what she asked me to do."

I ask, "Who did she tell?"

Patch shakes his head as if signaling he's done with the conversation, so Bash answers. "Sara told a few of her friends that he was rough with her, but she left out a key tidbit about consent. The townsfolk were radiant with gossip for months.

Our reputation was already shit, but hers was untarnished up to that point. It serves her right."

Patch kisses me. "I'm going to take a shower and read for a while."

"Lizzy said she might come over in a little while," I say to Patch and hope he picks up on my cue.

Without a speck of hesitation, he says, "I'll watch for her. I wouldn't want to leave that sweet, hot ass outside and risk it cooling off."

"You're such a romantic." I snicker as he makes his way to his bedroom.

Bash reaches across the table and glides his palm down my forearm. "So, now that you have the dress and shoes, and most of the other arrangements are in order, are you still nervous or has that passed?"

"Hmm. Passed, mostly. My tummy falls out when I think about walking in heels with all those eyes on me. But I picture you waiting to receive me, and I feel right again." Just after he pops a sizable chunk of potato in his mouth, I ask, "How about you? Are you nervous?"

My amusement from his struggle to quickly chew and swallow before he answers can't be stifled.

"I'm not at all nervous," he says with his eyes locked on mine as he takes a swig of beer. "Knowing you'll soon be Mrs. Goldilocks Bear is all I need to make me right as rain."

Teasingly, I ask, "What if I decide not to change my last name?"

One of his shoulders lifts as his lips twist. "I'm only teasing. It's your name and your decision to change it or not."

"Good answer." I stand and push mine and Patch's chairs under the table. "Can you rinse your dishes when you've finished? I'm taking a cue from Patch and going to lie in bed to read as well."

"I'll be in shortly," he says and returns his attention to his plate.

While Bash showers, I hear a knock at the front door and rush to greet her. Patch has already let her in by the time I get to the living room.

"You're here," I say, interrupting their whispers.

She and I hop up and down and quietly squeal as we hold hands.

Patch's upper lip quirks and his head shakes. "You two are the weirdest chicks I've ever known." His finger wags between us. "Seriously. You appear to be sexy women but act like high school girls."

She and I are in sync when we stick our tongues out at him as if we'd planned it. He smirks as he turns to walk back to his bedroom.

Lizzy stands with her hands on the waistband of her yoga pants and asks, "So, are you excited? I'm nervous."

My shoulders sag. "I was nervous before I talked with Patch about it. He might be a bohemian, but he's pretty good at advising when it comes to subjects of a sexual nature."

"Hmm. I'm heading in there, so maybe he has some words of wisdom for me, too."

She kicks off her shoes and leaves them in a heap in front of the door purposely because she knows it irritates Patch. She loves to annoy him.

She adds, "Speaking of Bash—even though his name didn't come up—where is he?"

"Oh, shit! He'll be getting out of the shower any minute. I'd better get back in bed."

She bounces on her toes and whispers, "I'll wait a while and then listen at your door. Now go before he sees us plotting."

I slip into bed and reclaim my book seconds before he opens the bathroom door. Before he blow dries his hair, he rubs a towel through it. He steals glances at me while I forego my book to admire his tall, lean, nearly naked form. He gestures as if to ask if I want his body, and I respond with a nod, my bottom lip pinched between my teeth.

Bash takes his time drying his chestnut hair before dragging a comb through it to contain his shaggy brown curls. Then he brushes his teeth painfully slowly while his long fingers glide down his tight tummy. His fingertips stop at the base of his semi-hard cock hidden behind a white towel. His eyes burn into mine before they squint from his quiet laughter. He shrugs innocently and turns to face the sink while he brushes his back teeth. Time drags an eternity before he spits and rinses.

To prepare, I kick the covers to the end of the bed, pull off my t-shirt nightie, and toss it to the floor. My arms and legs spread wide on the bed as giggles fill the room.

Bash hangs his towel on the back of the bathroom door, struts to the edge of the bed, and licks his lips. "Do you think I care if you starfish? You can lie there and do absolutely nothing if you wish, and I'll do whatever the fuck I want."

He growls as he kneels on the bed. As he leans in to kiss me, he eases himself between my spread legs. Plump, inviting lips press to my mound. The heat from his breath brushes over my clitoris, and my pussy tightens with anticipation.

Bash's tongue is hot, wet, and wide as it glides up and down my pussy, teasing my labia and clit as the tip explores my folds, setting me ablaze.

Having forgotten about Lizzy, I startle when she peeks into the bedroom. Thankfully, Bash's face is buried in my pussy and he didn't notice. She motions for me to flip so he's on his back, as we planned. She ducks back from view, and I run my fingers through his curls.

"I want you on your back so I can straddle your face."

His lips glisten with my arousal as they lift at their edges. "Fuck yeah! Ride my face, woman."

We shift positions: him on his back; me straddling his head, facing his cock. His long arms grip my waist to urge me to lower my pussy toward his mouth.

"Are you going to suck my cock while I suck this beautiful pussy?" His tongue begins its assault, and a hollowness lightens my body as if my stress has evaporated, leaving a gap.

With a low voice, I reply, "Something like that."

The grip of his palms on my waist urges my torso to lie flat against him, hoping I'll take his cock in my mouth. I swallow as much of him as I can take while my eyes lock on the door. I'm so aroused, and his mouth is playing with my pussy just right. Despite the huge cock head in my mouth, my moan sounds like a sweet song warming the surrounding air.

Lizzy's face slides into view, and I wave her in. Her walk is rushed but delicate and quiet like the stealthiest ninja. She pulls off her pale grey chemise, tosses it to the floor, and holds her hand over her mouth to restrain a giggle.

I sit up with my eyes wide, and I bite my lips between my teeth to restrain my laughter.

She waves her hands and rolls her shoulders before gently climbing onto the bed and straddling Bash.

His hands reach down and glide up her thighs, and he moans into my pussy. Bash mumbles something not meant for our ears and then ravishes me with fervor.

She and I look into each other's eyes and smile. With a faint whisper, she asks, "Are you sure?"

I nod my approval as Bash grips his rock-hard cock and holds it upright like a solid pipe. Lizzy eases herself down, engulfing his shaft inside her pussy. As she does, her lips part and her eyelids droop as an effortless moan escapes her.

This is so sexy.

Shadows bite through the glow of my nightstand lamp and dance across her pale skin. Her red hair topples forward as her face tips, as if his entering her is stealing her strength. Another moan fills the room, but it's Bash's muffled tone.

My hands span across Bash's abs as I lean forward and press my mouth to her forehead. I must taste her kiss. Her face lifts, and our lips meet. Small hands grip my cheeks to pull me in. Her skin and tongue are so much softer than men's.

Despite her delicate nature, her voracious kiss sets me on fire. Surely Bash can hear our feminine moans laced with desire.

Bash's moans vibrate my clit. His eager tongue and pillowy lips expertly stroke my stiff nub as if I'd given him instructions. If he keeps this up, it won't be long before I erupt, claiming my ecstasy, but it's something I'd rather prolong.

Lizzy sits straight up while her fingertips press to his flexed abdomen. His long fingers dig into her ass as his hips tilt forward and back, pushing his cock to her core. He rocks her hips forward and back; an easy pace, at first, just as he likes. Her eyes are closed, mouth gaping as moans carry on her quickening breath.

Something moves in the dark shadows by the doorway, grabbing my attention. Patch is leaning on the frame with his arms crossed over his chest, watching us. The bulge in his navy-blue pajama pants is proof of his arousal. A crooked grin meant just for me softens his typical stoic expression.

Bash maintains his grip on her ass as he grinds Lizzy against him to slow her pace. She tries to fuck him faster, but his hold on her slight frame is firm. If I know him at all, he's preparing to pound so viciously into her that he'll need to hold her for the sake of not humping her across the room.

Lizzy's head turns to see what holds my gaze. She smiles and moans when she sees Patch. He lifts his chin to acknowledge her.

Bash forces her pelvis to rock quicker, reclaiming her attention. Her moans grow louder with each thrust. He holds her body still and lifts his ass off the bed as he mercilessly plunges into her.

"Cum, Goldilocks," she whispers, and cups my breasts. "Cum with me."

My fingertips find her nipples and pinch and roll them, mimicking her assault on my nipple.

Between heavy breaths, I reply, "I thought you'd never ask."

Her smile's fleeting. The crease between her brows deepens as her eyelids pinch shut. Her mouth gapes, and each breath coincides with his brutal thrusts.

Despite Bash's rapid hot breaths, he maintains his assault on my burning, tingling clitoris. My mind grows quiet, and my body becomes lighter as the painful tickle threatening to shoot through my body from my swollen button grows more intense. The itchy desire for release is unbearable, and just as I think my mind and body can't take anymore, pleasure overwhelms my entire existence. As I float through the blackness of euphoria at the peak of utter bliss, Lizzy cries out.

My ecstasy comes to a sudden end, and each stroke of his tongue shoots pleasure daggers into my twitching clitoris. It's a hated sensation yet I can't get enough of it.

Bash hasn't eased his thrusts.

Lizzy's face transforms from a pained tightness to the softness of elation as she drifts away from herself into her ecstasy. Her moans halt along with her breaths.

Having had enough, my right leg lifts over Bash's reddened face, and I kneel on quivering legs on my side of the bed.

Bash smiles widely at me as his hands glide up Lizzy's waist to her perky breasts to pinch her nipples. His free hand reaches for my hair and pulls my face down to his. We kiss with a gentle passion while he continues to plunge into Lizzy with less force. His breaths are quick as he fills my mouth with his moans.

This is so fucking sexy! Why did we wait so long to do this?

Lizzy's fucking my fiancé... She's riding his cock and getting off on it. He's so excited. She's excited. I'm more excited than I've ever been.

Lizzy's lips press to my shoulder as her fingernails lightly glide down my back, awakening my flesh.

I turn my face to her and our tongues dance while Bash's ass collapses to the bed, exhausted from his efforts. His hips lazily rock as he watches us kiss. His feverish hand glides up my back while the other continues to grip Lizzy's hip.

His tone is genuine in his whisper. "You two are so fucking beautiful."

Lizzy grips his wrists by her hip and says, "Let me fuck you. I want you to cum."

"Not yet. I want to enjoy this," he replies, and his tongue pokes out to moisten his lips.

As sure as I am that he will not give her full control, he proves me wrong and releases her hips. His fingers weave together and rest behind his head on the pillow. His devilishly handsome face wears a wicked grin as his stare burns into hers.

Lizzy's feet cross over his thighs, spreading them slightly and pinning him to the bed with her weight. She uses the flexibility in her legs and waist to roll her hips. Each time she glides him out, his abdomen flexes, begging to get back inside her.

Bash's words ride a moan. "Oh, fuck! Ease your grip on my cock. You're too fucking tight." His blink holds as his head tilts back and his mouth gapes.

She and I share a glance before I take her nipple into my mouth and suck while I roll it with my tongue. I reach behind her and between Bash's legs to fondle his testicles.

He cries out, "Oh. My. Fucking. God." His ass muscles tighten, followed by his thighs and abs: a sure sign he's about to erupt.

Lizzy suddenly hops off him, leaving his glistening cock pointed at the sky, thick and rigid.

He groans. "Lizzy, that's cruel."

With a smug laugh, she leans down to whisper matter-of-factly, "You said you didn't want to cum yet. I was only following your wishes."

"Unless you two want to play with each other, I want Lizzy to squat over my face."

She and I smile at each other. She shrugs and suggests, "Maybe next time?"

Now that we're in the situation, I don't feel as anxious about going down on her. It's something I've wanted to try for some time. It surprises me that Lizzy's the one backing down. It's typically the opposite with us because she's much more daring than me.

"No," I say, and both sets of eyes widen. "Lizzy, lie on your back. I'm doing this."

Bash shifts over so she can lie in the middle of the bed. My heart pounds and my hands shake as I part her knees. Her vagina is inches from me, and the scent of her sex fills my nostrils. My pussy clenches and I suddenly realize my heart isn't pounding from being nervous but because I'm extremely aroused; my body knew it before I did.

Lizzy rises onto her elbows to watch my tongue reach her clitoris for the first time.

My lips press around it and engulf it. The silky flesh is hot and tastes slightly tangy, like my own pussy juices. The sensation of my lips gliding over her flaps while knowing how these movements feel isn't something I can explain. I simply love it. Her moan reminds me that it isn't my pussy I'm devouring.

Her head falls back when I apply suction and drag the bumpy side of my tongue up and down over the tiny nub peeking out from beneath its jelly-like protective hood. Her moan fills the room, and the sweet sound is reassurance that I'm doing it correctly.

The softness of her skin is like licking a gummy. It's bewildering how something so soft can have such firmness beneath layers of skin. Her blood-filled, aroused clit entertains me with a mix of silky and stiff. Her scent has seduced my mind and stolen it away from my wanton, twitching clitoris.

My eyelids part and the sight of him fucking her mouth while he fists her hair has my pussy dripping. Unable to resist, my fingers slip between my folds and gently stroke my slippery clit to ease the urgency for attention. Letting my thoughts roam and matching my finger movements with my tongue, it's like I'm licking my clit. The sensation is phenomenal.

Lizzy's hips jerk and her moans around his cock grow louder. Her chest rises and falls like a marathon runner. Bash yanks her mouth off his cock and she wails.

"I'm coming! I'm comi—"

Holy shit! I made my best friend have an orgasm with my mouth!

Lizzy's clit thickens and her vagina pulses as her orgasm ravishes her mind and body. My movements and tempo don't alter in the slightest until her jerking subsides and she tilts her hips away from me.

My smoldering lips peck up her silky tummy, pausing between her perky breasts. I lie between her legs and kiss her as lovers do.

Bash clears his throat, drawing our attention to the fact that he's still in the room. He's on his knees with his hand wrapped around his steely hard cock. While stroking it slowly, he asks, "Who wants to help me with this?"

As she sits up, Lizzy says, "We both do. Lie on your back."

Lizzy kneels between his spread knees and takes his balls one by one in her mouth. I engulf his cock as far down my throat as I can manage. His moans are lengthy and deep. His huge hands rest on our heads and occasionally stroke our hair while he savors the image of two women worshipping his genitals.

"So beautiful. I'm a lucky man."

We switch, and she takes his cock in her mouth while I lick and gently suck his testicles. It isn't more than a minute before he's teetering on the edge of bliss.

"I'm going to cum." His ass muscles tighten beneath him.

Lizzy grips the base of his cock and strokes while she bobs her mouth around the head.

His balls tighten toward his body. He pants four hard breaths and then falls silent as his head eases back to the bed. He jerks and ejaculates into Lizzy's mouth. In seconds, his cock withers in her grip, and he deflates. His arm flops over his eyes, and his chest rises and falls rapidly.

"That was so much fun!" I say as she and I lie on either side of him. "We have to do this again."

Lizzy wholeheartedly agrees.

"I need about fifteen minutes before I can go again," Bash says, and his palm glides up my back. "Maybe thirty."

Lizzy and I lie with our heads on his biceps and our fingers tracing the muscles on his trim tummy.

Curiously, she asks, "So, how was it for you? I mean, going down on me."

My smile is a bit more enthusiastic than hers. "I loved it right from the start. I thought it would be weird, but quite the opposite. Hearing your moans and knowing I was the cause was thrilling."

"I'll return the favor another day." She leans up on her elbow and places a tender kiss on Bash's lips. They part and she whispers, "You, sir, have a *fabulous* cock." He winks, and she turns her attention to me. "And your mouth is so soft." She sighs, kisses me, and then slips off the bed. "Okay, kids. I'm heading back to Patch's bed."

Bash snickers and scratches the top of his head. "He was watching us for a while. He's going to want to fuck you when you climb into his bed."

She flips the covers over us and waves her eyebrows. "Maybe I'll offer him a brain-melting blowjob."

"He loves to fuck, but I doubt he'll turn down a blowjob," I say, and straighten the covers over Bash's chest.

"Goodnight," she says, and closes our door as she leaves.

"That was my first threesome with two women. The best part was it was with the woman I love, and I've grown quite fond of Lizzy. I'm pretty sure Mack is head over heels in love with her. Maybe Patch, too."

"I think you're right." With my body snug against his, my arm flops over his chest and my forehead tucks against his neck.

He kisses the top of my head as his arm hugs my back to hold me tighter against his side. "How do you feel about seeing me with your friend? Did it bother you?"

"I wasn't sure how I'd feel. I'll admit that I was worried, but seeing you two together was thrilling. My pussy was so wet when I was licking her. It was exciting. We'll see how I feel about it tomorrow."

He whispers, "You didn't cum after you went down on her. Did you?"

I know where this is going. "No. I didn't."

He rolls me onto my back as he kisses me. "I suppose we should do something about that, huh?"

"Well, if you insist." I spread my legs and lace my fingers behind my head to copy how he looked earlier.

The humor in the gesture doesn't go unappreciated, and he snickers. "Oh, I insist."

GTBH

Chapter 4

It's been a few days since our exciting threesome. Not much has changed in my relationship with Lizzy, aside from us having a naughty little secret.

She's excited because Mack's supposed to arrive home today. The company that hired him doesn't need him for the next stages in the build, so we'll have him for about a week before he has to return.

Laura, my supervisor, pokes her head into the operating room just as Dr. Kacey's about to close Mrs. Koudell. She had a mass on her liver the size of a grape. Unfortunately, we're almost positive it's cancerous. Thankfully, I won't be present when the results come back and he has to tell her she's up against a battle for her life.

Laura holds a mask up to cover her mouth when she asks, "How'd it go?"

Dr. Kasey looks up at her and shakes his head, signaling it's not good news.

She shakes her head as if she knows the patient personally, and this news hurts her. After a heavy sigh, she clears her throat. "Goldilocks, was your paycheck correct? There was a mix-up in accounting and some people found errors."

As the doctor sutures the incision while I hold it closed, I reply, "I haven't looked at my pay stub. I'll do that when I'm finished and let you know."

She huffs and waves her hand. "Don't involve me any more than I already am. I'm only a messenger and don't want to be the middleman. If there's a problem, go upstairs to accounting because they're the people to talk to."

"I will, Laura. Thanks," I say as Dr. Kacey finishes the last stitch.

She leaves and so does the doctor, entrusting an unconscious Mrs. Koudell to the custody of the anesthesiologist and me.

Rebecca, the anesthetist, is just as miserable as Dr. Kacey, but I think it's the result of working with the miserable old goat for so many years. I've never seen that man smile.

Lizzy's been buried in paperwork since this morning, but she and I share our breaks, as we often do when we're on shift together. She finishes at five o'clock, but I'm working a double and won't be done until midnight.

I'll be in the maternity ward after four o'clock, and I love it there. Sure, there are screaming babies, but most of the patients are happy despite knowing their brand-new baby is going to suck their finances for years to come; not to mention their time, energy, and patience. That sweet-scented baby's head has a shelf-life—let the poop and snot begin.

I'm *not* ready for kids!

After rolling Mrs. Koudell to recovery, I sit at the nurse's station and fill out the reports. My feet are sore from standing all day and can't wait to get to maternity where I won't have to be on my feet constantly. I'll be watching over the babies, which isn't as difficult as it sounds. Newborn babies are easy; they sleep most of the time.

My next surgery isn't for half an hour, so there's time to get my pay stub from my purse and calculate my hours. With coffee in hand, I add my hours from my calendar on my phone and discover I'm short $87.23.

"Dammit! There goes my break." I hiss and storm up the stairs to the offices. A smiling woman in a red pantsuit directs me to the accountant's office. Before I look inside, I tap on the door frame.

"Goldilocks?" A familiar voice grabs my attention from my paycheck.

Surprise overwhelms my face. "Cody?"

Cody was one of my *parent-approved* boyfriends. We dated in high school for almost two years. He's a sweet guy and everyone loved him, but there was something about him that prevented me from giving him my heart.

We had sex a few times, and it was fun but quick. He didn't enjoy going down on me, and that was frustrating. He loved getting blowjobs, though. I stopped offering, and he didn't request them. He has a big cock and fucked hard, but he couldn't last more than two minutes on a good day. Our relationship ended the summer before I became a high school senior. He was angry about it, and we parted ways. I missed his friendship more than having him in the boyfriend category.

A few steps into his office, and I'm still stunned to see him here. "Wow! It's been a while. How are you and where did you disappear to after high school?"

He steps out from behind his desk and greets me, awkwardly; unsure whether to shake my hand or hug me. We settle with a handshake. He offers me a chair before returning behind his desk.

His palm smooths his blue-striped tie as he sits on the leather chair. "I'm doing well. After high school, I packed up and moved to California for a few years. I put myself through college while working three jobs. It was tough, and I ate a lot of bagged soups, but it was worth all the struggles." He studies my face, tips his head to the side, and weaves his fingers together on the desk in front of him. "So, how about you? What have you been up to aside from nursing?"

My eyebrows rise, and my head tips to match his. "Don't act like you haven't heard all the rumors. Everyone in this bullshit town has."

Cody leans back in his black leather chair, and it squeals. "I heard some things, but I tried not to listen to rumors." He leans forward and folds his hands together on the desk. "Just tell me you're happy. You deserve to be happy."

Now I remember why I dated him for so long: he's sweet and cares about people. "I'm happy. Busy with all the wedding planning and working, but happy."

His eyes shift to my empty ring finger. "No ring?"

"I leave it in my locker so I don't accidentally pull it off with a latex glove and toss it out. It happens more often than you'd think." I gesture toward the gold and diamond band on his finger. "You're married?"

He spins a picture frame on his desk, and my breath stills.

"This is my husband, L.J., and our twins, Ally and Amy. They're three and have yet to outgrow the terrible twos stage." He rights the frame to look at the photo and lowers his voice. "That's why I went to California. I knew what I wanted and, back then, there was no way I could emotionally handle the cruel judgments from the caveman mentality of the local-yocals."

"Caveman mentality. That's an accurate assessment." I point to the photo frame and add, "It all makes sense now. We got along so well, but the sex—" My face twists, as does his. "So, you came back. Why?"

He shrugs, and sadness fills his eyes. "My mother got sick, so I came to help her. She was sicker than she let on, and within six months, she was gone. She willed the house and property to me, and L.J. thought raising our kids in a small town would be safer than in a big city. So, here we are." His eyes widen. "And why are *you* back? If I recall correctly, you had big plans to leave for college and never return."

I glance up at the ceiling and my shoulders sag. "Before my last semester of college, I came home for a visit, fully expecting it to be my last time home. I decided to be a bad girl for one day by finding a Bear brother and having my way with him. Turns out, it was so good I kept going back for more. I fell in love with Bash."

He quickly corrects me. "You were always in love with Bash. It was more than a secret crush. Shit! *I* had a crush on all three of those boys, but I knew that would never come to fruition." His eyes roll as he pouts and leans forward to rest his elbows on his desk. "It was blatantly obvious Bash had a thing for you. I was so jealous of the way he looked at you when you weren't paying attention. You're a lucky woman."

"I'm grateful to have all of them in my life." I wave my pay stub between us and glare accusingly. "*Someone* fucked up my paycheck. I wonder who that could be, Mister Accountant."

He groans as I hand it to him. "Don't blame me. Jerry stepped in when I took a few days off. The girls and L.J. had that bad flu going around. He was in bed for two days, and the girls were an absolute nightmare; the poor things."

I always knew he'd be a good father.

"It's a bad flu. I hope they're fully recovered."

He nods and then tips his head back to look through the bifocals to study the computer screen. "Everyone's fine now, and luckily, I didn't catch it." He pauses and then quirks his mouth. "Jerry really messed this up. It's all straightforward, so how he managed to do *this* much baffles me. He's an accountant and should know this program." He taps a few keys. "Okay. You should have the money deposited into your account in a few hours, and you'll receive an additional pay stub with your next one. Is there anything else I can do for you?"

"No. Thank you for fixing that," I say as I take the paystub back from him and stuff it in my shirt pocket. "I'm so happy to see you again, and I'm thrilled your life morphed into something wonderful."

He stands and walks me to the door, only about ten steps from his desk. "Thank you, sweetheart. Come to chat any time. We should have lunch soon."

"I'd like that." Before I leave, I give him one last smile. "Take care of those kids."

"Will do. Take care of those hunky men," he whispers and winks.

Dammit! I'm going to be late for my next surgery!

***

The hours fly by quickly but slow down when I start my overtime on the maternity floor.

I've been rocking inconsolable newborns off and on for five hours. For three solid hours, while his exhausted mother slept, I've been cradling one particular little bald guy. Being less than a day old, he has an impressive set of lungs. But he's back with his mother now, as are the other two babies.

Being such a small hospital, there aren't often more than three births in a week, so it's typically quiet and the nights drag on. But there's something to say about the peacefulness of holding the tiny sleeping babies. It warms my heart to see how happy the parents are.

To stay awake, I've been at the nurses' station reading an erotic romance ebook on my phone. Linda, the night nurse supervisor, leans over the counter and startles me. The biggest problem with everyone wearing nursing shoes is they can easily sneak up unnoticed, whether or not they mean to.

In her cartoon-like, high-pitched voice, she asks, "Goldilocks, how's everyone doing?"

She wakes the computer screen and sifts through the evening's chart to review what I've written, which isn't much.

A yawn envelops my face as I shut off my phone and slip it into my pocket. "Crystal took a shower. Little boy Brensen cried for hours, and Leslie needed instruction in nursing her fussy little girl."

Without looking away from the screen, she says, "So, all is Q?"

Q stands for "quiet," which is a word nurses never use to describe the floor. It's bad luck and will likely change the circumstances shortly after it's spoken.

"Too Q. I'm barely keeping my eyes open." Again, I yawn and cross my arms over my chest as I pull my sweater closed.

Linda sits on the edge of the desk and pulls an apple out of her shirt pocket. "If you want to go home, you can. I'll be here doing paperwork, so there's no need for you to stay unless you want the hours."

Wedding dress. Shoes. Lingerie to wear beneath it.

"I could use the money, but I'd rather go home. It's been a long day."

"You were on the surgical floor this morning, right?" she asks, and I nod. "You've had a long go of it. Go home, rest, and prepare for another day."

"Thanks. I really appreciate this." I stand and stretch my arms over my head, which is a mistake. I have to clutch the counter until the stars, brought on from standing too quickly, clear from my vision. "I stood too quickly. Stars. I'm okay." I blow out a breath and release the counter. "I'm off tomorrow."

"Must be nice! I'm working every day for the next three weeks. Two nurses are on vacation, and too many staff are sick with that damn flu. More will come down with it over the next few weeks, I'm sure. Sometimes, being a supervisor sucks." She chuckles, and I tilt my head to show my sympathy.

"If you're stuck and need anyone to fill a shift, call me and I'll see if I can come in, okay? I'm off. Have a great night," I say, and take my leave.

The drive home is peaceful. With only a slivered moon hanging low, the shadows are dark, as is the road extending past where my headlights can reach. The blackness doesn't scare me, even when I'm on a deserted highway less traveled at 10:15 PM with no houses within half a kilometer off the main road.

A yellow mailbox with our address painted on its sides is the only thing to alert others to where the driveway is. I asked Bash to install one since the delivery people couldn't find us to bring our packages. Picking them up at the trading post proved tiresome.

The driveway is nearly half a kilometer long because it twists and turns almost the entire way. It was the easiest path to carve since there are many rocky cliffs, boulders, and one-hundred-year-old trees nobody wanted to cut down. I'm thankful they didn't. What trees were cut have been stored for later use in building projects like homes and furniture. The Bear brothers waste no trees.

The last turn before the road runs down the hill into our front yard nearly turns around on itself. The house is dark aside from a dim light in the living room, but the trees at the back of the house have an orange hue. Bash has a fire burning outside. Maybe Patch or Mack are over. They love sitting around a fire, having a few beers, and talking. I love listening to the stories of their youths.

I park beside a car I don't recognize and round the house. A woman is on her knees giving a blowjob to a man sitting on an Adirondack chair, but her hair is short and dark, unlike Lizzy's. Who is this woman and why is she blowing—

Wait! Bash?

What the fuck?

I yell, "Bash!"

The woman jolts upright, and Bash lurches forward. That's when I realize his eyes are covered with something black and his wrists are tied to the arms of the chair.

The shirtless woman stands and tries to cover her bra with her hands. As I near, I can see his cock is hard and wet with her saliva.

Sara Joyeau.

As I rush to close the distance, my fists are clenched and ready to swing. "Someone better tell me what the fuck is going on here."

Bash frantically pulls at his arms. "Untie me!"

I stop a few feet from her and nearly growl through feminine vengeance. "What are *you* doing here? And *what* the fuck are you doing with Bash, Sara?!"

Bash stills and increasingly louder, yells, "Sara? Untie me! Fucking untie me!"

Bash pulls his arms, likely bruising his wrists. She shrugs one shoulder and leans in toward his wrist.

I shriek, "Don't fucking touch him!"

She jolts back with her hands up defensively. I quickly yank what I realize is her shirt off his head, and she mumbles something, but I don't hear her.

Bash glares at her, then me, and back at her. His eyes narrow and his nostrils flare. "Why would you do this?"

Her eyes widen, and her hands come to rest on her hips. "You wanted me to."

His head shakes faster until he turns to look at me with fear in his eyes. "No! No, I didn't. She's lying! I wouldn't. Why would I?"

"If you didn't invite her, what the fuck is she doing here? And you look pretty willing with that raging erection." My glare locks on Sara, and she nervously tucks her hair behind her ear. Not that it stays.

While questioning Bash, my arm waves in her direction with her shirt clutched in my hand. "Of all people, it's fucking Sara! Why *her*?"

Realizing I'm still holding the makeshift blindfold, I grimace and toss it into the fire. She lurches forward to grab it but thinks better of it when the flame grabs hold of the hem almost immediately.

His voice is calm, but a blaze rages below the surface. "I swear to you, Goldie, I thought she was Lizzy. Please, untie me."

The way he stares at her has me wondering if he's blaming her when he invited her. Is she telling the truth, or is he? I want to believe him—I should—but her expression is so painful. She stares at him while he stares back, shaking his head slowly. I'm unsure of whom to believe.

She steps toward me but maintains a safe distance. "He came into the diner where I waitress on Friday nights and we started talking. We talked about some of the fun times we had, and that led to the topic of sex. He suggested we get together; that I come here and—"

He growls, "No fucking way, you goddamn lying *bitch*!" His voice softens to plead with me. "Goldie, why would I invite her here when you could come home at any minute? I'd have to be a stupid son-of-a-bitch to do that."

My mouth twists as my head tilts. "You weren't expecting me until after midnight. I'm home early. So, either you are a stupid son-of-a-bitch or she's a fucking rapist. Which is it?"

"I'm no rapist!" she sasses and folds her arms over her chest.

"Rapist is a bit too much, don't you think?" Bash suggests, and my surprised response has him shaking his head. "She didn't fuck me. It was a blowjob. Big deal. It just sucks it was her who did it."

She screeches. "You asked me to!"

"I did not!" he yells and pulls at the bindings. "Goldie, please untie me."

"Not yet," I say as my hand rises between us. "Where did she get the idea that you wanted her to blow you?"

His eyes close for several seconds as his mouth presses into a line. "We were talking about old times, including the sex we had together. I might have mentioned something about how great her blowjobs were—"

"Did you say that you *missed* her blowjobs?"

"In all honesty, I might have," he says and sounds defeated.

Ouch! Does that mean hers are better than mine? Do I suck at giving head? Pardon the pun. Did he invite her so he could finally get a good blowjob?

"He did," Sara says, and picks up her purse from behind Bash's chair. She looks down at Bash and says, "Don't call me."

As she storms off, I want more than anything to chase after her and beat the living hell out of her, but that isn't my style. Besides, I've never punched anyone.

"Goldie. I didn't tell her to come here. I wouldn't. If I wanted to have an affair, which I don't, I'm smart enough not to bring someone to our house." His hips shift forward in a last-ditch effort to pull his wrists free, but he fails. "Please, untie me."

"If you didn't want Sara, why did you let her tie you up and blind you?"

His head shakes as he flops back in the chair, extremely annoyed. "I fell asleep. I woke up to hands over my eyes. I heard, *Shh*, and then something was tied around my head. I couldn't see anything. When I reached to touch you or Lizzy, a hand took my wrist, held it to the armrest, and tied it. I thought you or Lizzy were playing a mystery bondage game. I was all for it, especially when my pants were yanked down and a hot mouth was sucking my cock. I'm not going to lie, it felt good. I didn't know it was her. She didn't speak."

"Did she fuck you?"

"No! But if you hadn't come home when you did, who knows what she would have done? That's a scary thought. She could've fucked me; maybe given me a disease, or—"

I whisper, "Or gotten pregnant."

His eyes close as his nostrils flare. His voice is soft, but the words are harsh. "I've never hit a woman before and would never actually do it, but I wish I could slap that fucking bitch into next week."

"So, it's a good thing I didn't untie you." I stand and struggle with the stockings she tied to each wrist and toss them into the fire beside her ashen shirt and watch them shrivel instantly.

Bash rubs his wrists and stands as he pulls up his pants. Looking down at me, he says, "For what it's worth, I'm sorry. Had I known it was her—" He pulls me into a hug, but I don't hug him back. "I shouldn't have talked with her at the restaurant. We used to be friends. Had I known she still has feelings for me, I would've avoided her like a plague."

My arms wrap around him, and I bury my face in his chest. "I know. I'm sorry I didn't believe you, but you have to admit the scene was pretty damning."

He grumbles, "Yeah. If I'd come home and saw you tied to a chair with one of your exes eating your pussy, I'd probably kill the fucking guy whether you invited him."

"Now that you mention exes... Cody's working in the accounting department at the hospital. You must remember him." My head tilts back to see his face lit with an orange hue from the flames.

Bash chuckles and backs away. His hands slip into the front pockets of his jeans. "Yeah. I remember him. He's the gay guy you dated for a few years."

Shocked, my arms rise at my sides. "What? You knew he was gay? I didn't know he was gay. Did everyone know but me?"

"I don't know about everyone else, but the way he stared at me wasn't like any woman-loving man I ever met." Bash sprays the fire with the hose, and smoke pours from the pit.

"He's married to a man, and they have twin girls. He was my best friend back then."

Bash laughs again. "Yeah, but I bet the sex was horrible."

My lips pinch between my teeth, and I nod with raised eyebrows. "He refused to go down on me. That should have been my first clue, but I wasn't thinking he could be gay. Anyway, I'm going inside. Boil your cock before you come to bed."

Halfway to the back porch, I turn and add, "If you ever talk to her again, I'm going to put on my pointy-toed boots and kick you in the balls."

He lifts his arm to acknowledge he heard me but doesn't turn around. Instead, he continues spraying the hot coals with water.

As I walk away, I hear him say, "Talk to her. Lose my balls. Got it."

Chapter 5

I was asleep by the time Bash came to bed. The long workday had exhausted me, and I couldn't keep my eyes open. My dream seemed to repeat a dozen times through the night: Sara was sucking Bash off or riding his cock, and they were both screaming through an earth-shattering orgasm. In the dreams, Bash wasn't blindfolded, and he was thoroughly enjoying her.

A sliver of sunshine beams through the gap in the drapes and crosses my closed eyes, waking me. I'm instantly angry as hell at Bash. Stupid, I know. It's not like he has any control over what I dream.

Bash is sitting on the porch with his heels perched on the railing, lounged back in his Adirondack chair while he holds a coffee mug. It must be cool outside because he's wearing a hoodie and steam floats from the mug's contents.

After filling a mug with coffee and wrapping the red and black plaid blanket around my shoulders, I join him.

With a soft kiss and a smile, I whisper, "Good morning."

"Good morning. How'd you sleep?"

After I sit on the second chair and arrange my blanket to cover my legs, I reply, "I'm mad as hell at you."

His eyebrows furrow with concern. Is he worried I'm still furious at him about last night?

To ease his concern, I shake my head. "Last night's event haunted my dreams. You were either getting sucked off or she was riding you."

He jokes, "Had it been Lizzy blowing me, it would've been a delightful dream."

"Sure, funny man. Go ahead and joke. I was furious in my dream and wanted to kill you both because you were enjoying it so much. Now the image of her fucking you is stuck in my brain forever."

His long fingers brush along my blanket-covered arm. "It was just a dream. What happened last night is over and done. We have to let it go, or it'll eat us up. Don't let her put a wedge between us, please. Again, I'm sorry it happened." His blue eyes hold a sadness within them, and I don't like it.

"It's not your fault. She raped you," I say, and sip my steaming coffee.

Exasperated, he scoffs. "Raped? No. She didn't rape me, Goldie. That's a bit of a stretch."

"No. It's not," I correct him and set my coffee on the stump we use as a table. "Turn it around. If a man tied a woman to a chair, blindfolded her, and ate her pussy under the disguise of her assuming it was her mate, would that not be rape?"

His eyes roll. "Of course! And I'd have to kill the fucker."

"Exactly!" My arms fling up and drop to my lap. "Mhm. I should have punched her lights out. It might have made me feel better."

"Thinking about it in the way you turned it around, she forced herself on me under false pretenses by concealing her identity, but I'm not going to the cops to have her arrested." He stands and stretches his long arms over his head. "I have to get ready for work. I'm only going to the paper for a few hours, and then I'll be home. I'm in the mood to write."

I'm excited to have him working on his manuscript again. He took a break because working at the paper was taking a lot of his time. Editing people's articles put a strain on his eyes, so he didn't want to work on his computer when he got home. His hours have since eased off now that most of the staff have recovered from the flu outbreak.

"You haven't written in a few weeks."

"And I miss it. Tonight, I'm determined to write at least a chapter." He smirks suggestively. "Unless you have plans for me."

"No plans to speak of." My shoulders lift, and I sip my coffee with wide, innocent eyes.

Bash squints as he assesses my face to see if I have something up my sleeve. Still unsure, he turns to walk into the house.

I ask, "Has Mack come home?"

Bash stops and turns as his hand rubs his strong abs under his sweatshirt. It lifts enough to show the waistband of his grey sweatpants hanging just above his cock. "He got in late last night. You should go see him, or we'll both go later. Maybe we'll order pizza and have a fire."

"Maybe I'll take a walk in the afternoon. There's laundry and other chores to do first," I say, and Bash disappears into the house.

A gust of wind drafts under the blanket, sending a shiver through me.

"Fuck this. I'm going in."

***

Two loads of laundry hang on the line outside. I love watching the white sheets swing in the cool gentle breeze as sunlight dances on the cotton. The windows are open to freshen the house now that it's warmer outside. The dusting is done, and I don't have to sweep because Bash bought one of those automatic robots that vacuum the floor. What's even better is it empties itself when it's full. Technology is awesome and mildly entertaining to watch while I eat a sandwich.

After a shower, I towel-dry my hair and slip into yoga pants and a long-sleeved plaid shirt that hangs low enough in the back to cover my butt. It's big and frumpy, perfect for my mood. Last night's marathon of dreams has left me tired.

With my hiking boots on, I trek along the trail leading to the main Bear house. It's a pleasant walk, and the sense of solitude the forest offers lifts my spirit. The smell of the mossy forest floor is more appealing to me than the scent of chocolate. I stop at the big boulder beside the river where I used to spend a lot of time when I was a kid and consider lying face down to watch the minnows swim between the small rock crevices. It would invoke a peacefulness in me, sure to calm my soul.

A flash of light catches my attention from up the river. With my knees on the boulder, I lean forward to see what caused it. Patch is fly-fishing. Each time he flings the rod, the line grabs the sunlight for only a second before the fly lands in the fast-moving water and the line sags onto the ripples.

Patch is lost in his thoughts, but his face is calm with a hint of a smile teasing the edges of his lips. He's in his element.

His jeans are snug on his thighs and address his strong ass with nothing less than perfection. His green and grey flannel shirt is unbuttoned. As he moves, it flips open, revealing a dark grey t-shirt snug against his thick chest but loose at his waist. I giggle when I see his tan hat has about a dozen different fly hooks pushed into the fabric.

"Hi," I say from a distance.

Patch doesn't like it when someone sneaks up on him. I jumped out to scare him once, and he stopped himself just before he punched me in the face. I'll never do that again. Announcing my presence outside of his arm's reach has been my goal after that.

He jolts and whips his head around, and his wide eyes blink several times. "Oh, hey. Where'd you come from?"

"Where do you think? My mother." My sarcasm has him turning to look at me. "Home."

"You could've been coming from work."

My arms lift from my sides. "I'd still have to park at home to follow the path here." Again, he looks at me, so I answer his original question. "I'm on my way to the main house to see Mack."

"He's not home," he says and flings the fly far into the stream. In silence, we watch the tide take it downstream. He pulls it up and does it again.

"Where is he?" I stand beside him and look into the water when something moves. A swarm of fish is clustered on a metal stringer. "Bass? How many?"

"Four so far. This is dinner tonight," he says in his low, deep voice.

I face him and *tsk* to show my disappointment. "Bash and I were going to buy pizza or something; takeout and a fire. But if you promised Mack fish—"

"Whatever will make you happy, beautiful woman," he says, winking over his shoulder. "So, now that your plans have changed and you won't be going to see Mack, what now?" His gaze scales my frame while he sports a sexy grin.

"Probably not what you're thinking." I cross my arms over my chest and shake my head.

He grunts disapprovingly.

I wave emphatically. "I caught—get this—Sara Joyeau blowing Bash last night."

Patch whips around to face me and glowers in a squint while a valley grooves between his brows. He's angry. "I better have just heard you wrong."

"It's not what you think. Well, it is. But—" I lift my hands to calm him because his face has flushed red. "I came home from work early last night, and Bash was at the fire blindfolded. His wrists were tied to the chair, and Sara was sucking his cock. He didn't know it was her because she snuck up on him and didn't speak. He thought she was Lizzy."

It's impossible to read Patch's stoic face. Is he angry, confused, or impressed with her ability to have her way with Bash without his knowledge, or does the image give him ideas on binding Lizzy or me to a chair? Maybe all of the above.

"Did he enjoy it?" he asks with no discernable tone before he turns back to the river to flip the fly he'd left to float downstream.

"He was until he heard me yell her name. He was furious. I wouldn't free him right away because I needed to know if he invited her or not. She said he did. Bash said he didn't. I choose to believe him." My hip juts to the left as my weight shifts to one leg. I rest my hands on my waist, and I gloat. "I threw her shirt in the fire."

"You should have decked her. A black eye or split lip would have her thinking twice about ever doing it again." Patch shakes his head and casts. "So, what happened next?"

My shoulders lift even though he isn't looking. "Nothing. I fell asleep."

Patch pulls in his line and sets the pole on the rocks so it's out of the water. He wipes his hands on his pants and is in no rush to get to me. When he does, not a second passes before his lips claim mine, and a wad of my damp hair is clutched in his fist. The heated passion I know to be Patch's way sets my body on fire with its raw, carnal lust.

He spins me to face away from him, nearly knocking me off balance. With my head under his control, he walks me toward a waist-high boulder. He yanks my yoga pants down just past my hips and pushes me to bend forward with my chest on the rock.

Yes! This is what I need: a hard, angry fuck under the warm sun while a cool breeze kisses my skin.

Patch rubs saliva-soaked fingers over my vagina and then immediately fills me with his steely hard cock. He thrusts punishingly rough, as if he hates me. It feels like he's punching so deep my belly button might pop out, and yet I want more. I want him to hurt me because the physical pain is easing the emotional pain I'm harboring from last night. My need for him outweighs the pain of my hair being pulled or my thighs scraping on the boulder.

The rushing water carries my scream downstream. "Fuck me! Yes! Hard! Please! Patch!"

His primitive grunts roll between his words, "That's right! Take my fucking cock, whore!" Patch releases my hair, but quickly wraps his hand around my throat. He pulls me up to whisper in my ear. "You're my fucking cunt. I own you. I'll take you whenever I want you. Don't cum until I say you can."

His hand slides around to the back of my neck and I'm pushed chest-down onto the boulder while he pounds into me with cruel thrusts, harder than ever.

This is *exactly* what I need. How does he always know whether I need rough sex or gentle love-making?

I reach between my thighs and the rock and rub my drenched clit with my index finger. He wants me to cum when he tells me to, but if I want to before he permits, I will. If he wants to punish me for it, I'll accept.

Patch's growls and pants are proof he's tiring, but his voice is still deep and powerful. "You want to cum?"

I'm on the verge of exploding, so I scream, "Yes, sir!"

His laugh is cruel, and his words are disappointing. "Fuck no!"

My orgasm hangs in the balance, and I must decide to wait for his approval or take my pleasure.

My orgasm owns me. It has my soul floating high into the sky. Up, up, up into the still blackness of nothing. It's magnificent. I'm sucked back from my bliss like a magnet drawn to metal by a hard slap to my right ass cheek, and it infuriates me.

Patch pushes into me while he holds my hips to keep me from squirming, and he fills me with his seed. Loud bellows erupt from his core, hushing the creatures in the wilderness. The comfort of his stillness silences my thoughts. The relief in his exhaustive exhale brings a satisfied smile to my face. Seconds pass before the sounds of life resumes around us.

I turn and sit on the rock as my palm wipes sweat from my forehead. Beads of sweat trickle from Patch's forehead and down his cheek as he stands before me with his cock and balls hanging over the gaping zipper of his jeans. He licks his lips and smiles as he uses what little strength he has to fasten them.

"Do you feel better? And don't think I'll let you off easy for defying me." He glares, cups my chin, and presses a kiss to my forehead. "Beautiful."

I smile and glance at the sky with a shrug of both shoulders. "You like it when I *disobey* you. But I feel better.

My pent-up anger has subsided. Was that your intention, or were you simply in the mood to fuck?"

He picks up his thermos and uncaps it, pours some into the cap, and hands it to me. It's unlikely to be water.

"Moonshine?"

Patch smirks. "Just a bit."

"It's not even noon!"

"Shut up and drink it. It'll do you some good." He winks a dangerous brown eye and flashes a crooked smile before taking a swig from the thermos. His lips pull back as he inhales. "Wooh! Damn, that's good."

After swallowing a small sip, my throat burns. It's hard to breathe. "Nope! Too early for me. Even at night, it'll still be too early. That shit will strip the paint off a car."

As he caps the thermos and stuffs it in his backpack, he says, "Hasn't yet."

"Don't be surprised if you have a bleeding ulcer one day, or worse."

"Last I checked, you're not my mother," he says, and winds the fishing line on his pole.

I laugh. "Good thing! I can't imagine having pushed your gigantic head out of my cooch."

Patch points at me and snickers. "Odds are if you have a Bear son, you *will* push one of these huge noggins out of your cooch. So, don't laugh too hard."

"If you ever want to be an uncle, you'll never threaten me with that again."

"Uncle? Shit! I want to be your baby-daddy," he says in a tone that's impossible to know whether he's joking or serious.

Patch as the father of my child? How would we explain that to everyone, let alone the child? And what about Mack? Would he want to father one of my children?

Bash... How would he feel about his brothers being called "Daddy" by a bunch of kids running around the house? What do I want? Do I even want kids? Do I want one with each man or just Bash's offspring?

No, just Bash.

Then again, I love them all. But—

His voice pulls me from the beginning stages of a panic attack. "Are you going to answer that?"

"What?" I ask sharply, and he points to my ringing phone in the mid-thigh pocket of my yoga pants. I answer it and say, "Hello."

A voice no deeper than Bash's rings in a comedic tone. "There's my girl! How the hell are you?"

"Mack! Hi. I'm good. I was on my way to see you but ran into Patch. He said you weren't home and then he otherwise occupied me, so I didn't have time to call."

He laughs. "That sounds like something Patch would do. I hope, at least, he was good."

"Vicious, actually." I squint accusingly at Patch.

He stands tall with his hands on his hips, wearing the gleaming smile of a proud stud.

My eyes roll before I ask Mack, "So, where are you?"

"I just got home and thought I should call you. I miss you, girlie." Mack sounds like he's doing something somewhat strenuous because his breath hitches now and then. "Are you still at the river?"

"Yeah," I say, and sit cross-legged on the boulder Patch fucked me against. "Are you coming here, or do you want me to come there?"

In stereo, I hear his voice come from the left while my phone rests against my right ear. "I'm already here." He slips his phone into his pants pocket and rushes to grab me and swing me around. "I missed you, Goldilocks."

"I missed you, too, but you were only gone for just over a week."

"A week is too long to be away from you," Mack says and sets me down before kissing me with the swoon-worthy tenderness this Bear brother has perfected.

Out of all the brothers, Mack is the most romantic. He's a kinky fucker who loves ass, but he's also gentle and sweet. Rarely is he rough during sex. I've heard stories of him wiping the floor with four men in a bar fight. He's a lover and a scrappy fighter, too. When I look into his seductive blue eyes, it's obvious how much he adores me.

"Have you talked to Lizzy?" I ask and rustle my fingers through his long, dark-brown hair. "When are you going to cut this mop?"

His head jerks back and his eyes widen. "No way! No one's cutting my hair. Lose that thought. It's not an unkempt mess. My hair is gorgeous, wavy, silky, and it suits my bone structure." He strikes a pose. Always the comedian.

Patch walks past him and gives him a swat on the back of his head. "You're such a girl."

An inch taller than Mack, Patch stands at 6'3" and has an extra thirty pounds of muscle from all his years of lumberjacking. He often teases Mack that he's gone soft from years sitting behind a desk at architecture school. They love each other dearly, but they're brothers, and boys will be boys.

"If I'm a girl, I'm a damn sexy lesbian!" Mack threatens to kick Patch in the ass, but Patch turns and glares before he can, so Mack feigns innocence. "I wasn't going to kick you. I lost my balance."

"Yeah, sure. Make yourself useful and get the fish." Patch strides down the path toward the main Bear house while Mack frowns.

"He leaves me with the smelly job. But, I suppose, since he caught them, I can carry and clean them."

He unhooks the stringer of fish from the stick wedged between rocks and pulls the chain from the water. His elbow protrudes as he bows toward me.

"May I escort you, my lady?"

"Most certainly." My arm slips through his, and we walk. "So, how was the site?"

"We're ahead of schedule, which is rare. I'm not needed for at least a week, but they'll let me know if I have to go back sooner. They're doing the electrical, and that's out of my wheelhouse. I can do it, but we hire certified electricians to keep things to code." He allows me to lead the way down the narrowest section of the path before offering his elbow when it widens. "How about you? What's new?"

"I came home from work early last night and Bash was tied to the chair by the fire while receiving a blowjob."

He smiles excitedly. "Really? Lizzy's having fun, I gather."

"No. Sara Joyeau," I say, and he steps in front of me, accidentally slapping my calf with a fish. "It's not like that. He was blindfolded and didn't know it was her. She was sneaky about it. He thought she was Lizzy. I threw her shirt into the fire. Patch said I should have decked her."

"You should have," he says angrily and continues walking beside me.

"She kept blaming him for inviting her. I believe him, not her. Something about that chick is off. She must be crazy."

Mack says, "There was a reason we had to let her go. Well, *I* had to let her go. She was *my* girlfriend. I always seem to pick the crazy ones."

"I was told she fell for Bash and no longer wanted to be sexual with Patch because she claimed he was too vicious and it frightened her."

He scoffs. "Something like that. She was showing up unannounced when she knew Bash would be home alone. She only came to see me when Bash was there, too. After a while, she didn't want me anymore, and she said she was terrified of Patch—probably because he saw through her bullshit. She wanted Bash, but he had no interest in dating her. When he realized what she was doing, he told her to keep her distance. She didn't like that. One night, she showed up in his bed, claiming she loved him and wanted to run away with him."

"But she was dating you," I say and climb over a fallen tree Patch has yet to clear after the recent storm.

Mack steps over it and says, "Supposedly. We had a family meeting and decided she had to go. That's the story in a nutshell." He releases my arm when we come to another narrow section of the path just before it opens up to the Bear house backyard. "My advice? Keep your distance from her. She's not right, and I wouldn't put it past her to hurt you."

My heart pounds a little harder, and my breath catches. "What? You think she'll hurt me?"

"Just stay away from her. And don't assume she's finished with all of this. She obviously still wants Bash. Now that she knows you're marrying him, she's desperate. Just be careful. Okay?"

Mack kisses my cheek before he flops the fish on the long table beside the porch they use for preparing their catches.

Bash didn't say anything about watching my back. Patch either. If that little bitch comes anywhere near me, I will gladly rearrange the nose on her face.

Chapter 6

While Mack cleans the fish and Patch is in the house, I pluck weeds from the garden and collect some potatoes, carrots, cucumbers, herbs, squash, peppers, and green onions.

While I wash the healthy harvest in the kitchen sink, Patch sweeps the kitchen. I step out of the way so he can sweep where I stood. As he passes, he pecks a kiss on my forehead.

"Sweet as sugar," he says, and winks.

I contradict him: "Sour as a lemon… at times."

"Not with me you aren't." He looks over his shoulder at me. "You know I'll spank a sour attitude out of you."

My clit twitches. I swear I can feel the heat of his palm on my ass, even though he's not near me. Recalling the intense pounding he gave me at the river doesn't ease my thoughts of bending over to accept a second fucking. A deep breath centers my mind on more general thoughts, like my stomach growling from hunger.

Mack startles me when he pauses his walk past me to kiss my neck. "Our garden is hearty this year."

I reply, "Mhm. Lots of yummies."

Mack flops the fish fillets in a deep bowl and pours milk over them before covering them and putting them in the fridge. "Will Bash be joining us for dinner, or is he staying late at the paper? Patch said he's been working a lot of long hours lately."

One of my shoulders lifts as I set a cucumber on the cutting board Patch most likely made and begin slicing. "He has. I wish he wouldn't work so much. I miss our time together. But so many people were off with the flu, and with the chief editor being on maternity leave, he's the next best editor."

"Is he still writing the obituaries?" Mack asks.

He sets a clear plastic tray with divided sections beside the cutting board and positions the cucumber slices in two rows. I would have just plopped them in a heap, but he's so particular I can't help but giggle.

"Yes. He's doing multiple jobs; hence the long hours, but he claims he won't be late tonight. We planned to order takeout to spoil you but fresh fish sounds better."

He kisses my neck again. "I'd rather eat you." His teeth nip at my neck.

I giggle like a smitten teenager and hate myself for it. I set the knife down and wipe my hands on the towel before flinging my arms around his neck. My lips peck his. We smile before we peck again.

He whispers, "I missed your lips. You have the prettiest bottom lip. I always want to suck it because it reminds me of your clitoris." His tongue glides along my bottom lip as he moans. "Yes. That's nice. I'd drop and make you cum all over my face, but my brother was recently inside you, so I'll wait until I've showered you."

Mack's gaze locks on my lips when I moan.

In a soft voice, I propose, "Later?"

He nods slowly as one side of his lip lifts into a sexy grin. All the brothers have similar seductive sneers despite their differently shaped lips.

"It's a date," Mack says and presses his lips to mine while he grips my ass. "I want this, too."

Why are my cheeks flushed? Having sex with Mack isn't a new thing for me. However, anal sex has always been high on my naughty, taboo list. It's possibly more taboo than having sex with three brothers and my female best friend. It's strange how my morals stand.

I kiss him once more before setting his neck free and teasing him. "We'll see."

Mack's head tips back while his eyes assess my body. He shifts his erection in his faded, torn-at-the-knee jeans. Should I rethink my decision to postpone sex? If only we had more time to play, I'd take him to the shower right now. I miss him, but these vegetables will not cut themselves.

He snickers and runs his hand under his t-shirt, lifting it to reveal a washboard tummy. He flexes to taunt me. Goddamn! That man is magazine-worthy-level of sexy.

I pull my eyes from his bulge and flip the towel at him. "Stop that."

"What? This?" Mack's hand glides down to his cock while he wears his typical joker-like smile. When I tilt my head, he points to his abs. "Maybe this? Want to touch? I mean, you can. It'll be a sacrifice on my part and I'll have to endure, but if it'll make you happy, I'll manage."

Fine! You want to play that game, I'm all in.

I close the gap between us and stare into his wanton, powder-blue eyes. My fingernails glide down his mountainous abs and then undo the button on his jeans. The further my hand goes down his pants, the lower his zipper slides down. His cock is hard and ready for whatever kinky shit I propose. My hand wraps around the shaft and gently strokes while I place a breathy kiss on his throat.

"Do you like this?" I ask in a sultry voice.

He moans. "You know I do."

"Would you like me to make you cum?"

Again, he moans. "Only after I make you cum."

"As tempting as that is," I pull my hand from his pants and quickly button and zip them before lightly slapping his cheek, "we have dinner to prepare."

In frustration, he licks his bottom lip and shakes his head. "You're a sinful temptress, and I love it, but you'll pay for this. You know that, right?"

With a snicker, I kiss him and say, "I look forward to it."

He watches me wash my hands and pick up the knife to cut the tomato before he runs his fingers through his hair to pull it off his face. As he walks away, he complains under his breath.

Patch's voice startles me. "Cut the tomatoes into thick slices."

When did he walk up behind me?

"Fuck! You scared me! You shouldn't scare people who have a knife in their hands!"

He slaps my ass. "You wouldn't stab me. You love me."

"I *do* love you, but automatic reactions are just that."

Patch kisses my forehead, and I'm forced to lean in when he pulls my head against his chest for another kiss on my hair. "You're fucking adorable."

Mack calls out from his bedroom, "Hey! You already had her, bohemian. Hands off! She promised to love *me* tonight."

I laugh when Patch pops his bottom lip out and I push it back in with my finger. "If Bash wants me tonight, he has first dibs, of course. But if he doesn't, and since Lizzy's working late, I promised Mack that he could tarnish my virtue."

"Girl, your virtue has long since tarnished," Patch says and bites into a slice of cucumber.

Patch cooks the sauce for the fish while I peel potatoes for him to boil. Mack has since changed his clothes to rid himself of the fishy smell gained from cleaning the catch.

Bash's truck chugs as it pulls in, and he shuts off the engine. I watch him through the kitchen window as he leaps up the porch steps two at a time. He whips open the screen door and struts through.

Patch yells, "Don't let it—" *Slam!* "Dammit, Bash! Were you born in a barn? Dick!"

Bash and Mack laugh.

Patch shakes his head and grumbles, "Goddamn kids!"

"How's my Goldie?" Bash asks as he nears me and gently sets a plastic grocery bag on the counter. His arms wrap around my back when I wrap my arms around his neck. Before he kisses me, his laughing blue eyes memorize my face.

He frees me, opens the bag, and removes two pies: apple and pumpkin. "I made dessert! It's the least I could do since you two are working so hard in the kitchen."

With a shake of my head, I ask, "You *made* dessert?"

"Well, I made the money that paid for them to be made by someone else. So, in a roundabout way, yes, I made them."

His goofy, extra-wide grin has his lips curled against his teeth to boast his pearly whites.

***

Dinner was delicious, and we had lots of laughs, as usual.

The brothers insist I sit with my feet up on the chair beside me while they clear the table and clean the kitchen; each man playing his role. Watching them move like a well-choreographed dance has my heart ready to burst. Not a moment passes where I don't appreciate how lucky I am that they accepted me into their family.

Bash sits his ass on the table near me and crosses his arms over his chest. He whispers, "Goldie, should we invite Mack to spend the night with us?"

Spend a night with two incredibly sexy men who want to share me both physically and emotionally? And their primary goal is my pleasure? Um, *yes!*

"Sure, as long as we don't make a marathon of it. My shift starts at ten."

His suggestive grin and hooded eyes are a dead giveaway to his intention to seduce me. His voice rises. "Hey, Mack. Do you want to spend the night with us? Well, not me, necessarily. But I'll be there."

I add, "As long as you promise I'll sleep at some point because I have to work in the morning."

Mack leans on the island and licks his lips while his sky-blue eyes remain fixed on me. "I'd love nothing more than to spend a few hours loving you up while you scream in ecstasy."

As brothers do, Bash takes a poke at Mack. "Don't fret. I'll be there to bring her to ecstasy when you fail to tickle her just right."

Mack laughs. "Make yourself useful and wash the table."

He throws a wet washcloth at Bash, but he catches it just before it splats on his blue t-shirt.

Patch playfully pouts. "Looks like I'll be spending the night reading with my cock in my hand."

From behind him, Patch throws his thick arm around Mack's neck and bends him over so he can rub his knuckles on the top of Mack's head. In retaliation, Mack's elbow meets Patch's abdomen, rewarding him with Patch's sudden grunt.

Patch releases him and steps back while sporting a toothy grin and laughing. His hand raises between them and the other rubs his belly where Mack elbowed him.

Mack laughs. "What's the matter, old man? Are you getting soft in the middle along with everywhere else? I hear limp-dick is a common issue with the elderly."

Patch scoffs. "I'm like the finest cheese, motherfucker. I get better with age."

Bash teases, "Yeah, and you smell like it, too."

Chapter 7

Bash and Mack won't let me wash myself in the shower. They soap me and wash my hair while I enjoy their spoils. To return the favor, I soap them and spend extra time on their cocks; stroking until they're hard as steel and moaning.

We dry ourselves, but they don't give me time to dry my hair. Instead, Mack twists his damp hair in a bun and then copies with mine. I love when he plays with my hair.

Bash takes my hand and leads me to the bed while Mack follows. Bash cradles my cheek in his palm and kisses me. My arm wraps around his back, and I lightly scratch. He moans and his fervent kiss intensifies.

I feel Mack's heat before his bare chest presses to my back. Even hotter than his skin, his full lips press to my neck. The heat from his exhale trails goosebumps onto my skin. His fingertips glide up my hips and waist and tease my nipples while his palms encircle my breasts.

My phone vibrates, but I ignore it. *Fuck off! I'm about to have the best sex of my life!*

Bash's phone vibrates after mine stops. After his stops, Mack's phone sings from atop his folded clothes on my dresser. All the kissing stops, and we reach for our phones.

While naked with an erection that could crush diamonds, Mack lifts the phone to his ear. "Hello." He's quiet for a moment before his eyes meet mine; their shape no longer screams sex. "I'll get her there." Another pause, and he swallows. "Okay. Thanks."

Bash's wide hand rubs my back when he hears my quivered exhale.

Mack hangs up and shakes his head before he tosses his phone on the dresser. "Goldie, that was Lizzy. Your dad's in the hospital. He had a heart attack."

No! Oh, God... no! We haven't worked out our differences. He can't leave me before we do. I love him. As much of an ass as he can be, I love him. He's my daddy; the man who raised me with tender words and stiff rules. He's always kept me safe. Please. Please, don't take him from me.

He crosses the room to help Bash steady me when all the blood leaves my face and my knees weaken. They sit me on the bed, and both men squat before me.

In a softer voice, Mack adds, "They've stabilized him, but she thinks you should see him. He's scheduled for surgery in the morning."

How much has the world shifted from a moment ago? From sex to sympathy in a few seconds.

My head shakes, hoping to unscramble the many thoughts spinning in my mind, and yet only one concern comes to the forefront. "We don't have a cardiothoracic surgeon in town."

Mack brushes his hot hand down my cool left arm to grab my attention. "There will be one here in the morning."

Bash rises from a squat position in front of me. "Let's get you dressed. We'll take you to see him."

"What if he dies? We haven't settled our issues. He's so disappointed in me. He can't die. He can't!"

Bash rushes to my closet and takes out my pastel blue, mid-calf length dress, and a pair of three-inch heels. He rethinks the heels, shakes his head, and exchanges them for a pair of flat black ballerina-style shoes. He hands me the bra I took off when I got home, and I quickly dress while my thoughts continue swirling in a panicked mess.

Bash drives my car after stopping at the main Bear house to pick up Patch. It takes half the time it normally does because Bash drives like a maniac, as usual. I won't complain about his lead foot; tonight, I'm grateful for it.

Once we're at the hospital, Mack addresses the nurse by name and flashes his sexy smile. Her cheeks flush a deep crimson and her thin bottom lip pinches between her teeth. But her attitude shifts back to professional when her eyes dart to meet the concern in mine. She knows me and who I'm here to see. She directs us to his room and shyly smiles when Mack winks at her.

I whisper, "Really, Mack?"

He shrugs innocently as he watches her walk away. Bash takes my hand to lead me to my father's room. Patch grips Mack's shoulders and gives him a little shove so he'll follow.

My hesitation to enter his room isn't because I'm worried Dad will go on another rant about how my life choices have ruined my good-girl reputation. The last time he was lying in a hospital bed for the same reason, he didn't look like the strong man I know him to be. When I walk through that door, he'll be weak and vulnerable; not my dad, but a failing body housing my father's tired spirit.

Patch pulls me into a hug and holds my head to his chest. He says nothing, which is perfect. He steps back and nods a silent reassurance that it'll be okay.

I push open the door. Mom's standing at the bedside of a man with grey-tinged skin and sunken eyes. The tubes and wires attached to him are familiar to me, but the steady beeping sound of a heartbeat that usually calms me has me anxiously awaiting each one. If the beep fails, so will he.

"Mom," I whisper, and she looks up.

At first, the pain of her concern makes her appear older than her fifty-two years. Like any mother who doesn't want her daughter to worry, a forced smile lifts her face.

"Goldilocks," she says before she hugs me tighter than usual. "I'm so happy you came. Dad's been asking for you. Our nurse, Lizzy, said she's your friend. She seems nice."

"Mom, are you okay?" She nods, and my eyes hesitantly veer toward my father. "How's Dad?"

She turns to look at him as her lips twist and she shrugs. "Well, he's holding his own. A surgeon's coming in the morning to—I don't know what he's going to do. What they said is a blur."

"Lizzy called us. She talked to Mack." More words stick in my throat, threatening to choke me.

I gesture to see if it's okay for me to go to his bedside. She nods, so I unhurriedly make my way to him. Dad looks worse now that I'm closer. It's obvious by his color that his oxygen levels are down. I assume he's asleep until he reaches up. I take his cool hand in both of mine.

"Goldilocks," he says in his fragile voice, which breaks my heart. "Thank you for coming. I want to talk to you."

Mom excuses herself and urges the brothers to follow her into the corridor.

He's slow to speak. "I'm sorry we argued. I shouldn't have struck you. Every day since I've regretted it and wanted to tell you so, but my damn pride got in the way."

"Dad, it's okay," I say while holding back a waterfall of tears.

"No! No, it's not." He frowns when he runs out of breath and has to pause. "Goldilocks, I love you. The moment you were born, I vowed to protect you. Those brothers aren't known for being respectable, and I thought a little tough love would make you see that." He coughs and then breathes slowly. The heartbeat monitor comforts me with its sounds. "Do you love him? Bash?"

My voice squeezes past the huge lump in my throat and threatens to choke me. "I do, Daddy. I love him enough to marry him."

He looks at the ring on my finger and the deepening crevice between his eyebrows cannot hide his disappointment. "I raised you to be a smart, independent woman with a mind of your own. I can't be angry about the decisions you make. If you're happy, I'm happy... even if I don't approve. You know what's best for you. Never forget that I love you." He struggles to bring his other hand across his body to pat my hands holding his. "Now, send that fiancé of yours in here. And I don't want you here all night worrying about me, so go home. Hug your mother first." I turn to walk away, and he calls out to me in his weakened voice. "Goldilocks, I'll be beside you when you walk down the aisle."

"You will?" I ask, and swear my heart skips a beat waiting for his nod. "Oh, Dad. Thank you so much!"

Those words mean everything to me. Agreeing to walk me down the aisle is a big deal because he was so against me dating the wild and out-of-control Bash Bear. He might not like it, but he's trying, and I couldn't be more delighted.

I squeal with excitement before I reluctantly leave his hospital room.

Mom and the three men turn and seem shocked that I'm not in tears. Bash takes my hand and is the first to return my smile.

"He's going to be okay because he promised to be beside me when I walk down the aisle."

"Yeah?" As if that's a tremendous weight off his back, Bash's shoulders relax and he pulls me into a hug. "You must be so happy, Goldie."

With my ear pressed to his chest, I whisper, "It's a big step for him. There's only one thing." I pull out of the hug and hold on to his forearms. "He wants to talk to you."

Bash's eyes widen and lock onto the door to Dad's room. His lips part and he cracks his knuckles. "What does he want?"

"There's only one way to find out," I say, and push open the door.

He sighs and his shoulders slump forward like a misbehaved student about to enter the principal's office. I close the door behind him to give them privacy.

My mom sits cross-legged on a chair mid-way through the row of five in the hall with Patch beside her, and he's holding her hand to comfort her. Mack reaches for my arm and pulls me into a hug.

He whispers, "Are you okay?"

I think my nod is a desperate attempt at convincing myself that I'm fine, but my tears spill forth onto his shirt. As pleased as I am about Dad's promise, the fear we might lose him before he can follow through is a real concern. He doesn't look well. If the surgeon cannot repair his heart, or Dad's too weak to handle sedation, he could die in surgery or never wake from the anesthetic.

Mack gently rocks me and says nothing as he holds me until I gather myself enough to dry my tears and be strong for my mother.

Mom smiles and stands as I approach. She hugs me, and in her comforting mom voice, says, "Don't worry. Things always work out the way they're supposed to. Nothing is by chance, baby girl."

Before I can stop myself from saying the one thing she really shouldn't hear from a nurse, I blurt, "He doesn't look good, Mom."

She nods, and her eyes search the hall behind me for nothing in particular. "I know. Once he has the surgery, he'll be okay."

I wish I were as confident as she is. My positivity isn't as strong because I've seen too many bodies fail after a second heart attack. No! I must stay positive.

I'll tell her about the good news. "He said—"

She interrupts and waves her hand between us as she steps back. "No. No! What you two talked about is between you two. I'm staying out of it." She smiles and takes my hands. "Just tell me you're happy."

"I am. I really am. He said I should go home," I say, and twist my mouth.

She laughs. "That sounds like your father. I suppose you should go home then. I'll call you in the morning to let you know when he goes in for his surgery."

Patch asks, "What time is he going in?"

Mom shakes her head. "It all lies on when the specialist's plane lands. I was told he should arrive by seven o'clock. He'll have to do his assessment first, so—" She shrugs and forces a smile. "I'll call you when I know."

Bash strolls out of the room and flashes a smile to ease my concern. "Okay. He wants us to go home. So, let's go." He offers my mom a hug, which she accepts, and then whispers, "Call me first if there are any changes. Okay?"

He thinks I didn't hear him and the insinuation behind those words. He means if my father dies.

She replies, "Don't worry. He'll be fine."

Bash says something to her in a softer whisper that I can't hear. Her hand pats his chest, and she steps back. She whispers something, and he nods. She hugs each of us and then goes back to my dad's bedside.

Bash wraps his arm around my shoulder. "Come on, Goldie. Let's get you home."

"Sitting here the whole night worrying won't do anyone any good," Mack says and leads the way to the elevator.

Patch remains silent, but his heavy work boots clomp loudly as he trails behind.

Chapter 8

The ride home carries with it a somber heaviness. But the love of these three men comforts me like warm pudding fresh off the stove. It's strange how that's what comes to mind: creamy chocolate pudding.

This one time, after a horrible day at school, my father sat me on the counter beside the stove and made pudding. I think I was about seven years old. I remember how quiet we were while I watched him stir the liquid until it was thick. He poured it into dishes and set them in the freezer. While the dessert cooled, we sat at the table and he listened to me tell him about how horrible someone was to me. After a few minutes, we ate them in silence. The outer layer was quite cool, but the inside was still hot. I loved the contrast.

I'll never forget the advice he gave me that day. He said that the bowls of pudding were a lot like people: the frozen exterior works hard to keep its warmth inside, but eventually, the heat softens the hard shell, allowing its warmth to flow. Basically, people can be cruel in order to protect themselves from emotional contact. But when someone breaks through, they'll find a fragile, scarred heart afraid of being rebroken. Their cruelness can be their frozen shell.

I've found that to be true with most people in that they present themselves as an asshole, but it's a shroud to protect their vulnerabilities. Dad explained it the way a seven-year-old would understand. When I was growing up, he was the best person in the world, and I adored him. Mom was amazing, too, but she was more strict. She had to be because Dad was a big softy and couldn't bring himself to punish me.

My hand cups my cheek when the phantom pain of him slapping me jerks away my happy memory. He was furious about me dating a Bear brother because he wanted his lily-white daughter to marry a *good boy*, not an out-of-control bad boy. The sensation of the slap is an emotional wound despite the physical handprint having long since vanished.

After dropping Patch at the main Bear house, Bash drives us to our house. I strip down and slip into bed. Bash and Mack aren't sure what to do. Their whispering in the hallway outside the bedroom isn't as hushed as they'd hoped. If they wanted secrecy, they should have stayed in the kitchen.

I call out, "Guys?" Both of them step into the bedroom. "Take your clothes off and make love to me."

They must have raced to see who could strip the fastest because seconds later, both men are pressed up against me: Bash in the front with my arm around his neck while he kisses me, and Mack behind me, kissing my shoulder and caressing my breasts as if relishing their milky flesh.

My face turns over my shoulder to kiss Mack. Bash's hot breath warms my flesh before each tender touch of his lips to my cool skin as he eases his way down my body, stripping me of the warm comfort his body offered. The air is chilly, but my core is hotter than an Alaskan sled dog on a tropical vacation.

My thoughts are not on my father as I lie on my bed. Their touches have stolen my fears and eased my tension with each kiss. This is what I need to get through the night. If they don't exhaust me, I won't sleep. I'll pace and chew my nails down to stubs.

Mack's hand holds my cheek as his lips and tongue bring heat to my mouth.

Bash spreads my legs and kisses my mound, sending shivers of heat outward. His hot, wet tongue slithers between my labia and over my clit, easing a moan from my soul. He's languid in his movements, intent on building my orgasm gradually. He wants me to feel everything and think nothing. Each brush of his tongue or lips edges me further from my thoughts, from my concerns about my father's wellbeing.

Mack collects something from the nightstand, and the absence of his lips is almost unbearable. Whatever he holds when he lies down alongside me is handed to Bash. Seconds later, Mack's kisses exude a fiery passion.

Bash gently sucks my clit and slips a finger into my ass. He gradually stretches it until two fingers, and then three, fit with relative ease.

Mack's kisses are more gentle now to allow my moans to escape. He knows I'm close to orgasm. Bash does, too, because he stops and slides up the bed. Mack leans back to allow Bash's super-heated lips bearing my scent to press to mine.

His kiss is gentle, but his need to be inside me has him rushing to settle between my thighs. He gently eases his erection into my eager slickness. Despite my inability to kiss him back because of the sudden invasion, he continues to kiss me. He leans his upper body on his left elbow on my right side to allow Mack access to my left breast to kiss and suckle my nipple. Heat shoots directly on my clitoris, and my pussy tightens around Bash's shaft.

Mack leans away and Bash grips my ass with one hand, the other under my back, and rolls onto his back, bringing me with him.

I sit up, straddled over his hips, and the scalding heat from his hands heats my thighs down to the bone. My hips rock above him with a slow rhythm. A tilt of my hips to allow my clitoris to brush along his tummy just right. I don't want to cum yet because I want to savor this moment, so I maintain the laziness of the moment.

Bash slides his legs together as he grips the back of my neck and pulls my face down to kiss him. His free arm hugs my back to hold me against his warm body. The mattress compresses on the outside of my calves, and I know Mack is preparing to enter my ass. Soon, I will be filled by two men I adore while they make love to me in a skillful, erotic dance sure to have me losing myself completely.

Bash slows his movements to allow Mack to ease himself into my ass. Perhaps today, Bash's need to glide inside me is so overwhelmingly desperate that attempting complete stillness, as he usually is at this stage, would be too torturous a feat.

The full length of Mack's penis stretches me so beautifully as he eases into me and holds his pelvis against my ass cheeks. His kiss on my spine between my shoulder blades sends shivers over my entire body.

I'm full, so beautifully complete. Goddamn! I love this sensation of two fiery bodies sandwiching me, filling me, being one with me.

Bash's firm body beneath grants me a sense of safety, like a boat's anchor in a vicious storm. Mack above ensures my soul won't float away as I fall into a weightless euphoria. Together they protect me when the fire grows too hot and threatens to explode me into a billion shards.

Being sandwiched between two powerful men warrants immobility, and I'm unable to contribute to their efforts. Bash's hips lift and lower while Mack fills me from behind. He leans over me. His breath is rapid and hot, waking my skin with tiny bumps and sending shudders throughout my entire being.

Bash tries to kiss me with loving tenderness, but it's impossible. His efforts, the added weight on his chest, and the struggle to prolong his growing need for release have him panting.

As one man glides in, the other eases out. The alternating rhythm is glorious. My thoughts are about as far away from real life as they can be. All I know is my pleasure and nothing else. Even the bodies using my body don't seem real. I am of no mind but of flesh.

Each time Bash lowers his hips, his strong Adonis belt brushes over my needy clitoris. I want him to move faster, and yet I don't want this intimate nearness to orgasm to end. If this moment continues forever while these men worship my body, mind, and soul, I wouldn't complain.

We move as one body, one heart, one soul, absent of conscious thought.

Bash holds me tighter against his chest, and my face tucks under his chin. My fists grip the bedsheet on either side of his head so I won't float away if the men should let me go. Bash quickens his thrusts upward. My deep, carnal wails merely overshadow their moans.

I'm lost in the glorious black abyss. This is total freedom. Bash's loud moan can be heard in the far distance, but it's enough to keep me grounded. My head lifts and my eyes open to see his face tense, as if he's in horrible pain. I gasp and shudder when my pussy spasms around his twitching shaft as his seed fills me.

Seconds later, Mack's arms hug my shoulders and pull my back up to his chest. He lifts me as he sits back on his calves with me straddling his thighs. He remains inside my ass while Bash slides out from beneath us. I'll miss the heat of his body and the sounds of his panting breaths.

Mack whispers behind my ear, "On your back."

As he frees me to my own power, I'm fully aware that my limbs are so weak they almost can't bear my weight. I flop onto my back beside Bash while he smiles lovingly.

Mack slips his inner elbows behind my knees and curls me up so his hands press on the bed beside my chest. He gazes into my eyes with his loving blue orbs as he slips his steely hard cock back into my ass. His moan is almost immediate, signaling he isn't far from falling victim to his pleasure.

His arm pulls free from my leg so he can cup my cheek in his palm. Soft lips kiss mine as his hips slowly gyrate. Both of my legs are freed, but I hold behind my knees to keep them in place. He rests his weight on his forearms beside my shoulders and looks into my eyes. His blink is long as his lips part and brows lift in their center. What a difference a few seconds make when his face bears the look of severe pain like I've never seen it. Several screamed moans vibrate my chest before his face softens. His body stiffens into the most handsome statue I've ever seen. His Adam's apple bobs, and then his lips part before he sags limply atop me, and his gasps resume.

We lie still for several minutes while Bash holds my hand and Mack lies half on top of me.

"That was perfect," I whisper to break the silence the stillness the night warrants. "I'm going to take a shower."

Two grunts have me laughing as I climb over Bash and peck a kiss to his lips. He smiles without opening his eyes.

After my shower, I consider slipping into bed between the two snoring men, but there's no way I'll get any sleep if I do. I slip my nightie on and search until I find my phone. My feet chill on the hardwood floor as I head to Patch's room. He's spending the night at the main Bear house.

The moon is bold enough to illuminate my path around the living room. My body eases under the cool, black duvet and my shiver has me missing the bodies I left in my bed. The pillow smells like Patch, and it's as if he's right beside me, protecting me as I sleep.

***

Morning comes too quickly, but the scent of breakfast cooking in the kitchen mixed with the aroma of a dark roast coffee blend has me sympathizing with my growling stomach.

Lizzy said she'd leave a note for our supervisor explaining what happened with my father and that I'm taking the day off to be there to support my mom when he goes in for his surgery.

As I leave the bedroom drowning in Patch's housecoat, the darkness bleeding through the windows has me shaking my head. They get up so damn early! The sun hasn't even risen yet!

"What time is it?" I ask even though the big clock to my left would answer the question.

"It's 5:30, Goldie," Bash says as he pours coffee into a mug and sets it in front of me when I sit at the island. "I woke up, and you weren't in bed. Sleeping with my brother didn't sit well since the fucker had his arm around me and his dick was inches from my ass."

Mack turns and raises his voice as his arms flop. "I was *asleep*! It's not like I was trying to fuck you. Christ! You make it sound so bad."

Bash exaggerates a nod. "It was bad. I don't want your cock anywhere near my ass."

While chuckling, Mack says, "My cock couldn't get past that mat of hair you got growing back there, so relax."

"I don't know!" Bash teases as his arms raise at his sides and his head tilts. "You've dated some hairy women. How do I know whether you like that kind of thing or not?"

Mack waves the spatula at Bash. "You know I d—"

"That's enough!" I cover my eyes. "It's too fucking early for your brotherly bantering. Please, just give a girl time to drink a coffee."

They both apologize and try to kiss my cheeks simultaneously, but I swat at them to back off. I'm tired and worried about my father's surgery, and how my mother could break while we wait. She's the strong one in our family, the keel that directs our ship. If she cracks, what do I do?

Mack rubs my back despite my recent protest at being touched and in an unoffending voice, says, "We thought you'd want to be up early so you can get to the hospital to relieve your mother. She's probably been there all night and could use a break to freshen up before he goes off to surgery."

My hand pats the one he's resting on my shoulder. "Thank you. I appreciate that. And yes, I want to be there for her."

Bash sets a plate of fruit in the center of the island before he gets the silverware, while Mack serves eggs, bacon, hash browns, and fried bologna, which is considered cuisine to a Bear boy. I'm not a fan, and they say I have no taste because of it.

After we've eaten and gotten dressed, Bash drives the three of us to the hospital. We would've picked Patch up on the way, but he has a pre-scheduled meeting at seven with his crew. Even though I told him he didn't have to be there, he promised to come to the hospital as soon as he could, but he asked us to keep him updated with any news.

Chapter 9

"Mom, how are you?" I ask, and she looks up from the steaming paper cup she holds. "Have they taken him in?"

She stands from the tan-colored plastic chair in the corridor outside of his room. Her puffy eyes don't hide her fears as she lifts her chin toward my father's room. She's quick to hug me.

"They're prepping him now."

The bareness of the beige paint on the closed door doesn't offer much emotion. Behind that door is my father, and he might leave us today. My stomach bottoms out, and everything around me spins. My butt meets the chair my mom was in. The warmth radiating from the plastic centers me.

Before she sits beside me, she offers Mack and Bash hugs.

To me, she asks, "Are you okay?" Her hand presses to my back when I shake my head. "Don't worry, sweetheart. He'll be back to his normal self in no time. Maybe he'll be better than he was before, more tolerant of the things he doesn't quite understand."

She smiles, wraps her arm around my shoulder, and presses a kiss to my forehead: the universal action of a loving mom.

She shouldn't be comforting me. I should be the one telling *her* it's going to be all right. Isn't that why I'm here?

"I know, Mom. Dad will be fine. I don't know the surgeon, but I've heard only good things." That's a lie. I've spoken to nobody about the doctor's reputation.

"She seems nice. She introduced herself to us and explained the surgery, along with the risks." Mom takes a deep breath and smiles despite the deep frown line revealing her worst fears. "He'll be fine. He's strong and too damn stubborn to die."

She giggles, but I can't manage a smile, let alone laugh.

"Does anyone want a coffee? I'm heading down to the cafeteria. Goldilocks?" Mack asks and reaches into the front pocket of his faded blue jeans and pulls out a twenty-dollar bill.

I nod with enthusiasm while Mom shakes her head and points to the steaming cup on the ledge. He turns to look at Bash, but he's distracted by the pretty brunette nurse down the hall. She's standing in front of the nurses' station, writing something on a chart.

Mack lightly slaps Bash's arm. "Hey, perv. Do you want a coffee?"

"Hmm?" Bash's attention shifts to Mack. "Oh. Ah, yeah. Thanks." His attention returns to the brunette.

What is it about her that holds his attention? She's pretty, but she isn't magazine-level gorgeous. Her dark brown hair twists into a messy bun atop her head. Her girl-next-door face bears no makeup. She's thick in the hips but her hourglass shape is movie star approved.

Mack follows Bash's line of sight and whispers something to him. Whatever he said has Bash grinning.

The nurse looks up at the men and smiles as if she knows them. She hands the chart to the nurse seated on the other side of the counter and stuffs her pen in her shirt pocket. Her hips sway as she makes her way toward them in her silent shoes. Mom and I remain seated, watching as if this is a scene in a soap opera about to unfold.

Mack is the first to hug her. "Hi, beautiful. How've you been?"

She steps back and then toward Bash. "Things are great with me. How are you two?" Her arms wrap around Bash and she says, "I hear you're getting married. I never thought you'd ever settle down."

Bash sets her free and shrugs before he turns to introduce me. "Clarice, this is my lovely fiancé, Goldilocks, and her beautiful mother—"

"We've met." She smiles at my mom and greets me with a handshake while her eyes assess my face. "So, you're the one who claimed his heart. I can see why; you certainly are beautiful. It's nice to meet you, Goldilocks."

Curious, I ask, "So, how do you know the guys?"

Her hands stuff into her pants pockets, and she rocks foot to foot while she considers how to answer that question. "Um, we met a few years ago."

Bash, trying to ease the situation, says, "Yeah. Ah, Mack and I met her when she tended to my sprained ankle. It hurt so much I thought it was broken." He tilts his head and smiles at me, but it doesn't meet his eyes. "We became," he shrugs, and his sight skirts to the ceiling, "friends."

Clarice nods, but her eyes don't glance my way. Instead, they shift from Bash to Mack. "But I haven't seen you two in... What? It's got to be two years, at least." The guys agree with mumbles, shrugs, and nods. It's obvious they've had sex with her. "Well, I should get going. It was nice to meet you, Goldilocks. Boys," she says with a sexual undertone while her eyes shift between them and her cheeks flush, "good to see you."

She nods to my mom and walks away with her thick hips swaying.

Bash looks everywhere but at her ass. Mack, on the other hand, doesn't hide his desirous thoughts and tilts his head as his lips pull inward to be held by his teeth.

The door to my father's room opens, and Mom and I shift our attention. Mack and Bash step back to allow the nurses to wheel out the stretcher.

The grey hue of my father's skin has worsened overnight. He looks awful despite the measures taken to improve his oxygen levels. The nurse in me knows this isn't good, but I'm also familiar with people making miraculous recoveries from illnesses believed to be fatal. So, there's always hope.

He's strong. He's my daddy. He has to live.

His weak arm lifts and my mother holds it in both of hers and he says what he always does. "I love you. You own my heart."

Mom lifts his oxygen mask for a quick kiss and whispers, "I love you. You own my heart, always and forever. Don't you dare leave me. I'll see you soon."

Dad smiles beneath his mask and reaches for me. "Goldilocks, I love you, too. You are my blood." He takes a few much-needed breaths. "Do what makes you happy. You're my daughter, and I could never not love you. I'm proud of the strong-minded woman you are. I shouldn't complain about the choices you make. We raised you to make your own choices. Just be happy. Okay?"

Tears drench my cheeks. That's all I ever wanted to hear from him, that he accepts me for me, and his love isn't restricted based on his moral approval. My lips press to his forehead, leaving a hint of shine from a tear.

"I love you, Daddy. I still need you, so don't go anywhere. Okay?"

His feeble laugh proves his fragility, but the smile he wears remains strong although veiled behind the oxygen mask.

To my surprise, he shakes the hands of Mack and Bash and asks Bash to take care of me. Bash swears with his hand held over his heart, and the nurses roll Dad's gurney down the hall and into an awaiting elevator. The doors close, and my chest cavity hollows.

Will my dad ever say my name again?

My phone chimes, startling me. I answer without looking at the name. I assume it's Patch checking on the progress.

Lizzy's sweet voice says, "Hi, love. How are you holding up?"

"I'm okay. They just took him down." I clear my throat and whisper to the guys that it's Lizzy calling. "Are you in surgery today?"

Her voice is more chipper than it should be under these circumstances. "Yeah. I'll be in with your dad. Don't worry, we'll take great care of him."

"Are you assisting?"

She sounds winded, as if she's walking quickly. "No. Dr. Janson and I will stand by in case they need extra hands." I hear the familiar squeal of the unoiled hinge on the scrub room door. "I have to let you go. Try not to worry. I'll update you when I can."

"Thank you, Lizzy." I hang up and slip the phone into the side pocket of my pale yellow dress. "Lizzy's going to be on standby in the OR with Dad. She said not to worry, that she'll take care of him."

Bash rubs my mom's back. "Why don't we go sit in the cafeteria? Have you had anything to eat?"

Mom shakes her head, so Bash escorts her toward the elevator while Mack and I follow.

His strong arm drapes over my shoulders and he kisses my temple as we walk. "It's going to be okay."

Is it?

The hours tick by. We've moved to the waiting room with the glass wall overlooking the golf course. Lizzy's come out twice to update us and reassure us he's doing well. Two of his ventricles have been bypassed, and they were working on the third the last time she came to update us, which was over an hour ago.

Lizzy and the surgeon enter the large waiting room and approach in silence as their nursing shoes make no sound on the slate floor; perhaps I'm numb and just can't hear. The doctor assures us my dad did well in surgery and has a 50/50 chance at a full recovery, but that the next twenty-four hours are crucial. She said he'll be in the ICU for at least a week, but she has to return to her hospital for scheduled surgeries and will leave him in the capable hands of our hospital staff. We thank her with handshakes before we see the back of her white coat rush off.

Lizzy hugs each of us while wearing a big smile. To me, she says, "He should be fine. He breezed through the surgery with no complications. I'm going to stay on as his primary as long as they'll allow me to."

My head shakes. "Is that a good idea? You've been on shift all night, but you want to stay even longer?"

"I caught catnaps in the break room last night, so I'm good to go. I'll stay until they tell me to leave." She shrugs and hugs me again. "Come! I'll bring you and your mom in to see him. Sorry, guys, you'll have to stay here."

She's peppy in her step as she leads us to his room in the ICU. Mom pauses at the door, and her breath catches. The initial view of the love of her life lying unconscious in a hospital bed while hooked to too many wires and tubes attached to beeping machines is just too overwhelming. She fights for a full breath and clings to the doorframe to keep herself steady.

My whisper is low and calm, which surprises me because my inner voice is screaming, "Mom, take a deep breath." I hold her free arm and rub her back. "When you're ready, we'll go in."

Her steps are dainty as a ballerina as she edges toward him. She places her hand over his. In the calmest whispers I've ever heard my mother utter, she says, "Love of my life, you're alive. You did well through the surgery, so don't quit now. I won't allow it. Keep fighting."

Some distance away, Lizzy stands with her hands in her pants pockets while she talks to Amelia, the head nurse for the ICU. The short, large-breasted woman changes an IV bag for the unconscious man on the bed across from my dad.

I've always thought of my father as being larger than life, but here he lies in a drug-induced sleep; vulnerable and weak. He looks smaller somehow. Will he again be my invincible hero?

Mom's bent over near his face and brushing her fingers through his short, dark hair while she speaks to him. Her words aren't meant for me. Besides, I want to know what makes Lizzy and Amelia look so worried.

"I'll be right back," I say to Mom and pat her back.

My come-hither finger waves at Lizzy, and she and Amelia follow me into the corridor.

"So, how is he? Don't sugar-coat it."

Before Lizzy can say anything, Amelia stuffs her hands in her shirt pockets at her thick waist, and in a husky voice says, "You know it's too soon to know for sure. If he holds out through the night, he'll likely be okay." Her lips press tightly together, awaiting my reaction.

I clear my throat and pause because my one-word question could bring information I don't want to know. "And?"

"It's too soon to tell," Amelia says and twists her mouth before she adds, "It'll be a struggle, but he's a fighter."

"Struggle? Is he struggling?" My heart pounds like a drum in my ears.

Amelia's voice softens. "His blood pressure is all over the place, but we're keeping a close eye on it." She pats my shoulder and excuses herself to check on another patient.

I'm grateful for her honesty, but I'm more worried now than I had been.

Lizzy says, "I'm going to watch him like a hawk. From what you've told me about your dad, he's stubborn and strong. Those are great qualities to have in situations like this. You know that." She takes my hands in hers. "I'm going to go pee and get some coffee while you're with your dad."

She smiles and is peppy in her stride as she disappears down the hall. Mom's silent as she holds Dad's hand. She can't hide the fear in her eyes from me despite her efforts.

Her voice starts strong. "What did they say, Goldilocks? And don't tell me they said he's fine. He doesn't look fine. Oh, God! What if he—"

My arms wrap around her shoulders as I stand beside her. "You have to stay strong and radiate good vibes. I don't know if he can hear you or not, but he needs you to be strong for him." She looks at me from the corners of her eyes. "Amelia said his blood pressure fluctuates but that it's early yet. This isn't uncommon, Mom. Give him twenty-four hours."

We stay by his bedside for a few hours while Mom talks to him about gardening, mostly. Watching the clock makes the hours seem longer. Bash has been in the waiting room and refuses to leave. Patch brought a box of donuts and bottles of water. He stayed for about an hour and then left with Mack.

"Goldilocks, go home," Mom says as she pats my thigh and stands. I stand and she adds, "It's almost dinnertime, and you've been here long enough. Thank your men for being so supportive. Now go. If anything changes, I'll call."

"Okay, but promise me you won't stay all night. You need to get your rest if you're going to be strong for him."

She reluctantly agrees and hugs me extra tight. She won't leave him.

Bash drives us home to our house, and I'm surprised to see Patch's truck parked out front. Patch and Mack made fish tacos for us, and they're delicious. The men leave around nine o'clock because Patch has to work early in the morning. Mack will go with him. I appreciate them giving me time alone with Bash.

We soak in the bath together and barely say a word. I prefer the silence so I can revisit my memories of better times with my father without interruption. After some time, we maintain the silence as we dry off and slip into bed.

Bash hugs me to his chest in bed. Despite my racing thoughts, I quickly drift off to sleep.

I jolt awake after dreaming that someone was watching Mack make love to me. I yelled for him to get off me, but he either couldn't hear me or didn't care to stop. The silhouetted man was pacing, obviously enraged by what he was witnessing. I felt ashamed of his judgment. Mack would distract my attention back to him and bring me close to orgasm, but each time my eyes left Mack's, I'd see the pacing man, and the awful feeling returned.

I lie still to catch my breath and listen to the consistent snores from the man to my left. The steady rhythm would be sedating if the dream hadn't shaken me. And now I have to pee!

My feet chill on the hardwood floor as I tiptoe out of the bedroom and close the door.

The sun's rising. Bash will awaken soon, and he'll be hungry. He's always hungry! I start by making a strong pot of coffee.

I'm almost finished making breakfast: scrambled eggs, bacon, sausage, hash browns, toast, fresh fruit wedges, and yogurt topped with blueberries. Bash strolls into the kitchen, rubbing his eyes. He's shirtless but wears his dark grey pajama bottoms and the navy-blue slippers I bought him, which he prefers to wear instead of socks.

He kisses me before he pours himself a coffee. "You're up early. Couldn't sleep?"

I place food on our plates and set them on the island. "I slept great until I had a nightmare, which I'm going to slap Mack for when I see him."

A smirk rises on his lips, and he chuckles. "What'd he do?"

As I take the silverware from the drawer and collect juice glasses from the cupboard, I explain, "He was making love to me and a man was watching, but he was extremely upset. Mack wouldn't get off. Instead, he tried to console me, but then I'd see the man again—" My entire body shivers, and I run my hands over my face to rid my mind of the memory.

Bash pours orange juice into our glasses. "You know what that dream was about. Don't you?"

As I cut into a juicy sausage, I swallow the flood of saliva the scent urged forth. "It's about my father. He disapproves of our strange dynamic, and that upsets me."

"Mhm," he mumbles and bites into a piece of bacon. "Have you heard anything from the hospital?"

"No news is good news. At least, that's what I'm telling myself."

Bash nods and takes another bite from the strip of bacon. "I'll take you to him after breakfast."

"Thank you for being so supportive," I say and watch his lips lift at their edges. "I promise not to slap Mack for his actions in my stupid dream."

I take my first bite of sausage, and my phone rings. My stomach feels cavernous when I see Lizzy's name on the caller ID.

If I'm peppy in my tone, she'll have good news. Right? "Hi, Lizzy-girl. How's my dad?" I'm met with silence. My mind spins and my voice drops to a whisper. "Lizzy? Are you there?"

"I'm here." There's a long pause. "Goldilocks, you should come to the hospital."

The sausage I swallowed launches back up into my throat, and I run to the garbage pail. Bash is behind me in seconds and tries to take the phone from me, but I hang onto it like my father's life depends on it.

I sink to the floor against the counter beside the garbage and whisper, "Tell me wha—"

I take deep breaths in through my nose and out my mouth to ease my stomach and stop the white stars in my eyes from growing so thick my brain will shut down. I need to know right now, so passing out won't do.

Lizzy clears her throat as if a lump could impede her words, and then her voice cracks. "It's not good news."

My body needs oxygen, but I can't inhale no matter how hard I try. My chest has caved in, and the floor threatens to swallow me whole.

I can't lose him. I just can't.

My words ramble quickly. "He said he wants to grow our relationship. He said he isn't angry with me anymore. He said he was going to walk me down the aisle. He said he loves me. He *said so*! Doesn't that mean he'll be sticking around? He *can't* leave me. Not now. Not ever."

Lizzy whispers, "I know."

"Is he—"

The word sticks in my throat. *Dead.* I can't say it.

Lizzy doesn't answer my question. "Just come. Your mom… She needs you."

Oh, God! No. Will someone wake me from this horrible nightmare? I must still be dreaming. Please, let me be dreaming.

"Is he brain-dead?" I ask and close my eyes, dreading her response. If she says he's okay and he isn't, I'll hear it in her voice.

In no discernable tone, she says, "Come now."

Without saying goodbye, I hang up. My thoughts race, and I toss my phone into the garbage without thinking. I rise off the floor and push a very concerned Bash away so I can get to the bedroom. My brain's telling me to run, but my legs can't bear it.

He follows and sets my phone on the bed. As I rush past him to toss the dress I pull from my closet onto the bed, he grabs hold of my shoulders and pulls me into a hug. It's the last thing I want. I need to get dressed. I need to get to the hospital to be with my mom. Before he leaves me, I need to say goodbye. But Bash refuses to let me go.

I'm numb and the tears don't fall. I honestly can't feel anything. Is this what people mean when someone dies and they say they're numb and it hasn't hit them yet? I've never felt this void of emotion. Maybe that's a good thing. I have to be strong for my mom and can't be an inconsolable puddle.

"What did Lizzy say?" Bash asks as he gently rocks us.

My head shakes and I force myself from his grasp. "We have to go. There's no time."

It's all he needs to hear to know she said nothing good. As he dresses in blue jeans, a light-blue t-shirt, and a navy hoodie, he calls the guys' phones and leaves messages to go to the hospital. We dress quickly and rush out the door. Bash insists on driving and holds my hand as he speeds the whole way. Strangely, when we arrive, I can't recall a minute of the drive. Everything from Lizzy's phone call to the moment I see my mom is shrouded in a grey blur.

My first word spoken since we left the house is, "Mom?"

She looks up from my father's bedside, and the stains of dried tears mark her face. Her eyes are more red and swollen than I've ever seen them. The pain of her shattered heart stabs a dagger through mine. The numbness that prevented my tears from falling has dissolved, and the flood begins.

Mom saunters toward me and wraps her arms around me, and I cling onto her while I visually assess my father through tear-blurred vision. She shushes me and rubs my back. Dad doesn't look right.

"Mom, are you okay?" I ask and groan as she sets me free. Her hands stroke down my arms. "I'm sorry. That was a dumb question. Of course, you aren't okay."

"No, baby girl. I'm not okay. But I will be, in time." She clings onto my left arm as we near my father's bedside.

Although his features look exactly like my father, it isn't him. His skin is grey, and he's far too still.

The machines aren't beeping to his heartbeat because the wires are disconnected. Where's his oxygen mask?

"Mom?"

I pull away and put my hand on Dad's chest and wait for it to rise. It doesn't.

"Mom? When?"

"About an hour ago," she whispers and eases out a lengthy breath. "I knew you'd be coming soon, and I didn't want you to race here and risk having an accident. I asked Lizzy not to call you."

"What? Lizzy's still here?"

There's no way the hospital would allow her to work this long. Mom tries to smile, but her face can't maintain it.

"She was exhausted, so I told her to go home shortly after you left last night. She came back around six this morning."

"So, she was here when he—" My mouth refuses to form the word *died*.

Mom nods and again tries to smile. "She wanted to call you, but I told her not to."

My hands shake as my fingers glide down Dad's forearm. The coolness of his skin reminds me he is indeed gone.

My voice shakes. "I should have been here. She promised she'd call me."

Bash rests his hands on my shoulders from behind me to offer his support. "Lizzy was obligated to follow your mother's request. You know she couldn't have called no matter how much she wanted to."

"I told her not to call you," Mom repeats herself and pulls me into a hug. "Be angry at me, not her."

"You promised *him*, but she made a promise to *me*." My head shakes because what Lizzy did is unforgivable. "She robbed me of the last few moments I could've had with my father. I'll never get that back."

Mom's voice grows more insistent. "He had a stroke about five hours ago. The doctors ran tests and concluded he was brain dead. He was already gone, Goldilocks. As per your father's wishes, I asked them to disconnect the machines."

"You let him go without calling me?" My two favorite women have betrayed me. "I should have been here."

The pain in her unassuming tone nearly breaks me. "He didn't want you here."

"You don't know that!"

She's so calm despite my furious rage. "I do, actually. We discussed it after his first heart attack. He made me promise not to have you here if I ever pulled the plug on his life. I promised him, Goldilocks." She swallows and whispers, "Now, say goodbye to your father."

My anger isn't helping her get through this, which is what I should be doing.

"I'm sorry, Mom. I'm going to miss him so much."

She whispers so low it's almost inaudible, "Me, too,"

In a sniveling mess of tears and snot, Mom and I say our last goodbyes. After we walk away, Bash leans toward my father's face and whispers something as he pats Dad's shoulder. He stands tall and nods before turning to follow us out the door. What did he say to him?

After we exit, two orderlies enter the room and close the door. They're prepping to transport his body. I've seen it happen many times.

***

Bash drives to Mom's house and shuts off the engine. We get out, but she stops us from following her inside.

"I need time alone," she says and turns her attention toward the house. "This is something I have to do by myself. I'll call you later."

Mom's much stronger than I'd be if Bash died, and we haven't been together all that long. I can't imagine how much she hurts after having lost the person she's spent most of her life with.

"Are you sure? I can sit outside if you need time in the house. I don't want to leave you. We should be here for you."

Bash asks, "You can come to our house if you aren't ready for this." He glances at the house that seems lonelier now. "We have a guest room, and you can stay as long as you'd like."

Mom steps toward him, and they hug. "No. But thank you for the offer. I have to do this now or I never will." She hugs me, and then her flat-soled boots thump the steps as she ascends.

Bash and I stand and wait to see if she'll change her mind and come back outside. After a few minutes pass and there's no movement, we get back in the car and drive home.

Bash pours me a hot bath and helps me in. He leaves the room to call his brothers with the news. Even though he whispers in another room, his voice travels, making the situation seem far too real.

My tears erupt, and the most horribly devastated wail escapes me.

Bash holds the phone to his ear as he opens the door, but quickly closes it to give me time to grieve.

I don't know how long I cry and beg the universe to go back a day. There's so much I want to tell him. We wasted too much time with our stubbornness. I'll never get that back. Wasted time; time his moral values and opinionated views stole from us. I just want my dad!

Patch and Mack come to the house as soon as they can. Each man takes turns hugging me in my bed. They don't say much, but they let me talk or cry as much as I want without interruption. It's exactly what I need.

They suddenly lost both of their parents when they were just kids. I can't imagine how awful that was for them. Who hugged them? They had no other family. Patch was only eighteen. Did he hold his younger brothers while they cried? Who held Patch? How did he survive without a shoulder to cry on?

Around six o'clock in the evening, I cry myself to sleep with my arms wrapped around Patch. When I wake, he's still holding me even though I've rolled onto my side to face away from him.

"There she is," he whispers when I roll to face him. His fingertips glide down my cheek to brush the hair off my face. "Are you hungry? The guys cooked."

"Can I ask you something?" He nods, and my fingers play with the neckline of his black t-shirt when I ask, "How did you survive your parents' deaths? Was anyone there for you emotionally?"

His voice is deep, even through a whisper. "I had brothers that needed me, so I couldn't break down. I had to step up and be a man. I went from a teenager who partied, drank, smoked, and was almost never home to being a mentor to two young teenagers. It was really hard. I'd do it again, but it was hellish at times. At least there was money, so that wasn't an issue. I couldn't have done it otherwise." He looks at me as if to memorize my face, but he doesn't wear a sympathetic mask, which I appreciate. "And no, nobody was there for me emotionally. There was a social worker who'd stop in to check on us, at first, but after I gained custody, she stopped calling. I'd walk into the woods and scream as loud as I could to work through my anger and frustration."

"Did it help?" I ask and picture myself screaming at the trees.

He nods and shrugs the shoulder I'm not leaning on. "Yeah, it did. So, are you hungry? I'm starving."

"I could eat."

Chapter 10

My fork doesn't make the journey to my mouth enough times to make a noticeable difference on my plate. Food doesn't interest me even though this lasagna is the best I've ever had. Even food won't fill the emptiness inside me.

Patch places his palm over my hand and says, "You should eat. I can make you something else if you don't like lasagna."

His eyes are kind, and his smile is sweet. All I want to do right now is kiss him. If I'm lost in his wild affection, surely I'll forget about my father, and not feel so much anger at Lizzy for not calling me to come to see him before he—

I can't even think of the word.

"It's delicious; my mother's dulls in comparison, but I'll deny it if you tell her I said so." My lips rise into a smile but sag quickly.

I set my fork on my plate and see that each handsome face looking at me bears an understanding of the pain I'm in. Their expressions don't hold pity, and this pleases me. I'm sure there will be plenty of upturned eyebrows, droopy eyes, and down-turned mouths in my future. The funeral is going to be brutal, and I'd give anything to not have to attend. I hate funerals, but I'll hate this one especially.

"I'm going to give my mom a call," I say, and a squeal announces I've slid my chair back. I try to smile at Mack but my lips don't lift. "Sorry. I know you worked hard at making this meal, but I don't feel like eating."

Mack stands, rounds the table, and wraps his thick arms around me. My face burrows in his tresses of freshly shampooed hair hanging down his chest.

"Don't worry about it. I'll wrap it and put it in the fridge. Maybe you'll be hungry later," Bash says as he steps up behind me and rubs my back before he takes my plate. "Call your mom. I'll bring tea." He pecks a kiss on my free cheek and leaves me in Mack's loving embrace.

Mack's lips press to the top of my hair and his hand strokes down my head before he releases me. "I'm going to drop some lasagna off at your mom's and then head home unless you need me here."

"No. I'll be fine."

He points his thumb over his shoulder at Patch and Bash standing at the counter. "Those two knuckleheads will take care of you. But if you need me—for any reason—call and I'll be here in no time."

"I promise." I kiss him before I walk away, letting the distance separate our hands.

Sitting on the bed with the lights dimmed, I stare out the window at the heavily shadowed forest and wonder where our souls go when we die. Is my father standing in this room watching me? If he is, I hope he leaves before I'm intimate with the guys. My head shakes to rid the thought.

My phone vibrates. Lizzy has texted again. This is the fifth time, and it'll be the fifth time I'll ignore her. If we speak, I just know something horrible will come out of my mouth. Words will be said that I don't mean, and that could ruin our friendship. I'm still angry, and I need to be angry at her because transferring it to my father is too painful.

He didn't want me there. I know this. It's still not fair.

Instead of talking to her, I call my mom.

"Mom, how are you holding up?" I ask and run my finger along the seam on the dark red, king-size duvet cover.

She sounds sullen, but I can hear soft music playing in the background. "I'm okay. How are you?"

That's so like her to worry about how I am when she just lost her husband.

"Sad. I can't eat. I slept, so that helped." I cross the room to the window and notice in my reflection how wrinkled my t-shirt is. "Did you eat? We have lasagna. Mack made it. He's getting ready to go home, but he's going to stop to bring you some."

"No. I'm not hungry. Thank you for offering." She takes a deep breath, and it rushes from her. "I've been on the phone since I got home. There are so many plans to be made. We had nothing prearranged. Some people do that—they pre-plan their funerals and burial so their families don't have to deal with it. We talked about it, but we never got around to it because we're still young and it didn't seem likely either of us would—"

She, too, can't say the word *die*.

Mom talks for the next fifteen minutes without me saying a word. It's okay for her to ramble if it's what she needs to do. She doesn't say much about anything important, but the tidbits of information must mean a great deal to her for her to be telling me now.

When there's a pause, I interrupt to ask, "Do you want me to come over?"

With enthusiasm, she says, "No, Goldilocks! Stay with your man, or men depending on who's with you."

"Mack's about to leave, but Bash and Patch are here. I don't know if Patch is staying over tonight or going back to the main house."

"Do you want him to stay?"

I breathe on the window to steam it and draw two smiley faces, but one isn't smiling. "I sleep well between him and Bash. Maybe I feel safer. I don't know. But I like it when he's here."

"You're a lucky woman, Goldilocks, to have three men madly in love with you. You're the envy of all the women in town. Of course, they won't confess to it, but many have whispered to me from the corners of their mouths." She snickers. "Can you imagine how the town is going to turn upside down when all three of your men are standing beside you in the greeting line at the funeral parlor? Each person will have to shake their hands and offer their sympathies."

She laughs with more enthusiasm. "I can't wait to watch their faces when certain people enter the room and realize what they have to do. Some have talked shit about those boys for far too many years to be nice to them now."

Don't I know it?! My whole life, I've heard so many awful lies about the Bear brothers that I thought they were truly bad. Very few of the stories spread were true. Now they talk about them and me and how they've tainted me with their wicked ways.

She asks, "Patch, Mack, and Bash are going to stand in the precession line, aren't they?"

She wants them to stand with us? All three of them?

"I don't think Dad would like that."

"Well, your dad isn't here right now. Is he?" Her words are sharp and spiteful, as if she's angry at him for leaving her. I suppose she's entitled to feel that way. "I'm going to take a bath and have a glass of wine; maybe two or three glasses. Goldilocks, take your men to bed and love them. Cherish them because you never know when they're going to leave you."

Her words of warning don't ease my broken heart because now I'm thinking about one of my guys d—

There's that word again.

"I love you, Mom. If you need me through the night, call. Promise you'll call."

"I promise," she says, and sighs again. I hear the familiar pop of a cork from a wine bottle. "*If* I need you, I'll call."

She makes me promise to eat something before she hangs up, but it's a vow I'll likely break. Food doesn't appeal to me. I want this feeling to stop; this sensation of being in a dream, a horrible dream I can't wake from.

Bash startles me when his hand fishes under my hair and grips the back of my neck to pull me into a hug. "Goldie, what can we do for you or your mom? We feel helpless. Mack just left with a plate of lasagna for your mom."

"She likes lasagna. However, she's about to get in the tub with a glass of wine. He might see her in a towel if she answers the door."

For some reason, this has me laughing. Nobody wants to see the mother of their girlfriend in a towel.

Girlfriend—is that what I am to Mack? Hmm, what would be my title for each man? How will they refer to our relationship when they'll have to introduce me to someone?

"I know what I want to do," I say, and look up into Bash's eyes which always look like he's seconds from bursting into laughter. "Patch gave me an idea."

I rush down the hall to the kitchen where Patch is washing dishes. His brows furrow when I take the dish towel from him and drop it on the counter. Then I take his hand and lead him to the door.

"Bash, I need you, too."

We put our hiking boots on and head outside, down the dark path to the river's edge. I stand on the big rock I claimed as my own many years ago, and I scream as loud as I can at the rushing river and into the darkness of the trees just past it.

I look over my shoulder and see Patch's arms crossed over his chest. The early evening moonlight peeking through the trees illuminates his wide smile. Bash's eyes are wide with confusion as they dart from me to Patch.

Again, I scream. This time, my wail is met with a thunderous roar. Patch is standing beside the rock with his mouth wide open, back arched and his face tipped upward. His hands cup around his mouth, amplifying his wail.

My laugh is muted by a wail directly behind me. Bash is also standing on the rock, screaming over my head. I take a deep breath and scream as my body curls in on itself. The action is foreign, but the release of pain is immeasurable. Each time I scream, the river steals a piece of the burdening heartache within me. The pain remains, but I'm no longer drowning from it. It's as if the earth and water around me understand my pain and want to share it with me.

I scream until my voice falls victim to heavy sobs. Bash's arms wrap around me, and Patch takes my hand. The calmness of the cool breeze contrasts with the rushing water, but the silence in the air soothes my soul. The fresh crispness of the night offers the promise of another morning, thus dissolving this horrible day and storing it in my memories where it'll no longer seem as painfully real.

"Okay. Now you two can take me home and make love to me," I say, and wipe my tears from my face.

Chapter 11

Bash swiftly scoops me off my feet and carries me home and into bed. Between the two of them, I'm kissed and gently caressed while I'm bared of my clothing. Bash rests himself between my legs and kisses me with soft, quick pecks. He eases his shaft into my pussy, and my breath catches.

He's unhurried in his rhythm. I feel every inch of him as he stretches my walls. Our kiss grows more needy at my urging. I grip his ass and pull him into me, but it's not enough. My legs wrap around his waist and my fingers dig into his back. I want more. Maybe I want it to hurt because I don't want to feel the pain in my heart.

He rolls to put me on top, giving me control. Without a second to waste, my hips rock fast and pound down onto him. I lean forward and press my hands on his chest to maintain my balance. Fire burns my clitoris as I press and rub the nub on his hard tummy muscles, inching me closer to the orgasmic numbness I seek.

What I'm doing isn't making love: it's a raw, selfish need. I'm angry, but the closer I get to climax, the more my rage melts away. My hips pound without concern for the welfare of the man beneath me.

Bash's hands press down on my thighs. "Goldie, stop. You're going to make me cum. Not yet, please!"

I ignore his warning, and seconds later, his moans sing about the room.

"Oh, fuck! Goldie!"

His body stiffens, so I pull his throbbing cock out of me, and press my wanton clit onto his heated shaft, which lies hard as steel against his abs, and then buck my hips. He cries out as his seed rushes through his cock in powerful spurts, further igniting the fire in my clit. Bash's grip on my thighs begs me to have pity on his sensitive, withering cock, and it frustrates me.

I was almost there.

"I'm sorry, Goldie. You didn't stop, and I couldn't hold back," Bash says, and his body jerks when I run my finger over the sensitive head of his cock.

Patch lunges at me and grabs my shoulders. In a flash, I'm chest down over Patch's thighs with his strong arm pressing onto my lower back to hold me in place.

I try to get up, but he won't release me. "Let me go!"

My feet kick and I push my upper body up with my arms but he shifts his elbow higher on my back, forcing my chest down. He's much stronger than me.

"Fuck off! Let me *go!*" This time my screams are ignored.

He remains silent, which is out of character for him. Surely he wants to tell me to shut up or call me a nasty name. We both like it when he does. Instead, his free hand cracks hard onto my ass cheek. My wail is met with more silence until the high-pitched clap of his hand on my other cheek sings. He alternates cheeks until both my eyes burn hot from tears. I might not sit for a week. I'm angrier now than when I was fucking Bash. But I needed that spanking.

Bash stands beside the bed with a towel around his waist and watches Patch punish me. He trusts Patch not to push me past what I can handle, and he knows he can't do this level of punishment as well as Patch can. He doesn't like to hurt me, but Patch gets off on making me scream. If I fight back, it entices him even more.

My scream is more of a growl as I twist my body and slap the side of Patch's face with the back of my hand. His arm relaxes enough that I can pull my ass away from him. Three times I slap his face before he's able to catch one of my arms to stop me. I'm so goddamn pissed off; not at him, but at my father for leaving us. I know this is why I'm angry enough to hurt Patch. If he were anyone else, I'd never push this hard.

But Patch gets off on it, and I'm sure he spanked me to get this reaction from me. He wants me to let my anger out.

With my face inches from his, I scream. I twist my wrist free and repetitively hit him anywhere I can while he tries to catch my arm.

Patch grabs a fistful of my hair to gain control of me. But I continue swinging. I don't see where I hit him, but it has to hurt. Good! He hurt me!

My hands press to his chest and try to push him away, but his lips press to mine. He's so rough I may bruise. I try to scream in protest, but his tongue fills my mouth, muffling me. To stop him, I pinch his nipple with my fingernails. How Patch can pick me up and spin me into position so easily while I slap and kick is impressive.

I'm on my hands and knees with my head in his control because he's still gripped onto my hair, and it hurts! He's behind me with his knees spread over my calves. He plunges his cock into me with one vicious thrust, sliding easily after having Bash's thick cock buried in me only moments ago.

He leans over me and growls. "You're my whore! I fucking own you! What do you call me?"

"A fucking asshole," I shout, knowing the only acceptable answer is *sir*. My elbow swings back, catching his ribs, and I'm rewarded with his grunt.

Patch's thick, powerful arm wraps around my side, pinning my arm against my body. He grabs my throat and pulls me up until my back presses against his front. My lower back arches to keep his cock inside me because I need it. I need him. I need this raw, heated battle for ownership, and he knows it.

Patch's breath is hot behind my ear. "Oh, I'm an asshole, huh? You have no idea how much of an asshole I can be. Hold tight, little cunt, I'm going to fuck you like I hate you."

Yes! Fuck me so hard that my problems disappear. Make it hurt so I'll feel it later because if I'm lucky, the memory will be enough to hold me distant from the emotional pain desperate to overwhelm me when the room falls quiet.

I struggle to yell because his hand is wrapped around my throat; holding, not squeezing. "Fuck you, asshole!"

"I'd rather fuck you, cunt!" he rages through clenched teeth and thrusts so hard my breath forces from my body.

Patch throws my cheek against the bed as he releases my hair and throat. My face bounces off the dark red duvet before my arms can get beneath me to prevent another faceplant. He makes good on his threat to fuck me like he hates me. He grips my hips firmly and pulls me back as he thrusts forward. My freshly spanked ass cheeks ache and my cervix is taking a hell of a beating. But it's exactly what I need.

How did he know?

I don't know how many times I've climaxed, and if you offered me ten million dollars to tell you how long he's been pounding into me, I wouldn't guess correctly. Time seems to stand still; at least, it does in my mind as I float in a perpetual bliss while my body is ravished and used by a man so powerful he sometimes scares me. But I love him, and he loves me. And I trust him with my life.

My eyelids part and I'm looking at dangerous dark-brown orbs surrounded by a sun-stained face dripping with sweat.

How and when did he get me on my back without me knowing?

His lips are curled in against his clenched teeth. My thighs are against my chest with my ankles on his shoulder. His hands press to the bed above each shoulder to prevent me from sliding away from him as he plunges into me with incredible force and speed.

Patch pushes into me and holds, and releases my legs to fall listlessly to the bed. He wipes the sweat from his face with his hand before he leans in to press his lips to mine with a tenderness not suiting for the situation. His tongue brushes my lips before exploring my mouth. Both of us are panting, but the easiness of his kiss soon relaxes our gasps.

As his weight shifts to his right elbow, his hips move slowly. His left hand gently explores my breast before moving along my ribs and settling under my ass. His slow and gentle movements allow my mind to drift into peacefulness. I can feel him; his heart and his love. He's pure and real, and we are bonded.

Patch moans before his body stiffens. He pulls his cock from me and pins it between our bodies as an orgasm takes his soul away from mine and into the blackness. The heat of his seed oozing down my waist proves his pleasure.

His eyes no longer look dangerous as they peer into mine.

He whispers, "I love you, Goldilocks. You have my fragile heart. You have my damaged soul. You have all of me. Please don't hurt me."

"I love you, Patch. You are in my heart, and I'll never take that for granted."

His kiss is quick.

Through a smile, I demand, "Now, get off me because we both need a shower. Any idea where Bash went?"

Patch sits back on his knees and looks around the dim room. "There you are."

As my jelly-like legs drop over the side of the bed, my smile is met with Bash's. Perhaps it's the lack of light that has his smile looking like it doesn't meet his eyes.

Bash stands and takes my hand and leads me to the shower. He warms the water before letting me into the glass box able to accommodate four people with ease. He washes my hair and my body. As I rinse it off, he asks, "Did you have fun?"

My nod and listless laugh please my fiancé, and his smile crinkles the edges of his eyes. "And how Patch was with you... Are you okay with that?"

"Are *you* okay with how Patch handled me? Did it scare you?" I ask as the hot water feels cool against my freshly spanked hot ass.

Bash's head tilts, almost meeting his lifted shoulder. "It was rough. I'll admit, I was a little worried he'd hurt you. But I know he'd never intentionally cause you harm. It's just... The way it looked was—"

"Scary? It was scary, but somehow Patch seems to read me. He knows what to do to get me out of my own way. I don't know how he knows, but he does."

Bash bites his cheek as he soaps his chest, but he doesn't say what his face tells me, that he doesn't feel like he measures up to his brother.

My hands press to his soapy chest. "I adore how you make love to me, and when you're rough, it's just as fucking incredible. It's just that sometimes I need a little cruelty with the roughness, and Patch has plenty of that to offer. He has a lot of deep-rooted anger that he uses as kindling to ignite his fuse. He's different from you; not better, not worse, just different. But you... I love you most. I always have. I just didn't know it."

His lips peck mine and his twisted smile eases my worry that we've upset him. With soap all over his body and shampoo in his hair, he pouts so I'll step aside to give him access to the water. The cool air awakens my nipples.

Once he's rinsed, he kisses me and steps out of the shower. I shake my head when he offers his hand to help me out.

"I want to stay here where it's hot and soothes my sore butt cheeks."

He nods and chooses a towel to dry himself off.

Patch steps in, ruining my alone time in the shower. "Can I get some of the water, or are you going to hog it all?"

"I might hog it." I smirk before I step back to allow him access to the water. "Can I ask you something?"

Being the smartass he is, he says, "You just did."

"Okay. I'm going to ask you something," I say as water pours over his head and his hand glides along his muscular chest. "Where do you hide that level of rage? I mean, you're always so composed. You had to have pulled that fury from somewhere."

"Don't let this happy-go-lucky attitude fool you. I'm a rotten motherfucker to the core." He snarls and picks up the soap.

"Happy-go-lucky? Nobody would ever refer to you as happy-go-lucky. Serene, at times. Hardened, definitely. But happy doesn't suit."

Patch looks to the ceiling and then nods to agree. "I have a lot of rage. What can I say?" He snickers as I slide past him and step out of the shower. He whistles and much to my dismay says, "I'm loving that red ass of yours."

Bash heated my dinner while I finished showering and insists I clear my plate. He and Patch drink a beer while I eat and laugh with them. It isn't until I'm snuggled between them and they're asleep when guilt hits me. I was laughing, and my father is…

This isn't the time for laughter.

Tears flow onto my pillow, but I maintain the silence in the room so I won't wake them. I need this time alone to weep, and I don't want them to coddle me.

Chapter 12

The sun peeks through the canopy of trees, painting blueish rays onto the greenery desiring to drink in its ultraviolet light. All I hear are the sounds of the forest and the soles of my hiking boots as they pat down the earth with each step I take toward my mother's home. I woke before the sun rose and waited until nine o'clock before I set out on my solo walk.

Lizzy texted only once this morning and begged me to call her.

Not yet. I just can't. Soon.

Bash went to work at the newspaper and says he's going to write the perfect obituary for my dad. I'm glad I don't have to write it.

Patch has an appointment at his lumberyard with a man who needs help choosing the right logs for him and his son to build a miniature log house for his three-year-old granddaughter. Patch was going to cancel, but I sent him on his way so I could have time to myself to cry or yell without sad or pitiful eyes watching or them trying to comfort me.

My childhood home looks the same as it did a few days ago, but I know it's emptier now that the happiness was stolen away. I knock and walk in. Mom appears from the bedroom and smiles with little effort. She's wearing a pink sweatsuit and big fuzzy slippers. Her shoulder-length hair spills from an unmanaged ponytail, and her swollen eyes rest above deep purple hues.

Her tone isn't as desolate as I'd imagined it would be. "Hi, Goldilocks. Did you sleep? Are you hungry?"

I shake my head and hug her. "The guys wouldn't let me up from the table until I ate breakfast, and I slept for a few hours last night. How about you?"

She shrugs and returns to the bedroom. I follow, curious about what she's doing. Four large boxes sit on her messy bed and house my father's clothing.

She's getting rid of my dad's things already? He hasn't been d—

It hasn't even been twenty-four hours.

Mom pulls a red t-shirt from his closet and looks at me while she folds it and tosses it into a box. "I know what you're thinking: it's too soon." Her hand presses to her forehead and the other rests on her hip. As they drop away, she adds, "I can't look at them. Each time I see anything that belongs to him, it feels like my guts are being ripped out. It's too painful."

I tip a box and look into it, seeing a lot of suits and dress shirts. "But you're getting rid of everything?"

She folds a light grey dress shirt I've seen my father wear many times and holds it while she stares at me with wide eyes. "I'm sorry. I just can't—" Her lips pull into a tight line and she closes her eyes as if she's desperate to maintain control. "If there's anything you want, you can have it. I'm keeping his pillow in an oversized zip-tight plastic bag so I can always have his scent." She tosses the dress shirt into a box and points to the red sweatshirt crumpled on the pillow. "And I'm keeping the sweatshirt. Anything else is yours."

Mom pulls his dark-green hoodie from the hanger, and I take it from her. "This. I want this."

Together, we empty Dad's belongings into boxes, tape them shut, and set them in the back of her SUV. She'll drop them off at the second-hand store the next time she's in town.

We sit in silence and stare at the sandwiches we made for lunch, neither of us wanting to eat more than a few bites. She suddenly stands and gets two beers from the fridge and opens them, handing one to me. We take them outside, leaving the sandwiches on the table.

The sun kisses my face, and it feels as good as the hot water from my shower this morning. The birds whistle as if nothing has changed, and the leaves on the trees sing their tunes to give a voice to the wind.

Mom's tone is soft and pulls my attention from my thoughts. "Everything has been arranged for his funeral. It will happen tomorrow. Dad wouldn't want us to drag it out. There will be only one viewing between noon and two, and he'll be taken for cremation from there. When it's all done, I'll bring his ashes back here. I'd like you here when I spread him around the yard and in the river." She tilts her head and grins when my face contorts. "It's what he wanted. It's what we both want, so you'll have to do it for me when I go."

"Oh, *God!* Please don't even talk about you leaving me, too. I'll fall apart if you do. One parent dy—" My voice cuts off before I can finish the word. "It's hard enough. Two would be unbearable. I need you. You can't go anywhere until after I have kids. Who's going to babysit?" I snicker, and her eyes widen. "Take it easy! I'm not pregnant and don't plan to be for quite a while."

"How are you going to work that? Will you have a baby by each of them or just Bash? You'll be married to Bash, but you're with all of them."

My fingers pick at the label on the bottle and I shrug. "I don't know. We discussed it briefly, but we didn't decide anything. When the time comes when we're ready to pop out some puppies, we'll figure it out then. Only fate knows what each man will be doing or who they'll be with when the time comes. Their girlfriends or wives—if they have them—might not want me to have their kids. I don't know. I really don't."

"Do you have your wedding plans arranged?"

My tummy flutters in a good way. "My wedding—" Dread suddenly drowns my happiness. "Dad won't be there to walk me down the aisle."

Mom and I fight back tears in silence. Who can I ask to be his substitute? Nobody can fill his place. If only I had a brother, uncle, or cousin. The faces of every man I've ever known breeze through my memory, but none measure up.

She suggests, "Why don't you ask Godfrey?"

My head shakes. "I don't know him all that well."

"He was your father's best friend," she says with a shrug. "He knew your father better than anyone other than me."

"But *I* don't know him well enough to have him give me away."

As if a lightbulb went off over her head, she excitedly says, "Ask Patch or Mack."

My eyes twitch, and a quirky smile has her understanding. "The person walking me down the aisle has to *give* me away. Neither of them wants to do that. Besides, Patch is officiating, and Mack is Bash's best man."

"Right!" She sips her beer and shrugs. "Well, you have time to think about it."

"You can do it."

Her brows pinch in the center. "A man traditionally fills the position."

"Yes. But it's my wedding, and I can do what I want." My hand presses to my chest as a breath fills my lungs. "Mom, will you do me the honor of walking me down the aisle? I can't think of a better person to fill Dad's shoes than the woman who knew him best."

The tears I held back spill over when she turns on the waterworks.

"I'd love to."

"Okay, that's settled. Let's drink another beer, shall we?"

As I rise, Mom gulps the last few sips and hands me the bottle before wiping her cheeks and taking a deep breath to prevent more from falling.

Four beers later, my eyes seem to float when I first try to focus, and I'm sure my words are slurring. "Well, I should go."

"Do you have to?" Mom asks with a slur in her words.

We both giggle as we enter the house. I failed to grasp the door's handle on my first attempt.

After using the washroom and hugging Mom, I set off to walk home and realize what little control I have over my extremities when I trip and nearly land on my face because my arms are too weak to break my fall. My shin is scraped and my forearm is going to have one hell of a bruise, but I can't stop laughing at my ridiculousness. Even the trees seem to laugh along with me as the wind tickles their leaves.

I feel good; happy. My eyes close as the familiar scent of moss tickles my nostrils.

My eyelids lift, and I screech. A man's face appears above me. Mack's long brown hair flows like a veil, framing his beautiful face. His smile is wide to reveal bright white, perfectly straight teeth. With his hands on his hips and a shake of his head, he asks, "What are you doing down there? Did you stop to take a nap?"

My laugh is louder than I'd planned. "Something like that." The last thing I want to admit to is being drunk enough to have fallen flat out. "Have you ever laid on the trail and looked up at the trees? They're tall and pretty."

He offers his hand, so I reach up and take it. In the blink of an eye, I'm on my feet with my head spinning like I'm on a ride at the fair. Mack's arms wrap around me to help keep me upright, and he's laughing.

"Stop laughing at me," I slur.

"You're fucking adorable," he says and turns me so we can walk this wide section of path with his arm over my shoulder and mine around the small of his back. He leans down and kisses my head. "How's your mom?"

"Drunk. We're both drunk." I laugh hard, but it soon fades. "She's okay, or at least seems so. The plans for his funeral are all set for tomorrow."

"Bash told me."

Confused, I ask, "How the hell did he know? I just found out a few hours ago."

"He wrote his obituary and texted us with the details." Mack kisses my head again.

A few moments pass as my thoughts weigh heavily on my spirit. This feeling is grey and horrible and I want it to stop. "Will you take me to my bed and make love to me?"

He whispers, "You're drunk."

"And that matters why?" I ask and giggle. "It's not like you haven't taken me to my bed before. In fact, I remember a few shower and outdoor scenes that would make a pornstar blush."

Mack chuckles, swoops me off my feet wedding style, and smiles down at me as he walks. "I'd love to take you to my bed and make love to you."

"Can you put me down? I can walk on my own two feet."

As my feet touch the ground, he says, "Oh? I don't know about that. What were you doing when I found you?"

I slap his arm playfully and lead the way down the thin path aimed toward the main Bear house and to his bed. Before we've even crossed the grassy yard, I've pulled off my dress and tossed it to Mack. I'm walking in my bra, panties, and hiking boots while Mack remains behind me, commenting on how delicious I look.

"Hey," he calls out, and I turn. He's naked aside from his boots. His clothes are spread out on the grass. "Get your gorgeous self over here."

I slink toward him with what I think are sexy strides as I fling my bra. His gaze drops to my breasts as his tongue moistens his puffy, sensual lips. I point to my chest, and he waves a come-hither finger. When I'm close enough, he reaches for my biceps and pulls me to him for a kiss that makes my head spin.

Goddamn, he's a great kisser, gorgeous, and built like a Mack truck, and he loves to please me. What more could a woman want? Well, Bash... but Mack is here and I need to keep this happy feeling going for as long as possible so my thoughts don't slip back into the grey zone.

I lie back and spread my legs, inviting him in. His eyes stay on mine, but his cock grows as he kneels between my thighs and kisses my breasts, my neck, and finally my lips. His hand glides down my ribs, up my thigh, and back down.

The sun warms my bare flesh as he removes my panties, boots, and socks. His soft, warm lips press to my labia before his tongue licks between them. The palms of his hands push the back of my thighs until they press to my torso, allowing him access to my ass as well.

I watch the sparse puffy clouds float past and the odd bird passing overhead while he performs the most sensual cunnilingus of all time. He gradually edges me closer to orgasm. With tender kisses, he licks from my clit to my asshole, his hot breath mixing with the gentle breeze.

Knowing someone could drive up at any moment adds an element of taboo that arouses me almost as much as having Mack's tongue tease my asshole or clit.

He sucks my erect clit and swishes his tongue back and forth so quickly that I can't stop myself from moaning. My body feels like it's going to explode from the heat and immense tickle leading from my clit to my belly button. I don't know what he does next, but it sets me ablaze in the most fantastic way. My body seizes beneath his tongue which feels like it's as big as his entire head.

I float through weightlessness as euphoria takes hold. Clarity gently comes into focus, but he already has me building to another climax. How? How is he doing this? What is he doing to me?

My fingers grip the grass, hoping it'll hold my body to the earth so I won't float up to the cloud passing overhead. Again, I'm stolen away to a place so magnificent surely only angels can go.

My soul is sucked back into my body with a gasp. The most unfeminine moans escape my chest in bursts. I sound like a wounded animal on the verge of death, and I couldn't stop if I wanted to.

Mack's cheek rests beside my gaping mouth. I hadn't realized he was between my legs and his shaft is buried deep inside me, pressing against my cervix. My face turns and our lips kiss like we're starving and this is the only way to earn nourishment. His chest presses down on mine with enough weight to hold me to the earth but not crush me into it.

My feet lock together over his back and squeeze his trim waist while my hands grip his muscular biceps resting on his elbows beside my head. Beautiful orbs matching the sky stare deep into my soul, comforting it while his flesh ravishes mine. I'm losing myself to this man. He's taken my heart and is caressing it lovingly.

The combination of Mack's hot breath on my cheek, his rock-hard body thumping against mine, and the gentle breeze that cools our skin are all I need to lose myself to circumstance.

His moans grow more intense until his muscles stiffen and his body gradually sags, nearly crushing me. His forehead rests on mine and he gasps and pants as his seed spills inside me.

"I love you so much, Goldilocks," Mack says, and gazes into my eyes while his thumb glides along my bottom lip. He leans in for a sweet kiss with closed lips before rolling off me.

I roll onto my tummy and lift onto my elbows. "I love you, too, Mack. You're so sweet to me. How could I not love you?"

He shifts onto his side to face me. "So, are you still angry at Lizzy? It's not her fault, you know."

"Mack, I appreciate you standing up for your girlfriend, but this is between her and me, and you shouldn't get involved. You'll end up stuck in the middle."

He sighs frustratedly and traces my spine down to my lower back with his fingertips. "You need to talk to her. She's your best friend, so you two—"

"Best friend? I thought we were, but my best friend would call to let me know my father was dying so I could come to the hospital to say goodbye. She robbed me of that, and I'll never get it back. I'll never get to hug him again or tell him I love him. I don't care that my mother told her not to call. It's no excuse! He's my father, and I had the right to know."

Mack flops on his back when I sit up and pull on my socks, underwear, and boots. Then I fetch my bra strewn on the recently mowed grass and put it on. My dress is mixed with his clothes but a quick shake solves that and I slip it over my head. Mack rushes to get dressed because he knows I'm about to rush off.

"Goldilocks, hang on a minute!" He grunts and hops while pulling on his sock before slipping his foot in his boot, and jogging to catch up to me on the trail leading to my house. "Wait! Let's talk about this."

I yell without turning or waiting for him to catch up. "What's there to talk about?"

"Goldilocks! Come on. Wait up." He struggles to hold his clothing while he walks wearing only one boot.

I stop and spin to face him with my hands on my hips and my weight resting on my left leg. My lips purse when he finally catches up. "Listen, Mack, this has nothing to do with you. I'm not upset with you. If I were, we wouldn't have done what we just did." My hands rest on his shoulders. He drops his belongings so he can hold my waist as we admire each other's faces. "I love Lizzy. I do. But I'm angry at the moment."

"She understands that, and that's why she's giving you some time. But, if you want to see her so you two can work it out, I'll be glad to mediate or—"

"I have her phone number, and I'm quite capable of operating my smartphone." My hand holds his cheek. "Do me a favor?" I wait for him to nod. "Stay out of it. Go home, Mack."

After a light slap to his face, I smile and rush down the path, leaving him behind.

***

My head is thumping from sobering up. Who knew I'd get a hangover during the day? I always thought sleep brought it on. I pop an ibuprofen and eat a peanut butter and jelly sandwich so the pill won't upset my stomach.

I climb onto my bed with an ice pack at the back of my neck and a damp washcloth on my forehead and close my eyes, hoping to escape reality.

Chapter 13

Men's voices speak low enough that I can't hear what they're saying, but it's enough to wake me. The room is dark except for the line of yellow light painted on the floor leading to the gap at the unlatched door. As quietly as I can, I sneak down the hall and hope the wood-slatted floor doesn't squeal to announce my presence.

"...and that's what you're going to do? Just like that?"

"Yeah, if the result is positive, you know I'll have to go."

The second voice is Patch's, but where will he be going, and what positive result?

"You can't leave," Bash says, and I hear movement in the kitchen. "What are we going to do if you're not here?"

Patch grumbles, "Why don't we just wait for the results? And, ah, don't mention anything to Goldilocks. At least, for now. Not until we know more ab—"

"Know more about what?" I ask as I round the corner into the kitchen, startling both men. "Patch, where are you going if there's a positive result? And what test are you taking?"

His face pales and his eyes drop to the counter and skirt up to Bash before he straightens his spine, looks at me, and says, "Paternity test."

"What the hell?" Is he a father? Who's the mom? How old is this kid? A hundred questions zip through my thoughts in an instant. "Are you a father?"

Patch's lips pinch into a line, and his head shakes once. "I don't know. There were two men she was with: not Bash or Mack. She can't find the other guy, so I'm up."

Bash hands me a mug of steaming coffee and leans down to kiss me. "Don't worry, Goldie. He'll take the test, and we'll go from there."

"No! I want to know what you'll do if it's positive. Are you going to leave me?" I shake my head and correct myself. "Us?"

"If he's my son, I want to be with him." Patch looks at Bash and then me before he clears his throat. "But I don't want to leave what we have here. I love my family."

A child? He might have a *child*. A boy? When did this happen? Who's the mom? Did they love each other?

Through my fog of questions, the only one I can think to ask is, "Would the mom be willing to move here? I mean, if you get along with her. You don't have to have a romantic relationship. It could just be so the kid can be around his dad."

"She moved across the country for a prestigious job and her life is there now. She's not coming back." His fingers run through his army-style hair and his tone deepens. "All I'm saying is that if she kept my son from me all this time, I'm not going to be fucking impressed."

I reach across the island and offer him my hand, which he takes and smiles crookedly. My voice softens. "Whatever happens, you know you have us in your corner."

Patch nods and I release his hand.

Bash's eyes scream his concern. He's worried Patch will leave if the test comes back with a positive match. Patch can't leave us.

Patch stands and takes four plates from the cabinet. "I'll go to the city tomorrow. There's a lab where the test is run on-site. I should have the results in a day or three. If I do it here and mail it out, it could take weeks."

Bash collects silverware and napkins, and Patch returns to get the salt, pepper, ketchup, and mayonnaise.

"I don't see any food, guys. What are we eating?"

Both men stop to look at me, but it's Bash who says, "We thought you'd cook tonight."

I'm shocked because they rarely let me cook. "Okay. Do you guys have a hankering for something in particular?"

Bash turns me to face him and pins me back against the island. He picks me up under my arms and sits me on the counter. "Yeah, I have a hankering for something Goldilocks-flavored."

There's a hint of something wicked in his grin as his hands glide up my thighs to expose my panties. It's now that I'm thankful I washed up after Mack fucked me. Bash's long fingers pull my panties aside and his fiery mouth presses to my pussy. I lean back to give him more access, and the reward is fabulous.

Not only is this sexy as hell, but watching Patch walk back and forth, setting the table and putting things away, only observing us now and then, adds to the excitement. It isn't two minutes before an orgasm has my hips gyrating on the counter.

Bash sets me down after pecking a pussy-scented kiss to my lips. It takes a minute for me to gather myself enough to ask them again what they want me to cook for dinner.

Mack flings open the door and storms in, bringing the crispness of a cool wind with him. Patch rushes to take the two bags of food from him and sets them on the table. Mack removes his jacket and boots before coming to stand before me with an expression that screams, *I'm sexy and you can't resist me.*

His voice is soft when he whispers, "I'm sorry if I pissed you off."

He's so damn gorgeous with those puppy-dog eyes. I have to let him off the hook. "I'm not angry with you, Mack. I told you that."

A toothy smile lights up his face and his thick arms fling around my neck and pull me into a hug. My hands stroke his strong back and I'm reminded of how romantically he fucked me under a late afternoon sun. My pussy clenches and I wonder if it's a residual effect from the recent orgasm or the favorable memory. I pull out of the hug and lightly slap his face while I smile and wink.

He wags his tongue at me. "Yes, Mistress Goldilocks. I've been a very bad boy. Punish me if you will." He pants like an excited dog.

My eyes roll, and I shake my head. "A mistress I am not. This girl is submissive all the way."

Patch walks past me and slaps my ass, eliciting a quick screech from me, which he finds entertaining. "Yeah, this little slut is full-on submissive; exactly how I like her."

Bash, not to be outdone, says, "Yeah, well, she makes sweet love to me and submits, so I have the best of both worlds. *And* she's wearing my ring!" He rubs his chest and holds his chin high as if boasting. Patch and Mack grab him and pretend to punch him while Mack holds him in a headlock. They're brothers!

I take the food out of the bags and set it around the table while the three of them laugh and yelp when something hurts. Several minutes later, all three of them have red faces, messy hair, and they're out of breath, but each is smiling. It's nice to see them so happy when it feels like our lives are falling apart.

If Patch moves away, we're all going to miss this.

***

Although not much talking fills the silence, dinner was excellent as it always is when we order Thai from the only Thai restaurant in town. Takeout was the best option since it's nearly impossible to get a table after five o'clock. There's often a line out the door of people waiting. Three restaurants filled the building across the street from the Thai restaurant: Mexican, Italian, and Middle Eastern, but none were successful. They all closed within three years of opening.

We're all sipping on a beer after we remove the dishes from the table when Patch speaks. "Mack, I found something out today that I told Bash as soon as I got the call." He points to me. "That little brat overheard, so she knows, too. I got a phone call telling me I might have a six-year-old son."

Six!

All eyes are on Mack as he sits stone-faced for about twenty seconds. "Julie?" Patch's subtle tilt of his head is enough confirmation for Mack. "Six, huh? What the fuck took her so long to tell you?"

Patch shrugs. "I don't know. That's something I may need to ask her."

Mack's finger points to Patch. "You said *may*."

Patch sits back in his chair and says, "Yeah. She isn't sure if he's mine. There was someone else." The way Mack's face pales has Patch snickering. "No, brother. He's not yours."

A heavy sigh escapes Mack as his hand washes down his face and hangs off his chin. "Thank fuck! I'm not mature enough to be anyone's dad. Can you imagine? I'd pity that kid."

When we stop laughing, Patch tells Mack about his plan to get tested tomorrow.

"Wait," I interrupt. "You can't go tomorrow. It's my dad's," the word sticks in my throat, "funeral."

"I haven't forgotten," Patch says in a sympathetic but deep voice. "I'll leave before sunrise and be at the funeral home when the doors open. Don't worry. I'll be back in plenty of time."

"It's a two-hour drive, Goldie," Bash says and takes my hand in his. "He'll be back with hours to spare."

The guys clean the dinner dishes, and I excuse myself to take a soak in the tub. A soft orange glow flickers as the flame dances on the candle. The gentle scent of lavender and vanilla essential oil has calmed my tears, and water hot enough to steam all the mirrors soothes my stressed body. Every once in a while, the brothers' laughter travels through the house, carrying with it peacefulness for my soul and a smile to my lips.

The memory of my father helping me with my math homework when I was young comes to mind. No matter how much he tried to break it down for me to understand, I couldn't grasp it. He sent me out to the garden to get thirty green beans. I thought he was hungry, but when I came back, he used the beans to teach me math. After that, it all made sense, and I never had trouble with math.

A light tap on the door pulls me from the fond memory. Mack's soft voice rings out just before the door pushes open. "Goldilocks, I'm heading out unless you'd like me to stay."

"Oh! You're leaving? I suppose it's getting late. I'll be fine." He kisses me as I sit up. "You'll be there tomorrow, right?"

"Of course," he replies and sits on the edge of the tub. "About tomorrow… are Patch and I supposed to stay in the back of the room so people won't spend all their time gossiping, or do you want us with you? We never did ask, and tomorrow doesn't seem like the time to do that."

"Mom and I want all three of you standing with us." His face scrunches with doubt. "No. It's true. She and I talked about it this morning. She insists you three be there for me. I want us to be supportive of each other."

His head tilts and his brows lift in their center. "And Lizzy? She loves you and you love her, even if you're angry with her. She said she's going to be there even if she has to stand in the back."

I'm not sure how I feel about that. Of course, I want her there, but I don't want to see her… or do I?

"My mom might have a hard time seeing her because she was there when he d—" Why can't I say the damn word? "I don't know what to do with Lizzy. I'm angry."

Mack slips his ass off the tub's edge and squats, resting his forearms on the edge and his chin on them. "Is it possible you're redirecting your anger onto Lizzy, but it isn't her you're angry at? Maybe you're angry at your father for leaving you and your mom. Or you're angry that you left the hospital and didn't stay with him."

My anger rises. "Are you saying I should have stayed or that I'm mad at my dad? Really?"

"Not exactly." He shifts onto his knees. "You couldn't have stayed with your dad the whole time and there was no reason to assume you shouldn't have gone home. The surgery went well, he was recovering, and your mom told you to go home. As for being angry at your dad for leaving... I meant that you're angry he's gone. I didn't mean it as he gave up. I'm sure he fought hard."

Am I really this angry at my father for leaving me?

I know it's not his fault for dying. Why did he have to leave me a week before my wedding? Am I angry he died *when* he did and not *that* he did? What the fuck is wrong with me?

"Anyway, love, I'm off." Mack stands and kisses my forehead. "Should I come here in the morning?"

I shake my head and swallow back my anger at myself for being angry at my father, or I'm angry at Lizzy, and God, too?

"I'll be at my mom's. You can either come there or meet us at the funeral home."

With another kiss to my head, he leaves while I watch his thick thighs flex all the way up to his round ass.

Shit! I'm thinking about sex while I'm having an inner debate over who I'm angry at because my father d— *Damn that word!*

* * *

I'm in bed reading when Bash enters the bedroom and smiles. "There's my Goldie-girl."

My book shuts as my head tilts and my brows lift. "Are you drunk?"

"Nah!" Bash says.

As he strips down, Patch strolls in wearing a pair of worn jeans. His bare feet slap the floor as he nears me. "Should I sleep here tonight, or do you want to be alone with Bash? I won't be offended if you choose the latter."

I set my book on the nightstand and slide to the middle of the bed. "I want you here with us."

As I slip down and pull the covers to my neck, Bash climbs into bed, and Patch strips off his pants and tosses them to the sofa chair by the big window overlooking the dark forest.

The hands of two wanton men glide up and down my body, touching me in places meant to ignite desire within me.

"Not tonight, boys," I whisper, and their hands come to rest on my tummy without argument.

I kiss each man and fall asleep quickly, only to dream of Lizzy on her knees with her hands clasped together, begging my forgiveness. Patch picks her up and kisses her like he's in love with her, and it angers me because he's supposed to be on my side and not hers. Bash kisses me, stands behind Lizzy, and then slips his hands around to cup her breasts. He bends down to press a tender kiss to her neck. Mack stands beside me, holds my hand, and tells me to move past it because they all love and desire her and that he doesn't want me to divide the group. Mack lets go of my hand so he can go to Lizzy and his brothers, leaving me alone with my anger.

My eyes, still heavy with sleep, open. The dream felt too real to ignore and I can't fall back to sleep. I know it was a dream, but the message is clear: she's my best friend, and she had to honor my mother's wishes by not calling me. My issue isn't with Lizzy, it's with my mother. Why did she do that? This is not the time to ask her; there may never be a good time.

It's five o'clock and I'm surprised the boys aren't awake yet. They're early risers.

The rising sun on the horizon has cast a temporary orange hue in the sky. Each moment I stand in front of this window and watch the morning come to fruition, the orange washes to yellow, and finally, the sky is blue. The light has yet to filter through the trees, so the shadows of the forest remain and I imagine the night creatures within them are scrambling to find their way home.

A hand comes around my waist, and I jolt with a loud yip. Coffee spills on the window and pools on the sill. Patch pulls some tissues from the box next to the sofa to soak it up.

"It's only me, Goldie."

"Don't call me that." I groan and check for a coffee stain on my nightie. Thankfully, it missed me.

His arm wraps around me beneath my breasts, and he kisses my messy hair. His breathing is loud and his breath hot on my head.

He whispers, "Today's going to be one of the toughest days of your life, but I promise you'll get through it. Each day after this one will get easier. As time passes, you're going to feel guilty for having not thought of your father for a few days. It's normal; it's how we get on with life." He turns me to face him and tucks a tress of hair from my cheek behind my ear. "You can cry, scream, throw yourself on the floor if you want. We won't judge you for it, but we'll be here for you if you want us to help you be strong. Lean on us because we've got you, and we have your mom, too."

My free arm wraps around Patch's waist, and he hugs my head to his chest. His powerful heart thuds a steady beat and it's soothing.

Bash calls out to us, "Anyone want pancakes?"

Patch kisses my head and takes my hand to lead me to the table. He gets me another coffee before helping Bash prepare breakfast by cutting strawberries and washing blueberries from the fridge we picked from the bush along the path a few days ago.

Chapter 14

I sit on Mom's bed while she dresses in her black pantyhose, black bra and panties, and the black dress she bought for old man Kinsley's funeral last fall. He was a miserable old man, but he was an avid churchgoer and my parents knew him well. They didn't like him much, but they felt obligated to attend. I think some people went just to make sure he was dead.

Mom looks defeated, as if she's been battling something for far too long and has finally accepted her loss. The black dress amplifies the paleness of her skin and the purple bags beneath her eyes. She sees me watching her reflection in the mirror and smiles softly, like that'll lighten the heaviness of the air threatening to crush us.

Bash and Mack are sitting at her kitchen table, sipping coffee and talking in a nearly whispered tone when Mom leaves her room and announces that we have to go.

Mack drives us in my car. Bash is in the passenger's seat, Mom and I in the back. She takes my hand and holds it while she watches the trees zip past through her window.

We arrive before anyone else, but I had expected Patch to be here waiting for us.

I lean to Bash and whisper, "Where's Patch?"

He shrugs and looks around the room, knowing full well he isn't here. "I don't know. I sent him a text about an hour ago and he wrote back saying he'll be late but he'll be here. I don't know what's going on."

Mack and Bash stand behind Mom and me when the man opens Dad's casket and we see what used to be my father. What lies there bears his resemblance, but his jowls are more prominent and he looks older. Maybe it's all the makeup they put on him. He'd roll his eyes to know he's wearing make-up.

Mom talks to the man while she fine-combs Dad's hair into place the same way he always did. With a sigh, she straightens his already perfect tie. She's on the brink of breaking down and this might be her way of keeping her emotions in check.

People dwindle in at first, but soon, the room is alive with whispers and the odd laugh and faces I don't recognize offering their condolences. Most of the visitors I recognize are churchgoers since my parents were at the church several times a week and ran multiple events to help raise money for faith-based charities.

So many of the people seem put off when they shake Bash or Mack's hand, as if doing so soils them, and it pisses me off. But now is not the time to make a scene.

Lizzy's next in line. Red-framed orbs pull at my heartstrings as her tear-stained face begs me to forgive her. She opens her mouth to say something but before she can, my arms are around her shoulders and my tears drip onto her red hair and lacy, long-sleeved, black shirt. She hugs me back and whispers her apology.

The line congests behind her, so she flashes an apologetic smile before she moves on to hug my mom. The two of them whisper condolences while hugging. A man's words—words I've heard a hundred times today—prevent me from hearing what they say. Four more hands meet mine and six hugs from people I recognize but have never uttered a word to before today.

Patch's hand brushes my back. I turn and sigh with relief that he's okay.

"I'm sorry. I got a flat tire, and the spare was also flat, so I had to walk." He grumbles and shakes his head. "It doesn't matter. I'm here now. Where would you like me to stand?"

I whisper, "Beside Mack is good."

He pats my back and takes his place.

I'm surprised to see Sebastian in line to shake Patch's hand. He cried like a baby when we broke up after only having dated for six months. He said he loved me and couldn't live without me, but here he is: alive and breathing. He was a parent-approved boy, despite his sexy body, chiseled features, and blonde wavy hair.

Does he know I'm dating all three men standing beside me? He wouldn't approve and certainly wouldn't have his hand now clutched in Mack's. Mack says something and Sebastian says something back. Mack releases his hand and smiles widely while he leans toward the man and whispers. He points to Bash—who's giving Mack his full attention—and then points to Patch.

Patch is about to shake the hand of the next man in line, but his attention is on Sebastian's face. Patch looks angry, but that's his resting expression.

Bash reaches his hand to Sebastian, and neither man smiles nor says a greeting as their hands briefly clutch. Sebastian's focus is on me and if his eyes could shoot daggers, I'd look like a porcupine.

Sebastian stands before me and licks his front teeth without opening his lips, and then whispers, "I'm sorry for your loss. Your father was a good man."

"Thank you," is all I can think to say. Should I shake his hand or hug him? He isn't initiating, so we stand like statues— me wide-eyed, and him glaring as if disgusted with me. To move him along, I add, "Thank you for coming."

He shuffles toward my mother and hugs her. They chat briefly before he makes his way past a gathering of four people to view my father. As I shake hands and greet people, my attention keeps pulling back to Sebastian until he leaves the room. If he still held feelings of love for me when he entered the room, they're gone now. What did Mack say to him?

I swear the whole town and most of the next have come and either shook my hand or hugged me. We've been standing here for almost two hours, and my feet and back are killing me.

The line has dwindled to only a few when I see another familiar face enter the room. As he nears us, he stops and his shoulders drop. His eyes shift from man to man to man before meeting mine. With a shake of his head, his lips purse. His eyes shift down the line of my men as he shakes his head and mouths the words *I can't.* He turns around and joins a group of mourners.

Jeff is another parent-approved guy I dated for over a year. We broke up shortly before I started dating the Bears, and he's obviously still bitter. It's too bad because I really liked him, but he bored the hell out of me. It's because of his boring sex that I set off that day to have sex with a Bear brother. I'd overheard the sexy stories women told when they thought I wasn't listening. I wanted to know what it was like to be ravished and fucked hard like a cheap whore. I wasn't disappointed on that day or any day since.

Bash must have been watching the interaction because he leans down and kisses the top of my head before he follows the man. They knew each other from high school. Jeff always frowned down on him as if he were scum. Bash thought Jeff was an asshole and unworthy of me.

They step away from the group of people, and the room seems to hush as too many eyes watch them. They chat quietly and don't seem to share angry words; there's no reason they would. But men will be men, and women will never fully understand the angst of testosterone.

They shake hands and Jeff leaves. Bash resumes standing by my side as if nothing happened. I elbow his arm and he looks down at me.

"I simply told him that if he wasn't here for the family, there was no reason for him to be here. He asked if I was going to marry you, and I told him we're engaged. He threatened that if I hurt you, he'll find me, and I won't breathe another day. The man still loves you, and I can't blame him for wanting to protect you. It's what I want, too."

Even Cody, another one of my ex-boyfriends, comes to offer his condolences. He's brought his husband along and introduces him to us. The guys are okay with Cody and his husband because Cody doesn't glare at them or give them the cold shoulder. He's upbeat and happy to meet them despite the circumstances. I enjoy meeting his husband, and I think we'd get along well if we were to spend any time together.

My mom's excited to see Cody but shocked to discover he's married to a man, considering he and I dated for two years and gave no indication that he played for the other team. I should have picked up on it. Why didn't I pick up on it?

There's no discussion about my ex-boyfriends, which is good because I've been watching and there were plenty of women who made their way down the line while they smiled and flirted as if they've been naked with at least one of them. Too many women! But I won't ask about them.

What happened before me doesn't matter. What happens from now on does.

***

The prayers and speeches from friends are lengthy. My back is sore from sitting on this stiff couch with Bash on one side of me and Mom on the other. Patch and Mack are in sofa chairs pushed up on either side of the couch. Mom holds my hand and Mack's. Patch sits quietly beside Bash. Each time I've looked at him, he seems lost in thought with his brows furrowed as if his thoughts burden him terribly. I can't help but wonder how the bloodwork for the paternity test went.

Lizzy sits behind Mack on one of the hard gray chairs, among some of my parent's friends. I want to sit and talk to her and apologize for getting so angry. I'll never forgive her for not telling me my father was dying, but—

Wait, I thought the whole word. My brain didn't cut it off. Have I reached the acceptance stage? Is that really a thing? Stages?

My father *died*. He's dead. Damn.

As if the world crushed in on me, all the pain I've been pretending isn't real erupts into a pitiful sobbing, gasping cry.

No amount of comforting can stop the pain from clawing its way out of me. Only time can heal this wound if it ever will.

While the speeches begin and the minister does his thing, I continue to cry until my tears run dry. I've given into it and sagged against Bash, utterly sapped of energy. I'm not numb anymore. I'm worn out.

A curtain is closed around the casket and the family's invited to say their last goodbyes before the lid is sealed and he's cremated, never to be seen in human form again. *Ever!* He'll be gone, and I'll never be able to touch him. He'll have to live solely in my memories and pictures. Will that be enough?

It'll have to be.

***

The wake is held at Mom's house. Some of their friends left the funeral early to set up food, rearrange furniture, and add extra chairs to make it more guest friendly. I'm not surprised to see most of the town has shown up to either express their remorse or simply to get an inside look at their house. It's a beautiful home, small but picturesque, with an A-frame design and excellent yard maintenance. Over the years, many people have asked me what it looks like inside.

It's been two hours, and people are still hanging around. I want them to leave. Mom looks tired and if I read her right, she wants them to leave, too. Through the window, I see Lizzy sitting on a chair near the apple tree with Mack and Patch. Bash has barely left my side and I wonder if he doesn't want to be left to the judgemental glances of the townsfolk who've misjudged him, or if he's trying to be supportive of me. Maybe both.

I fiddle with Bash's silky black tie while his fingers reach around the back of my neck to pull me to him enough that he can kiss my forehead. "Bash, I'm going to go talk to Lizzy… alone."

Bash smiles, pleased with my decision to settle things with her. He steps back with his hand on my back to usher me through a small gathering of people to the door and outside. He waits on the porch where nobody else stands, leans his elbows on the railing, and watches me cross the yard toward her.

Mack sees me approach and his lips move to say something, and Patch and Lizzy turn their heads. Patch stands and greets me with a hug, and Mack copies.

I ask, "Guys, can I have a moment with Lizzy?" Mack releases my hand, and they walk away side-by-side, Patch a few inches taller than Mack but wider in the shoulders. "Lizzy, are you okay?"

Her brows furrow, and she takes my hand as I sit in the dark green fold-out chair beside her. She replies, "Yeah, I'm okay, but I should be asking how you are?"

My eyes drop to our hands and my shoulders lift. "I don't know. I'm tired, mostly. In so many ways, I want this to be over, but when everyone leaves, that'll mean he's really gone. It doesn't make sense. I mean, I know he's gone, but—"

"I get it. When my favorite aunt died, I wanted everyone to fuck off and leave me alone. But when they did, I was alone to feel everything, and I hated it." Lizzy's eyes seem to sadden even though her lips lift into a smile. "She always lived with us, and she was like a second mother. It still hurts."

How long will I feel this crushing pain in my chest? If I were to fathom a guess, judging from Lizzy's eyes, I'd say it never goes away. I won't survive if this continues much longer. I'm barely hanging on as it is.

"Can you tell me about my dad's last hours? You owe me that," I say insistently, squinting.

She must sense our friendship depends on her telling me everything, whether she wants to or not. She swallows and explains as a medical professional, not my peppy friend: "When you left, he was stable, and he remained so for several hours. Your mom went downstairs to get something to eat. Within a few minutes, his heartbeat became erratic, and he went into cardiac arrest. We began resuscitation, but our efforts were futile."

The image of my mother leaving my dad's side plays over and over in my head. Why would she leave him?

No! I can't blame Mom. People letting go when their loved ones leave is common. I've seen it many times.

Lizzy's shoulders relax, and she speaks in the tenderest of voices, "I think your dad waited until you and your mom left before he slipped away"

My mind pictures his body struggling for breath, even though his soul has departed. Our bodies want to go on and will often gasp and make choking sounds. Sometimes, it's awful. As much as I wish I had been there for him, I'm glad I wasn't. I won't ask Lizzy about his actual death because I don't want to know the details.

"Thank you for telling me. I'm sorry I got so angry at you. It wasn't you that I was angry at, and it took me a while to figure that out. You're my best friend, and I'm thankful you were there with him when he... died." A cleansing breath helps ease the pain of the finality of that word—died. "Even though you didn't know him when he was alive, at least someone was there who really cared about the people he loved. Maybe that was a comfort to him. So, thank you for being there."

Lizzy leans in. I meet her, and we hug. She whispers, "I'm so sorry, Goldilocks. I'm so sorry you lost your daddy."

We sob into each other's hair until my back aches from leaning over the armrest. I sit at the edge of the chair and flatten the tummy of my black dress and admire the garden Dad was so proud of. Gardening was his way of de-stressing, and he was good at it. Mom's not as talented in the gardening department, so his masterpiece will eventually fall to ruin despite her efforts.

Lizzy swoops her red curls off her shoulders and stands with her hand out to me. "Should we go back inside? I'm sure your mother could use some intervention. You could take her to her bedroom to get her away from everyone for a few minutes. It helps."

I take her hand and just like that, we're back to being best friends. It was inevitable, but I have to redirect my anger where it belongs: into the universe. One day, my mom will leave me, too, but I pray that isn't until I'm eighty years old.

After the guests leave and her friends have cleaned all the mess and put the furniture back in place, the brothers, Lizzy, and I are the only people left. We toast Dad with a shot of his favorite whiskey before Mom abruptly kicks us out, saying that she wants to go to bed.

It's been a long day, and we're all exhausted. I spend the night between Bash and Lizzy, safely connected to them with our arms and legs. I don't have a nightmarish dream. Could that be because of my physical connection to people I love, because I survived the stress of Dad's funeral, or the simple fact that I let go of my anger?

And now I have to put my anguish on the back burner while I anticipate my wedding.

Chapter 15

Bash has left for work at the newspaper when I wake. A bonus to him working there is that a free newspaper is delivered to our front porch every morning. By the time I get up, the guys have already gone through it and refolded it wrong.

Our small town of less than three-thousand people doesn't make enough news to fill a paper, so recipes, book reviews, recommendations, and photos from around town fill the gaps. I like the recipes; not that I cook often enough to try any of them. Why would I cook? The guys love working in the kitchen.

Patch's voice fills the room, startling me. "Good morning, Goldilocks."

My hand holds over my thudding heart. "Good morning. I thought I was alone."

"Sorry to invade your alone time. I'll be out of here in a minute." Patch rushes about the kitchen to pack a lunch and fill his thermos with the rest of the coffee in the pot. I was going to drink that. He apologizes when he notices my twisted mouth. "Sorry. I'd make more, but I don't have time."

My eyes roll as I slip off the stool and round the island to make more coffee. Patch packs his bag with sandwiches, grapes, apples, salad, cookies, and yogurt, and then ensures his thermos is closed tightly before adding it to the bag and zipping it closed.

With the coffee dripping, I turn with my arms crossed over my chest and lean my back against the counter. "Hey. So, why were you late for the funeral? I'm not angry, just curious. Did the test not go well?"

Patch lifts his heavy backpack off the counter, carries it to the front door, and sets it down. He takes his orange reflective vest and slips it over his long-sleeved black shirt. The vest hangs open as he leans one elbow on the edge of the island.

"The test went well, but the drive home wasn't the best. My tire blew, and I went off the road. Thankfully, the ditch wasn't deep, so I was able to rock it out after I changed the tire. I got about fifteen kilometers and that damn spare lost air. I wasn't about to call Mack or Bash to come get me because I knew they'd be with you and you needed them more than I did. So, I walked to the next town and bought a used tire from the mechanic, and he was nice enough to drive me back to my truck."

"Why didn't you hitchhike? You're a big guy, so it's not like anyone would fuck with you."

Patch snickers and rubs his hand over his short, dark hair. "That's why nobody would pick me up. I tried to get a ride but the cars wouldn't stop, so I gave up and hoofed it. It was a hell of a jog." He slinks toward me while his dangerous brown eyes take in my bubble gum pink t-shirt nightie with the words *I Worship Coffee* written in bold white letters.

My hand presses to his chest to keep the distance between us. "Your excuse for not making a new pot of coffee was that you were in a hurry. Don't start something you can't finish." I laugh when he lifts my hand to his lips and kisses my palm as his eyes burn into mine and his firm body presses against me.

In a deep, sexy voice, he whispers, "I'm the boss, so I can be as late as I want." He steps back enough so his fingers can slip under the hem of my nightie and drags it up my body to bare my breasts. "And I'll do whatever the fuck I want to you. If I want to start and not finish, that's my prerogative. You're my little whore, or have you forgotten?" He winks, and I purse my lips to restrain a smile.

I wince, but my pussy clenches when he pinches both nipples. One side of his lip lifts because he knows what he's doing to me. His hands slip around my back and pull me away from the counter, and then grip my ass firmly.

"This is *my* ass, and I want it red and hot."

Patch spins me to face the counter and fists my hair, pushing my cheek to the counter to face away from him while he positions himself at my side.

Knowing what's coming, I grip the edge of the counter. My heart beats so fast it's making my head swoon. My body shakes with adrenaline as I anticipate the first crack of his wide, rough palm. It's too early in the morning for this. Isn't it?

His hot breath washes over my ear. "I'm going to give you ten spanks: fast and increasingly hard. Are you ready?"

Without pause, I whisper, "Yes, Sir."

My pussy's on fire and dripping wet by the time he lifts his hand off my ass only to slap both cheeks at once. It's so wide, he doesn't have to choose between my cheeks. There's no pause between slaps and by the time his hand lands for the tenth time, I'm moaning. My jaw quivers as he stands me up and turns me to face him. His lips press to mine and his body pins my back to the counter. His imprisoned erection presses into my tummy and I want to set it free, but my hands won't fit between us.

I beg when his lips leave mine, but his face hovers so near I can feel its heat. "Fuck me! Please, fuck me!"

Patch's thumbs gently wipe tears from my cheeks I hadn't realized had fallen.

He whispers, "No." He snickers with an evil undertone. "You can wait to have me. Keep in mind that I own your body, and I'll start whatever I want whenever I want."

"You're going to leave me like this?" My question is answered with his grunt. "Fine! I'll masturbate after you leave."

He kisses me so lovingly and then grips my chin between his thumb and forefinger. "No. You won't. That's an order."

My brows lift to question his demand. "An order? Really? You're ordering me around now?"

"Do you want to submit to me? If you do, you'll follow orders without question."

My lips twist and my eyes roll. "Fine! I won't masturbate. But you owe me!"

"I owe you?" he asks as he backs up and shoves his hand into his jeans to shift his erection to a more comfortable position. "Do I ever leave you unsatisfied?"

My laugh follows him as he makes his way to the door and slips his feet into his work boots. "Yes. You do. You've left me horny a few times, and I don't like it."

He glances up at me and laughs. "Oh, right. I suppose I have. Maybe you'll learn your position and stop testing me."

"My position?" I'm goading him because I want him to punish me with a hard, angry fuck. Hell yes! "And what is my position, exactly?"

"Submissive," he says and rests his hands on his knees. "You're my fucking submissive and I'm your dominant, and you wouldn't want it any other way." His smile glows with bright teeth contrasting with his tanned face.

I whisper through a grin I can't contain, "No. I wouldn't."

"Okay," he leans in to kiss me quickly and adds, "I'm late and it's paycheck day."

"Yeah, go." I swish my hands from my hips out in front of me, palms up. "Will we see you later?"

As he descends the steps on the wraparound porch, he says, "I'll let you know."

The last thing I want to do is sit around the house moping. I have two more days off work due to mourning, but if I don't keep busy, the idle time may cause my demise.

After a phone call to Mom to ask if she wants to go shopping or just get out of the house for a while, and she declines, I shower, dress, and drive to the mall. I spend several hours going from one store to another. The only things I've purchased are a red blouse for work, three-inch tan stiletto heels, stockings, and a tan bustier with panties and garters for play. This will be an inviting surprise to whatever man, or men, invades my bed this evening.

The thought of walking around the house in this outfit with these heels while Patch drools over me and I refuse him earns me a sense of power. My feminine wiles could possibly drive that man to submit. Okay. Maybe that's a pipedream, but I'll have his full attention. Tease me, will you?

I make my way through the grocery store with no need to rush. My cart's filled by the time I reach the cash-out. I'll be questioning some of the purchases later by asking myself, *What the hell were you thinking?*

The groceries are put away and the roast is in the crockpot with the potatoes, carrots, and onions, and it's only two o'clock.

I open my phone and tap Lizzy's phone number. She picks up on the second ring.

"Hi, girlfriend," she says, and drags out the *-iend* part.

"Hey! What are you up to?"

It sounds like she's in her car. "I'm driving home from work. Why? What's up?"

"Do you want to do a little day drinking?" I know her well enough to pull the phone away from my ear because she's about to yell.

"*Fuck yeah!* I'm on my way." Lizzy giggles and hangs up without another word.

With the blender on the counter filled with the ingredients for margaritas, I blend and dance to the quick beat of the music thumping through the house louder than it probably should be. Before I'm done pouring the icy mixture into two glasses, Lizzy bursts through the door, dancing while she sings along with the female singer.

She's in her green scrubs with her I.D. badge clamped to her pocket. Her purse swings from the long strap as she dances with her arms over her head, hips swaying, and red hair bouncing in a long ponytail. We dance until the song ends, and then I turn down the volume using the phone app Mack set up for me.

"Can I borrow some clothes?" Lizzy asks and heads toward my bedroom without waiting for my response, not that I would deny her request.

I choose a pair of black yoga pants and a purple and blue tie-dyed t-shirt while she has a quick shower to freshen up. She dresses and sets her hair free from the quick bun she's fashioned atop her head so she wouldn't get it wet. After she runs a brush through it a few times, red curls spill softly over her shoulders. If only my hair looked that amazing after being in a ponytail all day, but I could never get that lucky.

We sit outside on the porch and watch the river through the clearing while we drink and laugh like nothing changed when I foolishly blamed her for my pain. Storm clouds roll in while we're on our third margarita and laughing like fools at stupid things.

Lizzy suddenly remembers she's supposed to call Mack to let him know whether she plans to stop by the main house. She calls and giggles while she confirms his suspicion that she's been drinking. Before he hangs up, he says he's on his way.

We rush into the house, strip, and flop on the bed. By the time I feel his hot hand on my lower back, Lizzy's on her back with me on top in a sixty-nine position, and we're moaning from the pleasure we're inflicting on each other.

Between the alcohol, the laughs with Lizzy, and the sex, several hours have passed without my thoughts slipping to my father, and I'm grateful for the reprieve.

I climb off Lizzy and she spins so we're facing each other with a gap between us big enough to fit a naked, extremely aroused Mack.

His hips roll from his waist as he gets in a few dance steps and sings the end of the chorus of the song blasting throughout the house. Then he flops between us.

Lizzy and I laugh until her lips meet his and my lips wrap around the head of his cock. He moans into her mouth as his hand glides up my arm and rests at the base of my neck.

I straddle his hips and lower my pussy over his cock, taking him deep into me. His hand grabs onto my thigh, hoping to move me at a pace he prefers, but I'm on top and in control. He gives into my rhythm and eases his grip.

Lizzy stands and straddles his chest, facing me. She waves her brows and sticks out her tongue as her hips sway side to side teasingly. Mack stares up at her pussy while his finger buries between her wet folds. I lean forward and glide my tongue over her clitoris and tease the stiff nub with licks and flicks. Mack glides two fingers into her and fucks slowly and deliberately. Lizzy holds my head to help her with her balance and slowly bucks her hips.

Mack moans and whispers to himself, "What a fucking view this is." I look down when I hear the click of a camera and see Mack holding his phone and smiling. He clicks another picture and whispers, "This is a beautiful moment, and it needs to be captured."

I'm eager to see the pictures, but Lizzy tugs my hair to pull my attention back to the task of licking her clit. She moans and bucks her clit over my tongue until her body stiffens and vibrates. A loud moan from Mack follows. I'm not surprised when he grabs my hips to ease my pace. Was her orgasm enough to push him close to his own climax?

Lizzy's in the kitchen making more margaritas while I calmly ride Mack's cock and admire the photos he took. He's right; the view is incredible. I send the pictures to Bash and Patch in the group chat to tease them on Mack's behalf. Seconds later, the screen lights up with excited text messages and jealous comments.

Mack writes, *Fuck you. They're mine!* and tosses the phone onto the nightstand while he laughs.

We kiss as his arms wrap around my chest and I hold my hips still while his rock-hard cock remains imprisoned in my vagina.

"Okay, you two. Enough fucking, more drinking." She sets the tray of drinks beside Mack's phone and hands us each one after I climb off Mack and sit with my back against the footrest. Mack and Lizzy sit with their backs against the headrest while we talk about everything and nothing and drink until we've emptied our glasses.

Mack shifts onto his knees and grabs Lizzy's waist to pull her down until she's lying flat on her back while she squeals and laughs. He kisses each knee before he lies between her spread thighs, and kisses her while he makes love to her at a leisurely pace.

Several minutes pass, and Lizzy whispers something I didn't hear. Mack lifts off her and she leans over and opens the nightstand drawer to collect the small but powerful vibrator she knows I keep there. She hands it to me and bites her bottom lip.

What does she want me to do with this?

She flips onto her hands and knees and shoves a pillow under her hips before she lies face down. Mack bends over her and slips his erection into her pussy while one hand grips her hip. His hand glides up her waist to her breast where it stays and tweaks her nipple. This is Mack's favorite position, although he's usually fucking an asshole.

Now I know what she wants me to do.

Lizzy's legs are spread, as are Mack's, giving me free access to their genitals. The vibrator revs to life. I alternate between him and her to make sure to vibrate his perineal, balls, and the base of his cock, as well as her labia and clitoris. Both are on the edge of orgasm, but I don't want Mack to cum yet.

I grip Mack's upper thigh and push and pull until he gets the message that I want him to thrust faster. He thrusts down into her hard and fast while I hold the vibrator on the side of her clitoris. Lizzy reaches behind her and digs her fingernails into Mack's ass and screams her way through a climax until her breath holds and her body stiffens. Her pussy spasms around his cock and coats his shaft with her cum. My hand's dripping wet when I sit back and shut off the vibrator.

Mack kneels, and a panting Lizzy rolls out from beneath him and onto her back. He flips as he drops onto the warm spot Lizzy's body just vacated. His hands weave together behind his head. A crooked grin grows as if pleased with himself. His cock is still stiff and ready for whatever we want to do next. He's leaving it up to us, and I like that.

Lizzy sits up and slides down the bed. "Well, would you look at that gorgeous cock. It looks lonely. Maybe we should worship this glorious erection. What do you think, Goldilocks?"

"I agree; it definitely looks lonely, almost desperate for attention. Perhaps we should entertain it." My index finger presses to my chin and my eyes lift to the ceiling as if searching for an answer. "But how, I wonder?"

We both laugh when he says, "Ladies, I don't care what body part you touch it with. Just touch it. Pretty please."

"Since you asked so nicely," I say, bend forward, and gently suck one of his testicles in my mouth. I'm rewarded with his lengthy moan.

Lizzy's hair brushes over my cheek when she takes his cock in her mouth. Despite our mouths being full, we giggle.

Mack's palm mindlessly presses down on my shoulder while the other holds Lizzy's hair to keep the strands out of her way. He's considerate like that.

Her head bobs while I lick and suck his testicles. I turn on the vibrator and slip it between his ass cheeks, up against his asshole and perineal.

"Holy fuck! Oh, man! That feels fucking awesome." He moans with each strangled breath. His leg muscles tighten and his cock thickens. "Oh, fuck yeah! I'm going to cum. Holy fuck! I'm going to cum!" Mack's muscles tighten as his deep-throated groan sings through the room. His hand presses firmly on my shoulder as his fingertips dig in. "Ah! Ah! *Ah!* Yeah!"

Lizzy moans and sucks every last drop of cum from his shaft while he twitches, gasps, and chuckles under his breath. She and I sit up, and she wipes her lips while we smile at Mack the same way he smiled earlier: pleased with ourselves.

We shower and dress, and then sit on the deck to drink a beer. Lizzy has switched to water since she'll be driving home soon to pack an overnight bag so she can spend the night with Mack.

The two of them are getting close, and I wonder if one day we'll be preparing for *their* wedding. How great would that be to have her in our lives all the time? I love her and I think the guys do, too. If I were to judge by how they look at each other, I'd say they're in love. Neither has said it to the other. Not yet, but it's coming. I can feel it.

Chapter 16

Two weeks have passed. I'm standing in front of the foggy bathroom mirror wrapped in a towel. I wipe the steam from the mirror with a washcloth, and my hazy image stares back at me.

"In less than three hours, you'll be a married woman. You'll become Goldilocks Bear." I like the sound of that and say it again. "Goldilocks Bear. I could get used to that."

The truck with the chairs, tents, and tables, has already arrived and the workers have begun setting them up. Over the past few days, the weather's been sunny and warm but not too hot. This morning, the weather lady said we're expecting the same today. The tents are going up over the food preparation area at the cook's insistence. He fears a bird will *shat* in the food.

A small stage was set up yesterday afternoon for us to stand on for the ceremony. It'll be decorated with white roses like the ones my father grew in his garden he was so proud of. It's my little tribute to him.

Dad was supposed to walk me down the aisle. He said he would. It was the last thing he said to me. Mom will take his place. Mack is Bash's best man, and Patch will officiate. I can't wait to see them in tuxedos, again.

The memory of Mack and Patch standing and Bash on his knee before me with his mother's ring pinched between his trembling fingers is one of my most treasured. I can't wait to see them looking that fine again.

A knock on the door startles me. "Yes?"

Lizzy says, "Hey, girl! Let me in."

"It's open," I say, and rub lotion on my face.

She comes in and turns the fan on to rid the bathroom of the steam. "Oh, my God! My hair's going to go flat in here." She shoves the door wide open. "I'm leaving this open. How can you breathe in here?" I shrug and she squeals. "You're getting married today!" She squeals again, and this time my ears ring from it.

"Easy, woman! You're going to deafen me and I won't be able to hear when it's my turn to say *I do*."

"Seriously, it's fucking hot in here," she says and opens the window.

"They're setting up out there. They'll see me," I say, and shut the window as I pull the blind back down. "You're early. We have a few hours to go."

She hops on the counter and groans when her powder-pink sweatpants gain a small wet mark. "I know; I'm here to help you get ready. Isn't that what besties do? I'm your maid of honor, after all." Her legs swing and she leans forward with her palms on the edge of the counter. "So, what can I do to help?"

"You can make me a coffee with some sort of liquor, and don't be cheap with the liquor," I say, and drag a brush through my hair.

"I'm on it!" Lizzy rushes from the bathroom, leaving the door open.

It's not a problem since we're the only people in the house. Bash stayed the night with Patch and Mack at the main house.

Marcel will be here in an hour to make sure everything is prepared to his high standards. Personally, I don't care if the guests have to open their own chairs and choose to sit wherever they want. But Marcel has maps of where things need to go and a curriculum the hired staff must adhere to or suffer his wrath.

My hairdryer is blasting when Lizzy returns with two steaming mugs. All I can smell is the Irish cream. Even before I taste it I know we'll be giddy by the last sip. Good because I'm nervous.

Lizzy styles my hair in a partial updo with dangling curls and tiny teal-colored silk flowers to accent. She does a fabulous job, so I tell her she's missed her calling.

Next, she does my make-up. Again, I'm blown away. I can't stop staring at myself because I look like the 2.0 version of myself: a new design with serious upgrades.

While I'm still in my yoga pants and t-shirt, Lizzy insists I eat some toast before the dress goes on. It takes serious concentration to convince my body to swallow each bite. My stomach bears the brunt of my anxiety and doesn't want food.

Marcel calls out to me when he enters the house. Before I can reply, he jammers on about the plans and how I'm not to worry about anything because he has it all handled. By the time he reaches the bedroom where Lizzy and I are sitting cross-legged on the bed, he's out of breath.

"Oh, good! You're eating. Most brides forget to eat, and they're nauseous by the time they get to the altar. Of course, their nerves don't help the situation, but I always try to get them to—"

Lizzy interrupts him. "I'll be back in a minute."

It doesn't stop Marcel from continuing to ramble.

He disappears into the closet and returns with my dress dangling from a hanger. I did as he suggested and hung it in the bathroom, steamed it, and then hung it in the closet after it had dried. He steps back and admires the silk and lace with one hand on his cheek while his other arm crosses his chest.

He whispers, "My God! That's going to look so lovely on your figure. You'll be so sexy Bash won't be able to contain his—" Marcel's finger and eyes aim at his crotch.

"Marcel! You're so bad," I feign shyness. "But you might be right."

"You know it, girl! Now let me look at you." He steps back and eyes my make-up and hair. "Damn! You are so beautiful. It's true, I say that to all the brides, but I really mean it with you. Some brides wear too much make-up and damned if they don't look like they'd be better suited on a street corner. Sometimes less is more if you know what I mean."

Lizzy dances through the doorway with four empty flutes and a bottle of champagne. She fills three glasses and hands one to each of us. We toast to everything going smoothly, and if not smoothly, worthy of fond or funny memories.

While we dress, Marcel makes himself scarce, but we can hear him firing off orders to the staff before he's even off the porch.

Lizzy's dress is teal and silky: an off-the-shoulder, form-fitting to the hips, knee-length in the front, swooping almost to the floor in the back and has a deep plunge to reveal the small of her back. She's astonishingly beautiful.

We laugh because of the alcohol as she helps me into my dress. While she laces the back of my gown, I watch the workers through the window scurry like scared ants to rearrange the chairs at Marcel's insistence.

Mack's friend I've only met twice offered to shuttle people from either Mom's house or the main Bear house. We don't have enough cleared ground for all the cars and the sixty-two guests, so this was a great alternative.

Mom steps out of the Bronco and smiles as she speaks with the driver. She nods and stands, clutching a tote bag and her purse while she takes a moment to watch the busy help. She's stunning in her knee-length dusty rose and white dress. Having seen enough, she ascends the stairs and disappears under the overhang.

Mom calls out, "Goldilocks?"

Lizzy replies, "We're in here."

Her dusty rose-colored, two-inch heels clack on the hardwood floor as she approaches. She walks in and stops. Her gaze wanders down my gown and her breath catches. "My God… You are so beautiful." Her hand rises to cover her mouth as her eyes pool with glistening tears. She looks away and waves that hand. "No! I will not cry and ruin my make-up."

Lizzy taps my shoulder. "You're all done."

My stocking-clad feet carry me across the room to Mom on my tiptoes so I won't trip on the lengthy gown.

"You look beautiful," I say as she sets her belongings on the long dresser beside the door. We hug and step back to adore each other's appearances. "That dress shows off those bazoongas and your trim waist. And your make-up and hair are impeccable."

I lied because she looks tired, and her eyes are red and puffy from crying. It's obvious she didn't sleep much last night. My heart sinks when I picture her lying in bed with her arm stretched across to my dad's side while she cries.

No! Stop thinking like that... make-up!

"Do you want something to drink?" I ask as Lizzy wraps her arms around my mom.

"Good morning. Are you excited?" Lizzy asks.

They part, and Mom smiles wide. "I'm a little nervous that I won't make it through without bursting into tears, but I'm going to do my best."

Lizzy pouts and says, "If you cry, I'll cry, too. So, *don't* cry. Okay?"

Mom pats her arm, tilts her head, and shuts her eyes momentarily. It was a gesture, not a promise. "So, what can I do to help? I mean, it doesn't look like you need any help. Wow! You are stunning! Your father would be—"

All three of us nearly choke, fighting back our tears, but Lizzy saves us from falling apart. "We need more champagne."

Mom presses her hand to her tummy and lets out a lengthy breath. "I'd love that."

Lizzy fills the fourth glass and hands it to her. She anticipated my mother coming, and that's why she brought four glasses, not three.

After a long sip, Mom says, "I stopped in to see the boys. Goldilocks, hopefully, this doesn't make you angry, but they're terribly hung over. Mack ran to the bathroom to vomit when Patch set a plate with eggs, hash browns, bacon, and toast in front of him. Bash struggled to swallow each bite, but he didn't vomit."

"No! Come on! Seriously? I knew they'd be drinking last night, but I thought they'd be smarter about it." My groan is very unbecoming of a bride-to-be. "If Mack pukes while standing behind Bash, I might leave my position to give him a slap." My laughter fills the room along with Mom's and Lizzy's. "All I have to say is that someone had better get it all on video."

Lizzy's arms spread and wave before they open wide to make the announcement. "We could put it in a contest and win money: *Best man vomits on groom at wedding.*" Her mouth forms an "O" before her arms drop to her sides. "No! That wouldn't be funny. I mean, it would, but after the fact… Maybe, like, in ten years from now."

"I'm sure he'll be fine by then," Mom says and glides her palm along the lacy embellishing on my arm sleeve. "This gown is gorgeous!"

"Thank you." I turn to gaze at it in the full-length mirror. "I saw it and knew it had to be mine."

It hugs my curves perfectly. The guys are going to love it. I'll try to remember to look at their crotches to see if they *really* love it, as Marcel suggested.

Marcel rushes into the house and sees Mom, Lizzy, and me standing at the island sipping champagne. He sings, "Okay, ladies! It's almost time!"

His hand reaches out to my Mom while his other clutches a tablet. He leads her to the door and points to the altar while he explains something.

Mack walks in, and he's dashing in his black, double-breasted tuxedo. His bowtie and pocket square match Lizzy's teal dress and the flowers in my hair. The vest doesn't button straight up the middle. Instead, they rise from the center to the right with the fourth button stopping a few inches above the pocket. It's a different, fancier style that suits Mack's personality perfectly.

He takes Mom's hands and leans in to kiss her cheek. She says something to him, and he snickers and nods.

He sees me, and his cheery grin gradually sags while his eyes drink me in. Mindlessly, he crosses the room and stops an arm's length from me. "Holy... Wow! I... You're... Goddamn!" His wide, bright-blue orbs meet mine, and he swallows before he whispers, "I want to kiss you so badly right now." His voice drops to a groan. "I mean, *really* kiss you."

With a slight tip of my head and in a sweet voice, I whisper, "You'll smear my lipstick." My cheeks flush when his head shakes and his eyes gesture toward my pussy. "Stop that! My mom is standing right over there."

Mack turns to see where Mom is and whispers, "She knows about us. Besides, she's talking to Marcel."

His eyes shift to Lizzy when she steps up beside me. His hand holds over his heart as he savors her beauty.

"Goddamn beautiful. Mhm! You look mouth-wateringly delicious, like the finest dessert. I'm *definitely* kissing you; lipstick be damned."

He leans down and kisses her with a gentle peck so he doesn't smear her lipstick. He's such a gentleman.

She wipes the trace of her lipstick off his lips and whispers, "You can kiss me anywhere you'd like, but it'll have to wait. First, we have to get this gal to the altar." She points to me with her thumb.

As if suddenly waking to the realization of why we're all dressed up, Mack steps back as his palm smooths his vest. "Oh, shit! Yes, of course."

He wears the cutest sexy grin as he leaves us. He runs his hand down my mom's arm to get her attention as he says something to her.

Lizzy hands me a bouquet of flowers. She and Mack designed them and wouldn't tell me anything about it.

Amid lace closely matching that of my dress is a light batting of green sprigs one would find in the forest. Four big white roses surround the most beautiful blood-red rose I've ever seen. My fingertip traces one of the velvety petals, and my eyes pool with tears.

"No! No, no, *no*!" Lizzy says, and quickly and brutally pinches the backside of my bicep.

"Ouch! What the fuck, Lizzy?"

As if I should know why, she sarcastically says, "You can't cry right now! You're about to go on."

"Yeah, but now I want to cry because that hurts." I rub the rising bruise and frown.

"Big baby," she teases and then smiles as she covers the bouquet with her hands so I won't see it, even though I'm holding it. "Without crying, what do you think?"

"But this is so beautiful! I love it so much. You're the best friend a woman could have. I love you!"

My arms fling around her neck. I mean it! I love her more than any friend I've ever had.

"Okay! Okay! You're crushing my curls, woman!" she barks, and I set her free. Her voice softens and she whispers, "You're the red one."

"And you and the boys are white." I swallow the lump in my throat and whisper, "It's perfect."

Her hands clap once. "Okay! Let's get this show on the road."

Lizzi's arm bends at the elbow, so I slip mine into it. She hands me off to Mom and then dances with excitement while waving her less busy bouquet with smaller roses and less greenery.

Marcel lifts a walkie-talkie to his mouth and says, "Queue the music."

Chapter 17

Gentle music sings from the many speakers. Marcel waits with his hand on Lizzy's shoulder while he watches out the door. I'm not sure what he's waiting for. He tucks back into the house and waggles his fingers.

Nearly singing, he says, "Strut your stuff, gorgeous."

Lizzy dances a little jig, sobers up, and then steps outside, across the porch, and down the steps. Mom hasn't looked at me. She's focused out the open door while she takes deep breaths in through her nose and out her mouth.

"Mom, are you okay?"

She remains focused. Through a forced smile that doesn't meet her wearied eyes, she says, "I will be." She swallows and takes a deep breath. "Your beauty always impressed your dad. If he were here today, he'd be in tears. I just know it. Despite what you think, he was pleased you found someone to love; not so much for how many lovers you found. Nonetheless, he would've been proud as a peacock to walk you down the aisle."

She turns her head to look at me when I pull my arm from hers to wipe my tears before they stream down my cheeks and wash away my makeup.

"Goldilocks, no! Don't cry, baby."

A sob escapes me. "Why would you say all of that right now? Oh, my God! I'm a mess."

Marcel turns to investigate the commotion. With wide eyes and the intention to resolve whatever issue has risen, he rushes toward me, pulls a tissue from the sleeve of his pale blue jacket, and blots my tears.

He whispers, "How do you shoot a blue elephant?"

Confused, I ask, "What?"

"How do you shoot a blue elephant?"

I shrug. "I don't know. With a gun, I suppose."

"Yes. With a blue-elephant gun. How do you shoot a pink elephant?"

Still unsure why he's asking me stupid questions, I reply, "With a pink-elephant gun?"

He stops blotting when my tears cease. "No, silly girl. You squeeze his trunk until he turns blue and shoot him with the blue-elephant gun." He shrugs and rolls his eyes when our response is a titter. "It's lame, I know. But it's the only joke I can remember. It worked because you're not crying anymore... Just in time. You're on, sweetheart."

The *Wedding March* song plays loudly and disappears into the forest. The guests have stood to their feet.

I squeeze Marcel's hand before releasing it, and then slip my other arm around my mom's, and say, "Thank you, Marcel. You saved the day yet again."

He smiles and waves his arm. "Go, child! They aren't going to wait forever."

"Mom, if you let me fall, I'm taking you down with me."

We laugh and plan our steps methodically. My heart is racing, and my legs feel rubbery as we descend the steps, arm in arm. *Please don't fall!*

I'm thankful my feet are on solid ground, but when I look up, more eyes than I'm comfortable with are fixed on me. I feel heavier because of them, and my legs won't move.

Mom hugs my arm a little tighter to grab my attention. "Breathe, Goldilocks. Focus on your husband."

The people fade away as I take in each man standing at the altar: Mack, Patch, and finally Bash.

Deep breaths keep me from wanting to run down the aisle and into Bash's arms, bury my face in his chest, and make the spotlight on me disappear. No. I am about to marry the most wonderful man in the world. This is a moment in my life I'll never forget. It's a moment to be savored.

A deep breath fills my lungs, and I look at Mom. Her smile is genuine, and it reminds me of every smile she's ever given my father. Love. Pure, honest love.

I have to look away before I burst into tears.

As we near the altar, a giggle escapes me. Mom wasn't kidding when she said the Bear brothers are hung over. Mack is the only one of the three men who doesn't have purple bags under his eyes, but he's just as pale as Patch and Bash.

Mack smiles proudly since he's already ogled me. Bash and Patch haven't blinked. Both men have their hands together and over their crotches. Is that to hide their excitement or to keep them out of their pockets?

Bash and Patch wear matching tuxedos to what Mack wears, but Bash's kerchief is white and his boutonniere is a white rose, and Mack and Patch's roses are teal. How lucky am I to have them love me as much as they do? I don't think that amount of luck can be measured.

Goddamn! They are a trio of sexy men. How often is it that all the brothers in a family are gorgeous? There's usually one of them that's just so-so, but that's not the case with the Bear boys.

At the front of the aisle, Mom and I sigh with relief that we didn't trip and we snicker. She kisses my cheek and reaches for Bash's hand to give it a quick squeeze. To my surprise, she takes my hand and joins it with Bash's. She steps back and salutes us.

"She's all yours," she says rather loudly, and the crowd bursts into laughter.

It takes me a second to realize she was joking to lighten the mood—it's something my father would've done.

"If you insist." Bash smiles and hugs my mom with his free arm.

She sits in the front row beside my dad's best friend, Godfrey, and despite her smile, tears spill.

Bash whispers to me, "I'm the luckiest man in the world."

Our eyes meet, and I'm instantly lost in his piercing blue pools, glossy from happiness. I have no idea what Patch is saying, despite his rumbling voice. A microphone he does not need. I can hear his words, but they aren't registering as something I should bother to comprehend.

"Bash," Patch says and taps Bash's arm to get his attention.

"What? Oh, yeah," Bash says and then clears his throat before looking back at me.

My heart is pounding so hard, and yet I hear nothing but his words surrounded by complete silence. No matter how hard I try to swallow the massive lump threatening to erupt from my throat into an ocean of tears, I can't. The best I can do is take a deep breath and ease it out slowly.

He's so handsome.

In high school, when I had a massive crush on the oh-so-cute Bash Bear, never had I dreamed of this moment. Wild sex with him was the fantasy, but unlikely. Love never crossed my mind. But here I stand, proving my younger self wrong because he *does* love me. He honestly and truly loves me. His eyes tell me so.

"Goldie, from the moment I first set my eyes on your beautiful face, I knew you were the only woman for me even though we were just kids. You were shy and steered away from me whenever I tried to talk to you, but I never gave up hope. My pull to you only grew stronger the older we got, but you still showed me no interest. When I thought all hope was lost, there you were. All it took was one moment alone where you couldn't avoid me." Bash pauses to lick his lips.

The memory of the first time I went to the Bear house has me grinning and blushing. After being intimate with Patch in the forest, and then Mack in the bedroom, I found myself sitting beside Bash on the bed. I was nude, hugging a sheet, and still breathing heavily after Mack pleasured me. I thought for sure Bash would cast me aside and call me a nasty name, but he was kind, caring, and completely accepting of my time with his brothers. In fact, he didn't care about that at all. He confessed his feelings for me, and I finally let him know how much I liked him from afar. That's where it all began—our love story.

Bash continues, "You said you've always felt the same pull toward me. That was the best day ever." Sobs escape me when his tears spill down his cheeks. He makes no attempt to wipe them away. "Standing here, about to share rings with you, *this* moment—right now—is the best moment of my life."

Patch whispers, "Mack, the rings."

Mack hands the rings to Patch, and Patch hands one to Bash, who pauses with the ring at the tip of my left ring finger.

Bash whispers through his tears, "Goldie, do you accept this ring as a token of my eternal love?"

I whisper, "Yes. I do," and he slips it on my finger.

My excitement has me wanting to scream, but the shimmer of the diamonds reflecting from the bright sun steals my attention. The band molds perfectly with the diamond engagement ring, but it looks newer than his mother's engagement ring. And it's absolutely stunning!

Patch draws my attention with a whisper. "Goldilocks."

How the fuck am I going to talk with this enormous lump in my throat? His speech was smooth and flawless. How can mine compare to that when I didn't prepare one?

"Bash, I can't tell you how many times I kissed your picture in my yearbook. I'm surprised the page hasn't worn away. You were not the kind of boy a girl like me was supposed to be seen with, but I always hoped *you* would see *me*. One day, I gained enough courage to take a walk on the wild side, and that walk ended with you beside me. The way you looked at me and how you said my name was all the proof I needed to know how you felt about me. You woke me from my cookie-cutter life and showed me that love can be free of guilt, expansive, and comes in many forms. I am so in love with you, so I would be honored to marry you today."

Patch hands me a ring and smiles down at me with flushed cheeks and glassy eyes. Is he fighting back tears? No, dammit! He's my rock; he can't cry!

The lump I've suppressed so well until now erupts into a flood of tears. I can't see his finger, and talking above a high-pitched whisper proves impossible. "Bash, if you marry me today, I vow to love you and always be by your side when our dreams steal us away."

Bash made me promise to always be beside him in bed every night. He said he was okay with me being intimate with his brothers, but I had to promise each night would be spent dreaming beside him. That was his only rule. And now I've vowed to be his, and he's about to vow to be mine.

"Do you accept this ring and all it represents?"

Bash whispers, "Yes. Goldie. A thousand times, yes."

Patch clears his throat, and says, "By the power vested in me from the online course I took," he pauses while people chuckle, "I now pronounce you husband and wife. Bash, kiss your beautiful wife, or I will."

Without hesitation, Bash presses his lips to mine while his hand cups the back of my neck, and the other hugs my body against his. Our lips part, and my arms fling around his neck. He looks steady and in control of himself, but his body's shaking. He's more nervous than me. Somehow that's comforting.

My new husband releases me, and I turn and hug Lizzy, who's cried herself a puddle. She sets me free, and Patch hugs and kisses me before he snuffs his runny nose. Bash hugs Patch after I'm set free.

Mack wraps his arms around me. We hug for a few seconds before he steps back and cups my cheeks. His red, puffy eyes remind me of his hangover, but he smiles, and all is well in the world. He kisses me softly, but not too lovingly, so the guests aren't uncomfortable and those who don't know of our intimate dynamic won't pick up on it. Today is not the day to shock people.

Bash gently tugs my hand, but I pause to hug a red-faced Mom before he leads me toward the house while people cheer and clap. He scoops me up wedding-style and carries me up the steps and into the house and then kicks the door shut behind him with his foot. He kisses me before he sets me down.

Bash laughs and opens the door to our wedding party which followed us down the aisle. His arms lift from his sides and they laugh.

He turns to me with dry eyes and a wide and toothy smile. "Mrs. Goldilocks Bear, thank you for marrying me."

My right shoulder lifts as my head tilts toward it and my lips twist. "I wasn't doing anything else today." I smile back and whisper, "Mr. Bash Bear, my husband, I like how you said my name."

"My wife..." He moans and pulls me against him for another kiss as people flow inside to congratulate us.

After Lizzy pulls me away from the excited guests so we can touch up our make-up, we set off to the pre-chosen locations for photos. This allows time for the guests to get drinks, mingle, and find a table, since we didn't want a seating plan. We return an hour later and our hired help brings out the first course.

After dinner but before the desserts are served, speeches commence.

Patch's speech mentions their parents, and that brings Bash and Mack near tears. He adds in a few funny anecdotes about raising Bash and Mack that bring back their cheerfulness.

It's Mack's speech that has our guests erupting into fits of laughter. Not only is he romantic and so handsome he's almost pretty, but he's funny, too.

Lizzy follows Mack; she has people laughing at first, but soon the laughter fades. She cries while talking about how much she treasures the friendships she found in all of us.

Nobody's surprised Mom doesn't make a speech. There's no way she'd get through it without mentioning my father, and that would likely break her into a million pieces. It's too soon.

The guests are eating their choice of either a chocolate lava cake or tiramisu when Bash takes my hand and leads us to the microphone perched like a lonely soldier guarding the small stage. My heart pounds when I stop beside my new husband. The many conversations halt and silence grows while too many eyes lock onto us.

Bash clears his throat and speaks into the microphone. "First, I'd like to thank all of you for coming to join us as we embark on our union as husband and wife. I still can't believe she said yes. And even more shocking is that she showed up today. I thought she'd wise up and run in the opposite direction." He sighs and runs his fingers through his hair as if he's relieved, and the audience laughs. He kisses my hand and the audience coos. "There are so many people I want to thank. I mean; my brothers, Mack and Patch, Lizzy as maid of honor, and Goldie's mom, of course."

Bash pats his chest over his heart, and Mom smiles and repeats his motions. For whatever reason, he doesn't mention my father. Maybe he thinks it'll be too painful for all of us.

He adds, "Can we get a shout-out to Marcel, our wedding planner? He put this whole thing together and deserves our applause."

People clap and cheer, and Bash leans down to me to ask if I want to say anything.

At first, I don't, but then I pull his sleeve to get his attention and nod. He steps aside from the microphone and tips it down for me. My voice is soft. If I try to speak louder, I won't make it through what I want to say.

"Bash did a great job of thanking everyone, but if he left anyone out, I apologize. Um," a deep breath fills my lungs and I smile at Mom, who's already fighting back tears, "as you all know, my father passed away not long ago. It's been incredibly difficult on Mom and me, but with the support of family and friends, we're making it through. Dad and I weren't seeing eye-to-eye for some time, but after his first heart attack, we were trying to work through our issues. When he woke from his surgery after the second attack, we talked and decided we didn't want tension between us. The last thing he said to me was that he couldn't wait to walk me down the aisle."

I have to look over people's heads because their flow of tears will probably push me over the edge and I won't be able to finish my thought. "Thank you, Mom, for standing in his place. That had to be challenging for you, but you did it with grace and laughter. You're an amazing person, and I love you, Mom."

Mom stands and comes toward me, so I step down and meet her halfway. We hug and our guests stand and clap, but I hear only Mom's breath. She holds me so tight and we cry like nobody's watching. Bash's arms wrap around us both. Seconds later, Patch, Mack, and Lizzy's arms join in the huddle.

Patch's voice is the only one to roar over the applause. "I love this family."

Mom bursts into laughter. "Okay! Okay! Goldilocks, I can see why you love these guys so much."

***

The night is spent dancing, with laughter and drunken storytelling. The whole day was perfect; better than I'd imagined it would be.

I was nervous about dancing to romantic belly-rubbing music with Patch or Mack. I feared there'd be disapproving stares and whispers, but nobody seemed to care. Then again, the men held my attention with either their eyes or smooth dance moves, so I didn't think to look at any faces.

I can't ever recall feeling so loved and accepted by so many people. Not once did I feel shamed or judged. It was fabulous; better than anything I could've hoped for.

Some of the guests my mom insisted we invite were friends with Dad. I wasn't sure if they'd be supportive because they knew about the tumultuous relationship between Dad and me. Surprisingly, none of them gave us so much as a side glance, not even the most judgemental couple among the avid churchgoers, Lou and Cece. I was shocked to see them in attendance at the reception. I was sure they'd cancel at the last minute or just not come. When I saw them talking and laughing with Mack and Bash shortly after dessert, I could almost feel my dad's hand on my shoulder and hear him telling me something he always said: *"People's hearts are bigger than you think, kiddo."*

Chapter 18

Patch got his paternity test results back, and they proved he wasn't the father. He told everyone he was happy that he doesn't have a son living across the country he has never met, but there was a sadness in his eyes he fought hard to suppress. A few days after he found out, he had a few too many drinks and told me there was a small part of him that was disappointed he doesn't have a son.

He said he wishes to have a child one day and hopes I'll be their mother, but if that isn't on my agenda, he'll love mine and Bash's children as if they were his own. He loves me and I him, and we both love Bash and Mack and Lizzy.

I'm thrilled he won't be moving away. The thought of losing him for any reason makes my heart ache. I love him very much.

As for children, who knows what the future holds?

Maybe one day we'll stop all birth control—pulling the goalie as Bash says—and we'll see what happens. If we do that, we won't know whose baby I give birth to. But I don't know if I want to go that route; it might be too difficult for the child to comprehend, and they might get picked on by other children. School life is hard enough to survive with a positive paternity, so why would I want to make it harder on them?

It's been two months since we returned from the surprise honeymoon Patch and Mack secretly arranged for us. I never thought I'd get a chance to go to Australia, but we went and it was so much better than I'd imagined. We spent two weeks traveling and taking in many exciting experiences. By the end of each day, my face hurt from smiling so much and we were exhausted.

Lizzy moved into the main house with Mack. Patch continues to alternate between our house and the main house: mine and Bash's bed, and Lizzy and Mack's. We wouldn't want it any other way. Our arrangement hasn't changed in that we can have sex with whomever we want in our little family.

When the time comes when Lizzy or I want to pop out a few offspring, we'll decide who baby we want to carry. I love them all, but Bash is my husband, and having a mini-Bash running around the house doesn't sound as terrifying as it once did. That won't be for at least a year.

Will I want to have Patch's baby, too? I don't know. Maybe Mack's? Hmm…

I love Patch and don't want to share him with anyone other than Lizzy, but I know it's selfish to feel that way. One day, sharing his brother's wives may not be enough for him. If he finds someone he wants to call *his*, I won't stand in his way even if my heart breaks to let him go. Hopefully, the person he falls for will fit into our lives like a puzzle piece we didn't know was missing, and the six of us will become one big loving family. He deserves to be happy like me and Bash or Mack and Lizzy. Will he find someone? It's a question that lingers in all our minds.

For now, we have each other and love freely. It's all we need, but we know tomorrow may throw us a curveball and take us in a different direction. The thought of us breaking apart scares me, but if someone decides they've had enough, we will accept their decision knowing it didn't come easily.

The brothers, Lizzy, and my mom talk and laugh while I sit on the deck in an Adirondack chair, face tipped up toward the sun, my feet resting on the log railing, and thankful to the universe for granting me such wonderful people to share my life with.

"Hey, Goldilocks!" Lizzy's voice grabs my attention. My eyes open to see her beside me in another chair. "Mack took me for a walk in the woods this afternoon. We had a picnic under the canopy of trees. It was so quiet and sedate;

absolutely beautiful. We made love for an hour and then… this happened."

My hand shades my eyes from the sun, but I squint when light shimmers from atop her hand. Her hand comes into focus and I see a brilliant diamond ring on her finger. Her smile is wide. We both squeal, grabbing the attention of Mom and the guys.

"Does everyone know already? Am I the last to know?" I ask excitedly, but she shakes her head.

Mack smiles and announces, "I know I didn't mention this before it happened, but I wanted this to be something Lizzy and I shared together as a couple. Show them, honey."

"We're engaged!" Lizzy jumps up and squeals.

She showcases the ring on her hand, exciting everyone. We all knew it would happen sooner rather than later because they're madly in love.

After hugs from everyone, she turns to ask, "Goldilocks, will you be my matron of honor? Please?"

My arms wrap around her neck, and she hugs me back. "Do you even have to ask?"

Mack says, "Patch, will you be my best man or would you prefer to officiate *our* wedding, too?" His arm swings between Patch and Bash as he laughs. "How about I let the two of you fight it out?"

With a seriously mean expression, Patch steps toward Bash with his hands up in fists. Bash accepts the challenge and takes a fighter's stance. Both men burst into laughter.

Bash says, "I'm his best man."

"No way! It's my turn to be the best man. You can be the best man for my wedding."

Patch growls like a vicious animal and rushes toward Bash, but Bash jumps out of the way. Both men are laughing when Bash runs off the porch.

As he runs, he yells, "Who the fuck would want to marry a miserable prick like you? I can picture you as the grouchy old fuck yelling at people to get off his lawn while your thirty cats follow you around."

Patch chases Bash across the yard but he'll never catch him. Bash is way too fast.

Laughing and out of breath, Patch stops chasing and yells, "Yeah! Run away, chicken boy! I'll ravish your wife and send the cats your way."

As quirky as we may seem to outsiders, we're happy. We're almost always laughing, but when one of us struggles, the rest are there to hold them up. As a bonus, we're never lonely and always have people to share in our special moments. I wouldn't want it any other way.

My life is playing out completely differently than I could've imagined it would.

Sometimes, the path you start out on can take an unexpected hard right turn. The decision to follow can bring on a rough ride. For me, taking the path that led to the Bear brothers wasn't always an easy one, but I wouldn't change a moment of it.

The End

Thank you for reading the Naughty Goldie series.

If you loved this series, tell other potential readers by leaving a review on your book purchasing site.

Feel free to boast the book online and tag Pebbles Lacasse.

Great reviews help authors find more readers interested in this genre, and earn promotional opportunities. In doing so, this book could become a best-seller, with your review posted below for all to read.

The more books authors sell, the more they can afford to write, professionally edit, create fabulous covers, and promote, so you can enjoy the many stories they desire to create for you.

The Naughty Goldie Series
https://books2read.com/Naughty-Goldie-set

Goldilocks & the Three Bear Brothers, Book 1
https://books2read.com/Goldilocks-BookOne

Goldilocks & the Three Bear Brothers: Trifecta, Book 2
https://books2read.com/Goldilocks-BookTwo

Goldilocks & The Three Bear Brothers: Overture, Book 3
https://books2read.com/Goldilocks-BookThree

Goldilocks & The Three Bear Brothers, Liberated, Book 4
https://books2read.com/Goldilocks-BookFour

About Pebbles Lacasse

Pebbles is a contemporary romance and erotica author. She leans toward writing bad boys desiring women who didn't know they have a kinky side. However, she's also known for her women with a dominant nature, and a secret yearning to be loved. Her books and short stories often take her readers into the BDSM lifestyle while revolving around real-life issues, and there's always a happy ending. The captivating stories of romance, love, and tender moments keep her readers coming back for more.

As someone living with Porphyria, Pebbles stays indoors to avoid UV light which gives her plenty of time to write. That's not to say she doesn't love "glamping," fishing, kayaking, and swimming, she just has to do it with protective clothing. If there's something she wants to do, she'll find a way to make it happen.

Pebbles is very family oriented. She and her husband raised their children in southern Ontario where she was born and remains to this day. A 150 lbs Mastiff takes up a lot of room in their home and in their hearts. His best friends are the two rescue cats that think they own the house. The chickens couldn't care less about him until he chases them when they come too close to his outdoor toys.

Discover more about Pebbles on her website
https://www.pebbleslacasse.com

Free short story with newsletter subscription:
https://bit.ly/pebbleskinkynews

Keep swiping for more books you may enjoy!

More Books by Pebbles Lacasse

Full Novels & Series
My Wife and Master Jake
Broken Charm

The Complete My JoeSmith Collection Boxed Set:
    My JoeSmith: Anonymity, Book One
    My JoeSmith: Anonymity, Book Two
    My JoeSmith: Nurture, Book Three
    My JoeSmith: Unity, Book Four
The Coaching Rayna Two Book Series:
    Coaching Rayna, Book One
    Coaching Rayna: Bound Hearts, Book Two
The Naughty Goldie Series:
    Goldilocks & The Three Bear Brothers, Book One
    Goldilocks & The Three Bear Brothers: Trifecta, Book Two
    Goldilocks & The Three Bear Brothers: Overture, Book Three
    Goldilocks & The Three Bear Brothers, Book Four
    Rule Breakers: My Best Friend's Brother, Book One

Short Stories
Little Miss Muffet
Hello Officer
Mistress Rabbit
A Run with Charley
Carter's Mistress
Still Waters Burn Deep

Dominatrix for Hire

Anthologies
Quarantined: A Boxed Set of Pandemic
Proportions – Still Waters Burn Deep

To read teasers and see book cover photoshoot
photos by Pebbles,
visit https://www.PebblesLacasse.com

Connect with Pebbles

Facebook
https://www.facebook.com/PebblesLacasseEroticRomanc
eWriter/

Facebook Group
www.facebook.com/groups/pebbleslacasseandfriendsgro
up/

Newsletter sign-up
https://bit.ly/pebbleskinkynews

Website
https://www.pebbleslacasse.com

Instagram
https://www.instagram.com/pebbleslacasse/

Twitter
https://twitter.com/pebbleslacasse

Goodreads
http://bit.ly/Goodreads_2y5xJji

Bookbub
https://www.bookbub.com/profile/pebbles-lacasse

Amazon
https://www.amazon.com/author/pebbleslacasse

Youtube
https://www.youtube.com/channel/UC3Jb8ofSw0m3TFn
4cMWu5dw

Subscribe to Pebbles' Newsletter

Sign up to receive Pebbles Lacasse's newsletter and receive a free short story to welcome you. Be among the first to read teasers from the books she's writing, learn what Pebbles does to keep her busy when she isn't writing her steamy novels, discover the captivating authors she's reading, be led to books with similar genres grouped together just for readers like you, and other crazy antics.

https://bit.ly/pebbleskinkynews

Join Pebbles' Team

Would you like to be a valued member of my **_ARC team_**? Advanced Readers receive copies of my soon-to-be published novels to read with the promise to leave reviews by the date set by Pebbles.

*You'll get **my books for FREE** forever as long as you leave reviews!*

Sound like a good deal?

https://forms.gle/gseo39XRubENVWjA9

Why Do I Write BDSM Erotic Romance?

Erotica captivates me and for this reason I write it. It's not all about sex, much like real life. It's the romance, love and tender touches that keep us coming back for more. We all want to be loved, adored and cherished. BDSM gives us all of that and more. Yes, it can be cold and emotionless, but it doesn't have to be. My books show the pain and pleasure associated with the BDSM lifestyle, but they also show the unbreakable, loving commitment between the Dom and Sub. The trust built by this play is undeniable.

Thus, I love to write BDSM Erotic Romance.

Always, Pebbles Lacasse
https://www.pebbleslacasse.com